"Put the boys on the phone, or I call in the FBI right now."

Nick's threat was met with silence.

Becky had moved to his side, standing so close she could probably hear the hammering of his heart. She didn't touch him, but somehow it made him stronger just to have her near.

Nick hadn't realized until that moment how tightly he'd been holding on to the phone, as if it were a tenuous tether to his sons.

Becky sunk onto the couch. Her shudders dissolved into sobs.

Nick could stand it no longer. He crossed the room and dropped to the sofa beside her. He wound an arm around her shoulders, hoping she wouldn't push him away.

Her head fell to his chest. "Get them back, Nick. Just get them back."

JOANNA WAYNE

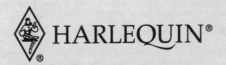

COLTS RUN CROSS

HARLEQUIN®

TORONTO • NEW YORK • LONDON
AMSTERDAM • PARIS • SYDNEY • HAMBURG
STOCKHOLM • ATHENS • TOKYO • MILAN • MADRID
PRAGUE • WARSAW • BUDAPEST • AUCKLAND

To mothers everywhere who know what it means to love
a child more than life itself. And to every woman who's
ever found that special man whose love is worth fighting
for. Here's to Christmas, miracles and love.

Recycling programs
for this product may
not exist in your area.

ISBN-13: 978-0-373-88870-2
ISBN-10:   0-373-88870-8

MIRACLE AT COLTS RUN CROSS

Copyright © 2008 by Jo Ann Vest

www.eHarlequin.com

Printed in U.S.A.

ABOUT THE AUTHOR

Joanna Wayne was born and raised in Shreveport, Louisiana, and received her undergraduate and graduate degrees from LSU-Shreveport. She moved to New Orleans in 1984, and it was there that she attended her first writing class and joined her first professional writing organization. Her first novel, *Deep in the Bayou,* was published in 1994.

Now, dozens of published books later, Joanna has made a name for herself as being on the cutting edge of romantic suspense in both series and single-title novels. She has been on the Waldenbooks Bestselling List for romance and has won many industry awards. She is a popular speaker at writing organizations and local community functions and has taught creative writing at the University of New Orleans Metropolitan College.

She currently resides in a small community forty miles north of Houston, Texas, with her husband. Though she still has many family and emotional ties to Louisiana, she loves living in the Lone Star state. You may write Joanna at P.O. Box 265, Montgomery, Texas 77356.

Books by Joanna Wayne

HARLEQUIN INTRIGUE

753—AS DARKNESS FELL*
771—JUST BEFORE DAWN*
795—A FATHER'S DUTY
867—SECURITY MEASURES
888—THE AMULET
942—A CLANDESTINE AFFAIR
955—MAVERICK CHRISTMAS
975—24/7
1001—24 KARAT AMMUNITION**
1019—TEXAS GUN SMOKE**
1041—POINT BLANK PROTECTOR**
1065—LOADED**
1096—MIRACLE AT COLTS RUN CROSS**

*Hidden Passions: Full Moon Madness
**Four Brothers of Colts Run Cross

CAST OF CHARACTERS

Becky Ridgely—The oldest Collingsworth daughter and the mother of twin sons Derrick and David. She's filed for divorce from Nick Ridgely but she's far from over him.

Nick Ridgely—Star receiver for the Dallas Cowboys. Football is the one thing he always does right, until an injury threatens to end his career.

David and Derrick Ridgely—Twin eight-year-old sons of Nick and Becky.

Lenora Collingsworth—Mother of Becky and matriarch of the Collingsworth clan.

Langston, Matt, Bart and Zach Collingsworth—Becky's brothers. Langston runs Collingsworth Oil, Matt and Bart manage Jack's Bluff Ranch and Zach is a local sheriff's deputy.

Jaime Collingsworth—Becky's younger, unmarried sister who also lives on the ranch.

Jeremiah Collingsworth—Becky's much-loved and cantankerous grandfather.

Trish, Jaclyn, Kali and Shelly—The wives of Langston, Bart, Zach and Matt, respectively. Shelly was formerly an FBI agent.

Sam Contrella—FBI agent called in to work the kidnapping, a specialist in abductions involving children.

Evie Parker—FBI agent who is a master of disguises.

Hermann Grazier and Bruce Cotton—Hunters who had the misfortune of running into the kidnapper.

The kidnapper—An ex con who'll do anything for money.

Chapter One

Becky Ridgely grabbed her denim jacket from the hook and swung out the back door. A light mist made the air seem much cooler than the predicted fifty-degree high for the day. The gust of wind that caught her off guard didn't help, but she'd had to escape the house or sink even deeper into the blue funk that had a killer grip on her mood.

In a matter of weeks, her divorce from Nick would be final. Their marriage that had begun with a fiery blast of passion and excitement she'd thought would never cool had dissolved into a pile of ashes.

Nonetheless, Nick Ridgely, star receiver for the Dallas Cowboys, was in her living room on the Sunday before Christmas, as large as life on the new big-screen TV and claiming the attention of her entire family. She could understand it of their twin sons. At eight years of age, Nick was David and Derrick's hero. She'd never take that away from them.

But you'd think the rest of the family could show a little sensitivity for her feelings. But no, even her sister and her mother were glued to the set as if winning were paramount to gaining world peace or at least finding a cure for cancer.

Did no one but her get that this was just a stupid game?

Most definitely Nick didn't. For more than half of every year, he put everything he had into football. His time. His energy. His enthusiasm. His dedication. She and the boys were saddled with the leftovers. Some women settled for that. She couldn't, which is why she'd left him and moved back to the family ranch.

Her family liked Nick. Everyone did. And he was a good husband and father in many ways. He didn't drink too much. He had never done drugs, not even in college when all their friends were trying it.

He disdained the use of steroids and would never use the shortcut to improve performance. He didn't cheat on her, though several gossip magazines had connected him to Brianna Campbell, slut starlet, since they had been separated.

But his one serious fault was the wedge that had driven them apart. Once preparation for football season started, he shut her out of his life so completely that she could have been invisible. Oh, he pretended to listen to her or the boys at times, but it was surface only.

His always-ready excuse was that his mind was on the upcoming season or game. The message was that it mattered more than they did. She'd lived with the rejection as long as she could tolerate it, and then she left.

"Mom."

She turned at the panicked voice of her son Derrick. He'd pushed through the back door and was standing on the top step, his face a ghostly white.

She raced to him. "What's the matter, sweetheart?"

"Dad's hurt."

"He probably just had the breath knocked out of him," she said.

"No, it's bad, Mom. Really bad. He's not moving."

She put her arm around Derrick's shoulder as they hurried back to the family room where the earlier cheers had turned deathly silent.

The screen defied her to denounce Derrick's

fears. Nick was on his back, his helmet off and lying at a cockeyed angle beside him. Several trainers leaned over him. A half dozen of his teammates were clustered behind them, concern sketched into their faces.

Becky took a deep breath as reality sank in and panic rocked her equilibrium. "What happened?"

"He went up for the ball and got tackled below the waist," Bart said.

Before her brother could say more, the network flashed the replay. A cold shudder climbed her spine as she watched Nick get flipped in midair. He slammed to the ground at an angle that seemed to drive his head and the back of his neck into the hard turf.

His eyes were open, but he had yet to move his arms or legs. Players from the other team joined the circle of players that had formed around him. A few had bowed in prayer. They all looked worried.

"Those guys know what it means to take a hit like that," her brother Langston said. "No player likes to see another one get seriously hurt."

"Yet they go at each other like raging animals." The frustration had flown from Becky's mouth before she could stop it. The stares of her family bore into her, no doubt mistaking her exasperation for a lack of empathy. But they hadn't lived with Nick's obsession for pushing his mind and body to the limit week after week.

"I only meant that it's almost inevitable that players get hurt considering the intensity of the game."

The family grew silent. The announcer droned on and on about Nick's not moving as the trainers strapped him to a backboard and attached a C-collar to support his neck.

David scooted close to the TV and put his hand on the corner of the screen. "Come on, Dad. You'll be all right. You gotta be all right."

"I got hurt bad the first time I played in a real game," Derrick said. "I wanted to cry, but I didn't 'cause the other players make fun of you if you do."

Becky had never wanted her sons to play football, but had given in to their pleadings this year when they turned eight. Nick had always just expected they'd play and spent half the time he was with them practicing the basic skills of the game. It was yet another bone of contention between them.

They showed the replay again while Nick was taken from the field. All of the announcers were in on the act now, concentrating on the grisly possible outcomes from such an injury.

"The fans would love it if Nick could wave a farewell but he still hasn't moved his arms or legs."

"It doesn't look good. It would be terrible to see the career of a player with Nick Ridgely's talent end like this."

"Did you hear that?" Derrick said. "The announcer said Daddy might not ever play football again."

Becky grabbed the remote and muted the sound. "They don't know. They're not doctors. Most likely Daddy has a bad sprain."

"Your father's taken lots of blows and he's never let one get the best of him yet," her brother Bart said, trying as Becky had to calm the boys.

"We better get up there and check on him," David said. "He might need us."

"You have school tomorrow," Becky said, quickly squashing that idea.

"We can miss," the boys protested in unison.

"It's only half a day," Derrick said. "A bunch of kids won't even be there. Ellen Michaels left Saturday to go visit her grandmother in Alabama for Christmas."

"You have practice for the church Christmas

pageant right after school lets out. Mrs. Evans is counting on you."

Becky knew that missing school in the morning wouldn't be a problem. They would have been out all week had they not lost so many days during hurricane season.

They'd been lucky and hadn't received anything but strong winds and excessive rain from two separate storms that had come ashore to the west of them, but if the school board erred, it was always on the side of caution.

Still, if Nick was seriously hurt, the hospital would be no place for the boys. And if he wasn't, he'd be too preoccupied with getting back in the game to notice.

"You can call Daddy later when he's feeling better."

"But you're going to go to Dallas, aren't you, Momma? Daddy's gonna need somebody there with him."

"I can fly you up in the Cessna," Langston said, offering his private jet. He'd done that before when Nick had been hurt, once even all the way to Green Bay.

But that was when she and Nick were at least making a stab at the marriage. Things had become really strained between them since the divorce proceedings had officially begun. She doubted he'd want her there now.

"Thanks," she said, "but I'm sure Nick's in good hands."

"Maybe you should hold off on that decision until after you've talked to him," her mother said.

"Right," Bart said. "They'll know a lot more after he's X-rayed." The others in the room nodded in agreement.

Becky left the room when the game got back underway. Anxiety had turned to acid in her stomach, and she felt nauseous as she climbed the stairs and went to her private quarters on the second floor of the big house.

Too bad she couldn't cut off her emotions the way a divorce cut off a marriage, but love had a way of hanging on long after it served any useful purpose. Nick would always be the father of her children, but hopefully one day her love for him would be just a memory.

But she wouldn't go to Nick, not unless he asked her to, and she was almost certain that wasn't going to happen. They'd both crossed a line when the divorce papers had been filed. From now on, the only bond between them was their sons.

BECKY CALLED the hospital twice during the hours immediately following Nick's injury. Once he'd still been in the emergency room. The second time he'd been having X-rays. The only real information she'd received was that he had regained movement in his arms and legs.

Her anxiety level had eased considerably with that bit of news, as had everyone else's in the family. The boys still wanted to talk to him, but she'd waited until they were getting ready for bed before trying to reach him again.

Hopefully by now the doctors would have finished with the required tests and Nick would feel like talking to them. Regardless, Nick would play down the pain when talking to her and especially when talking to the boys.

That was his way. Say the right things. Keep his true feelings and worries inside him. It was a considerate trait in a father. It was a cop-out for a husband.

And bitterness stunk in a wife. It was time she accepted things the way they were and moved past the resentment.

"Can you connect me to the room of Nick Ridgely?" she asked when the hospital operator answered.

"He's only taking calls from family members

at this time. I've been told to tell all other callers that he is resting comfortably and has recovered full movement in his arms and legs."

Becky had expected that. No doubt the hospital was being bombarded with calls from reporters. "This is his wife."

"Please wait while I put you through to his room, Mrs. Ridgely."

A female voice answered, likely a nurse. "Nick Ridgely's room. If this is a reporter, shame on you for disturbing him."

"This is Becky Ridgely. I'm calling to check on my husband."

"Oops, sorry. It's just that the reporters keep getting through. You don't know how persistent they can be."

Actually, she did. "Is Nick able to talk?"

"He can, but the doctor wants him to stay quiet. I can give him a message."

"I was hoping he could say a word to his sons. They're really worried about him, and I'm not sure they'll sleep well unless he tells them he's okay."

"He isn't okay. His arms are burning like crazy."

This was definitely not a nurse. "To whom am I speaking?"

"Brianna Campbell."

The name hit like a quick slap to the face. He could have waited until the divorce was final to play hot bachelor. If not for her, then for David and Derrick.

"Do you want to leave a message?"

"Yes, tell Nick he can…" She took a quick breath and swallowed her anger as David returned from the bathroom where he'd been brushing his teeth. "No message." Saved from sounding like a jealous wench by the timely appearance of her son.

"Okay, I'll just tell Nick you called, Mrs. Ridgely."

She heard Nick's garbled protest in the background.

"Wait. He's insisting I hand him the phone."

Nice of him to bother.

"Becky."

Her name was slurred—no doubt from pain meds. Derrick had joined them as well now, and both boys had climbed into their twin beds.

"The boys are worried about you."

"Yeah. I knew they would be. I was just

waiting to call until I was thinking and talking a bit straighter. Were they watching the game?"

"They always watch your games, Nick."

"Good boys. I miss them."

So he always said, but she wasn't going there with him right now. "How are you?"

"I have the feeling back in my arms and legs. They burned like they were on fire for a bit, but they're better now. The E.R. doc said that was the neurons firing back up so I figure that's a good sign."

"Is there a diagnosis?"

"They think I have a spinal cord contusion. They make it sound serious, but you know doctors. They like complications and two-dollar terms no one else can understand. I'll be fine."

He didn't sound it. He was talking so slowly she could have read the newspaper between sentences. "Do you feel like saying good-night to David and Derrick?"

"Sure. Put them on. I need some cheering up."

That's what she thought Brianna was for. She put the boys on speakerphone so they could both talk at once. Nick made light of the injury, like she'd known he would, and started joking with the boys as if this was just a regular Sunday night post-game chat.

He loved his sons. He even loved her in his own way. It just wasn't enough. She backed from the room as an ache the size of Texas settled in her heart.

MORNING CAME early at Jack's Bluff Ranch, and the sun was still below the horizon when Becky climbed from her bed. She'd had very little sleep, and her emotions were running on empty. Still she managed a smile as she padded into her sons' room to get them up and ready for school.

"Okay, sleepyheads, time to rock and roll."

"Already?" Derrick groaned and buried his head in his pillow.

David rubbed his eyes with his fists and yawned widely as he kicked off his covers. "How come you always say time to rock and roll when we're just going to school?"

"Tradition. That's what your grandma used to say to me."

"Grandma said that?"

"Yes, she did. "Now up and at 'em. She said that, too. And wear something warm. It's about twenty degrees colder than yesterday."

"I wish it would snow," Derrick said as he rummaged through the top drawer of his chest and came up with a red-and-white-striped rugby shirt.

"It never snows in Colts Run Cross," David said.

"Not never, but rarely," Becky agreed. But a cold front did occasionally reach this far south. Today the high would only be in the mid-forties with a chance of thundershowers.

"Have you talked to Daddy this morning?" Derrick asked.

"No, and I don't think we should bother him with phone calls this early. Now get dressed, and I'll see you at breakfast."

Juanita was already at work in the kitchen and had been for over a half hour. Becky had heard the family cook drive up. She'd heard every sound since about 3:00 a.m. when she'd woken to a ridiculous nightmare about Nick's getting hit so hard his helmet had flown off—with his head inside it.

Crazy, but anxiety had always sabotaged her dreams with weird and frightening images. Some people smoked cigarettes or drank or got hives when they were worried. She had nightmares. Over the last ten years, Nick had starred in about ninety-nine percent of them.

Juanita was sliding thick slices of bacon into

a large skillet when Becky strode into the kitchen in her pink sweats and fuzzy slippers and poured herself a bracing cup of hot coffee.

The usually jovial Juanita stopped the task and stared soulfully at Becky. "I'm sorry to hear about Nick."

"Thanks." She hoped she would let it go at that.

"I brought the newspaper in. Nick's picture is on the front page."

The front page and no doubt all the morning newscasts, as well. Nick would be the main topic of conversation at half the breakfast tables in Texas this morning.

"The article said he may be out for the rest of the season," Juanita said.

"The rest of the season could be only a game or two depending on whether or not Dallas wins its play-off games, but I don't think anyone knows how long Nick will be on injured reserve."

"I'm sure the boys are upset."

"They talked to him last night, and he assured them he was fine. So I'd appreciate if you didn't mention the article in the paper. They need to go to school and concentrate on their studies."

"Kids at school will talk," Juanita said. "Maybe it would be best if you show them the article and prepare them."

Becky sighed. "You're right. I should have thought of that myself."

Juanita had been with them so long that she seemed like an extension of the family. She fit right in with the Collingsworth clan, none of whom had ever strayed far from Colts Run Cross.

And if Juanita had been helpful before, she'd been a godsend since Becky's mother, Lenora, had started filling in as CEO for Becky's grandfather, Jeremiah, after his stroke. Thankfully he was back in the office a few days a week now, and Lenora was completing some projects she'd started and easing her way out of the job that would eventually go to Langston. As Jeremiah said, he had oil in his blood.

Jack's Bluff was the second largest ranch in Texas. Becky's brothers Bart and Matt managed the ranch, and both had their own houses on the spread where they lived with their wives.

Her youngest brother, Zach, had recently surprised them all by falling madly in love with a new neighbor, marrying and also taking his first real job. He was now a deputy, in training for the county's new special crimes unit. He and his wife, Kali, lived on her horse ranch.

And though her oldest brother Langston lived

with his family in Houston, close to Collings-worth Oil where he served as president for the company, he had a weekend cabin on the ranch.

Her younger sister, Jaime, who'd never married or apparently given any thought to settling down or taking a serious job, lived in the big house with Becky and the boys, along with Becky's mother, Lenora, and Jeremiah, their grandfather. Jeremiah was currently re-covering from a lingering case of the flu that hadn't been deterred by this year's flu shot.

Commune might have been a better term for the conglomeration of inhabitants. Becky hadn't planned to stay forever when she'd left Nick and returned to the ranch, but the ranch had a way of reclaiming its own.

The boys missed their father, but they were happy here. More important, they were safe from the kinds of problems that plagued kids growing up in the city.

Becky took her coffee and walked to the den. Almost impulsively, she reached for the remote and flipped on the TV. She was caught off guard as a picture of Nick with David and Derrick flashed across the screen.

Anger rose in her throat. How dare they put her boys' pictures on TV without her permission? Both she and Nick had always been determined to keep them out of the limelight.

"Nick Ridgely's estranged wife Becky is one of the Collingsworths of Collingsworth Oil and Jack's Bluff Ranch. His twin sons Derrick and David live on the ranch with their mother. There's been no word from them on Nick's potentially career-ending injury."

She heard the back door open and Bart's voice as he called to Juanita about the terrific odors coming from the kitchen. Becky switched off the TV quickly and joined them in the kitchen. It would be nice to make it through breakfast without a mention of Nick, but she knew that was too much to hope for.

The next best thing was to head her family off at the pass and keep them from upsetting Derrick and David with new doubts about their father's condition. Nick had left things on a positive note, and she planned to keep them there.

The phone rang, and she inwardly grimaced. Where there's a way, there would be a reporter with questions. And once they started, there would be no letup. Whether she liked it or not, she and her family, especially her sons, were about to be caught in the brutal glare of the public eye.

BULL STARED in the mirror as he yanked on his jeans. "Hell of a looker you are to be living like this," he muttered to himself. Without bothering to zip his pants, he padded barefoot across the littered floor of the tiny bedroom and down the short hall to the bathroom.

After he finished in the john, he stumbled sleepily to the kitchen, pushed last night's leftovers out of his way and started a pot of coffee. This was a piss-poor way to live but still better than that crummy halfway house he'd been stuck in until last week.

And the price was right. Free, unless you counted the food he donated to the roaches and rats that homesteaded here. The cabin had been in his family for years, but he was only passing through until he came up with a plan to get enough money to start over in Mexico.

His parole officer expected him to get a job. Yeah, right. Everyone was just jumping for joy at the chance to hire a man fresh out of prison for stabbing a pregnant woman while in the throes of road rage. No matter that she deserved it.

He stamped his feet to get his blood moving and fight the chill. The cabin was without any heat except what he could get from turning on the oven, and he didn't have the propane to waste on that. The only reason he had electricity was because he'd worked for the power company in his earlier life just long enough to learn how to connect to the current and steal the watts he needed.

Once the coffee was brewing, he started the daily search for the remote. If he didn't know better, he'd swear the rats hid it every night while he was sleeping. This time it turned up under the blanket he'd huddled under to watch the late show last night.

The TV came to life just as the local station broke in with a news flash. He turned up the volume to get the full story. It was all about Nick Ridgely. Apparently he'd gotten seriously injured in Sunday's game. Like who gave a damn about Nick Ridgely?

They showed a picture of him with his sons. Cute kids. But then they would be. Nick was married to Becky Collingsworth. He still had sordid dreams about her in those short little skirts and sweaters that showed off her perky breasts.

But the bitch had never given him the time of day. The announcer referred to her as Nick's estranged wife. Apparently she'd dumped him. Or maybe he'd dumped her. Either way they were both fixed for life, lived like Texas royalty with money to burn while he lived in this dump. The little money he'd stashed away before prison was nearly gone.

No cash. No job. Nothing but a parole officer who kept him pinned down like a tiger in a cage.

Bull's muscles tightened as perverted possibilities skittered through his mind. He went back to the kitchen for coffee, took a long sip and cursed himself silently for even considering doing something that could land him right back in prison.

Still the thoughts persisted and started taking definite shape as the image of Nick Ridgely's twin sons seared into his mind.

Chapter Two

"Too bad about your dad."

"Yeah, man. Tough."

Derrick joined the boys entering the school after recess. "I talked to him last night. He'll be back and better than ever."

"That's not what they said on TV this morning."

David pushed into the line beside them. "Yeah, but they don't know. My mother said they're just making news."

"Well, my daddy said neck injuries are the worst kind. Anyway, I'm sorry he got hurt,"

"Me, too," Butch Kelly added. "I'd be scared to death if it was my dad."

"It's not like he's crippled or anything," David said. "He just took a hit."

Janie Thomas squeezed in beside Derrick.

"They put your picture on TV, too. My big sister thinks you're cute."

"Yeah, David, you're cute," Derrick mocked, making his voice sound like a girl.

"You look just like me, you clown. If I'm cute, you are, too."

David followed Derrick to their lockers. They were side by side because they were assigned in alphabetical order. He shrugged out of his jacket and took off the Dallas Cowboys cap his dad had gotten signed by all his teammates. Derrick had one, too. His was white. David's was blue. He wore it everywhere he went.

"Are you worried about Daddy?" Derrick asked.

"I am now," David admitted. "Do you think he might really be hurt too bad to ever play again?"

"I don't know. I think we should ask Uncle Langston to fly us to Dallas to check on him."

"Momma said we couldn't go."

"She said we couldn't miss school, but he could fly us up there at noon, and we could be home by bedtime, like he did when he took us to watch Daddy play the Giants back in October."

David shrugged. "Yeah. Maybe, but I bet Momma's still going to say no."

"We ought to call Uncle Langston. He might talk her into it."

"We'd miss practicing for the pageant."

"So what?" Derrick scoffed. "How much practice does it take to be a shepherd?"

"I'm the little drummer boy."

"Big deal. You just follow the music. I say we call him. The worse thing he can do is say no."

"The office won't let us use the phone unless it's an emergency."

"Our daddy might be hurt bad," Derrick said. "That's an emergency."

"You're right. Let's go call Uncle Langston now. Maybe he'll check us out early, and we won't have to do math."

"I like that plan. I hate multiplication. It's stupid to do all that work when you can just punch it in the calculator and get the answer right away."

The boys went straight to the office. The good news was that Mrs. Gravits, who worked behind the desk, let them use the phone to call their uncle. The bad news was that Langston wasn't in.

They left a message with his secretary saying they really needed to fly to Dallas today.

BECKY DROVE up to the church ten minutes before the scheduled time for practice to end.

Several mothers were already waiting, parked in the back lot nearest the educational building. Her friend Mary Jo McFee waved from her car. Becky waved back.

Normally she would have walked over and spent the ten minutes of waiting time chatting, but she knew that conversation today with anyone would mean answering questions about Nick, and she wasn't up to that.

As it was, the phone at the big house had rung almost constantly since breakfast, and Matt had wranglers guarding the gate to keep the media vultures off ranch property. A couple of photographers had almost gotten to the house before they were turned back.

Becky leaned back and tried to relax before she faced her energetic sons who'd no doubt have new questions of their own about their father. Five minutes later, a couple of girls came out of the church. Mary Jo's daughter was one of them.

A couple of boys came next, and less than a minute later, the rest of the kids came pouring out the door. Some ran to waiting cars; the ones who lived nearby started walking away in small groups.

Two boys climbed on the low retaining wall

between the church and the parking lot. A couple of girls pulled books from their book bags and started reading. But there was no sign of David and Derrick.

Becky waited as a steady group of cars arrived to pick up the waiting children. Her cell phone rang just as the last kid left in a black pickup truck.

She checked the ID and decided not to answer when she didn't recognize the caller. Probably yet another reporter, though she had no idea how they kept getting her cell phone number.

She dropped the phone into the compartment between the front seats, her impatience growing thin. Any other day, her sons would have been the first ones out.

The slight irritation turned to mild apprehension when Rachel Evans, the church's part-time youth coordinator, stepped out the door and started walking toward the only other car in the parking lot. Rachel was in charge of the practice and never left until all the children had been picked up.

Rachel noticed Becky and changed direction, walking toward her white Mercedes. Becky lowered her window.

"I'm sorry to hear about Nick," Rachel said.

"I guess the boys were too upset to come for practice, not that I blame them."

Becky's apprehension swelled. "Weren't they here?"

"No. Some of the boys said they were flying to Dallas to see their father."

"There must be some mistake. The boys were supposed to be here. Why did their friends think they were going to Dallas?"

"They said that their uncle Langston had picked them up and was taking them in his private jet. In fact, Eddie Mason said he saw them getting into their uncle's car."

Langston would never pick up the boys at school without letting her know, much less fly them to Dallas. But maybe he'd tried to get in touch with her and kept getting a busy signal. Maybe he'd left a message and she hadn't gotten it. Maybe…

Rachel was staring at her, probably thinking she was a very incompetent mother not to know where her sons were. "I'll give Langston a call."

Rachel nodded. "I'm sure you'll find this is all just some kind of miscommunication. It frequently happens when everyone is stressed."

Becky nodded as Rachel walked away, no doubt in a hurry to pick up her own toddler daughter from day care. Becky's pulse rate was climbing steadily as she picked up her phone and punched in Langston's private number. She'd about given up hope of his answering when she heard his hello.

"Where are you, Langston?"

"In the office. Why? What's up?"

"It's the boys. Are they with you?"

"No, why would you think they were?"

"I'm at the church to pick them up from pageant practice, but they're not here."

"Maybe they caught a ride home with someone else."

"No, I just talked to Rachel Evans. She said they never showed up."

"Maybe they forgot about practice and got on the school bus."

"If they had, they would have been home before I left to pick them up. Rachel Evans said that some of the boys at practice mentioned that you were flying David and Derrick to Dallas."

"No. I had a message from David asking me to fly them up there, but I only got it about twenty minutes ago. I was in a meeting all day."

The apprehension took full hold now, and Becky started shaking so hard she could barely hold on to the phone. "If you didn't pick them up, who did?"

"Not mother. She's still here at the office. Did you talk to Bart and Matt—or even Zach?"

"No, but they never pick up the boys unless I ask them to. I'm scared, Langston."

"Try to stay calm, Becky. I'm sure they're fine and this is all a harmless mix-up. Call the ranch. See if they're there."

"And if they're not?"

"Then call Zach. Have him meet you at the church, and don't do anything until he gets there. In the meantime, let me know if you hear anything."

Hot tears welled in the back of Becky's eyes, but she willed them to stay there.

Becky called the big house first, just in case the boys had caught a ride back to the ranch. Juanita was the only one there, and just as Becky had feared, the boys weren't home. She hung up quickly and then punched in Zach's number. He was a deputy now, he'd know what to do. He didn't pick up, but she left a frantic message for him to return her call at once.

Her phone rang again, the jangle of it crackling along her frazzled nerves. This time it was

Nick. He was the last person she wanted to talk to now. Still, she took the call.

"Becky, it's Nick," he said, identifying himself as if she wouldn't recognize his voice after a decade of marriage. "Where are the boys?"

She heard the panic in his voice and knew he'd heard. "Did Langston call you?"

"I haven't talked to Langston, but this is very important, Becky. Do you know where the boys are? Are they with you?"

Her blood turned to ice. "What's going on, Nick?"

"Are the boys with you?" he asked again with new urgency in his voice.

"No. I'm at the church. I came to pick them up after their practice for the Christmas pageant, but they're not here. They never showed up."

Nick let loose with a string of muttered curses. "Are you by yourself?"

"Yes, but if you have anything to say, just…"

"I got a phone call a few minutes ago. It was from a man claiming he has the boys with him."

"Who?"

"I don't know. All he said was that he'd call back and that I'd best be ready to deal. I think they've been abducted."

No. Her sons couldn't be kidnapped. This couldn't be happening. She couldn't think, couldn't function. Couldn't breathe.

"We have to find them, Nick."

"We will. Just don't fall apart on me, Becky. We can't make any mistakes."

But she was falling apart, more with every agonizing heartbeat. "They'll be afraid. He might…" God, she couldn't let her mind go there or she'd never get through this. "We have to get them back at once. If it takes every penny either of us has, I don't care. I just want David and Derrick back."

"I'm leaving the hospital now. I'll meet you at Jack's Bluff as soon as I can get there."

"Langston can fly up and get you."

"I can get a chartered flight even quicker. Now go home and stay there in case the man calls you."

She swallowed hard. "I'll call Zach."

"I don't want the sheriff's department in on this, Becky. Not them or any other law enforcement agency, at least until after we talk."

"Don't be ridiculous, Nick. Zach can put out an AMBER Alert and have everyone in the state looking for this madman. And for the record, you don't get to call all the shots, even if it is your fault they're missing."

"Don't start with the blame, Becky, not now." His voice broke. He was hurting and probably as scared as she was.

But this was his fault. He was the one in the news, his name and face all over the TV and every newspaper in the state. And it was him the abductor had called for a ransom.

"The caller said that if we go to the cops, he'll…"

Nick stopped, leaving the sentence unfinished, though the meaning was crystal clear even in Becky's traumatized mind. Nausea hit with a vengeance. She dropped the phone, stepped out of the car and threw up in the parking lot. Weak and unnerved, she finally leaned against the car and gulped in a steadying breath of brisk air.

She would find out who took the twins, and whatever it took, she'd get them back. And heaven help Nick Ridgely if he got in her way.

NICK SHIFTED again, trying to find a way to get comfortable in the four-man helicopter he'd hired to fly him directly to the ranch's helipad. Pain shot through his neck and shoulders with each vibration, but no matter how bad it got, he wouldn't go back on the pain meds. He needed his mind perfectly clear to deal with the situation.

Becky had been quick to hurl the blame at him for the twins' abduction. He couldn't fault her for that. She'd always been determined to protect David and Derrick from the notoriety his career had brought him. She wanted them to have a normal life with solid values. She wanted them safe from the kind of sick person who had them now.

According to the attending physician who'd protested his leaving the hospital, his career could be over. Strapped with the fears of the moment, even that seemed inconsequential.

The pilot landed the helicopter approximately one hundred yards from the big house. Nick grabbed his quickly packed duffel bag, thanked the pilot and jumped out. He walked quickly, breaking into a jog as he neared the house.

He'd come by helicopter before. Then the boys had been watching, and the minute the chopper landed they'd raced to greet him. Their absence now sucked the breath from his lungs. By the time he reached the house, Bart and Matt were standing on the porch, their faces more drawn than he'd ever seen them.

He hoped Becky had kept this from the police, but he knew she wouldn't keep it from her family. Nor would he have wanted that. The

Collingsworth brothers, the fearsome four as he'd called them when he'd first started dating Becky, were a powerful squad, and he'd be glad to have them on his side.

He put out his hand to shake Matt's as he stepped on the wide front porch, and then his gaze settled on Becky. She was standing just inside the door, her silhouette backlit by the huge, rustic chandelier that dominated the foyer. She looked far more fragile than the last time he'd seen her, the day she'd told him she was through with being his wife.

He ached to take her in his arms, needed that closeness now more than he'd ever needed it before. Her words of blame shot through his mind, and he held back. Rejection from her might annihilate the tenuous hold he had on his own emotions.

"Glad you made it so quickly," Matt said, his voice level and his handshake firm, though the drawn look to his face and the jut of his jaw were clear indicators of his apprehension.

Bart clapped Nick's shoulder. "Have you heard any more from the abductor?"

"Not a word."

"The family's waiting inside," Matt said. "We should join them."

Nick nodded. Becky had left the door by the time they entered. He followed Bart and Matt into the huge den. The family Collingsworth had gathered en masse—except for Langston's daughter, Gina, and the ill Jeremiah—filling the comfortable sofas and chairs.

Becky was standing near the hearth, and the heat from the blaze in the fireplace flushed her face. Her arms were pulled tight across her chest as if she were holding herself together. She looked at him questioningly, and his stomach rolled with a million unfamiliar emotions.

"He hasn't called back," he said, answering her unspoken question.

She started to shake, and he went to her, steadying her in the crook of his arm until she regrouped and pulled away.

Zach stood. It was the first time Nick had seen him in his khaki deputy's uniform, and he was struck with the added maturity the attire provided.

Zach propped a booted foot on the hearth. "We need an action plan."

"I made a fresh pot of coffee," Bart's wife, Jaclyn, said. "I'll get it."

Langston's wife, Trish, handed their six-month-old son, Randy, off to his dad. "I'll help."

"This is what I've pieced together so far,"

Zach said. "Eddie Mason said that he saw the boys get into a car right after school let out, apparently when they were walking to the church."

"Has anyone talked to Eddie?" Langston asked.

"Not yet. At this point I'm following Nick's instructions to hold off, but I think it's imperative that we get a description of the car."

"I agree," Matt's wife, Shelly, said. "That information could be critical. So is speed in getting the search under way. That's one thing I definitely learned while with the CIA."

Nick's cell phone rang. The room grew deathly quiet. He checked the caller ID. Unavailable. His hands were clammy as he punched the button to take the call.

"Just listen. No questions."

His gut hardened to a painful knot. There was no mistaking the abductor's voice.

Chapter Three

"Here's the deal. Five million in small denominations, unmarked, and a flight into Mexico on
the Collingsworth's private jet."

All doable, though it surprised Nick for the
man to mention the private jet. It made him
wonder if the man could live in Colts Run
Cross. "Before I agree to anything, I want to
talk to my sons."

"No can do."

Nick's body flexed involuntarily. "Why not?"

"They're not with me at the moment."

Dread kicked inside him, but it had fury for
company. "Either I talk to the boys and know
they're safe, or there will be no deal of any kind."

"You're not calling the plays, Ridgely."

"Put the boys on the phone, or I call in the FBI
right now." It was a bluff at this point, but he certainly hadn't ruled out that option. His threat was

met with silence, a match for the still, breathless tension that surrounded him.

"Screw yourself." The man's voice reverberated with anger.

Nick waited. Angry or not, if the boys were alive and safe, the guy wouldn't blow this deal by refusing to let him talk to them—not if he was sane. And heaven help them if he wasn't. There would be no way of predicting the behavior of a crazy man.

Becky had moved to his side, standing so close she could probably hear the hammering of his heart. She didn't touch him, but somehow it made him stronger just to have her near.

"I'll call you back in a half hour." He broke the connection before Nick could respond.

Nick hadn't realized until that moment how tightly he'd been holding on to the phone, as if it were a tenuous tether to his sons. He walked to the window and stared out at the wintry view of bare branches mixed with the green needles of the towering pines, keenly aware that everyone in the room was watching and judging his actions.

Before his marriage had hit the rocks, he'd considered himself as an integral part of the close-knit Collingsworth clan. On the last few visits, the tensions between him and Becky had left him feeling as if he were hovering on the outer rim.

Today all he felt was relief that he was among people who loved his sons and whom he knew would put their lives on the line in a second to save them. Still, he was the father. The final responsibility rested with him.

Trish and Jaclyn returned with the coffee. He waited until they'd served it before he delivered the abductor's message—word for word—or as close as he could remember them. No one interrupted, not even Becky, though she seemed to grow more distraught at every syllable he uttered.

She dropped to the sofa next to her mother. Lenora reached over and took her daughter's hands, cradling them in hers.

"I'm really uneasy with a no-cops policy," Langston said. "There's a lot of knowledge about situations like this that we're not tapping into. I could call Aidan Jefferies. This is out of his jurisdiction, but he's a hell of a homicide detective, and I know he's had experience with abductions as well."

"I think we should let the sheriff's department handle this," Zach said. "We can put out an AMBER Alert, question anyone who may have seen the boys get into the abductor's car and start investigating any child molesters presently living in the area."

Nick's insides coated in acid at the mention of child molesters, though he'd already thought the same. But his gut feeling led him in another direction. "It seems likely that the abduction was a spur-of-the-moment decision spawned by the media attention yesterday, maybe someone desperate for cash."

"That makes sense," Bart agreed. "The man probably saw the boys' picture on TV."

"No sane person would let a picture of Nick and the twins lead them to kidnapping," Matt said.

Nick shoved his hands into his pockets. "That's my concern and the reason I hate to blow off his demand that we not bring in the authorities. The guy could be a mental case tottering on the edge."

"How will the abductor know if you talk to the cops?" Jaime asked. "I mean as long as they don't come roaring out here in squad cars or show up at the door in uniform."

"If we bring in law enforcement, the kidnapping could get leaked to the media," Nick said. "I don't think we can risk that—at least not yet."

Lenora leaned forward. "But surely it wouldn't hurt for Zach to do some unofficial investigating."

Nick was amazed at how well his mother-in-law was holding up under this. He knew how much she loved David and Derrick, yet she had a quiet strength about her that he envied. Thank God she was here for Becky since his wife didn't seem to want any comfort or reassurance from him.

"I could fly under the radar," Zach answered, "but we've got to agree on what we're doing here."

"I say pay him off, get the boys back and then we hunt the bastard down," Matt said.

"I'd like to see the FBI brought in," Langston countered. "I have connections. I can make a call right now and have someone come out here from the agency. But Nick and Becky are the ones with the deciding votes. I know I'd make the decisions if it was Gina or little Randy here." He kissed the top of his son's head.

"Where is Gina now?" Jaclyn asked. "Does she know about the abduction?"

"Not yet," Trish said. "She's spending the night in Houston with a girlfriend from her high school who's hosting a Christmas party tonight."

"With a protection service secretly watching her and the house she's in," Langston said. "I'm taking no chances until this crazed abductor is apprehended."

"I curse myself a hundred times an hour for not thinking to do that," Nick said.

Jaime walked over and placed a hand on Nick's arm. "Don't blame yourself for this. How could you possibly have foreseen something so bizarre?"

Jaime was Zach's twin sister. She was the party girl, but Nick had always suspected she had a lot more depth to her than she let on.

"Would you all just stop talking?" Becky said. Her voice broke, and her whole body began to shake. "My boys are missing, and I want them back. I want them home and in their beds. I want…" Her ranting and shudders dissolved into sobs.

Nick could stand it no longer. He crossed the room and dropped to the sofa beside her. He wound an arm around her shoulders, hoping she wouldn't push him away.

Her head fell to his chest. "Get them back, Nick. Just get them back."

"I will." It was a promise he'd keep or die trying.

Lenora got up from her seat on the other side of Becky. "I think we should give Nick and Becky some time alone."

"Sure," Zach said, "but remember that every second counts in a kidnapping."

Nick had never been more aware of anything in his life.

BECKY FELT as if she were suspended in time, stuck in the horrifying moment when Nick had first told her the boys had been abducted. She pulled away from Nick and tried desperately to regain a semblance of control as the others filed from the room. "I can't stand doing nothing, Nick. I need to know that someone is out there looking for David and Derrick."

"The abductor was adamant that we not go to the police."

"And in the meantime, what about my sons? What's happening to them?"

"The kidnapper wants money, Becky. He's made that clear almost from the second he took them. There's no reason for him to hurt them as long as we cooperate."

"Since when do you know so much about kidnappers? Since when do you know about anything except football?"

"Please don't do this, Becky. It won't help us to tear each other down."

His gaze sought out hers, and she turned

away, unable to deal with his pain when hers was so intense.

"I know I'm not all that good with reading people," he said, "but I'm convinced this was a spur-of-the-moment decision with the kidnapper. My guess is he's desperate for money. And desperate men commit irrational acts when pushed against the wall. That's why I don't want to push. I just want to give him the money and bring the boys home."

"And you really think you can pull this off without David and Derrick getting hurt?"

"I think working without the cops is our best chance of doing that."

Nick's face was drawn into hard lines that made him look much older than his thirty-two years. It was odd that she'd never thought of him as aging, though she was keenly aware of it in herself. He was constantly in training, keeping up his speed, agility and strength with the rigorous exercise routine that had kept him at the top of his game.

His boyish good looks and charm had come to him naturally and required nothing but his presence to make them work. But even those were lost tonight in the torment that haunted his eyes.

"If he puts the boys on the phone, I want to talk to them," she said.

"I don't know how much time he'll give us with them."

"Then put the phone on speaker."

"He'll be able to tell and will probably think I have a cop listening in."

She knew he was right, and yet the frustration started swelling in her chest again until it felt like her heart might burst from the pressure. "Are you certain you don't know the abductor, Nick, or at least have some idea who he is?"

"Of course not. Why would you think that?"

Actually, she had no idea where that idea had come from, but now that she'd voiced it, it wasn't all that far-fetched. The man had contacted Nick on his cell phone. He'd had to get that number from somewhere.

And he'd known where the boys went to school. She was certain the morning newscast hadn't mentioned that and was pretty sure that none of the others would have given out that type of information.

"Was the voice disguised?"

"I don't think so."

"Did you get any feel for the man's age?"

"No. He's not a kid, but beyond that, it's impossible to say. He tries to sound tough, but his tone wavers at times. So does the timbre, as if he's getting overly excited or nervous and doesn't want me to know it. That's another reason I think he really just wants to get the money and get out. If we convince him we'll cooperate with him fully, I think this could be over in a matter of hours."

She ached to believe he was right. "Okay, Nick. I'll agree to holding off on calling the police or the FBI until he calls again. But if we don't talk to the boys, or if he's hurt them in any way, the deal is off."

"That's all I'm asking, Becky."

His cell phone rang again. She tensed, and the quick intake of breath was choking. He shook his head, a signal that it wasn't the kidnapper. The disappointment laid a crushing weight on her chest.

"I can't talk now. I'll have to call you back later."

Probably Brianna. Becky dropped to the sofa and lowered her head, cradling it in her hands as a new wave of vertigo left her too off balance to stand.

Just keep David and Derrick safe, she prayed silently. If she was granted that, she'd never complain about anything again.

DAVID SUCKED the ketchup from a greasy French fry before stuffing it into his mouth. He chewed and swallowed. Momma didn't like for him to talk with his mouth full. "I don't think you really are my daddy's friend," he said, as he dipped the next fry.

"See, that's where you're wrong. I talked to your daddy when I was outside unloading the two-by-fours from the top of my car. He's real eager to see you boys."

Derrick wiped a dab of mayonnaise from his chin and sat his half-eaten cheeseburger in the middle of the paper wrapper he'd spread out in front of him. "Then how come you didn't take us to Uncle Langston like you said you were going to do?"

"I told you, there was a little misunderstanding, but you'll get to see your daddy soon enough, as long as he cooperates."

"What's that supposed to mean?" David drew a circle in his ketchup with his last fry. He always ate his fries first. Then he ate the meat off the burger. He hated buns.

"It means your Dad and I are working out a deal. He comes up with cash. You go home."

The fry slipped from David's finger and

plopped into the puddle of ketchup. "Have we been kidnapped?"

"No, no. Nothing like that. This is just a business deal, and you're the collateral."

"How much cash are you trying to get from Daddy?"

"Just a little pocket money. Five million. Do you think you're worth that?"

David choked and had to spit out the fry he was eating. His allowance was only a dollar a week, and when he'd asked for that super skateboard with all the fancy stuff on it the last time they went to Houston, Momma had said it was too expensive. And that didn't cost even a hundred dollars.

He didn't figure anybody had five million dollars except the Queen of England and maybe that woman who wrote the Harry Potter books. He and Derrick were in big trouble. He looked at his twin brother and could tell he was thinking the same thing.

Derrick jumped up from the rickety chair. "I'm getting out of here right now." He sprinted across the room, heading for the back door.

The guy with the dirty denim jacket grabbed his arm and twisted it behind his back until Derrick yelped in pain.

David ran over and kicked the man in his shins. The guy let go of Derrick and grabbed David. "You kick me again, and I'll take a belt to you, you hear me, boy? You won't have an inch of flesh that's not bruised."

"Then don't you hurt my brother."

Surprisingly the guy laughed. "So you two stick together, eh." Then he stopped smiling and his face turned red. "Let's get one thing straight. I don't want to hurt either one of you, but you try anything funny and I'll lock you in the bathroom and leave you there until this deal is done, do you understand?"

"Sure, I understand," Derrick said. "You're a criminal."

"Right, so don't even think of trying to escape. Besides, even if you did escape, you'd be so lost no one would ever find you but the snakes and buzzards."

"You hurt us and my daddy and uncles will kill you," David said. He was trying hard to act like he wasn't afraid, but he was plenty scared. Not for him but for his brother. Derrick didn't like to listen to anybody, and he might do something stupid.

"I'm treating you good, now aren't I?" the man said. "I bought you hamburgers and fries just like you said you wanted."

"Yeah, but you told us we were coming here to meet Uncle Langston so he could fly us to Dallas."

"I lied. Now I'm going to let you talk to your dad, but you have to tell him how good I'm treating you. And that's all you say. Tell him you're fine and that you want to come home. That way he'll close the deal, and this will all be over."

David nodded. He wanted to talk to Daddy. He wanted that real bad. He didn't like being kidnapped, and he didn't like this cabin. He didn't even want to go to visit his dad at the hospital now. He just wanted to go back to Jack's Bluff. But if he made this man mad, he might never get back.

The man took the cell phone from his pocket and started punching the buttons, whistling the same tune he'd been whistling when he'd picked them up in the car. David put his arm around Derrick's shoulders. He'd do what the man said for now, but he'd find a way out of this. Fast. He wasn't missing Christmas.

THIRTY MINUTES later, there was still no return call. Nick paced the floor, the pain from his injury shooting up his back and settling like smoldering embers in his shoulders and neck.

He welcomed the pain. It was familiar and deserved. He'd willingly taken the risks that playing ball in the NFL carried with it.

His boys didn't deserve this mess they were in and neither did Becky. She might have turned against him, but she'd always been a terrific mother. She was the mainstay for both his sons— steady, constant, yet filled with a love of life.

The same Becky he'd fallen so madly in love with from the first day he'd spotted her jogging across the campus in a pair of tight blue running shorts and showing off the best pair of legs he'd ever seen. He'd asked her out for beers and pizza that very night. To his utter amazement, she'd said yes.

The phone vibrated in his clammy hand an instant before its piercing ring shattered the ominous silence surrounding them. No ID information. His muscles tensed as he took the call.

"Nice that you're so available these days, Nick. Who'd have ever thought you could call a famous Dallas Cowboys receiver and get him on the first ring?"

His grip tightened on the phone. "Are my boys with you?"

"Still don't like talking to people like me, though, do you, Nick Ridgely? Your sons are standing next to me. You can have thirty seconds with each boy."

"Their mother wants to speak to them as well."

"Thirty seconds. You guys divvy it up any way you like. Maybe Brianna Campbell can take a turn, too."

Go to hell! The words hammered against Nick's skull, but never left his mouth. The rotten piece of scum held all the power, and he couldn't risk riling him.

"Daddy."

His heart stopped beating for excruciating moments and then slammed into his chest. "Hi, Derrick. Good to hear your voice."

Becky was at his side in an instant, her eyes begging him for reassurance. He nodded but held on to the phone.

"David and I got kidnapped. Momma's gonna be mad 'cause we got in the car with a stranger, but we thought he was Uncle Langston's friend."

"Mom's not mad, son. Are you okay? Has he hurt you?"

"Not really. He didn't buy the kind of hamburgers we like, though, and he doesn't have much of a TV. It gets lines in it all the time."

A sorry TV. Nick swallowed hard as relief

rushed through him. If that was their biggest complaint, he'd called this right. The guy wasn't a child molester. Now Nick just had to get the bastard the money and get the boys back before the situation worsened.

"Momma wants to say hello."

Tears filled Becky's eyes as she reached for the phone. "Are you okay, sweetheart?"

Nick could only hear her side of the conversation, but he could hear the relief in her voice when she realized as he had that their sons were apparently unhurt.

"Daddy and I are taking care of everything. You'll be back with us soon." There was a short pause, and then she whispered I love you and was apparently handed off to David.

"No, David, I'm not mad. I just want you home with me. Daddy's fine. He's here at the ranch. You'll see both of us soon. Are you warm? Did you get enough to eat? Okay, you can talk to Daddy. I love you."

She handed Nick the phone. His time was almost up with the boys, but now that he knew they were safe, it was the abductor he wanted to talk to. The quicker they made the exchange of his sons for money, the less likely they'd have complications.

"Satisfied?" the man asked after letting Nick have only a sentence or two with David.

"For now, but I mean what I said that you'd best not hurt them."

"Yeah, big guy. I'm doing my part. Now it's time for you to do yours."

"I'm ready."

"I'll give you twenty-four hours to get the cash together. Let's see, that will make it at 4:00 p.m. tomorrow."

"I won't need that long."

"Let's leave it at that for now. And have the plane ready."

"Where do you want to meet?"

"I'll call you in the morning with the details. And, remember, no cops or you'll be very, very sorry."

"I'm doing this your way, but if you hurt my sons, I swear I'll track you down, tear your heart out and feed it to the livestock."

"Just get the money and the plane."

Nick held on to the phone after the connection was broken, staring into the flames and the crackling logs in the big stone fireplace. His boys were safe, but he wouldn't breathe easy until they were back on the ranch.

He told Becky what the abductor had said.

She cringed even though there was basically nothing new in the kidnapper's demands.

"And that's all?" she asked. "We just hand over the money and he releases the boys?"

"Apparently."

"Then we don't need twenty-four hours. The bank knows I'm good for the funds even if I don't have that much in totally liquid assets. If that's not good enough, my brothers and mother will sign any documents the bank requires."

"I told him we'd have the ransom sooner, but I'll get the money," Nick said, his tone more adamant than he'd intended.

"This isn't about you, Nick, and I couldn't care less about some silly pride thing you seem to have going. I just want David and Derrick home—and safe."

"Don't you think that's what I want?"

She shrugged and walked away, stopping to stand near the blazing fire. She warmed her hands before turning to meet his gaze.

"I don't know what you want anymore, Nick. Maybe I never did."

"No, I guess maybe you didn't."

And that summed up their ten years of marriage. Nothing could compare with the torment of the abduction, but still knowing he was losing Becky cut straight to the heart. He might deserve this, but he didn't see how.

Bart stepped into the den. "Mother gave Juanita the week off so that she didn't have to explain to her about the kidnapping, but the ladies made sandwiches and warmed soup. Can I get you some?"

"I can't eat," Becky said, "but we've finished up in here. Tell mother I'm going to my room for a while—and that I really need to be alone."

"Sure."

Being alone was the last thing Nick needed. And oddly, the soup sounded good. "I'll join you. I just need a minute to wash up."

"You're holding your neck at a funny angle," Bart said. "You must still be in a lot of pain from that hit you took yesterday."

"Some, but don't talk about it. I figure if I ignore it, it will give up and go away." He didn't believe that for a second, but still he'd leave the pain meds in his duffel bag. He was in the middle of the biggest game of his life, and he had to be completely alert.

DERRICK LAY in the twin bed and stared into the blackness. It was so dark he couldn't even see David though he was just a few feet away. There was a window, but the weird guy who'd brought them here had nailed boards over it so they couldn't escape while he was sleeping.

This was all Derrick's fault. He should have known Uncle Langston wouldn't send someone to get them who looked like this guy. But then he didn't look so different from some of the cowboys who worked at the ranch. Some of them had tattoos, too, and they were good wranglers and nice people. Uncle Nick and Uncle Matt said so.

Only the guy hadn't mentioned Uncle Langston until Derrick did. He just stopped the car and called them by name. Then Derrick had asked him if he was there to take them to the hangar where Uncle Langston kept his jet. He said yes and told them to get in. Derrick had hopped in first.

All his fault, so he had to come up with a plan to get them out of here before this crazy guy started twisting their arms behind their backs again. Grown men weren't supposed to hurt kids.

Christmas was Friday. Their pageant was Christmas Eve. He had to come up with an escape plan fast.

He was smart for a third grader. He made A's, well except in math. He figured math didn't really matter if you were going to be a football player. He'd never once seen his dad working multiplication problems.

They could blindside the kidnapper and knock him out with a skillet. He'd seen that once on a TV show. Or sneak into his room while he was asleep and tie him up with the sheets. Only he and David were locked in the bedroom, and if they tried to break the door down he'd hear them.

But they could…

He closed his eyes and then opened them suddenly as the plan appeared like magic in his mind. He climbed out of the bed in the dark and felt his way to David's bed, sliding his hands across the covers until his fingers brushed his brother's arm.

"David." He kept his voice low but shook him awake. "We don't have to worry about Daddy getting five million dollars. I know how we can escape."

Chapter Four

As it turned out, getting five million dollars in cash on short notice was more of a problem than any of them had anticipated. Nick had the funds but not in liquid assets. Converting it to cash would incur time that they didn't have.

Finally, it had been Langston who'd arranged the transaction through the business account of Collingsworth Oil. Becky wasn't sure how Langston had explained his need for so much money in small denominations, but apparently he had, or else the bank didn't ask questions of their larger business accounts.

Becky and Nick were on their way into Houston to pick up the money from one of the main branches now. Nick was still in obvious pain from Sunday's injury, so Becky was at the wheel and fighting the noonday traffic. Nick was holding his head at a weird angle and massaging the back of his neck.

"Do you have something to take for the pain?" she asked.

"Back at the ranch, but I'm not taking anything that affects my judgment."

Becky took the freeway exit to the downtown area. The city was decorated for the holidays with huge wreaths on the fronts of buildings and storefronts and holiday displays in all the shop windows. The light changed to red, and she stopped near the corner where a Salvation Army worker was standing by her kettle and ringing a large red bell.

The spirit of the season came crashing down on Becky like blankets of gloom. Ever since the boys were old enough to tear wrapping paper from a present, Christmas had been her favorite time of year. She loved the carols and decorations, the boys' excitement and the traditions.

They always decorated the tree before dinner on Christmas Eve. The entire family took part, but David and Derrick had more fun than anyone even though they spent as much time sneaking fudge from the kitchen as they did hanging ornaments.

Then, as far back as Becky could remember,

they'd had hot tamales and Texas chili on Christmas Eve before leaving for the community Christmas pageant at their church. It was the highlight of the evening with even the eggnog, hot chocolate and desserts that followed taking a backseat.

"Derrick has a speaking part in the Christmas pageant, and David plays his drum." She didn't know why she'd blurted that out except that the thought of Christmas without them was unbearable.

"They'll be there for it," Nick said. "The boys will be back with us by tonight."

She wanted desperately to believe that, but the cold, hard knots of doubt wouldn't let go. The light changed again, and she sped through the intersection, eager to get the money in hand.

"I'd like to be here for the pageant," Nick said. "And for Christmas morning, too."

The old resentment surged. "Don't you have a big game in Chicago on Saturday?" Even when he hadn't been cleared to dress out, he'd always traveled with the team.

"I'll miss the game," he said.

"Are you feeling guilty, Nick?"

"I just think it's important that I be here for Christmas this year. Can we just leave it at that?"

She spotted the bank ahead and determinedly forced her bitterness aside. She parked the car in a lot across the street from the bank. Nick paid the attendant while she grabbed the large valises they'd bought for the money and locked the car door. When they left the bank, an armed guard in street clothes would walk them to the car.

"I'll take those," Nick said, joining her and slipping the bags from her arm.

He slung the strap over his left shoulder and linked his right arm with hers. An incredible feeling of déjà vu swept over her. Walking arm in arm with Nick, the valise over his shoulder, a feeling of urgency burned inside both of them.

Like the night they'd rushed to the hospital for the twins to be born. Her water had broken and she'd been propelled into labor with strong contractions that came much faster than normal. Nick had flown into action, trying to be tough but clearly as frightened as she was. But he'd stayed with her every second.

The image of him holding both the boys in his arms minutes after they were born pushed its way into her mind. His smile. His wet eyes. The tenderness when he'd kissed her and thanked her for giving him the world. She shivered as the memories took hold.

Nick let his hand slip down to encase hers. "It's going to be okay, baby. This is all going to be okay."

But who was Nick to promise a happy ending?

DAVID WAS CURLED UP in a smelly old chair with stains all over it. He looked like he was asleep, but Derrick saw his eyes move every now and then and figured he was just faking it, probably thinking about Derrick's stupid plan.

It had sounded great in the dark. The kidnapper couldn't watch them every second. He had to go to the bathroom and when he did, they'd raise one of the windows, kick out the screen and make a run for it.

They were fast. Derrick had won the relay race at school field day last year, and David had come in second. The kidnapper wouldn't have a chance to catch them if they had a head start. Sure, they might get lost in the woods, but Derrick wasn't worried about that. Uncle Matt had taken them camping lots of times and taught them all about survival. They'd find their way back to the road and wave down a passing car. Super easy.

Problem was that while they were locked in the bedroom last night, the kidnapper had nailed wood over the rest of the windows. That had made Derrick really mad, but he wasn't giving up. He just needed a better plan. He'd seen all the *Home Alone* movies a bunch of times. If that kid could take care of himself, so could Derrick and David.

In fact he and David could do it better. There were two of them and only one jerky kidnapper. That's why he wasn't really all that afraid. He'd let them out of the bedroom this morning, but the house was sealed tight. The kidnapper had the key to the front door and the back door was nailed shut.

The guy was lying on the lumpy old sofa now, whistling that same weird tune he was always whistling and watching a movie on the old TV that kept fading in and out. It looked like it could be a hundred years old, except their neighbor Billy Mack had told him they didn't have television back then.

Derrick waited for the commercial. The guy always hollered for him to shut up if he talked during the show. An advertisement for Dodge trucks popped up on the screen.

"How come you live out here all by yourself?"

"'Cause I'm not filthy rich like your parents."

"You could get a job and make some money."

"Don't get smart with me, kid."

"I wasn't."

The picture on the screen started rolling, and the man went over to fiddle with the knobs again. When that didn't work, he took the screwdriver from his back pocket and made a few adjustments on the back of the set. The picture steadied. He went back to the sofa and dropped the screwdriver onto the table next to him, beneath a heavy lamp that had scratch marks all over it.

Derrick walked over and propped on the edge of the sofa. He picked up the screwdriver and ran his fingers along the tapered tip. "Did you kidnap us 'cause our daddy's a superstar?"

"Who told you he was a superstar?"

"Nobody, but he is. He's been to the Pro Bowl three times."

"Is that what it takes these days for a kid to like his old man? You gotta be a superstar?"

"No," Derrick said. "You just have to love your kids like you're supposed to. Didn't your daddy love you?"

"Yeah. So much he beat me every time he got drunk and yelled at me when he was sober. Now, shut up. My show's back on."

"What about your mom?" Derrick asked, ignoring the man's comments to shut up.

"What about her?"

"Did she take care of you?"

"Yeah, sure, sometimes. When she was around. Enough with the questions. I didn't need nobody when I was a kid and don't need nobody now."

"Then why don't you just let us go?"

The guy didn't answer. But Derrick knew he wasn't going to let them go until he had the money from their parents, and he didn't see how Momma and Daddy would get five million dollars.

Derrick got up and walked to the kitchen though there was nothing in there to eat. They'd finished off the last two burgers for breakfast this morning. That had been hours ago. He wondered what Juanita was cooking for lunch.

He opened the refrigerator and looked at the empty shelves. That's when he heard the yell, a high-pitched shriek that sounded as if someone had their arm torn off at the shoulder. Derrick took off for the living room and then stopped in the doorway staring at the blood pooling on the floor by the couch.

Now he was scared.

"Quick, grab the door key out of his pocket, and get your jacket. We gotta get out of here," David yelled.

Derrick didn't move. He just stared at the kidnapper. The man was sprawled out on the floor behind the television set, blood pouring from a cut on the back of his head. The lamp was lying on the floor next to him, its shade at a cockeyed angle. "What happened?"

"He was tinkering with the TV, and I snuck up on him and hit him with the lamp."

"Do you think he's dead?"

"I don't know. C'mon. We have to get out of here now."

Derrick leaned over the man. He'd seen a dead cow before, but he'd never seen a dead man. It creeped him out, but he reached into the front pocket of the man's trousers and retrieved his key ring.

Derrick wasn't sure which one opened the door, so he tossed the key ring to David. He still wasn't sure if the man was breathing, but he could hear his own heart. It sounded like a banging drum.

David had found the right key and had the door open when Derrick saw the man's hand move. He wasn't dead, just knocked out. And when he came to, he was going to be roaring mad. Time to haul it.

Derrick picked up the screwdriver and

grabbed his jacket from the back of a chair. He didn't know why he needed the tool, but it seemed like a good idea to have it. He took off running as fast as he could, finally catching up with David at the edge of the woods. They kept running, tripping over roots and getting hung up in branches and vines.

Derrick's legs started to ache. His chest hurt, too. And he was thirsty. He was glad when David stopped and leaned against a tree trunk.

"Do you think he's chasing us?" Derrick asked when he'd caught his breath enough to talk.

"He thinks he's getting five million dollars for us," David said. "What do you think?"

"Yeah, but you hurt him bad."

"Nah. I knocked him out, but his legs will still work when he comes to. We have to keep moving and try to find a road."

"We should have stolen his cell phone," Derrick said. "Then we could have called Momma or Daddy or 911."

"Yeah, but we didn't. So we gotta keep on the move. I don't want to spend the night in the woods."

"We can do it if we have to." Derrick tried to sound brave since he hadn't done much toward helping them escape. "We've slept under the stars before when we were camping with Uncle Matt."

"We had food then," David said. "And lanterns."

And Uncle Matt, though neither of them mentioned that now. Derrick jumped at a sound like cracking twigs in the distance. And then they heard the man's voice calling their names.

"Keep up with me," David called, and he was off again with Derrick right behind him. "I don't want to have to really hurt that man."

Chapter Five

The fragrant smell of pine filled the house, just as it had every day since last Saturday when Lenora's sons had helped her drape the mantel and staircase with the fresh cut greenery. Her much-handled nativity was carefully placed along the top of the piano where they always gathered to sing carols after church on Christmas Eve.

Randolph, Lenora's deceased husband, had spent hours in his workshop, first cutting out and then coating each of the nativity figures with lead-free paint for Langston's first Christmas. The set had been a favorite of all her children from the time they were toddlers and first heard the story of the birth of the baby Jesus. David and Derrick had spent their share of time moving the figures around and playing with the miniature sheep, cattle and camels as well.

The house was almost the way it had always

been mere days before Christmas—except that it was shrouded in anxiety and the season's joviality was hushed by the burden of heavy hearts. Only Jaime was making a stab at normalcy. She was sitting on the floor by the hearth, tape, scissors and rolls of shiny Christmas wrap at her elbow.

Christmas in the Collingsworth family had never been a time for lavish spending. When her children had been growing up, Lenora and Randolph had insisted that the focus of the season be on love and sharing with those less fortunate.

It was a tradition that had stuck, and instead of rabid shopping that they could well afford, each member of the family always put a lot of thought and frequently a lot of time and effort into their gifts.

Lenora's treats for her family had been carefully selected and wrapped weeks ago, but today she couldn't remember anything she'd bought except the skateboards the boys had picked out and begged for on a recent Houston shopping trip.

The front door to the house opened, and Lenora hurried into the hallway. Hopefully this time it would be Becky and Nick returning with the ransom money and not some pushy reporter who'd managed to bypass the guards at the gate.

Earlier today, one had cut down part of the fence to get on the property. Jim Bob had spotted him and sent him packing quickly enough. Like Matt said, if all their wranglers were as dependable as Jim Bob, running the ranch would be play.

"The money's in hand," Nick called, holding up a large valise. "Now all we need is that phone call."

"Then you haven't heard from the abductor today?"

"Not a word," Becky said, the weight of the situation dragging her voice the way it pulled at her face and painted dark circles beneath her eyes.

"I'll fix you a plate," Lenora said. "Trish and Jaclyn made chicken pasta and a salad for lunch."

Becky shook her head. "None for me. We stopped for lunch in Houston."

"Which she ate two bites of," Nick said.

He was sick over the boys but obviously worried about Becky as well. He was a good man, cocky and fun loving and sometimes she thought he had a football for a heart, but her sons liked Nick and that said a lot about his character. Lenora had always been sure he and

Becky would work out their differences and make their marriage work.

But Becky was stubborn, always had been, and once she made up her mind about something, she developed a severe case of tunnel vision that never let her see another side.

She was a loving mother, though, generous to a fault. And unlike Jaime, she was seemingly unaware of her beauty or the fact that men were instantly attracted to her, as much for her grace and intellect as her stunning looks.

But stubborn, nonetheless. She'd no doubt inherited that trait from her grandfather. Jeremiah was the most hardheaded man Lenora had ever seen in her life. She'd be hard pressed to explain why everyone loved him. They just did. So did she.

Lenora and Nick followed Becky into the den.

Becky stopped next to the stack of wrapped gifts. "What are you doing?"

Jaime stuck a large red bow to a package. "Wrapping presents."

"How can you?" Becky's voice shook with unchecked emotion. "How can you go on like nothing's wrong when David and Derrick are in the hands of some madman?"

Jaime pulled a strip of tape from the dispenser. "Because I won't let myself believe that they're not going to walk though that door tonight with you and Nick, safe and excited to be home. When they do, they'll expect presents to shake and try to guess what's inside."

"But what if you're wrong? What if they don't come home tonight? What if…" Becky exploded, kicking one of the presents. It skidded across the thick rug and onto the wooden floor before thudding against the wall.

Jaime jumped up, dropping the roll of ribbon she'd just picked up as she pulled her sister into her arms. "Oh, Becky, you have to have faith that the boys are safe. We all do. We *have* to believe."

Both sisters were in tears now, holding on to each other while the fire crackled in the huge stone fireplace and streams of red satin entangled their feet. Tears burned at the back of Lenora's eyes. Jaime never ceased to amaze her. She'd never loved either daughter more.

NICK BACKED out of the den and went to the kitchen to get a cup of coffee though he was already so jumpy he could barely sit in one place for over five minutes. That and the ache in his neck and shoulders had made the ride back to the ranch pure torture.

There was a plate of homemade peanut butter cookies next to the coffeepot. There were always homemade cookies at Jack's Bluff. Juanita kept the freezer stuffed with them.

He picked up one. Still warm. One of his sisters-in-law must have done the baking honors in Juanita's absence. Everyone wanted to help. Everyone needed to keep busy.

He'd married into one terrific family—and then he'd blown it. How had he ever let things between him and Becky get to this point?

Who was he fooling? He'd known from the very beginning he wasn't the man Becky thought he was. She'd seen in him what she wanted to see, loved a man who hadn't really existed. It had just been a matter of time before she saw him for the fake he really was.

If anything, he'd loved Becky too much. He still did. There wasn't a day he didn't miss having her in his life, not a night that he didn't long to have her in his bed and in his arms. He couldn't even imagine making love to another woman.

But he'd never expected to bring this kind of terror into all their lives. If he hadn't gotten hurt… If they hadn't shown the boys' picture on TV… If the boys hadn't had to go to school

Monday to make up for those lost hurricane days instead of already being out for the holidays...

So many ifs, but the biggest one now was if he was doing the right thing in not going to the police or trying to bring the FBI in on this. He wanted to believe he was right, but the longer this took, the more the doubts tormented him. What if he was wrong and the man never called back?

He put the cookie to his lips, then pulled his hand away and dropped the morsel into the trash. His stomach was still struggling to digest the ham sandwich he'd forced down at lunch. He was filling a pottery mug with the strong coffee when his cell phone jangled.

The coffee spilled over his fingers as he set the cup down, stuck his hand into his pocket and gripped the phone. He answered without bothering to check the caller ID. "Hello."

"This is Dr. Cambridge's nurse. I'm calling for Nick Ridgely."

Damn. The doctor's office. They'd badger him about getting back to the hospital so that they could finish the tests. The head trainer for the team had already called him about the same thing twice today. He didn't have time for this.

"This is Nick Ridgely, but I'm expecting a

very important call and can't tie up my phone right now."

"This is an important call, Mr. Ridgely. The doctor needs to speak with you. Hold on. He's right here."

The seconds Nick waited seemed interminable. His phone line needed to remain open.

"We didn't meet, but I'm one of the staff neurosurgeons at the hospital where you were treated Sunday night. My colleague Dr. Krause asked me to review your records."

"I understand, but I can't talk now. I'll have to call you back later."

The doctor kept talking. "You left the hospital in a hurry."

"There was a family emergency. I signed the AMA form."

"I understand that. Are you still in a lot of pain?"

"Some." To put it mildly. To put it more accurately, the pain was constant, but waiting for a call from the abductor was a thousand times worse.

"I can't stress enough how important it is for you to check back in the hospital, Mr. Ridgely. It's urgent that we get a CAT scan and an MRI."

"Yeah, right. I'll do that one day next week."

"I don't think you understand the seriousness or potential damage you may suffer from your injury."

"Okay, give it to me straight—and fast. What's the worse that can happen?"

"The X-rays indicate that you may have a unilateral locked facet. It's not a common injury even in football, but it happens when the neck is flexed and rotated at the same time. The risk is that the spine may be unstable and can slip. Any sudden movement or bending of your neck could leave you paralyzed."

Nick fought the urge to slam a fist into the wall. He couldn't deal with this now. He had a contusion or whatever the hell the E.R. doc had said the other night. He just needed time for it to heal and he'd be fine. If it was something worse, he'd surely know it.

"Thanks for calling, Dr. Cambridge. I'll come back in for the tests as soon as I can."

It wasn't until the conversation was over and the connection broken that he realized Becky was standing in the doorway to the kitchen watching him. He had no idea how much of the conversation she'd heard.

"What's wrong?" she asked.

He shook his head. "Nothing." He needed to play this cool for her sake, though he felt anything but.

"Who was on the phone?"

"Dr. Cambridge reminding me that he needs to check out my neck in a few days."

"That's all?"

"That's it."

"You're lying, Nick. I heard the apprehension in your voice when you were on the phone, and it's written all over your face now."

"It's no big deal, Becky. I may miss a game or two." He turned his back on her and stamped toward the back door, not bothering to grab a jacket. Had it been freezing he doubted he'd feel the cold. How could he when he was sinking into hell?

Paralysis. A devil of a diagnosis to hold over a man whose sons were in danger. It wasn't like he could just walk away from the kidnapping. He'd be careful. No sudden moves. That was the best he could do.

NICK HAD SHUT her out again, just like always. Becky had seen his face when he was talking to the doctor. The news had been bad, but instead of sharing with her, he'd stalked out the back door to deal with his problems without her.

It shouldn't matter so much in light of all that was going on. It shouldn't but it did, maybe because of what they were going through.

He expected her to lean on him, but he was not about to let himself need any emotional support from her. Not about to admit that he was upset over some damn football injury that he admitted wasn't serious.

Maybe he found it easier to confide in Brianna.

Anger and bitterness pooled in Becky's stomach until she stormed out the back door and down the steps. When she spotted Nick walking toward the stables, she ran to catch up with him. He turned, saw that it was her footfalls he'd heard and kept walking.

He didn't stop until he reached the railed fence that surrounded the riding arena. He propped his elbows on the top rung and stared straight ahead as if there were something to see.

A gust of wind cut through Becky's thin cotton shirt, and she hugged her arms around her chest as she approached him. Her nerves were raw, her composure diminished to the point she had to hold on to the railing to keep steady. "What was that about?"

"I don't know what you're talking about."

"Your rushing off to brood over your injury instead of telling me what the doctor said."

"I'm not brooding."

"I think you are. All that talk of being here for Christmas with the boys was just your guilt talking, wasn't it? Well, if you think I'm worried about your career while my boys are missing, you're dead wrong."

"The thought never entered my mind. But just for the record, do you actually think I'm *not* going through hell every second David and Derrick are with that lunatic?"

"I don't know what you're feeling, Nick, but whatever it is, I'm sure football and your star performance is involved in it."

She stepped away, realizing she said too much. She let her temper and vulnerability get the better of her.

Nick grabbed her arm and held her, his gaze so intense his dark eyes seemed to be searing into hers. "I won't contest the divorce any longer, Becky. I'll sign whatever you say."

She shivered as he kicked at a clod of dirt before releasing her and walking away. The finality of their relationship had never felt so real. But it was what she wanted. Holding on to a corpse wouldn't bring it back to life.

The analogy sent new chills up her spine to eventually settle deep in her bones. She forced herself to follow Nick back to the house.

The boys' safety was all that mattered, and Nick and his cell phone were her one link to her sons. No matter how she and Nick felt about each other, they had to get through this together.

BULL MUTTERED a new series of curses with every step he made in the growing darkness. His head felt as if it were splitting open and his brains were draining into the huge knot that had formed around the cut on the back of his head.

The blood had matted in his hair, and when he touched the wound, it felt like the sticky mess that had passed for oatmeal in the penitentiary. It gagged him, and he'd thrown up once, though the nausea was probably more from the throbbing pain at the base of his skull than the repulsive feel of his bloody scalp.

He'd never expected Nick's sons would go violent on him. They had to get their nasty streak from their father. Big-shot NFL receiver. No wonder Becky had separated from him.

He stopped and leaned against a tree trunk,

gasping for air and trying to get his bearings before he was the one lost in these stinking woods. The image of Becky fixed in his murky mind until he dissolved into a fit of coughing.

He had to find those boys. Nick would never pay off if he couldn't produce them. No money. No flight to Mexico.

Worse, if the kids got free, they'd be able to identify him and he'd end up back in prison. No way he could let that happen. He had to find the vicious little devils before they reached the highway and flagged down a passing motorist.

Just his luck they'd been too smart to head back down the dirt road near the cabin to the highway. If they had, he could have taken his car and easily caught them before they reached help.

But the prints of their tennis shoes had led straight into the woods. He'd been able to track them easily at first, before they'd reached higher, dryer ground. Half the time they'd wandered in larger and larger circles—which meant they couldn't be that far away now.

But it was getting darker, and he'd lost all sight of their trail a good half hour ago.

An owl hooted overhead, claiming his hunting grounds for the night. Well, the dumb bird would have to share it. Something slithered at his feet. It was too cold for snakes to be slinking though the pine straw, but still he tensed as he searched the ground.

He didn't see the escaping creature, but he saw something a whole lot better. A screwdriver. He picked it up and rolled the amber handle around in his hand. It was his, all right, at least it was the one he used to constantly tinker with that piece-of-crap TV.

Apparently the boys had taken it with them when they'd gone on the run. Which meant they'd been in this exact spot, likely minutes ago. His heart began to pound, bringing more pain but still urging him on. It was almost as if he could smell the boys now.

This time when he got them in hand, there would be no more Mr. Nice Guy. He wouldn't be made a fool of twice.

The twenty-four hours were up. Nick would be waiting for his call. He might be the rich, NFL superstar, but there wouldn't be one damn thing he could do but wait.

Besting Nick Ridgely was almost as good a prize as the cash.

Chapter Six

The twenty-four hour mark came and went with no word from the abductor. By eight-thirty Tuesday night, Becky felt as if every breath took supreme effort and every heartbeat pumped new agony into her veins. Earlier the family den in the big house had been crackling with anticipation and conversation.

Even then every phrase and syllable had sounded forced, brave attempts to keep the mood positive. The family was all still present, but the silence now was like an icy spray that froze the oxygen in the still, heavy air.

They'd done everything the abductor had asked. The ransom was waiting. The plane was ready to go. Langston was planning to fly the plane himself, and Zach would go along as copilot.

But with each tick of the clock, the dread swelled. So did the doubts.

Following Nick's wishes to leave the cops out of this might have been a monumental mistake. Had they put out an instant AMBER Alert, the boys might be home tonight, sleeping in their own beds. No one was blaming him, but she was certain he was second-guessing himself though they'd barely spoken since her blow up this afternoon.

Nick walked to the hearth and propped both hands on the mantel, leaning close even though the earlier blaze had died to glowing embers. His face was drawn, his neck corded from muscles that looked taut enough to break.

Zach walked over to stand beside him. Blackie padded over to Becky and cocked his head to the side; the lab's dark, soulful eyes peered into hers. She patted his head absently, sure that he not only missed his masters but sensed the tension.

Zach put a hand on Nick's shoulder. "I can get the ball rolling with police involvement anytime you say. All you have to do is give me the word."

Nick nodded.

"Another option might be to hire a team of private investigators," Matt said.

"Or we could get a search party organized," Bart added. "There's not a man in the county who wouldn't be out there right now going door to door to see if anyone's seen David and Derrick or knows anything about the abduction."

"And then the media circus would take over," Langston said. "But maybe that would help flush this guy out. I just don't know."

"That's the problem," Nick said. "There's no way to know."

"Why doesn't he call?" Becky lamented out loud, saying what they all were thinking. "If he wants the money, why doesn't he call?" The terror tore at her throat and her voice.

Jaime came over and settled on the arm of her chair, slipping an arm around Becky's shoulders. "He's going to call, sis. He may be rethinking the exchange, but he's going to call."

"You don't know that. Those are just empty words."

Trish walked in with a plate of oatmeal cookies and a bowl of sliced apples. She set them on the coffee table and slid onto the sofa beside Langston.

"Becky and I have to talk," Nick said.

"We'll clear out," Jaime said, "and give you a little privacy."

"No." Becky stood and struggled for a grip on her composure. "All of you stay as long as you want. I need some fresh air. Nick and I can take a walk."

Nick nodded again. "I'm not discounting any of your advice, guys. And I'll tell you this, I don't know of a single person on earth I'd rather have in this with me than the Collingsworth clan. That includes the FBI or any police force in the world."

"But don't rule any of that out," Langston reminded him. "It's not either/or. You can have us and professionals."

Becky paused to give her mother's hand a squeeze as she passed her. "Keep praying," she whispered.

"Always."

This time Becky stopped for a jacket and took a flashlight from the rack by the back door. She didn't wait for Nick, but she heard the crinkle of leather as he pulled on his own jacket and followed her.

She noticed everything, the creaking of the top step when she put her foot on it, the rustle of the wind in the oak trees, the sting of cold air on her cheeks.

It was as if the totality of her being had been crammed into this moment and the decisions they were about to make. Her boys' safe return, their very lives might depend on what she and Nick did in the next few minutes and the next few hours. She wouldn't leave this all to him the way she had earlier.

Nick caught up with her hurried stride and fell in beside her. "I thought we'd hear from the abductor by now. I was sure he just wanted his hands on the money as soon as possible."

"And now you've changed your mind?" she asked, fighting her frustration.

"Not entirely. There's no reason for him not to call us if it's the ransom he wants. He may have met with complications."

"How complicated can it be to make a phone call?"

"He could be driving somewhere to use a public phone or to buy one with limited minutes from the convenience store. He'll want to make sure we can't use the phone to find him before he's ready to close the deal. Maybe he got caught in traffic."

"You think he's just driving around with our boys in the car? How is he keeping them quiet? He might have them drugged them or locked them up in the trunk. Maybe that's why he said they weren't available the first time he called."

Her voice climbed steadily higher. Worse, she wasn't even sure she was making sense, but terrifying possibilities were storming her mind.

"Maybe he's just enjoying his power to keep us on edge," he countered.

"More than he'd enjoy five million dollars in his hand?" No. If this were only about the money, he would have called. They could have delivered it to him tonight. He could be in Mexico. This could all be over.

"We can't just sit here and do nothing, Nick. He might be taking the boys out of the country or taking them who knows where. The longer we wait, the more difficult it will be to track him down. And…"

The rest of the sentence was swallowed by the growing lump in her throat. Nick put a hand on her shoulder. Her chest constricted painfully at his touch. She needed his strength, needed him. Yet she couldn't let herself lean on him. Reluctantly, she pulled away.

"Does my touch bother you that much, Becky?"

Yes, in ways she couldn't deal with in this situation. "I'm just trying to get through this, Nick. I have to be strong."

"We're in this together."

"I can't very well ignore that, can I, Nick, since you're the one the abductor contacts—or doesn't contact. You're the one making the decisions." The bitterness crept into her voice. She wished it hadn't, but there was too much at risk here to worry about that now.

Nick's cell phone rang. Becky's heart jumped to her throat. Please let it be the abductor. *Please let him be ready to give her back her sons.*

Nick's hello was firm, in control. She held her breath then released a sharp, painful exhale when she heard the agitation in Nick's voice.

Something was wrong. Her legs went weak, but somehow she kept standing, her mind grasping for meaning in every word Nick spoke. "HELLO, NICKY BOY. I guess you realize by now that there's been a slight delay in our plans."

The cocky bastard. He was enjoying their torment. Nick's teeth ground together and his muscles clenched. "You said five million in small bills and a flight out of the country. I'm ready to meet those demands, so let's get this over and done with."

"Not so fast, champ. The boys are asleep. You don't want me dragging them out in the middle of the night, do you? Besides, I have a couple of things I need to take care of before I tell America *adios*."

"I want my boys, and I want them now. Tell me where to meet you or I go to the cops."

"That would be a major mistake if you want to get them back alive."

"Let me talk to them."

"I told you they're sleeping. I'll have them call you in the morning. We'll talk specifics then. But there is one other thing. I've decided I need a hostage with me on the flight to Mexico. You know, someone to be sure you don't plan any tricks like aborting the flight once you have your sons. I'm thinking having Becky along would be a great insurance plan."

Nick's body went rigid. "My wife is not a bargaining tool."

"Why not? You've already replaced her with Brianna Campbell. You're surely not so selfish as to deny me the pleasure of her company on a short flight."

"Five million. Do you want it or not?"

"You do realize that you're not calling the shots here, Nick. I want Becky on that plane. If there's any funny stuff, she takes a bullet. That way I know you won't have an armed greeting party waiting for me when we land."

"You want a hostage, you can have me. That's my best offer."

"I'll sleep on it and let you know in the morning."

"Let me talk to the boys." The menacing click of the phone as it disconnected swallowed his demand. Nick stood still, his back ramrod straight, numb to the pain from his injury.

"What's wrong?" Becky demanded.

"Change in plans," he said.

"What kind of change?"

"Let's go to the porch. I talk better when I'm sitting." And he needed a minute to digest the kidnapper's new demand. Not that he'd even consider letting Becky get on a plane with that lunatic, even if she agreed. Their divorce wasn't final yet. She was still his wife and the mother of his sons.

She was still his to protect.

A LITTLE MORE than a half hour later, Nick and Becky sat down at the big oak table in the dining room with the core members of the Collingsworth family around them. The somber mood was foreign to the familiar setting where Nick had joined in many family celebrations and marvelous Sunday brunches.

The room was virtually unchanged from the way it had looked the Sunday morning he and Becky had officially announced their engagement, though it had been almost totally destroyed in the explosion this past summer.

That day the entire family had almost lost their lives for the sin of befriending and trusting the wrong man. Had it not been for the quick thinking of Matt's wife, Shelly, they would have been obliterated, his sons along with them.

If there was any weakness in the Collingsworths, it was their willingness to see the best in people. They'd certainly done that with Nick. Tonight that trust felt like weights pressing into his chest. He'd insisted on laying out the game plan, on going with his instincts. He'd made critical mistakes.

He'd failed the people who needed him most. Not for the first time and the memories that admittance unleashed were attacking him full force.

Langston took the seat at the head of the table. Lenora sat at the other end. Becky sat between him and Zach on one side of the table. Jaime, Bart, Matt and his wife, Shelly, sat opposite them. Jeremiah was still keeping to his room and had not been apprised of the situation.

Had the elderly gentleman with the temper of Attila the Hun and the determination of a bull known, Nick was certain he'd have been right there with them.

Becky had specifically requested Shelly's presence. Her CIA experience might be invaluable. The other wives had suggested they not be part of the decision-making process though they were there to help in any way they could. The solidarity of the Collingsworths in crisis was nothing short of astonishing.

Nick was fairly certain the room had never been this quiet before. It was as if all of them were holding their collective breaths waiting to hear what Becky had to say. She'd held up so well on the porch that Nick had feared she was slipping into shock.

That wasn't the case. She was stronger than he'd ever known. Courageous. Determined. And ready to fight. She was a hell of a woman. Always had been. Maybe her strength had been their downfall, though it was definitely helping to hold him together now.

Nick filled the family in with the basics of his latest conversation with the abductor, minus the information about his wanting Becky for a hostage. He hadn't even mentioned that to her.

It wasn't an option, so there was no reason to bring it up for discussion.

The family listened without interrupting until he was through, but he could sense the dread imbedding more deeply in their souls as he talked.

"I obviously misjudged the situation," Nick said. "I should have listened to the rest of you in the first place."

"Not necessarily," Shelly offered, the tone of her voice indicating the observation was more than sympathy. "You sensed the man was desperate and acting on impulse after seeing the boys' picture on the news. First instincts are frequently right on target. But that same impulsiveness might also make him edgy after the fact, and he may fear he's walking into a trap, thus his hesitance to make the exchange."

"But wouldn't his being on the edge make him even more dangerous?" Jaime asked. "Wouldn't that be more reason to move on this quickly and with every weapon in the arsenal?"

Shelly nodded. "Especially since we can't accurately judge the man's mental condition. But at the same time, we don't want to do anything to cause him to hurt the boys."

"Which is what might happen if we let the

media get hold of this," Becky said. "Nick and I have talked and made the decision that we can't take that risk."

"So what are you saying?" Zach asked. "That you don't want police involvement? If so, I think you're making a big mistake."

"No, we just want to keep this as quiet as possible. We're open to suggestions."

Zach nodded. "At the very least, we need an APB out to all the law enforcement officers in at least a three-state area to be on the lookout for David and Derrick. And we need to contact the border patrol."

"I'd say that's top priority," Matt said. "We can't let him take the boys into Mexico."

They were talking prevention, but for all they knew, the man could have crossed that border with David and Derrick hours ago. That, too, would be Nick's fault. No one said it, but they all knew it.

"With that much law enforcement involved, word of the abduction is going to leak to the media," Langston said.

"Not necessarily," Zach said. "At least not before we can track the boys down. Everyone takes crime involving kids seriously. Besides, I think it's a risk we have to take."

"And we need a description of that car that Eddie Mason saw them getting into," Lenora said.

"I've got you covered there," Zach said.

"Black Oldsmobile sedan. An old one, an eighties model he thought. Dent in back right fender with patch of rust showing through. No hubcaps."

"When did you talk to Eddie Mason?" Nick asked. "I thought we'd agreed you wouldn't."

"I didn't. There are more subtle ways to get information. I just mentioned to the crossing guard that someone had reported seeing a group of teenagers speeding though the area on Monday about the time school let out and asked if he'd seen it. When he said no, I asked if he'd noticed any unfamiliar cars in the area."

"Did he say he saw David and Derrick get into the Oldsmobile?"

"No, but he said the car had driven by the school a few times before the closing bell. That made him suspicious, and he was about to call in a report to the sheriff's department when the bell rang and the kids came pouring out."

"Then we don't know if that's the same car," Matt said.

"We wouldn't if he'd left it at that, but when I asked if he'd seen the car again, he said that when he got a break from the crossing duties he spotted the same car parked across the street from the church.

"Two boys climbed in and the driver pulled away, so he figured it was just a relative who didn't know the rule about where to pick up students."

"Did he say anything about the driver?"

"That he wasn't a teenager and he wasn't speeding, since he thought that's what I was investigating. Said the driver looked to be in his late twenties, maybe older, but he'd just gotten a glimpse of him."

"Thanks," Nick said. "At least we have that much to go on."

"I'd still like to call my contact at the FBI," Langston said, "and get his take on this."

"I agree," Shelly said.

"And so do Nick and I," Becky said. "We've made that decision."

Becky had suggested it first, and Nick had been in total agreement. He'd forced himself to believe things would never get this far, that if he followed the abductor's orders to the letter his boys would be home tonight. Now the terrifying possibilities he'd worked so hard to keep at bay filled his mind.

It had to be the same for Becky. He ached to reach out to her in spite of their run-in this afternoon, but he couldn't face a rebuff right now. This was all so damn hard, their years together counting for nothing.

Nick took a deep breath and exhaled slowly. They were passing the point of no return as far as following the abductor's orders, but he couldn't stall any longer. "Call your friend at the bureau, Langston."

"You've got it." Langston stood and left the room to make the call without waiting for the rest of the decisions to be made.

"What about Zach?" Bart asked. "What do you want him to do? I'd put as much faith in him as I would the bureau—not that I don't think you should use them, too."

"Let's see what Langston finds out and then decide about that," Nick said.

"What if he's already crossed the border into Mexico? Then what?"

A choking knot clogged Nick's throat when he saw the fright in Becky's haunted eyes.

"Alert the border patrol to be on the watch for the car and them," Nick said. "See if we need to hire our own people to make sure he doesn't get that far. Do whatever it takes."

"In the meantime, I'm taking a drive and looking for an old rusted, dented, navy Oldsmobile," Matt said. "Sitting here doing nothing is maddening."

"I'm with you," Bart said.

"I'll stick to my prayers," Lenora said. She walked over and put her arm around Becky. "You need some rest, sweetheart."

"I can't sleep, Mother."

"Then just come and lie down in my room for awhile. Exhaustion won't help the boys or your decision-making abilities."

Jaime and Shelly left with them, leaving only Nick and Zach at the table.

Zach stood and walked to the window, staring into the darkness before turning back to Nick. "Are you sure you've told us everything?"

Nick hesitated, but he knew he could trust Zach. "The kidnapper wants to take Becky as hostage when Langston flies him to Mexico."

"That's interesting."

"Don't tell me you think that's a good idea."

"No, absolutely not. I just wonder if it's possible he knows Becky."

Nick trailed his fingers up and down his neck, keeping the pressure light. "What are you getting at?"

"Just that if he knows Becky, that would narrow the suspects down considerably."

"I'm not sure how. Half the people in Houston know Becky or at least know of her. The Collingsworths are too active in local charities and arts foundations for them not to have heard of her."

"Yes, but half the people in America know who you are."

"Good point. He did call Becky by name, but that doesn't really prove he's had contact with her."

"Are you sure he didn't say anything that might give us a hint as to where he is?"

"No."

"Does he have a Texas accent?"

"Definitely."

"How was the grammar?"

"I don't see how this is helping."

"It could give us an idea of his background."

"His language is rough around the edges. Some slang. Nothing particularly unusual."

"I hate to even bring this up, but I've checked the files of all the registered people guilty of sex crimes living in this and neighboring counties. There aren't many in our immediate area, and I've made routine calls on all of them without giving any indication that I was investigating a crime. None of them have the boys with them. Of course that doesn't guarantee they aren't involved."

"Thanks, Zach. I really appreciate your efforts."

"The boys may be my nephews, but I don't think I could love them more if they were my own. They're great kids."

"Yeah." They were Nick's own, yet Zach had probably seen more of them this last year than he had. That said a lot for his quality of fatherhood, a point that Becky had been stressing for years.

Zach walked over to Nick and delivered a manly punch to the forearm. "I know this is tough, but hang in there, buddy. The boys are counting on you."

Langston stepped back into the doorway. "The FBI is sending out an agent from Houston who specializes in abductions. He'll be here in a matter of hours. Nick and Becky should probably try to get some sleep in the meantime."

"Fast work," Zach commented. "Pays to have friends in high places."

"Pays to have friends period," Langston said. And it paid to have the clout of the Collingsworths on your side. Nick had to hold on to the faith that it and Lenora's prayers would be enough.

"LOOK," DAVID SAID.

"At what?" Derrick stumbled though the brush, hurrying to catch up with his twin brother. He was tired of walking. They should have come to a road hours ago. He wished he had his compass or that he'd paid more attention when Uncle Zach had been teaching him about using the stars to find your way home if you got lost in the woods.

"Look, through those trees. Somebody must live there."

"Oh, man! Am I glad to see that!" He was beginning to think they were going to be stuck out here all night—or until the kidnapper found them, which would be a lot worse.

They kept walking until they got a better look at the place. "Do you think somebody lives there?" David asked. "I don't see any cars around."

"It looks kind of empty, all right. But if there's a mobile home there has to be a road for people to get here. We can follow it to the highway."

"Yeah, and if someone lives there but isn't home, there still might be food."

"And water," Derrick added. "I'm really thirsty."

"Let's check it out."

"Maybe they have a phone, and we can call Mom to come get us."

"Now, that's what I'm talking about." David took off at a dead run toward the mobile home with Derrick on his heels. Before he got there, he slid to a stop, grabbing Derrick's arm and almost making him fall.

"What's wrong?" Derrick asked.

"Suppose the kidnapper is in there waiting for us?"

"Why would he be? He didn't know we'd come this way."

"Still, he just might be in there. Or a friend of his might live there."

"We'll peek through the window before we go inside," Derrick said. He led the way, marching as if they were soldiers. When he got closer to the house, he sneaked to the side and rose up to the tips of his toes so he could see inside the window.

"Well?" David whispered.

"Gimme a minute. It's dark in there." But there was a stream of moonlight lighting the area right in front of the window. Derrick didn't see anybody, and the place was quiet.

"I think it's all clear," he said, still keeping his voice low just in case. "Let's grab a broken limb for a weapon, but I don't think we'll need it. If the kidnapper were here, he would have left the light on to lure us in. And if somebody else is here, they'll help us get home."

They grabbed the sticks and climbed the three steps to a porch so small it wouldn't have held them and Blackie.

David knocked. Nobody answered. "Hey, anybody in there?" Still no response. He tried the knob. "It's locked."

Derrick propped his weapon against the house. "Then I guess we'll have to break in."

"We could go to jail for that."

Derrick shook his head. "Naw. We've escaped from a kidnapper. They'll just be talking about how brave we are."

"How do we get in?"

"We can break out a window."

"I was just about to say that," David said.

"Sure you were."

"I was, 'cause see that big rock out by the road. We can hurl it through the glass."

"But you better let me throw it," Derrick said,

"'cause I can chuck it harder than you can." He wasn't sure that was right, but if they got into trouble for breaking out the window, he should face it since he suggested they break in.

David got the rock and handed it to him. He threw it as hard as he could. The rock went right through the pane, and glass shattered and scattered all over the ground.

"I'll heft you up to my shoulders," Derrick said. "You can reach in and unlock the window."

David took off his jacket and wrapped it around his right hand and arm so he wouldn't get cut. David was good at thinking of stuff like that. Once he was on Derrick's shoulders, he knocked out the rest of the window and just climbed through. "I'll unlock the door for you," he called, then disappeared into the dark house.

By the time Derrick got back around to the front door, it was standing open and the lights were on. The mobile home smelled like wet, dirty socks but it had furniture. Old stuff.

"Let's check out the kitchen," David said.

Derrick was right behind him. The refrigerator was mostly empty except for a few slices of cheese. There were a bunch of bottles of water though. Derrick took one for himself and handed one to David. He swallowed half of his in one gulp.

"There's sodas, too," he said. He opened the door to the freezer. There were bunches of packages of meat. "Ice cream sandwiches," he said, pulling out the box of frozen treats.

David crawled up on the countertop to reach the higher shelves. "Not much in here but canned stuff. Chili. Chicken noodle soup." He shoved the cans around to reach to the back of the shelf. "And two cans of spaghetti with franks like Dad made one time at his house. All we need is a can opener and a pan to warm it."

"Now you're talking." This was starting to feel like an adventure. "Spaghetti and ice-cream sandwiches for dessert?" Derrick took another long swig of his water as he opened another cabinet. "I found a pan."

"Yeah, I was so hungry I almost forgot about that. David jumped down from the counter. "But I think I'll have dessert first." He grabbed an ice cream sandwich and took off to search for the phone.

They both had dessert first, but David didn't find a phone. Derrick was still plenty hungry when the canned pasta and sauce was ready.

They divided it up into two big bowls and took them to the small table.

"Tastes just like Dad's," David said.

"Yeah, but not as good as Grandma's or Juanita's."

"You think Blackie misses us?"

"Yeah," Derrick said. "I wish he was here. We could sic him on the kidnapper."

"We don't need that. We got away all by ourselves. I think my screwdriver idea fooled him into going the wrong way to look for us after we took off our shoes and walked in the creek so he'd lose our tracks."

"Yeah, but that water was really cold." Derrick finished his food. He'd planned to eat another ice cream sandwich, but he was too full. He might have a soda, though. He spied a rope on a nail on the wall. He walked over, picked it up and tied a slipknot like he did when he practiced calf roping. "Do you think we should sleep here tonight?"

"I don't think so. The kidnapper might show up and grab us in our sleep. We better keep walking and try to reach a highway. We could follow that road outside but stay in the woods in case the kidnapper comes driving down it looking for us."

"I hope we get home in time for the Christmas pageant," Derrick said. "We could tell everybody how we escaped."

"The girls will think we're superheroes."

"Cool."

Derrick swung the rope, lassoing the back of an empty chair. "We should probably get going. The ice cream would melt if we tried to take it with us, but we can take some soda and water in our jacket pockets. I think I'll take the rope, too."

He put his jacket back on, rolled the rope and tucked it away in the big inside pocket. He stuffed the rest of his pockets with water. "I look fat," he said.

"Did you hear that?"

Derrick listened, and there it was. Whistling. The same stupid song the kidnapper always whistled. The adventure wasn't fun anymore.

Chapter Seven

The house was quiet, shrouded in a dismal dread that felt as if they'd been plucked from Jack's Bluff Ranch and dropped on a cold, dark planet. Lenora felt the desperation and ached for her dead husband the way she hadn't in a long, long time.

Not a day went by that she didn't miss him. Not the ferocious shredding of her heart kind of pain she had suffered the first months after his death. She couldn't have survived over two decades of that. Now it was a more a melancholy vacuum that even her marvelous family couldn't completely fill.

Lenora stood at the front door watching as the rear lights of Trish's car faded in the distance. She was taking Gina and her infant son, Randy, back to their cabin for the night so that the baby could sleep in his crib. Trish was a good mother and knew her baby and especially her teenage daughter needed a break from the fear and tension that saturated the big house.

Gina was taking this really hard, her usually high teenage spirits scraping the bottom. She'd spent most of the afternoon lying listless on the floor or out walking with Blackie. Lenora's granddaughter looked as woeful as the nine-month-old pup.

When Zach's wife, Kali, had gone back to their ranch to check on a new foal, she'd brought Blackie's brother Chideaux back to Jack's Bluff with her. In an emotional crunch, two loving dogs were always better than one, and both Lenora and Kali had insisted Gina take the dogs with her for the night.

Bart's wife, Jaclyn, had left with Trish. Nick had insisted she try to get a good night's sleep for the sake of their unborn daughter. The rest of the family was still inside, waiting. Endlessly waiting.

As if drawn into the darkness and the solitude of the Texas night, Lenora pushed out the front door, her footfalls sounding on the wooden planks of the porch. The night air was brisk but not cold. The temperature had climbed into the sixties this afternoon, not unusual for December in this part of Texas. The low tonight would only be in the upper forties.

Wherever the boys were, they would likely be warm enough. But were they safe? Did they have food? Were they afraid?

Lenora started toward the porch swing but then changed her direction, descending the steps instead. The noises and smells of the night wrapped around her like the arm of an old friend as she took the well-worn, moonlit path to the huge oak tree where she'd laid Randolph to rest so long ago.

She fell to her knees at the tombstone and rested her head against the smooth marker as salty tears pushed from her eyes.

"Oh, Randolph. I miss you so desperately. If you were here, you'd take control. You'd know how to get our precious grandsons back." Her tears fell harder as her words shifted to a prayer.

"I trust you, God. I always have. I try not to ask for much, but I'm pleading with you to watch over David and Derrick. I'll bear anything you lay on me without complaining, but please bring my grandsons home safely."

Minutes later, the sobs and tears subsided and soothing warmth seeped inside her. She felt as if Randolph had reached from the grave and cradled her in his arms, giving her new hope.

She stayed at the grave site until her knees ached from being pressed into the grassy earth. She had no clear concept of how much time had passed before she started back toward the house.

She saw only the shadow outlined in the moonlight near the house, but she knew it was Becky. She hurried toward her, wondering if Becky had come looking for her, hoping it was with good news.

Becky looked up as Lenora approached. "Mom, what are you doing out here all by yourself?"

Odd to hear it put that way when she'd felt anything but alone. She walked over and clasped Becky's hand. "I went for a walk. Are you okay?"

"No. I'm afraid."

"I know, sweetheart. You're doing all you can. You have to trust God with the rest."

"I wish I had the faith you do, but I don't."

And more reassurances that the boys were going to be fine would sound trite and placating to Becky. "When you talked to the boys they sounded fine," she said, going for evidence Becky couldn't deny. "There's no reason to think that's changed."

"Then why didn't the kidnapper let us talk to them the last time he called? And why doesn't he call again?"

"I don't know. Maybe he can't get to a phone he trusts. Maybe he fell asleep."

"I should have never listened to Nick. I should have had an AMBER Alert go out right away. I should have called in the FBI sooner. Nick doesn't know anything about dealing with kidnappers."

The bitterness in her voice cut straight to Lenora's heart. "Don't be so hard on Nick, Becky. No one could have known the kidnapper wouldn't call as he said. Nick loves the boys. You know that."

"I suppose—in his way."

"That's the only way any of us can love—in our own way. You need Nick in this, Becky, and he needs you."

"Why would he need me? Haven't you heard? He has Brianna Campbell."

"I don't believe anything they print in those gossip magazines, certainly not that."

"It's more than gossip. She answered the phone when I called his hospital room after the accident."

Lenora swallowed hard. She had never given

up on Becky and Nick getting back together, not even when the divorce papers were filed. They'd loved each other so much once. How could they throw their marriage away when they had two precious sons who needed them both?

Divorce was right for some people. She accepted that—but not for Becky and Nick.

The conversation was interrupted by the sound of a car engine and the illumination from the headlights of an approaching car. An unfamiliar black sedan pulled up in the drive and stopped a few feet from where they were standing. A lone man climbed out and started toward them.

The FBI had apparently arrived.

DERRICK TWISTED his hands and tried to loosen the duct tape that bound his wrists behind his back. No luck. His ankles were bound, too. Same with David. Worse, the goon had put David in the bedroom and left Derrick on the lumpy sofa so they couldn't even talk to each other.

He and David tried to run away when they'd heard that stupid whistling. They would have made it, too, if David hadn't tripped while running for the back door. Derrick had come back to help him, and that's when the man had grabbed both of them and put a killer grip around their necks with his muscular arms.

They'd tried to fight him off, but he was too strong for them. He'd locked David in the bathroom at the mobile home and dragged Derrick to the kitchen where he'd found the duct tape. Then he'd left them both tied up and locked in the bathroom while he'd gone back to his cabin for his grungy old car.

Now they were worse off than they'd been before they'd escaped. Derrick blamed himself for that. He should have been smart enough to just grab some food and water and clear out of that mobile home before the kidnapper had found them and brought them back to his cabin.

The kidnapper stomped on a giant roach crawling across the floor.

"I'm hungry," Derrick said. He wasn't, but he hoped the abductor would leave them alone again and go after food. That would give him some time to come up with a better escape plan, one where they wouldn't get caught.

"You think I care if you brats starve? You're lucky I didn't beat you to death for attacking me and running off."

"You beat us and you'll be sorry. My daddy is probably going to kill you anyway."

"I'm not scared of your daddy or your rich uncles, either."

If that was true, the guy was dumber than he looked. The only problem was that neither his daddy nor his uncles knew where to find them.

"Cut out the yakking," the kidnapper said. "I'm going to call your parents, and when I get them on the line, you tell them I'm treating you well."

"Why would I tell them that when you got me and David tied up?"

"'Cause I'm telling you to. And because if you don't, I'll take this belt off and stripe your behinds with it the same way my daddy used to do to me."

"Really? Your dad did that?"

"Every Saturday night when he got drunk. Sometimes in between, if I didn't jump fast enough to suit him."

Derrick didn't like the kidnapper, but still, he kind of felt sorry for him. He couldn't even imagine his dad beating up on him or David. "Do you have a brother?"

"Nope. My mother ran off right after I was born, and nobody else was stupid enough to marry my father."

The kidnapper kicked one of the empty beer cans he'd just drained and sent it flying over

Derrick's head. It landed in the part of the room where the table and chairs and kitchen stuff were.

"How come you don't put your cans in the trash like other people?"

"How come you don't mind your own business?" He pulled his cell phone from his pocket and started punching buttons. A few seconds and a bunch of cussing later, he hurled the phone against the wall. It broke into what looked like at least a hundred pieces.

"What did you do that for? You said you were going to call Daddy."

"Friggin' phone's used up."

"They don't get used up. Mom uses hers all the time, and it still works."

"Miss Becky has enough money to buy a better phone than I do."

"Just take us home, why don't you?" Derrick said. "My parents will pay the ransom, and then you'll have money to buy all the phones you want."

"I'll get the ransom. Don't you worry about that."

But the guy looked plenty worried. And mad. "So what are you gonna do now?" Derrick asked.

"Get another phone. I'll be out for a while.

Don't try anything stupid. I won't be near as forgiving next time."

He shoved his burly arms into his ripped denim jacket and stamped outside, the key clicking as he locked the door behind him. Derrick waited until he heard the car drive away before maneuvering himself into a sitting position and turning toward the locked bedroom door.

"David, are you okay in there?"

"I guess so. I heard a car start. Did the kidnapper leave?"

"Yeah."

"Good. I hope he never comes back."

"He'll be back. He just went to get a phone so he can call Daddy. Can you get the tape off your wrists?"

"Nope. I can barely wiggle my fingers."

"Same here."

"If we had something sharp to rub up against, we could cut the tape off," David said. "You know, like a knife."

"Right," Derrick agreed. "Or any kind of jagged edge." He wiggled off the sofa and leaned against it for support until he got his balance. Once done, he started shuffling his way to the kitchen. "I'll check out the kitchen.

You look around in there. But try not to fall. It might be hard to get back up."

"Okay, but there's not much in here."

Derrick should have better luck in the kitchen, but he'd have to work fast. One of the drawers was slightly ajar. He could see a knife inside it but didn't see any way he could pick it up.

A daddy longlegs scurried across the floor and crawled over his toes. He couldn't move his foot to kick it off. Another thing, the kidnapper had taken their shoes away from them so that if they escaped again, they'd have to run barefoot through the woods. Like that would stop them.

He needed a jagged edge, and he needed it fast.

SAM COTRELLA had been with the FBI for ten years now. He'd never planned to become a resident expert in dealing with child abductions. It had just happened over time, starting with his first kidnapping case in Ohio over five years ago.

Most of his cases had turned out well. A few hadn't. Those were the ones that came back to haunt him at moments like this. They were also the reason he knew there was no time to waste even though it was almost midnight.

He settled in the family den with Nick and Becky Ridgely and tried to size up the situation as best he could as they filled him in on the details. Becky's brother Zach, a local deputy, and her sister-in-law Shelly, formerly a CIA agent, were in the room, as well.

The rest of the family had left the room at his suggestion. Nick and Becky could fill them in later, but too many people talking while he was getting specifics often confused the issue.

"The man Langston talked to said you'd worked abductions before," Nick said once he'd given the rundown on what had happened and how they'd handled the situation to this point.

"Several. You might remember the Graham case in Houston last year."

"I remember it," Becky said. "A fourth-grade girl was abducted by one of her father's employees."

Nick looked puzzled. "I don't remember that."

"You wouldn't," Becky quipped. "It was during football season."

The tension in the room swelled to new proportions. Sam knew from the basic information he'd been given before arriving that the missing twins' parents were separated. He'd worked in situations like that before, too. The strain between them would not make this any easier.

"Julie Graham was the daughter of a Houston

CEO," Sam explained. "A disgruntled employee with a history of mental illness abducted her from the park near their house while the nanny was tending to a younger sibling."

Nick leaned in closer, his muscles taut. "How did you get her back?"

"The father turned over the money at the agreed-upon time and location, and once Julie was safe, we came down on him with a SWAT team we'd put in place. The abductor tried to shoot his way out and was killed in the exchange of gunfire."

"I don't want gunfire," Becky said. "I don't want to take any chances."

"We never *want* gunfire," Sam said. "But the girl was never in danger. We'll negotiate a plan of exchange that focuses on keeping the boys safe."

"There's not much to negotiate," Nick said. "I have the money. He can have it. All I want is my sons."

"So what exactly do you expect from the FBI?" Sam asked.

"I want you to find David and Derrick in case the kidnapper doesn't call."

"My gut feeling is that he will call," Sam said. "He wants the money. That's what this is about. Otherwise he wouldn't have made that phone call about the ransom so soon after the boys were in his possession."

"That seems reasonable," Becky agreed. "But Nick told him we have the money and he didn't seem in any hurry to get it. And he wouldn't let us talk to the boys."

That worried Sam, as well. There could be several explanations for not letting them communicate with their sons but most obvious was that the boys were in no condition to assure their parents they were safe. No use to point that out. Both Nick and Becky were well aware of the danger their sons were in.

His goal now was to convince them that they needed his guidance all the way.

"If you do exactly as the kidnapper wants, we may not be able to protect your sons. That's why we need to negotiate and why you need to let me veto any arrangements for the exchange that I don't think are feasible."

Becky pulled her bare feet into the chair with her and hugged her knees close to her chest. She looked a lot like a vulnerable little girl herself in that position. Sam could only imagine how hard this had been on her—and the worst might be yet to come.

"The kidnapper promised that we'd get

David and Derrick back safely if we cooperated," Becky said. "I guess we were fools to believe him."

"You were frightened parents," Shelly countered. "That's why we need Agent Cotrella's expertise."

"I'm still not sure how this works," Nick said. "Are you saying we should tell him you're from the FBI and that he'll have to negotiate with you? I'll tell you up front that if that's the plan, I don't like it."

Sam swiveled the desk chair so that he was looking directly at Nick. "The abductor won't even know I'm here. I'll listen in on the calls and guide you through the conversation by feeding you information, but you'll do the talking."

"If we put the phone on speaker, he'll immediately suspect police or FBI involvement."

Sam nodded. In spite of his reluctance to call in the FBI, Nick had a good grasp of the situation. "I have a two-man tech team on the way," Sam said. "They'll put attachments on the phone that will allow me to listen in to your calls without the kidnapper suspecting anything."

"Can they trace a cell call from a prepaid phone?"

"Maybe not to the exact location, but they'll be

able to identify the general area where the calls are originating."

"And this equipment will prevent the kidnapper from having any inkling that his calls are being monitored?" Nick asked.

"He won't be able to detect any difference in the sound of his voice or yours."

"He's been calling Nick's cell phone," Becky said.

"We'll monitor both your cell phones and the house phone," Sam said. "He may change up in an attempt to keep you off guard. Now let's get down to the specifics of negotiation. Up to this point, you've let him make most of the decisions. It's time you threw in a few demands of your own."

Apprehension darkened Becky's blue eyes. "What kind of demands?"

"Make it clear to him that the plane will absolutely not leave the ground until the boys are back with you."

Nick bristled. "You're damn right it won't. The guy can't be so crazy he doesn't know that."

"Assume nothing. He may try to ensure his safe arrival in Mexico by taking one of the boys on the plane as his hostage."

"Surely, he wouldn't," Becky said.

"You'd think, but I had a case in Nebraska a couple of years ago where the kidnapper had abducted a sister and brother. He gave the parents the sister in exchange for the money and told him that once he was sure there were no tricks, he'd tell them where their son was."

"And did he?" Shelly asked.

"No. Once he had the money, he had no reason to cooperate. He left the boy with an accomplice, who decided to ask for more money. That's when the FBI was called in on the case."

"Do we still provide the plane and the pilots?" Nick asked. "As per his instructions?"

"You can provide the plane. The FBI will take care of the pilots."

"Fine by me," Nick said. "But the boys will be released to me. I'll have it no other way."

Sam nodded. Cool-in-the-clutch Ridgely. That's how one sportswriter had described him. Sam had an idea that calm resolve would be tested as never before by the time this was over. But Sam's job went better with optimism. He would ensure the focus stayed on bringing David and Derrick home alive.

For Christmas.

For a brief second Sam let his mind wander to his own kids at home snuggled in their beds with visions of Christmas morning dancing in their heads.

He'd do all he could to make certain this had a happy ending, but the longer this took, the more the possibility of failure increased. The twins had already been in the hands of the abductor for more than thirty hours.

NICK PACED the small downstairs study that Sam Cotrella had chosen for his operations room. The guy seemed to know his stuff and didn't come off as too cocksure of himself. Nick liked that about him, the same way he liked those qualities in his teammates.

Teammates. That was another problem— minor when compared to his sons but nagging, nonetheless. They kept calling and trying to find out what in the hell was going on with him. They were baffled. A few were downright angry and had accused him of going soft and sabotaging their chances of making the play-offs.

The NFL was a business and multimillion-dollar receivers did not just up and walk out of a hospital without a doctor's clearance.

He'd stalled everyone off with feeble excuses. He was resting at home while the swelling went down and he got the pain under control. He'd miss Sunday's game but would be ready to work out with the team on Monday. Things were under control.

That was the biggest lie of all. It was 3:00 a.m. and still no word from the son of a bitch who had his sons. Things had never been more out of control. As for the rest of his life, that hell would just have to wait.

The house was quiet, but Nick doubted there was much sound sleeping going on. Every time he stepped into the kitchen for a cup of coffee, there was a new group of family members sitting around the table.

Growing up the way he had, he'd never even imagined there were families like the Collingsworths. They had their differences, but when trouble appeared, they stuck together like superglue.

He'd miss them when the divorce was over. Not the way he'd miss Becky. Not the way he already missed her, even with her lying a few feet away, sleeping restlessly on the brown tweed sofa.

His gaze fixed on her, and a potent ache clogged his throat, making it difficult to swallow. He walked over and covered her with the knitted throw that was lying near her feet.

She snuggled into it the way she'd once snuggled against him on cold, wintry nights.

Before he'd let things deteriorate to the point she could barely stand to be near him.

A sharp pain started in his shoulder and crept into his back, growing worse when he tried to take a deep breath. He grimaced and started to the kitchen for a glass of water.

The piercing ring of his cell phone stopped him. His body grew numb, his feet frozen to the floor as he waited for the agreed-on signal from Sam to take a call. It was late. Not even his teammates would call at this hour.

The caller ID said Marilyn Close. He looked to Sam, who'd walked up behind him. "I don't know anyone by that name."

"Take the call anyway. The kidnapper could be using a stolen phone."

Becky jumped to a sitting position and grabbed for the earphones that would let her listen in on the conversation if the call was from the abductor. Sam's were already in place. He took a deep breath and took the call.

And then the panic he'd worked to keep in check exploded inside him. The voice was the kidnapper's, but Nick was certain something was seriously wrong.

Chapter Eight

"You're lucky those brats of yours are still breathing."

The abductor's voice slurred as if he were drunk or on drugs, his anger seeming to vibrate through the phone into Nick's brain.

"If you've hurt them, I'll kill you." The words left his mouth before he remembered Sam's orders that he was to wait for a nod or instructions before responding. Even if he had remembered, he doubted he could have held back.

"Your threats don't scare me, Nick Ridgely. Are you ready to pay up?"

Sam nodded.

"I have the money you asked for."

"All five million?"

"Yes, in fifties and twenties, just as you instructed. Now I want to talk to my sons."

"But you're not in control here, are you, big shot? So listen up and do exactly as I say."

Sam mouthed the words for him to insist.

"I'm not doing anything unless you let me talk to my boys," Nick said, keeping his voice dead level.

The abductor spewed a string of vile curses. "Then I'm through talking to you. Put Becky on the phone."

Nick's muscles clenched. His fury went nuclear and would have resulted in some curses of his own had Sam Cotrella not been there motioning Nick to give the phone to Becky.

Reluctantly he did so, exchanging the phone for her headphones as Sam made quick notes on the yellow pad he was holding in front of her.

She read his question into the phone with a control that surprised Nick. "Do I know you?"

"You did once. Back in your rah-rah days. Maybe we'll just have us a grand little reunion on that plane to Mexico."

Sam quickly scribbled the response. Becky read it into the receiver. "I don't know what you're talking about."

"I don't trust your husband. I want you on that plane with me when I flee the country—my insurance that I actually get to Mexico a free man with money in hand."

Nick mouthed the words "no way," but Sam was already scribbling a different answer on his pad.

Becky nodded. "Deal," she said. "But the plane won't take off until I know both boys are safe."

"That's the deal I offered."

"We can meet at the airport in Houston where my brother Langston keeps his private jet."

"No. I'll tell you where we meet. You have the plane ready to go. I'll call you and let you know when."

Sam scribbled. Becky read. "Why wait? What's wrong with now?"

"I got this high going on, baby. If you were here, we could be having a real good time. Guess that fun will just have to wait until we're on your brother's jet."

Nick grabbed a pen, wrote out his own instructions and pushed them in front of Sam.

Becky is not getting on that plane with him.

Sam waved him off and nodded to Becky to follow the instructions he'd just written.

"What time will you call?"

"When I'm good and ready. Have the money, a pilot and you. If there's anyone else present or if I even suspect you've called the cops in on this, the deal is off and the boys are corpses. You got that?"

"The boys can't just be left at the airport on their own. Nick will need to be there," she said.

"Fine, bring Nick. Maybe I'll get his autograph."

The man laughed as if this were all some big joke. If Nick could have gotten his hands on his throat right then, he could have strangled him without a second thought.

"Let me talk to my sons," Becky insisted again.

"They're not exactly with me right now, sweetheart. They're kind of tied up somewhere else, but don't you worry. They're just fine. But you should have taught those little brats some manners. If I wasn't so nice, they'd be in big trouble."

"Don't hurt them," she begged, this time speaking on her own. "We'll give you everything you ask. Just please don't hurt them."

But the kidnapper didn't hear her plea. He'd already broken the connection.

"We'll have to move fast on this," Sam said, already punching in numbers on his cell phone.

Nick wasn't giving in that easily. "I don't know what you're thinking, but Becky is not going anywhere with that scumbag."

"Of course not," Sam said. "All the people in that plane will be FBI. A dozen more agents will be on the ground either hidden from view or posing as airport crew. Now, can you get Zach in here? Shelly, too. I can use their help in taking care of a few things. While you're at it, get Langston as well so we can verify information about his aircraft."

"I want to be there when he releases David and Derrick," Becky said.

"We'll talk about it," Sam said as he started giving orders to whomever it was he'd called.

"I don't want you there," Nick said. He knew the statement had come out too much like an order the second he saw the rebellious expression on Becky's face.

"I didn't ask for your permission," she said.

"I know," he said, this time going for appeasement. "I just don't want to add to the risk."

Thankfully, she let the confrontation dissolve without an argument. The wheels were turning again. His sons, *their* sons could be home in a matter of hours. Nick wouldn't breathe easy until they were.

Then the rest of his life could come crashing down on top of him—one heartbreak at a time.

BULL DROPPED the phone to the seat beside him as he crossed the bridge heading back to the dilapidated cabin where he'd left the boys. He'd planned on buying another prepaid model from a convenience store in Livingston, but luck and fast thinking had saved him the money.

He'd stopped at an all-night truck stop on Highway 59 where he knew he could buy a fifth of cheap whiskey and some joints from the night manager. Under the table so to speak, though everyone in these parts seemed to know where to go for after-hours booze or a quick fix.

The phone had been easy pickings from a broad who'd stopped for coffee and left her phone sitting next to her cup and cigarettes while she went to the bathroom. He'd palmed it on his way out. She'd probably have it disconnected before he used it again, but that was okay. He'd stop at a pay phone next time—one on his way to meet Nick Ridgely.

The fifth of cheap whiskey was almost gone now. He shouldn't have started it before he made the call, but his head had been still pounding from the blow he'd taken from the boys that morning, and he needed something to kill it. Once he'd started, he'd stayed with it.

Women, drugs and booze. That had always

been his downfall. But in a few more hours he'd have plenty of money to buy all he wanted. Not cheap booze or tawdry women, either. He'd have the best that five million could buy.

The car's wheels hit the shoulder and skidded completely off the roadbed. He yanked it back to the middle of the narrow strip of asphalt.

Slow down, buddy. Stay focused. Your next turn is coming up, and then it's just a few more miles back to the cabin.

The car swerved again. He could barely keep his eyes open, but he had to keep driving. He didn't dare leave those Ridgely brats alone any longer than he had to. They were his ticket out of here.

Just him, the pilot and Becky. He couldn't wait to get his hands on her—and all over her. She probably wasn't as hot as she'd been in high school in that sexy little cheerleading outfit. Firm little tits pushing at the fabric. He couldn't count all the nights he'd gotten his rocks off thinking of those.

She'd ignored him then. She wouldn't have that option now.

His turn was just ahead. He put on his brakes and slowed almost to a stop before turning on yet another winding, narrow road, this one dirt and half washed-out and with potholes big enough to bury a man.

Then a few more miles and he'd make the last turn onto the red clay trail that meandered back to the old fishing cabin. The place had belonged to his grandpappy back before the creek had dried up and become clogged with logs and trash.

His dad had brought him fishing out here a few times when he was a kid. The last time had been his seventh birthday, but he remembered it as if it was yesterday. His father had gotten the poles and bait from the car, then proceeded to get falling-down drunk.

His dad had hooked him with the jagged end of his fishing hook, then kicked him until he was black and blue for crying when he yanked it loose, tearing a bloody hole in his flesh as he did.

It was the first time he'd thought about killing his dad, years before he actually did it. That had been a long, long time ago, and no one had ever suspected him of murder.

Bull's eyes closed. A second later he slammed into a tree.

"THE LAST phone call was made from somewhere in the area of Livingston, Texas, from a phone belonging to Marilyn Close of Longview.

I've got someone checking her out as we speak," Sam announced, once the entire family had gathered in the cozy kitchen. The room smelled of coffee and the spicy apricot coffee cake Lenora had just pulled from the oven.

"I bake and pray," she'd said. "My way of holding together."

He would never have called a family conference at 1:30 a.m., but apparently none of the Collingsworths had done much sleeping since the boys' abduction. Now that he had all four of Becky's brothers, plus a few of the women, in attendance, he was glad to have them aboard.

They not only worked as a seamless team but they were smart and all willing to do whatever it took to get David and Derrick home safely. Families like that didn't come along every day, especially when they were also one of the wealthiest families in Texas.

"It's likely the phone was stolen," he continued, "but at least we know the general area where the abductor must be holding the boys."

"I say we start combing that area for them at daybreak," Zach said.

"Can you take care of that while still keeping the kidnapping quiet?" Sam asked.

"Absolutely."

"Then go to it." Sam made a couple more notes on his pad.

Nick stirred a bit of cream into his coffee. "What about the fact that the man seems to know Becky? Shouldn't we be checking into that?"

"He didn't say how he knew me," Becky said. "He could have been lying."

"We can't assume he's lying," Nick insisted, "and if he does know you I don't see how he'll be fooled by an FBI agent who's impersonating you."

"You'd be surprised how easy that is to achieve," Sam said, "as long as we keep the agent at a distance until the boys are with you."

"Do we know who that agent will be?" Langston asked.

Sam nodded and sipped his coffee. "All taken care of. Her name's Evie Parker, and not only is she petite like Becky but she's a master with undercover disguises. She has her own collection of wigs in every color. When I talked to her, she said she could fool Becky's mother as long as she didn't have to stand too close. However, that might be a slight exaggeration."

"But she hasn't even seen me," Becky protested.

"She has your picture."

"How?"

"I snapped it with my cell phone and sent it to her. She's on her way here now, flying in from Dallas with our pilot. They'll land at the same place Langston keeps his private jet in case there's no time for us to get together before that. She'll get a car and drive out here from there if there's time."

Sam had a feeling there would be plenty of time and that this was not going to play out exactly as it was being scripted. Just a hunch, but his hunches had a history of being right more often than they were wrong. Agent's intuition.

That and the fact that the kidnapper had been drunk when he called. The guy was obviously losing control of the situation. The question was *why?* He hoped the answer had nothing to do with the physical condition of David and Derrick.

"He must have known Becky in high school," Jaime said, "assuming rah-rah days refers to her being a cheerleader. She wasn't one in college."

"Good thinking."

"What can we do to help?" Matt asked.

"I need copies of Becky's high school yearbooks. I'd like her to peruse them and see if any of the guys stir bad feelings."

"My yearbooks are packed away in the attic."

Matt stood up. "I'll bring them down."

"I'll go with Matt," Bart said. "There are lots of boxes in the attic. Finding the right one could take a while."

Becky stuck a fork into the slice of coffee cake her mother had set in front of her. "I'm not sure what you mean by bad feelings."

"Perhaps someone you had problems with. Maybe a guy who had a crush on you that you didn't share. Maybe someone who aggravated you or even seemed creepy to you. We're grasping at whatever we can find," Sam admitted.

"I don't remember anyone like that attending Colts Run Cross High."

"Sometimes pictures can jog a memory. Have you ever been stalked?"

Becky hesitated. "Not exactly."

Not the answer Sam was expecting. "I'll need more than that."

She laid the fork back down and reached for the mug of hot coffee, sipping slowly before answering. "Right after I started college I met this guy in my freshman psychology class who I could have sworn was following me around campus. He never asked me out— not that I would have gone. He had zero personality. But he always seemed to be around, staring at me from a distance. It freaked me out big-time."

"Did you say anything to him about your concerns?"

"I thought about it, but before it came to that, he dropped out of school. But the really weird thing is, a few weeks ago I saw a man who reminded me of him in Colts Run Cross."

Sam saw the clench of Nick's jaw. Unless Sam was misreading the signals, he was more tuned in to his wife than Sam would have expected under the circumstances. And he was definitely protective of her.

His guess was that Nick Ridgely was not the one who'd initiated the divorce, though he might have made some dumb mistake that caused Becky to give up on him. Men with hero status had temptation thrown at them left and right.

Sam waited for Becky to elaborate on the man who'd reminded her of the college stalker. She didn't. "Do you think it could have been the same man?"

"I don't think so. It was more the feeling I got when I noticed him staring at me than his appearance. Not the old cliché about undressing me with his eyes, but more like the one about spiders crawling across the skin."

"Did you only see him that once?"

"Yes, and then only for a few seconds. I'd stopped at Thompson's Grocery to pick up a few items, and he was checking out in front of me. I'm almost positive he's not from around here. I would have seen him before—or since."

"Definitely weird," Sam agreed. "I'll need a description of him and as many specifics about the psych class as you remember. I'll have someone check the school records and see if we can get a roster for that class. You may recognize his name if you see it printed."

"I can sit with her while she skims her yearbooks," Shelly offered. "I can jot down her description of the man she saw in the store and make notes on anyone else of interest."

"I'd appreciate that." It would relieve Sam to go over the exchange plans with the other agents who'd be involved. "And Nick, you and Becky should try to get a little rest as soon as she finishes taking a look at those yearbooks. I doubt we'll be hearing from the abductor again before morning. He's probably sleeping it off right now."

"Is that everything?" Becky asked.

"For now." But Sam would have felt a lot better about this if the kidnapper had let Nick or Becky talk to their sons. Not hearing their voices raised a whole new set of questions with possibilities none of them wanted to consider.

NICK WALKED to the family den and stared out the window as the dawning light of a new day dissolved the night.

Wednesday morning. Two days before Christmas. His heart twisted as if it were trying to wrench itself from his chest. Becky stirred from her position on the sofa but didn't open her eyes.

He'd tried to talk her into going to her room for at least a few hours, but she wouldn't venture that far from him and his phone. Not only did she want the chance to hear her sons' voices but she wanted to be there if the kidnapper asked to speak to her again. Had it been left up to her, she'd have willingly climbed on the plane with the kidnapper in exchange for David and Derrick's safety.

Except for Zach, he hadn't seen the rest of the family in the past few hours. Zach had to be running on empty, but he'd left a half hour ago to get started on trying to locate the kidnapper and the boys. Sam had the FBI on the mission, as well. To Nick, it sounded like trying to find a particular face in a game-day crowd of seventy thousand.

Still, Nick envied their chance to do something useful. He would rather be doing anything other than pacing and waiting for the damned phone to ring.

He walked to the bookcase and studied the rows of family photographs. He picked up one and held it closer so that he could make out the details in the dim morning light.

In it, the boys were no more than four. David was crawling through a pile of wrapped presents. Derrick was on tiptoe reaching to hang an ornament on the Collingsworth Christmas tree. One of the many Christmases Nick had missed due to being on the road for an upcoming game.

Not that they hadn't always celebrated again when he got home, but nonetheless, he'd missed the actual day the same way he'd missed lots of big moments in their lives. School plays. Derrick's first touchdown on the parks department youth team. David's first win in the local rodeo's youth barrel riding competition.

Becky had captured the moments for him on film. At the time that had seemed enough. No. Who was he kidding? At the time, he'd been so involved with his own life, with the drive to win and the excitement of the upcoming game that what happened back home barely scratched his consciousness.

"What time is it?"

Becky's sleep-husky voice cut through his thoughts. When he turned, he saw that she'd kicked off the blanket and was sitting up, raking her fingers through her disheveled hair with one hand and clenching a throw pillow with the other. Her torment was tangible, a heaviness that filled the air like thick, poisonous smoke.

Nick glanced at his watch. "Six-twenty."

"You'd think he'd call."

"He's probably still sleeping it off."

"If he'd only let us talk to the boys, if I just knew they were safe, that they aren't being mistreated or abused, I could handle this."

"Don't think those things," he pleaded, though the same fears were eating away at him. He ached to drop to the sofa beside her and cradle her in his arms. In spite of his words about not contesting the divorce, it wasn't what he wanted. He wanted things to be the way they were in the beginning—when she loved him as much as he loved her.

Mostly he wished he had a chance to make up for everything he'd missed with his sons. He dropped to the edge of the leather hassock, waiting until Becky let her gaze lock with his.

Finally the question torturing his heart found its way to his tongue. "Am I a terrible father, Becky?"

BECKY FOUGHT the urge to lash out at Nick, to hurl all her frustration and fear at him. But it would only be a temporary release, a cruel, punishing sting that would do neither of them any good.

She opted to choose her words carefully. "David and Derrick love you," she said honestly. "You're their hero."

"A hero, but I'm not much of a caretaker. I'm not there for them to do the little things other fathers do, like go to their ball games or help with their homework, at least not on a full-time basis."

Surely he didn't expect her to contradict that. Yet one look into his haunted eyes, and she couldn't add to his guilt and pain. What purpose could it possibly serve?

"You love them," she said, willing to let it drop at that.

"It's not enough, is it? Not for the boys and definitely not for you. I'm away too much. You said it yourself a thousand times."

She dropped the pillow and clasped her hands

in her lap. "It was never just your physical absence, Nick. Even when we were together during the season, you weren't really there. You pulled away emotionally. I know it sounds crazy, but I felt betrayed, as if football were your lover."

Nick shrugged and looked away. "NFL football is demanding."

"So is life, Nick."

And she had never been able to simply turn off their marriage and life together the way he had. Never once had she become so immersed in anything that she didn't need to reach out and touch him, if not in person then by letting their souls touch in some meaningful way on the phone.

Not so with Nick. It was as if they existed on different planets during football season, and the expanse of space that separated them couldn't be bridged. Not even when they'd made love. That had probably hurt most of all.

"Things are going to change, Becky. When we get the boys back, things will change. That's a promise." He reached over and took her hands in his.

"I hope so, Nick, for your sake and the boys." But he'd made those promises before, always when his back was up against the wall. To give him credit, he'd probably even tried to change. But then football season would start, and he'd fall into the consuming drive to be the best receiver in the league all over again.

"I just want the boys home safely," she said. "I can't think beyond that."

"I know." Nick reached up and tangled his fingers in her hair, his thumb brushing her earlobe.

It would be so nice to wrap herself in his arms and have him hold her. Just hold her, but she couldn't let herself. Her mother would say she was stubborn. Too much like Jeremiah.

But it was more than stubbornness that made her keep Nick at arm's length when she ached for the comfort of his arms. It was survival.

She looked up as heavy footfalls trod down the hallway and stopped at the doorway. Sam was standing there.

"There's been a new development."

The slump of his shoulders told her the news would not be good.

Chapter Nine

"We haven't been able to acquire the log from your freshman psychology class in college," Sam said, "but we ran a routine computer check on males who were in your high school at the same time you were there."

Becky sucked in a ragged breath. "Then I hope you found a more promising suspect than I did by looking at old yearbooks."

"We had some luck." Sam handed her a computer printout with two names followed by sketchy information obviously gleaned from police files. She scanned the data quickly.

The first one was Tim Gillespie, a male Caucasian who recently went bankrupt due to gambling debts he'd incurred along the Mississippi coast. The name was only vaguely familiar. She checked his age. "He would have been two years ahead of me. I don't actually re-member him."

"Not surprising," Sam said. "According to what we have on him, he only lived in the area a few months."

"His family may have been migrant farm workers," Becky said. "We always had several of those who rotated in and out according to what crops were being harvested at the time."

"He's a long-shot suspect," Sam admitted. He tapped the second name. "What about Adam Leniestier? He's been arrested three times, always for some kind of get-rich-quick scam."

Adam she remembered well. "I dated him a few times my junior year," she said. "He was a con man even then, always a charmer and con-stantly trying to get someone to do his homework for him, but he was never in any real trouble."

"He's obviously progressed, but still guilty of nothing that's put him behind bars for any extended period of time."

Nick leaned closer to read over her shoulder. "Stealing credit cards from girlfriends and writing hot checks. That sounds worthy of a jail term to me."

"Not if he sweet-talks the girlfriends into withdrawing the complaint," Sam said.

Becky kept reading. "According to this, he did serve a few months for bilking FEMA out of money after Katrina."

"Right," Sam said. "He claimed he lost everything. Truth was he was living in New Jersey at the time."

"His dad still lives in Colts Run Cross," Becky said. "Mr. Leniestier goes to our church and works for the highway department, but Adam's mother divorced him right after high school and I haven't seen Adam since."

"Still, he sounds like the kind of man who might try to pull off a kidnapping." Nick slid the printout closer. "Except that it says here he's living in Denver now."

Becky considered the logistics. "If Adam got the idea for the kidnapping after seeing you get injured on Sunday, he'd have had to move fast."

Sam nodded and rubbed the tendons in his neck. "We checked. There's no record of his taking a flight to Texas."

"He could have driven all night," Nick said, "or bought a ticket using a fake ID."

"Distinct possibilities," Sam agreed. "We're following up on him, but I don't think he's our man."

Becky got the impression Sam hadn't told them everything yet. "Is there another suspect?"

His eyes narrowed. "Do you recall a student in your class named Jake Hawkins?"

This time the name triggered disturbing memories. "I remember him."

"What can you tell us about him?"

"He moved to Colts Run Cross my senior year—too late to be included in the yearbooks. He seemed nice enough, but…"

"But what?" Nick asked when she hesitated, his voice hoarse and edgy.

"He never talked about his parents, but he moved in with his grandmother, Nancy Hawkins. She was a retired schoolteacher, the kind of teacher students loved to hate. Anyway, she died from a fall on her stairs right after Jake started living with her, and some of the kids claimed he murdered her."

"He was never arrested for that," Sam said.

"No. The police said it was an accident, but you know how rumors are. They just get started and take on a life of their own, especially since Jake wouldn't talk to anyone about the accident after that—not even at the funeral. I don't know where he went to live after his grandmother died."

Nick stepped away from Becky, but closer to Sam. "What do you have on him?"

"He spent three years in a state penitentiary for attacking a pregnant woman in a case of road rage on I-20 near Dallas. Apparently she rear-ended him, and he yanked her out of the car and stabbed her repeatedly with his pocketknife. The woman didn't die or lose the baby, but she spent a month in the hospital. Jake was paroled two months ago."

"Was he in the Huntsville facility?"

Sam nodded.

"So he's likely still nearby." Nick rammed his right fist into the palm of his left hand. "Damn. That's just the kind of lunatic who might kidnap two young boys on an impulse."

"Wouldn't his parole officer know where to find him?" Becky asked.

"Unfortunately, he's already broken the conditions of his parole by moving from his original address without letting anyone know where he was relocating."

"So he could be anywhere," Becky said.

"Yes, and unfortunately, there's more."

Her legs grew wobbly, and she dropped back to the sofa. More. Always more. "What now?"

"The prison psychologist was the only one who

didn't recommend parole. He felt Jake was still capable of violence when provoked. He believed Jake to be emotionally unstable, prone to irrational rage and generally angry with the world."

Becky fought the burgeoning dread, but she had to face facts. "In other words, he's a dangerous sociopath."

"Find Jake Hawkins," Nick said. "I don't care what it takes. Just find him, or I will if I have to hire a whole damn army of men to track him down."

"We don't know that he's our guy," Sam reiterated.

"Find him anyway."

Given to irrational rage when provoked. And nothing would likely provoke him faster than finding out that they'd called in the FBI. And the longer this went on, the more likely he was to discover that fact.

Becky felt the stirrings of vertigo. Why didn't that damn phone ring?

"Derrick."

Derrick jerked awake instantly at the sound of his name. His eyes darted about the room as he came to terms with where he was and why he couldn't move his hands.

He remembered turning the faucet with his head and running water over his wrists to try to loosen the tape. It hadn't worked. Neither had rubbing his wrists back and forth across the edge of the TV. He didn't remember falling asleep on the sofa, but he must have.

"Wake up, Derrick, and talk to me."

"I am awake." He held his breath expecting to hear the kidnapper yell at them to shut up. There was nothing. Surely the guy was still gone to get a phone. Maybe he wasn't coming back.

"What's going on out there?" David asked.

"Nothing." Derrick wiggled his way to a standing position and wished he could go to the bathroom. He needed to real bad. "Are you doing okay in there?"

"Kind of. Where's the kidnapper?"

"I don't see or hear him. I don't think he came back last night."

"Then I'm doing great. I have the tape off my wrists and almost off my feet."

"You're kidding, right?"

"No, I fell asleep, but then I woke up and started looking for something sharp. There's a nail sticking out of my headboard. I rubbed against it until I finally cut through the duct tape. Oh, jeez!"

"What's wrong?"

"The last of the tape came off my ankle. Felt like the skin was going to come off with it, but it's okay now."

Derrick heard a clunk that he figured was David sliding off the bed. He started working his way toward the door that separated them. He was glad he wasn't an inchworm that had to move this slowly all the time. He heard David rattling the doorknob.

David groaned and muttered a word their mother would have a fit if she'd heard him say. "I can't get out of here."

"I'm sure the kidnapper took the key with him." Even if he hadn't, Derrick couldn't have reached the padlock near the top of the door frame, and he sure couldn't climb on a chair with his feet bound.

Derrick had never seen a padlock on a bedroom door before, and he figured the guy had put it there just to lock them in.

"I'll have to break the door down," David said, "like the guy did in that movie we watched with Grandpa the other night."

"He had something to ram it with," Derrick said. And he hated to say it, but the actor was a lot bigger and stronger than David.

"There's an old Indian statue in here. It's

made of iron, I think, like that dinner bell Bart hung on the back porch. I can hammer the door down with it, I bet."

Derrick backed out of the way as the statue crashed into the wood. The old wood cracked and splintered. Not enough that he could see David through the hole, but a few more hits and he might be able to.

The statue crashed into the wood again, and this time there was an opening big enough he could have pushed his fist through it. The kidnapper would be super mad when he saw that. They'd best be long gone.

"Hurry," he called.

This time when the metal crashed against the door, the statue broke right through and ended up on Derrick's side. David grabbed the splintered wood and tore it away until he could climb right through.

"Grab a knife and cut me loose," Derrick said. "We have to get out of here before that stupid kidnapper gets back and goes ape."

"Yeah. We gotta move fast. He may be out kidnapping more kids."

"We'll escape and come back and save them."

"That would be cool. Then we'd really get our pictures in the newspaper."

"We might even get to be on TV."

David grabbed a kitchen knife from one of the drawers under the counter. Derrick turned so his brother could reach his wrists.

"Boy, this sure works better than a nail."

Derrick wiggled his fingers as the tape came loose, and David peeled it from his wrists. "I'll do my own ankles," he said, reaching for the handle of the knife.

"Good, 'cause I got to go to the bathroom."

In practically no time, Derrick's feet were free, as well.

He gave a whoop and kicked one of the beer cans that littered the floor the way he'd seen the kidnapper do. It crashed into the wall and clattered to the floor as Derrick rushed to the bathroom to take care of business.

David was at the refrigerator when Derrick made it back to the kitchen. "There's a couple bottles of water," he said as he grabbed one and twisted off the top. "I say we drink this one and save the other until later."

"Okay. You drink first. Is there anything else in there?"

"Beer."

"Mom would kill us if we drank that."

"There's ketchup and some bread. We can make a ketchup sandwich. I like those."

"For breakfast?"

"Better than oatmeal."

Derrick pulled an opened package of pretzels from the cabinet. That was all there was except for a couple of cans of tuna with easy-open tops, some crackers and a package of uncooked lima beans. He stuffed everything except the beans into the pockets of his jacket just in case they got lost again.

David was waiting at the door. "I wish we had our shoes."

"I just wish we had a key," Derrick said, suddenly realizing that they'd have to break down the front door as well to get out of the house. He grabbed the Indian statue from the floor and had it hefted above his head when he saw David pull the rope from his inside jacket pocket. He let the statue slip from his hands and crash to the floor.

"Do you want me to break the door?" David asked.

"Not yet. I'm thinking maybe we shouldn't escape."

"Are you loony? I'm escaping and right now." David dropped the rope and grabbed the statue, grunting as he hoisted it over his head.

"If we run, we might just get lost again and the kidnapper could find us like before."

"And if we don't escape, we'll be stuck here with ketchup sandwiches for Christmas."

"Not if we're waiting for the kidnapper when he comes back. He thinks we're all tied up, so he won't be expecting anything." The plan kind of took shape as he talked. He liked it better all the time. "You could lasso him and pull him down, and I could hit him over the head with the statue and knock him out again. Then we could get the phone he went after and call Mom and Dad to come get us."

David held on to the statue. "What if I miss when I try to lasso him?"

"Then I'll still hit him and knock him out. I'll be behind the door. You can be perched on top of a chair, ready to throw the rope as he walks in."

"I don't know," David said.

"Well, I do. We'll outsmart him. You know, like *Home Alone*. That way we won't have to run around in the woods barefoot trying to find the way back to the highway."

"How are we going to tell Mom and Dad how to come get us when we don't even know where we are?"

"Then we'll call 911. They can find you

anywhere. We'll be home in plenty of time for Christmas Eve."

David swung the rope. "Okay, but we have to get ready for action. The kidnapper might walk in that door any second."

Derrick's heart was beating fast. But they could do it. He knew they could. And it would sure feel good to see Mom and Dad walk through that door together.

He just wished the together part would last forever. Divorce was like having a "parent-napper" steal your dad and keep him for most of every year.

THE TWO MEN stamped along side by side. They'd been hunting together for more than forty years, ever since they'd married sisters. Their wives loved holiday gatherings. Hermann and Bruce loved getting away from the hustle and bustle and occasionally even killing a buck.

They'd gotten a late start this morning. Too much whiskey last night. Sun was full up now, but there was still time to bag a big one if they were lucky.

"What the Sam Hill?"

Bruce shouldered his rifle and stared into the woods. "I don't see anything."

"Over there." Hermann pointed toward the half-washed-out dirt road they'd driven in on. The front of a black car was wrapped around a pine tree.

"Lucky bastard if he walked away from that."

Hermann trudged toward the wreck. "Don't look like it's been there too long. Not rusted out—well, except for that spot on the back fender, and that's an old dent."

Bruce was fifty pounds lighter than Hermann, mostly because the sister he'd married was a lousy cook. He overtook Hermann, reaching the car first. Hermann was only a step behind.

The driver was slouched over the steering wheel, not moving. Blood smeared the side window and was clotted in a clump of hair on the side of his head.

Hermann moved so as to get a better look. "This must have happened in the last few hours. If the man's dead, I bet he's not even cold yet. Color's too good."

He eased the door open. The smell of cheap whiskey and marijuana hit him in the face.

"Guess that explains why he collided with the tree," Bruce said.

"Yep. Poor bastard didn't even get to finish his stash." Hermann pulled two joints from the man's shirt pocket and stuffed them into his own. "For later." He felt for a pulse. "Heart's ticking."

"He's just sleeping off a drug and booze stupor. Do you think we should call for an ambulance?"

"If we do, we'll get stuck out here for hours waiting for them to show up and then have to talk to some meddlesome country bumpkin sheriff," Hermann said. "And we'll have to deal with this codger if he wakes up. And he ain't gonna be in a good mood when he finds I lifted his doobies."

Bruce leaned in and put a hand on the man's back. The man groaned and jerked but didn't open his eyes. "We could call 911, just in case he's hurt worse than he looks."

"If you call, they'll have your name and number, so you're still gonna get involved whether you like it or not."

"Guess you're right. Gotta wonder what he was doing out here in the middle of nowhere, though."

"Probably getting away from a wife who's a dry-hole gusher just like we're married to."

"You're not telling me nothing I don't know. Mary Sue can talk the horns off a billy goat." Bruce slid his hand down the back of the seat and lifted the injured man's wallet from his pocket.

"What are you doing now?"

"I'm just checking to see if he has some ID on him." He opened the wallet and looked in the money sleeve. "Guy's broker than we are."

"Well, I'm not contributing to the cause," Hermann said, his eyes already peeled for game. "Are we going to hunt or not?"

"Wait, here's an ID. A driver's license, just issued two months ago to Jake Hawkins. Age thirty-two. Address in Huntsville, Texas."

"That's not more than forty-five minutes from here. He'll find his way home when he comes back to the real world."

"Hey, what's this buried in the back?" Bruce pulled out two hundred-dollar bills and unfolded them. "What do you know? The guy's not totally busted." He started to refold the bills, then stopped.

Hermann put his hand on his brother-in-law's shoulder. "Are you thinking what I'm thinking?"

"Damn straight, I am. He's just going to waste it on booze and drugs. In a way you could think of it like we're doing him a favor to take it."

"If you put it that way…" Hermann grinned, though he felt a bit uneasy. He'd never stolen money before—unless you counted cheating on your taxes.

"One for me and one for you." Bruce handed

Hermann his hundred. "Now, this is what I call a successful hunting trip."

"And we haven't even spotted a whitetail."

They walked off, not bothering to shut the car door behind them. A jaybird jeered from a tree branch over their head. A rabbit scurried from one thick clump of underbrush, only to disappear into another one.

And an elegant buck with an impressive rack stepped into the clearing mere yards away. Hermann found him in the sight of his rifle and poised his finger on the trigger.

But the crack of gunfire did not come from his gun. He spun around in time to see Bruce fall to the ground in a pool of blood. And then the second bullet fired.

ODORS OF COFFEE, bacon, sausage, eggs, grits and biscuits wafted from the kitchen as Nick and Sam joined the Collingsworth family in the dining room. It held one table in the house large enough for all of them to fit around. The table was new, but was an almost-exact replica built by Matt and Bart to replace the one lost in the fire and explosion that had barely missed taking all their lives.

The Collingsworths had been through a lot

together. It didn't surprise Nick at all that they would hang together in this.

Nick took the chair to the left of Becky while Zach's wife, Kali, squeezed into the chair on Becky's left.

"I talked to Zach on the drive over here," Kali said. "He's in the Point Blank area, showing Jake Hawkins's picture around and hoping someone there may know where to find him. But he's not mentioning the kidnapping," she added quickly. "He's saying the guy jumped parole, which is the truth."

"Good," Nick said. Not that they knew for certain Jake was behind the kidnapping, but he was definitely the most likely suspect that had surfaced.

"Did Zach get any sleep last night?" Becky asked.

"Not much, but Zach can go longer without sleep than anyone I know. When I was in danger last winter, there were nights when he barely closed his eyes."

Matt forked a couple of sausage patties from the serving platter before passing it on. "Bart, Langston and I are cutting out of here in a few minutes. We're all taking our own trucks up to the Point Blank area."

"To do what?" Becky asked.

"Help Zach. There's a lot of back roads up there and not a lot of extra deputies. It was Sam's idea," Langston said. "And it definitely beats sitting around here doing nothing."

Jaime pushed away from the table. "Why just you guys? I can drive and ask questions. David and Derrick are my nephews, too."

"You'll never pass for a deputy tracking down a parole jumper," Nick said.

"Maybe not, but I'll come a lot closer to getting men to talk to me than you guys will. And I can look like a deputy if I want. I have a pair of khaki chinos and a boring jacket I can wear." She turned to Sam. "What do you say Mr. FBI agent? Would you buy that I'm a deputy?"

"Not unless you're wearing heat on your hip."

"I not only have a pistol but I'm an excellent marksman," she said.

"And so am I," Shelly said. "I'll go with you."

"Is that a good idea?" Lenora asked.

"Time is of the essence," Sam said.

He let it go at that, but as far as Nick was concerned the solemnity in his tone said a lot more. The boys had been missing almost two full days now, and they hadn't actually talked to them since shortly after the kidnapping. They had the ransom. It was the kidnapper who kept changing his tune.

Something was obviously wrong. And if he knew that, so did Becky and the rest of her family. They were walking that thin line between anxiety and outright panic.

Nick managed to get down a few bites of food. Becky didn't. She stared into space as if she couldn't even bear to look at the spoonful of scrambled egg she'd put on her plate.

Nick hated to see her hurting like this, hated that he hadn't protected their sons better. Hated that the only comfort he could offer were empty phrases.

His phone rang. The room grew deathly silent. Nick checked the caller ID. "Out of area."

Sam nodded, and Nick took the call even as he, Becky and Sam hurried back to the study.

He answered with his name. "Nick Ridgely."

"Good. You're just the man I want to talk to."

His coach. Not the man he wanted to talk to. Nick motioned for Sam and Becky to ignore the call. "I'm sorry I haven't gotten back to you, but I'm involved in a family emergency that I can't leave. It should be resolved soon, and I'll rush back to Dallas the minute it is and have the MRI and the CAT scan the neurologist ordered."

"This isn't like you, Nick. Why don't you level with me about what's going on?"

"Would it help if I said this was literally a matter of life and death?"

"It helps. I really need for you to say more."

"Look, I know I'm breaking the terms of my contract. You can fine me whatever you think is fair."

"I don't want to fine you. I want you to check back in the hospital. From what I hear from the doctor, you're not only in danger of never playing again but of risking paralysis."

"I think he's overreacting, but I'll have the tests run. Soon. Hopefully tomorrow."

Nick glanced at Becky. Damn. She was still wearing the earphones. He didn't want to get into this with her. Not now. "I can't talk now, Coach. I'll get back to you soon."

"Don't wait too long."

"No. I won't." Nick broke the connection before Becky heard more. She'd already heard too much.

She stared at him with a haunted look in her red and swollen eyes that ripped away the last of his tenuous control.

"Were you ever going to tell me the truth,

Nick, or was all that talk about you changing just another broken promise?"

She was right. If he was ever going to change, the time was now. Only, there were some secrets he could never share.

Chapter Ten

Paralyzed. It was a fear every wife of a professional football player lived with, but it had never seemed this frighteningly real. Becky clasped the back of a chair. The nervous adrenaline she'd lived with since the boys' disappearance dissolved, throwing her balance off kilter.

"You told me you were fine," she accused, "that all you needed was a few days' rest."

"You had enough to deal with without adding my troubles to the list."

"Your troubles? You make it sound as if we're talking about the common cold." She struggled for a deep breath to steady her emotions and clear her mind. "You should be in the hospital."

"No, I should be here. The tests can wait until the boys are safe."

"I don't get it," she said, trying to make sense of the incredible. "You were in the hospital from early Sunday evening until Monday noon. Surely that was enough time for them to do a CAT scan and an MRI."

"The machine was down, so that had to wait until morning. And then the team decided to fly in a neurologist from California who specializes in sports injuries resulting in severe trauma to the neck and spinal cord. He wanted to be there to supervise everything."

"So they did nothing for you that night?"

"They gave me pain medication, kept me comfortable, took X-rays. The usual."

"But no prognosis of any kind?"

"The E.R. doctor said I most likely had a central spinal cord contusion. That's not necessarily serious."

No, not serious at all. Only possible paralysis. "Don't gloss over this as if I'm worrying over nothing. I may be your wife in name only at this point, but I'm still your wife. I think I deserve to know exactly what the doctors told you in the hospital."

"In the first place, I'm not glossing over anything. I've set my priorities. Getting the boys back is number one on that list. In the second place, I've had MRIs and CAT scans before. The doctors order them if there's any doubt. It's called preventing malpractice suits. Their worries never amounted to anything before, and I don't expect them to this time. I know my body. I'm not in that much pain."

He nailed her with a penetrating stare. "And in the third place, you're my wife in name only because you chose for it to be that way. You stopped living with me. Stopped letting me touch or make love to you. You're the one who filed for divorce. I've fought it every damn step of the way." His voice had become strained, hoarse with emotion.

He was right on all counts, but he was the one who'd repeatedly shut her out of his life, just as he'd done again by keeping his medical condition from her—as if it were none of her concern.

Her heart twisted, and a raging need settled in her chest. She didn't know how she felt anymore except that she couldn't bear to think of Nick's being seriously injured. "I don't want to argue with you, Nick. Just tell me what the doctors told you."

"Fair enough." He crossed the room and stepped into her space, so close she could feel his warm breath as he took her hand and pulled her into the chair she'd been using for support. "Sit down, and I'll explain what I know."

He pulled a chair up close to hers. "I took a bad hit. I'm not denying that."

"I know. I saw the replay." And the horror of watching him motionless for long, agonizing minutes was a feeling she'd never forget. "You must have been in terrible pain."

"I didn't feel anything. That's what made it so alarming for me and the trainers who rushed onto the field."

Even admitting that much was a first for Nick. He always had to be tougher than anyone else, thought any sign of weakness on the field was for rookies or sissies.

"When did the feeling return?"

"Not until I was at the hospital and through with the X-rays. I told you that on the phone when you called."

"Exactly what is a central spinal cord contusion?"

"If you want the medically correct description, you'll have to go to the doctor for that."

"I'll take layman's terms. I just want to know what you're up against."

"I'm up against a possibly deranged kidnapper."

"Nick…"

"Right. You want facts. Your way. As best I

can understand it, a spinal cord contusion happens when something thumps the spine and a bruise occurs. If it improves, no problem."

"And if it worsens?"

"Then the circulation to the spinal cord is affected."

"And you could wind up paralyzed." She shuddered and clasped her hands tightly to keep them from shaking. She'd thought she could handle this, but the images of Nick as a paraplegic or worse were making her physically ill.

Nick took her balled-up hands in his. "It didn't worsen, Becky. I'm here with you. You can see that I'm fine."

"Then why is the doctor who called yesterday and your coach so concerned?"

"The doctor is concerned that the spine might still be unstable and that if it were to receive another blow, it could still slip and cause complications. But, he doesn't know my body like I do. I've taken thousands of hits. I'd know if this were more than a routine injury. I'll go in and have all the tests he wants when the boys are safe. For now, just trust me with this."

Hot, salty tears burned at the back of her eyes. Their marriage might be over, but Nick was the father of her sons. She'd never stopped loving him. That's not what the divorce was about.

Nick caught an escaping tear with a brush of his thumb on her cheek. "How did we get here, Becky? How did we get to the place where we can't touch or hold each other when faced with the most frightening time in our life? And I'm not talking about my injury."

How? She'd gone over and over those reasons both with him and in her own mind, but at this minute, they didn't seem all that important. They would matter again when all of this was over. When David and Derrick were safe. When Nick was back on the playing field going on with his life, that didn't include her.

But right now, she needed him so much it hurt. She slipped her arms around his neck and held on tight.

BULL HAD the mother of all hangovers. It felt as if someone were hammering nails into his skull as he dragged the men's bodies into the woods. He hadn't intended to shoot them. He'd just gone nuts when he realized they were robbing him.

Blown a fuse the way he had on the highway that day when the pregnant woman had cut in too close and forced him into the guardrail. That's how it was with him. Something snapped and he went crazy. Drinking and drugs made it worse.

He'd made a big mistake getting drunk and high last night when the biggest deal of his life was in the making. Five million dollars ransom for a couple of bratty boys he wouldn't have given two cents for. He should have already made the exchange by now. Should be in Mexico drinking a margarita with a pretty *señorita.*

Instead he was sweating like a pig and trying to cover up a couple of stupid murders. The man was heavier than he looked, and Jake's arms ached from maneuvering the deadweight through the heavy underbrush. And after this he still had another one to go. Then he'd have to find a way to cover up the blood. It wouldn't do to have the bodies found before he was long gone.

He had one of the men's phones and a set of car keys. He wasn't sure where their vehicle was parked, but he doubted it was far from here. Their boots weren't muddy enough for them to have been out here long. Besides, with that little shower they must have gotten while he was out of it last night, their trail should be easy enough to follow.

Too bad it hadn't rained before those Collingsworth kids had escaped. He could have found the little snots in no time and saved himself a lot of trouble. But he didn't have to worry about them now. They were tied up and locked in. They weren't going anywhere without him.

All he needed was to make the call to Nick Ridgely and have them meet him at Lone Star Executive Airport in Conroe. But he'd have to move quickly. In fact, he should make that call right now and then just bury the phone with the bodies.

Once these corpses were found, this area would be crawling with cops. He damn sure wasn't going back to prison on double murder charges. A man could die behind bars for that.

Which meant if there were any complications before the exchange, he'd have to kill the Ridgely boys so that they couldn't identify him. And then he'd find his own way to Mexico. He'd be poor, but poor and on the run beat death row by a country mile.

EVIE PARKER arrived just after 9:00 a.m. carrying a medium-size tan piece of luggage and a grim expression that fit the chilly undercurrent that hung over the big house like a dark shroud. She was petite with ash-blond hair, razor cut to hug the nape of her neck.

Becky was immediately impressed with her

professionalism and her warmth. Those two traits didn't always go hand in hand. She wasn't sure about her ability to take Becky's place in the plane, however. Their size was similar. Their facial features weren't.

"What's with the paparazzi outside your gate?" Evie asked once the introductions were over. "Did word of the kidnappings leak out?"

"They're here hounding Nick," Sam explained. "He's a star receiver for the Cowboys. He was injured in last Sunday's game."

"My brother-in-law Matt Collingsworth assigned a few Rangers to guard duty to keep the media hounds at bay," Nick said. "The cowboys didn't hassle you when you arrived, did they? I'd told them we were expecting you."

"They were very efficient. They checked my credentials and waved me right through."

Trish brought a plate of warmed coffee cake and a pot of coffee to the study as Sam caught Evie up to speed on the negotiation progress or lack thereof and on the attempts to identify and locate suspects.

Evie sipped the coffee. "Then you don't have a real lead as to Jake Hawkins's whereabouts?"

"Not yet," Sam acknowledged. Crumbs showered his shirt as he bit into a chunk of coffee cake. He brushed them to the floor with the palm of his hand. "But he's only a suspect at this point. We have nothing to tie him directly to the crime. All we know is that he has a criminal record and he went to the same high school as Becky."

"For a few months," Becky added.

"So our best bet would be to get a call from the kidnapper," Evie said.

"I couldn't agree more," Becky said. "But one other thing while we're on the subject. No matter who the kidnapper is, if it turns out he has seen me recently, I find it difficult to think he'll believe you're me."

Sam leaned back in his chair. "That's only because you haven't seen Evie's disguise mastery at work. Once she's done, even Nick may have difficulty telling the two of you apart."

Becky motioned toward the suitcase. "And everything you need for that transformation is in there."

"No. Some will come from your closet and dressing room. I'll wear the outfit you choose and apply your makeup. My bag contains a couple of blond wigs that I matched to your picture and materials for altering my facial features."

"You can alter your facial features?"

"Nothing dramatic, but minor adjustments. I

took lessons from a Hollywood makeup artist who's worked on a lot of major films. You'd be surprised how easy it is to acquire a specific look. But I don't think we'll have to do much altering this time. Makeup, hair and clothing will pretty much do it."

Becky still had her doubts. "I guess seeing is believing."

Nick pushed up the sleeve of his black T-shirt and glanced at his watch. "How long will this transformation take?"

"I like to have an hour, but I can work faster if I have to."

"I once saw her put on twenty pounds and some serious wrinkles in under twenty minutes," Sam said.

"Was the kidnapper fooled?"

"Yes, and she managed to take his gun away from him and apprehend him. He's still in jail."

Becky's cell phone rang, startling her and running clawing fingers over her nerves. She checked the ID. "It's a friend from Colts Run Cross," she said, letting it ring. She'd avoided taking most of her calls since the boys' disappearance. Eventually she'd have to return some of them but not yet. Making small talk under the circumstances would be torturous if not impossible.

Evie finished her coffee and set her empty cup on the desk next to Sam's. "Shall we get started, Becky?"

"I'm ready, but still a bit apprehensive about your taking my place on the plane."

Sam rubbed his chin thoughtfully, though his facial expression never changed. "Evie has to take your place, Becky. It's too risky for you to go with the kidnapper. I couldn't guarantee your safety."

"I'm not worried about *my* safety."

"I am," Nick said.

Not his call, but she wouldn't argue the point until she saw what Evie could do with a wig and some war paint. "I'll have the walkie-talkie with me." She held it up to make her point. "Let me know immediately if the kidnapper calls."

"Absolutely," Sam said. "Hang in there. We're making progress, whether it seems like it or not."

She wasn't fooled. He might keep up an optimistic front, but the ticking clock was wearing down all their confidence, his included.

Nick followed her to the door. When they reached it, he took her hand, tentatively as if expecting her to yank it away. "I know you're uneasy with this, Becky, but you can't get on that plane with that crackpot. Don't even toy with that idea."

She tried to pull away, not wanting to argue with him and knowing she could make no promises.

His grip tightened. "Be reasonable. The boys will need you here with them." He met her gaze, his own fears written in every line of his face. "So do I, and I can't face going through all this again while you're riding the wild blue yonder with a lunatic."

He was talking like a husband, as if the bonds between them were strong and loving. She wanted to trust that, but his need for her had always been short-lived, dissolving completely when football season claimed his mind, body and soul. Only now his season might have come to a permanent end and…

And she couldn't deal with any of this now. The stakes for her sons were too high. She took the stairs with Evie, praying with every step that her boys were safe.

NICK'S CELL phone rang at exactly 10:18 a.m. The caller ID said Hermann Grazier. He didn't recognize the name, but something deep inside him shouted that this was the call he'd been waiting for. This time he didn't wait for Sam's thumbs-up to answer.

"Nick Ridgely," he said, answering with his name as he frequently did.

"It's time for the show."

Adrenaline rushed Nick's system, speeding his heart until it felt as if it might burst from his chest. He pushed the button on the walkie-talkie to let Becky know the kidnapper had made contact.

"I'm ready," Nick said.

"Then listen and get this straight. One screwup on your part and you'll be burying your sons for Christmas."

Nick had never hated a man more. "Which airport?"

"Lone Star Executive in Conroe."

That would work. In fact, Langston had already mentioned it as a possibility. Langston would fly them by a helicopter—which was already waiting on the ranch helipad—to the small reliever airport northwest of Houston, where his plane and the FBI pilot by the name of Pete Halifax and two additional agents were waiting. Then it would be a very short hop to Conroe.

"We can meet you there in an hour."

"You do that. Have the money and the pilot on the plane with the engine running. When I show up, have Becky standing near the plane. I'll release the boys when I see her, but I'll be armed. One foul-up and I'll shoot to kill. I'll get at least one of the three before you get me. I might even get lucky and get them all.

"I'll call when I get there, and you can direct me to the waiting jet. Just remember. Double-cross me once I'm on that plane and bang bang, your sons' mother is dead."

Sam nodded at Nick for him to accept the conditions.

"Everything will be just as we agreed," Nick said. "Now, let me talk to my sons."

"I'd like to do that, Nick, I really would, but we have a little problem."

Nick's fists knotted. His stomach followed suit. "What kind of problem?"

"They're not exactly with me at the moment. They're much too annoying for me to hang out with all the time. You really should teach them some manners."

"Where are they?"

"Telling you that would kind of void my bargaining powers, don't you think?"

"I want to talk to them and know they're safe and that you actually still have them before I turn over the money."

"You'll know soon enough. Meet me at the airport, Nick. My rules. No cops. One hour."

Nick was reaching for Sam's rapidly scribbled note when the connection went dead.

"I'm calling him back," Sam said. "Demand he let you talk to David and Derrick."

One touch of the sophisticated machinery Sam was manning had the kidnapper's phone ringing. There was no answer.

Becky yanked off her earphones and dropped them to the desk. "We're doing what he said. I don't care what either of you think. They're my sons. He says they're safe, and I have to believe that."

Sam grimaced. "Not the best scenario but this is manageable. So, you heard the woman. Time for the games to begin. The boys should be home by dinner."

Nick could sense Becky's apprehension, though she'd become more animated than at any time since this had all begun. He hated that he wouldn't be with her for the ride to Conroe, but she'd be with Sam. He'd keep her safe.

They went over the plans again. Sam would call the shots outside the plane. Pete would be the one in control inside the plane. Pete would pretend to have a problem while preparing for takeoff. As soon as the kidnapper was distracted, the two agents hiding in the food compartment of the plane would rush out, and between the four of them, they'd disarm and apprehend their target.

It sounded simple, but Nick knew that just like a Sunday game plan, one mistake could turn victory to defeat. But unlike a football game, failure to succeed could be deadly.

"I'll get Langston," Becky said.

"Right," Nick agreed, "and tell your mother to rev up the Christmas plans. This is going to be the best Christmas in the history of all Collingsworth Christmases. And I don't plan to miss a second of it."

Nick put out a hand to Sam as Becky disappeared through the door. "If we get David and Derrick back safely, we'll owe it all to you. Now, just take care of my wife. I'm leaving her in your hands."

"I'll do my best. She's a terrific woman. You're a lucky man."

"Damn lucky."

But luck or not, he might end up losing her to a ridiculous divorce. He didn't know how to keep her. And he couldn't call in the FBI for that.

Chapter Eleven

Becky felt miles removed from the action and frustrated with her inability to know what was going on. She was standing at a window in a cargo company facility that was owned by the family of one of Bart's fraternity brothers during his college days.

Nick had explained that with the paparazzi clamoring after him since his accident, she was merely trying to avoid unwanted attention and endless questions while waiting to board a chartered jet. Perhaps that was why the workers had pretty much ignored her except for offering a soft drink when she'd arrived.

She sipped the diet cola from the can and shifted for a better look at Langston's plane. She was too far away to see any movement around it except for two businessmen climbing into a jet belonging to a local charter service.

She checked her watch again. Ten minutes past the appointed time. Still no sign of the kidnapper or David and Derrick.

Nick was on the plane with Evie and Pete. She'd learned from Sam on the way here that Pete was a top-notch agent who'd been a fighter pilot in the navy before leaving the service to join the Bureau. Sam claimed that he, Evie and the two agents who were hidden away were the perfect team to apprehend the abductor.

Sam was inside the waiting area, just a few yards away from the plane, posing as a businessman waiting to catch a charter flight.

Her phone rang. She recognized the number as Sam's and murmured a breathless hello.

"I just heard from Pete. There's been no word as yet. Nick wanted me to let you know."

Frustration rolled in her stomach and ground along her nerve endings. "He should be here. We did everything he said."

Only, that wasn't quite true. He'd ordered them not to call in law enforcement. They'd gone to the FBI. "Maybe he knows he's being set up."

"That's extremely unlikely. Don't start panicking, Becky. We have what he wants. There's no reason not to be optimistic."

None except that her sons were nowhere in

sight. Her cell phone beeped. "I'm getting another call."

"It's probably Nick, though he'll be calling on Evie's or Pete's phone. We're leaving Nick's open for the kidnapper."

"Okay. Keep your fingers crossed. Keep everything you have crossed." She broke that connection and took the incoming call.

"All systems are go, here. Are you okay?" Nick's voice was strained, though he was obviously striving for upbeat.

"No," she answered honestly. She checked her watch again. Time had never moved so slowly. "Maybe this isn't the right airport."

"It's the right airport. Lone Star Executive in Conroe, Texas. He was perfectly clear on that. Take deep breaths and try to stay calm."

"Not going to happen."

"You've been great so far, Becky. Don't fall apart when we're this close to having the worst behind us."

If the demented abductor showed up. There truly was no reason for him not to, yet the dread seemed to be swelling inside her like an angry virus that was consuming her lungs. "Let me know the second you hear something."

"Will do. And, Becky…" His voice became a raspy whisper that faded to silence.

"What is it?"

"When this is over, when the boys are safe, we need to talk about us."

Her heart seemed to burst to life only to immediately shrivel back inside the cocoon where she'd hidden it away over the last painful months. They were both vulnerable now. Afraid for their sons. Treading panic. Double jeopardy for him with his future in football so unsure.

But she couldn't bear to start thinking their marriage could work again only to have those hopes slashed the second he went back to the team. Filing for the divorce had been like cutting her heart from her body. She'd put up a front during the day only to cry herself to sleep on countless nights, aching to crawl into his arms one more time. But she needed more than he could give.

She took a deep breath wishing it could steady her soul. "We'll see." She couldn't promise more than that.

"HERMANN GRAZIER is a construction worker who lives in Livingston, Texas. His wife is a schoolteacher at a public elementary school. They have two children, a boy aged twelve and a girl aged nine. No criminal record and no reason to think he is involved in the boys' abduction."

"Any explanation for how the kidnapper came in possession of Mr. Grazier's phone?" Nick paced the small plane as he carried on the conversation with Zach, his eyes constantly peering out the window for any sign of David and Derrick. Their arrival was officially—he glanced at his watch—forty-six minutes past due.

"Mrs. Grazier says he had the cell phone last night when they went out to dinner. She knows because he called his mother from the restaurant. She thinks he took it with him this morning, but when she tried to call him, there was no answer."

"Where is he supposed to be today?"

"Deer hunting with her sister's husband. Her sister's family drove over from Birmingham, Alabama, yesterday for the Christmas holidays. They take turns visiting each other's homes every year and the men always spend at least one day hunting."

"Tradition." Nick mumbled the word, then wondered why. He couldn't care less about Hermann Grazier's traditions, and he was sick to his soul of clues that went nowhere and negotiations that were ignored.

Damn. He'd preached staying calm to Becky, but he was losing it fast. "Where is he hunting?"

"His wife didn't know, but the phone call came from somewhere near Oakhurst, Texas, just a few miles east of the area where the last call was made from. There have been no calls made on the phone since the one made to you by the kidnapper. And if the phone is turned on at the present time, it's lost the connection with the network."

"So basically we know nothing."

"I'm working every angle I can, while I'm saddled with keeping the kidnapping a secret."

"It won't matter anyway if this exchange takes place." Nick almost choked on the *if.* This had to take place. Everything the kidnapper had asked for was ready and waiting. Accompanied by FBI agents, but he was certain the kidnapper didn't know that. If he had, he'd have never set up the meeting to start with.

"You still think we should have gone with the AMBER Alert and full-scale search, don't you, Zach?"

"What do I know? The boys will probably come hopping across the tarmac toward the plane any minute now. We'll all be celebrating back at the big house by dark."

It sounded good. But the clock was ticking. The drive from the Oakhurst area where the call originated to the airport in Conroe shouldn't have taken more than an hour tops. "Did you give the information you just gave me to Sam?"

"I did. He's the one who gave me Pete's number so I could call you. I knew you'd be keeping your line open."

"Have you talked to Becky?"

"I did, but I didn't mention anything about Hermann Grazier to her. She's a meltdown waiting to happen. I'm not sure how much more she can take."

Neither was Nick and that was slicing away at his control like the sharp edge of a machete. They needed action. They needed their sons' boisterous antics. Needed to hear their laughter ringing in their ears.

They needed one lousy break.

He finished the conversation and went back to pacing. After another hour had passed, even Evie and Pete had given up on trying to reassure him.

Two hours later the kidnapper had still not made contact. Nick walked away from the plane and called Becky. He needed to hear her voice.

Most of all he needed her with him. He didn't have to go back on the plane. He could drive her home, and Sam could ride with Pete and Evie.

He made the call, but he was too late. Jaime had already come for her and was driving her back to the big house. He'd call her on the way home, though. It was time they pulled out all the stops.

Nick picked up his pace as he walked to the area where Sam was waiting. From out of the blue, something felt as if it had snapped in his back and white-hot pain shot up his spine. The doctor's warning echoed in his mind. He ignored it. The negotiations were a bust, but he couldn't give up. He had to find David and Derrick. For them. For Becky. For anything in life to ever matter again.

"I'VE LOOKED in every pocket. He doesn't have a phone."

Derrick dropped the cold rag he was using to soak up the oozing blood from the kidnapper's shoulder. "He has to have a phone. That's what he went after."

"Well, he must have just bought whiskey instead."

The kidnapper mumbled something that sounded like more of the bad words he'd been shouting before David had stuffed a cotton wash-cloth into his mouth to gag him.

Derrick picked up the almost empty roll of duct tape and tossed it to the sofa. The kidnapper was on the floor, right where he'd fallen when David had lassoed him and yanked him down like a mean calf.

Derrick had done the real damage, though, popping him over the back of the head with the Indian statue. Well, mostly he'd caught his shoulder, but it had left him howling in pain while Derrick bound his wrists and ankles just the way the kidnapper had bound theirs yesterday.

Then, just to make sure he stayed put, they'd tied the end of the rope to the leg of the sofa. He'd have to drag that around with him if he moved. Pretty cool. Derrick couldn't wait to tell his friends how they'd tricked the grown bully.

"I bet Janie Thomas tries to kiss me at the Christmas pageant when I tell how we captured this jerk," Derrick said.

"Ugh."

"I won't let her, but I bet she'll want to."

"How come she'll want to kiss you? I'm the one who lassoed the kidnapper."

"Yeah, but you wouldn't pick her for your kick ball team in PE."

"She can't catch. Can't kick, either."

"But she's hot."

"You don't even know what hot means."

"Do so."

David scratched the itch where the tape had irritated his right ankle. "Forget Janie. What do we do now that there's no phone?"

"We'll have to try to find our way back to the main road."

"What if we just get lost again?"

"We won't," Derrick said. At least he hoped they wouldn't. It had been pretty scary out there roaming around lost, especially in the dark. "But this time we won't have anyone chasing us. The kidnapper will be right here waiting on the cops."

The kidnapper started flopping his body around. His face got so red that Derrick thought he might be choking. He pulled the rag from the guy's mouth.

The man spit on the floor and then started cursing them out again.

David got down on one knee and held the rag over the man's head. "If you don't quit saying all those bad words, I'll put the stopper back in."

The man spit again, this time aiming it at

David. It missed, and it ended up dribbling off his own cheek. Served him right.

"Neither one of you have a lick of sense. If you did, you'd be bargaining with me for part of the five million your parents are paying to get you back."

"Yeah, right, like our parents have that kind of money."

"You're Collingsworths. Your family has more money than God. Just your daddy's bonus is probably in the millions."

"That can't be right," David said. "Mom said those skateboards we wanted were too expensive."

"And that we were too young for them," Derrick added, to be fair.

"She's just stingy," the kidnapper said. "Anyway I already called them. They're on their way here right now to bring me the money and take you back to the ranch. I say you get this tape off of me and we make a deal."

"I say you're crazy," David said.

"Yeah, why would we even believe you that our parents are on their way here?"

"Did you think I was just going to keep you brats around forever? That's the whole point of a kidnapping. They give me ransom money. I give them you, and then I walk away."

That part made sense. And if Momma and Daddy were on their way here, they'd be the crazy ones if they went off and got lost again trying to find their way to the main highway or to find help.

Derrick motioned to David to follow him outside.

"You could buy a lot of skateboards with your share of the money," the kidnapper called after them. "And I'd sneak it to you so that your parents would never know you were involved. You'd be the richest kids in school."

"No way! Janie Thomas is the richest kid in school. Her dad owns the grocery store."

"Well, at least give me a drink of water before you leave."

"We aren't leaving—not yet anyway. And there's not any water except that gross stuff that comes out of the tap." And Derrick and David were way too smart to drink that stuff.

"There's plenty of bottled water. You just have to know where to find it. There's some food, too. Untie me, and I'll tell you where it is. You help me get the ransom. I help you. It's the way the world works. Smart kids like you should know that."

They ignored him, stepped onto the porch and closed the door behind them. A clap of thunder rattled the windows of the cabin. The wind had picked up, and the clouds turned dark. It was going to rain again. They'd get soaked if they left now.

"Do you think he's telling the truth about our parents coming to get us?" David asked.

Derrick knocked a cricket from the rickety banister. "I don't know. He didn't come back with a phone, so I guess that means he could have used a pay phone to tell them where to bring the money."

"He left here in that old black car and came back in a new one." David walked down the steps and leaned against the vehicle. "What do you make of that?"

"I don't know. Maybe he stole it to make his getaway after he gets the money."

"Football players do make a lot of money, so maybe Daddy is going to pay the ransom." David hurried back to the porch as the first drops of rain splattered his head.

"I guess we could wait a little while and see

if Momma and Daddy come. It's not like the kidnapper is going to do anything to us now."

"Right," David agreed. "No way we'd be stupid enough to cut him free, and if he tries anything, I have his pistol."

"Which we should probably keep with us at all times." Instead of on the table where they'd left it when they came out here. Lightning lit up the gray sky followed by booming thunder. The rain fell harder.

"If we go now, we'll get drenched anyway," Derrick decided out loud. "I don't want to be sick during the holiday break."

"Me, either. Let's go see if we can find that water. Or I'll have to start drinking the rain."

"Food would be good, too."

"Yeah. I can't wait to get home."

BECKY TRUDGED the few steps, hating to step into the big house. Her family would try to console her, but they'd feel the same crushing sense of fear and defeat that had haunted her since she'd first realized that the kidnapper was not going to show.

Lenora opened the door. She pulled Becky into her arms and, though she was no doubt trying to be brave, her hot tears wet Becky's neck.

"Please, Mom. I know you mean to help, but I can't handle this now. I just need to be alone."

"I understand, sweetheart. But you can't give up. We'll find the boys. We'll all help, and we won't give up until David and Derrick are back here with us."

Words. Just words. The smell of chocolate chip cookies hit Becky's nostrils and sent her stomach into feverish rolls. She ran for the bathroom, making it just in time to fill the toilet with green bile and the little nourishment she'd been able to force down that day. When she could hold her head up without the bathroom spinning, she went to the sink and splashed her face with cold water.

Reaching the towel, her fingers brushed a crystal bowl filled with shimmering red and gold ornaments. The sight of the bright decoration sent her over the edge, and before she could stop herself, she'd swept the bowl to the tile floor in a crash of broken glass and a stampede of rolling iridescent balls.

She sank to the floor, her body gripped by mind-numbing shudders. A crimson stream trickled down her leg. She'd cut herself, but she didn't feel anything but the scream gurgling in her throat.

The bathroom filled with people. Someone's arms went around her shoulders. Someone's hands tended her wound. The bile rose up in her throat again, and a wave of nausea gripped and tightened her stomach.

"Leave me alone. Please, just leave me alone."

"I'm here now. I'll take over."

Nick's voice rose above the noise and confusion.

"Go away," she said.

He didn't. The others did.

Tears were streaming down Becky's face now, and her heart felt as if it had died inside her chest.

Nick's arms wrapped around her, and he lifted her as if she were a small child.

"It's okay, baby. You have every right to cry, throw fits, scream. You do whatever helps."

She closed her eyes tightly and buried her face in his chest as he carried her up the stairs. The fight slowly went out of her but not the heartbreak of knowing every second that passed was taking her sons further away from her.

Nick pushed into her bedroom, yanked back the pale yellow coverlet and laid her on the sheets. "You need some rest. Lenora's calling the doctor to see if he'll prescribe something to help you sleep."

"I don't need pills. I need David and Derrick to come home."

Nick sat down on the bed beside her. "I just talked to Zach. He's following our latest dictates and going full speed ahead now like you told him you wanted when the kidnapper didn't show. The sheriff's department has put out an AMBER Alert and is faxing pictures of the boys to every law enforcement office in the state. He and Sam will coordinate the investigation together from this point on."

"This is some kind of bitter reprisal against one of us, Nick. It has to be someone who hates us and wants to get back at us the way Melvin Rogers did when he tried to blow up the big house with all of us in it."

"Melvin failed. So will this man."

"But this man has our sons." She started to shake again, the sobs beginning somewhere deep inside her and fighting their way to the surface.

Nick kicked out of his shoes and climbed into bed beside her. He wrapped around her spoon-style, his broad chest fitting against her back. Just like old times. Only nothing was like old times and would never be again. She grabbed quick, sobering breaths and then pulled away.

"Please just let me hold you, Becky. I can't do this alone. Neither can you."

She ached to slide back into his arms, but the cold bitterness of reality wouldn't let her. She turned to face him, clinging to the same stubborn pride that had kept her going even before the boys were abducted.

"I wasn't the one who tore us apart, Nick." She was being a shrew but this all hurt so much. She couldn't hold all her feelings inside and not choke on the anguish. The kidnapping. Knowing that Nick's need for her could never last. "You chose football over the boys and me. You chose being a star over being a husband and dad."

"It was never like that, Becky."

"Then how was it, Nick? Tell me how it was when you decided to treat me as if I were as invisible as the cheers you craved, because it felt like total rejection to me."

"It felt like survival to me, Becky."

Nick slid his feet to the floor and walked away from the bed, stopping at the window and staring into the dismal, gray afternoon sky. She'd never be satisfied short of the truth, never be satisfied until she sent him back to the darkest corners of his miserable youth.

Not that he'd ever fully escaped it. Not that he could and therein lay the roots of all their problems. He'd tried desperately to move past his tainted history, had buried it so deep that not even the news media had discovered it.

But the shame was still inside him, taunting him and reminding him that he would never be good enough for Becky. That he'd never come close to measuring up to Collingsworth standards.

Her brothers could always be counted on to do what was right. They'd never turn their back on a woman in trouble. Simple truths they lived by. The basics that set them apart from the crowd.

Well, he wasn't a Collingsworth and never would be. He should just accept that and let Becky go on with the divorce and on with her life.

Becky sat up in bed, her eyes wide and accusing. "Just admit it, Nick. Say I wasn't enough woman for you. Say you deserved someone like Brianna Campbell to sport around and play celebrity with. Tell me there were dozens of Briannas. Damn it, just say something."

"Brianna? You think our problems have something to do with the likes of her?"

"She was in your hospital room when I called."

"I didn't invite her. She just showed up."

"But you have been dating her."

"A friend of hers is going out with one of our

running backs. The four of us had dinner together one night. If that constitutes a date, then I'm guilty. But dinner is all it was." He shoved his hair back from his face and went back to stand at the head of the bed.

"I could have lots of women, Becky. It goes with the territory. I've never wanted anyone but you, not since the first night we…"

The first night they'd made love. The memories rushed his mind now, so intense his body reacted in unwanted ways. He concentrated on killing the telltale stirrings that would only make this worse. "There's never been anyone but you, Becky."

She shivered and wrapped her arms around her chest. "I almost wish there had been other women, Nick. They would have been easier to compete with than football."

He nodded, knowing she was right on some level even though it wasn't what she thought. "Football wasn't my mistress, Becky. It was my life, at least I thought that until faced with losing David and Derrick."

He wrapped his hands around the bedpost, wishing he had a football in them right now. Only he might never have one in them again, at least not as an NFL player. He was losing everything. How the hell could the truth hurt him anymore?

"I'm not who you think I am, Becky."

"What are you saying?"

"My father didn't die while fighting insurgents in the Middle East. My mother didn't die of cancer."

"I don't understand."

No, how could she? She knew only the fabricated version of his life, the fairy tale he'd concocted when he'd gone to live with the last foster family. His muscles bunched and throbbed as his thoughts hurdled into the past.

"My father attacked my mother in a drunken fit of rage when I was six years old. It wasn't the first time he'd hit her, and I'm sure it wouldn't have been the last. Only this time I was going to protect her. I went to the kitchen and got our longest knife.

"But I wasn't fast enough. When he slammed his fist into her stomach, she stumbled into the knife I was holding. I was going to protect her. Instead I killed her."

Becky slid from the bed and stood beside him. Her face had turned pale but her shoulders were squared, her stare unrelenting. "Why didn't you tell me this before?"

"The same reason I never told anyone. I wanted to forget it had ever happened. I thought about telling you time and time again, but you're a Collingsworth. Your family reeks of perfection. I didn't want your pity or theirs. I never wanted anyone's pity. Football made sure I never got it."

"But that was all so long ago, Nick. You've proved yourself over and over since then. Besides, you were just a kid, and none of that was your fault."

"You'd think, but it doesn't work that way. Football was the only thing I ever truly excelled at. It made me feel like I was somebody. And once I'm on the field I can't settle for less than perfection. No matter what I know logically, it's like I'm driven, the same as when I played high school and then college ball. I have to be better than everyone else to be good enough."

"You should have told me. It would have helped me understand."

"I'm telling you now. I want a chance to make us work, Becky. Just a chance, that's all I'm asking. But a real chance where you live with me even when things get tough, and you don't go running back to the ranch."

She leaned into him, resting her head on his chest. He circled her with his arms and buried his face in her sweet-smelling hair.

"Oh, Nick. I want to say yes, but…I need time," she whispered, finally pulling away.

It wasn't the answer he wanted. But it was probably better than he deserved.

Becky's phone rang. She grabbed for it and checked the caller ID. "It's Zach."

"HAVE YOU found out something new?" Becky asked before Zach had opportunity to return her greeting.

"I'm not sure. Some kids on four-wheelers out riding in the area near where the phone call was made found a car with its front end wrapped around a tree. They called the information in to the local sheriff's department. Two deputies are there now."

"That's all? Just a wrecked car?"

"I think the car may be the one used to abduct David and Derrick."

A collision would explain why the kidnapper didn't show. But… "Where are the boys? Have you checked the local hospitals? Was there blood?"

"We're checking the hospitals now. There's no sign of blood in the car, but the vehicle fits the description of the one that picked up the boys on Monday, and deputies have found two pairs of kids' sneakers in the floor of the backseat."

"What size? What brand?"

She swallowed hard at Zach's answers. "The

shoes have to be theirs, Zach. I'm coming out there."

"That's not necessary. You should stay home in case the kidnapper makes contact again. Besides, there are law enforcement personnel on the scene, and I'm heading there with Bart and Matt as we speak. I'll keep you abreast of any new information as soon as I get it."

"No. I'm coming out there." She might not be any help, but if her sons were in the area, then she wanted to be there, too. "I'll need exact directions."

"Okay, but let me talk to Nick first."

"I don't need his permission."

"I know that."

She handed the phone to Nick and went straight to her closet, stretching to her tiptoes to reach the plain overnight bag she'd bought this fall. She had no intention of coming home until this was settled and she had her sons.

She dropped the bag to the bed, then leaned over Nick's shoulder to see what he was writing on the notepad she kept on her nightstand.

"Directions to the wrecked car," he mouthed without taking the pen from the paper.

Hopefully that meant she'd get no argument from him. She left him on the phone with Zach and went to the bathroom to start packing the basic necessities. Her reflection in the mirror stopped her cold.

She looked ten years older than she had before the abduction. New wrinkles had made deep grooves around her puffy eyes. Her cheeks looked sallow, her lips drawn, the bottom one cracked. She'd always chewed on it when she was nervous. And she was worlds beyond nervous now.

A light rain splattered on the bathroom window. She'd best take boots and rain gear. But the boys didn't even have shoes. The thought sent her determined attitude plummeting back to the abyss of dread.

But if they'd found the kidnapper's car then the boys had to be nearby.

Maybe wet. Maybe hungry. But safe. She wouldn't allow herself to think of them any other way.

When she returned to the bedroom, Nick was studying his notes. "We can be there in approximately an hour," he said, as if their going together was something they'd already agreed on.

"You can't go, Nick. You have to stay here with Sam."

He shoved a stray lock of her hair behind her ear. "Sam can come along if he likes, but I've had it with waiting around for this lunatic. I'm going after David and Derrick. I wish to hell I'd done that in the first place."

"You have to think of your neck and spine, Nick. You should stay here tonight and rest."

"My neck and spine are nonissues in this."

"Not according to Dr. Cambridge or your coach."

"Let it go, Becky. I'll check with Sam and let him know what's up. Can you be ready to leave in fifteen minutes?"

"I can be ready in ten."

"Have your mother and Jaime pack some sandwiches and a couple of thermoses of coffee, enough for your brothers and anyone else involved in the search. This might turn into a long, cold, wet night."

He started to walk away, then stopped to touch her cheek and let his eyes lock with hers. His gaze was penetrating and questioning. "I won't let you down, Becky. I hope you can believe that."

Her breath caught. He'd bared his soul to her, and now his eyes were pleading with her for something in return. A look that told him things had changed between them. A promise that she could start fresh.

She wanted so badly to give it. Already she

felt her walls crumbling. But she'd built up those expectations time and time again over the last ten years only to have them sink into pools of regret. Would they ever be able to get past the heartbreak?

"I LIED to you," Bull said. "Your parents aren't coming out here to get you. Obviously they don't think you're worth the ransom. Now that I've seen what brats you are, I can see why."

"You better stop lying to us, or you're gonna be sorry."

Derrick knotted his little fists as if he thought one of them could actually cause Bull misery. His punch couldn't. His and his brother's stupid cowboy and Indian trick had. But they hadn't done as much to blow the deal as those two bodies in the woods were going to do.

Bull had been certain he could trick the boys into setting him free, but they were as smart and determined as they were devilish. They weren't going to buy into his schemes, and they weren't going to give him a chance to escape—not as long as David was pointing Bull's own gun at his head. The little imp would be just spunky enough to shoot him, too.

He couldn't break free as long as they were in the cabin. That's why he needed to get rid of them. If a couple of eight-year-old boys could cut their way out of tightly wound duct tape, then surely he could do the same and a lot quicker.

Time wasn't on his side. If he hadn't given in to the rage and been so quick to pull that trigger, he could have still pulled this off.

But dead bodies brought cops, and the leaves he'd piled over them had surely washed away in the rain. That left him one option.

"So you kids gonna hang around here with me all night?"

"Nope," Derrick said. "We're leaving now, and when we come back, we're bringing our daddy and our uncles, and you will be sorry you ever kidnapped us."

He was sorry already, but they wouldn't be bringing anybody back. Once they were out of here, he'd free himself, then escape and track them down. He'd kill both of them before they had a chance to identify him. Luckily he had the hunters' rifles stuffed in the trunk of their Jeep. A pistol belonging to one of the men was still in the glove compartment.

He watched as they pulled on their jackets and got ready to leave. They were probably nice enough kids when they hadn't been kidnapped. Too bad they had to die so young.

Chapter Twelve

Jaime started filling the everyday glasses with ice water. "I don't know why we even pretend to have meals. It's not as if anyone is going to take more than a few bites. Even Blackie's not eating."

"We need food," Lenora said, "especially Jaclyn. Pregnant women can't do without proper nutrition." And Lenora needed the routine of familiar activities that required no concentration. She could have prepared the soup and ham sandwiches they were having tonight in her sleep—if she were doing any sleeping.

She'd finally dozed off a couple hours ago only to be wakened by a nightmare starring the boys.

"Are we eating in the kitchen again?"

Lenora nodded. The kitchen had a warmth the dining room lacked except when the whole family crowded around the big oak table.

"How many place settings do we need?"

"One for everyone who's not out searching for David and Derrick—except Jeremiah." Fortunately Lenora's father-in-law was still taking his meals upstairs, though he was feeing much better today.

Pulling him into this would add another layer of strain on all of them—especially Jeremiah. He'd made a miraculous recovery from his massive stroke over a year and a half ago, but she certainly didn't want to risk another one.

"I thought Kali went back to her ranch," Jaime said.

"She did, but only to check on her horses. She said she wouldn't be long. And Jaclyn is watching Randy while Trish is horseback riding with Gina."

"I'm glad," Jaime said. "Gina really needed to get out of the house for awhile. She had her own meltdown today when we got the news that the kidnapper didn't show."

"No one mentioned that to me."

"Because you have enough on your own plate, Mom." Jaime stopped to kiss Lenora's cheek as she sashayed by her with silverware.

So they were protecting her the way she was trying to protect them. Sometimes terrible things like this tore families apart. This one seemed to be pulling them all together. If it did that for Becky and Nick, it would be a blessing. But nothing would feel like a blessing until the boys were safe.

"I think we should all be out searching," Jaime said.

"I know you do. You've said that a dozen times over the last hour."

"We always pull together when something bad happens in this family. I don't see why it should be any different now."

"Zach thinks the situation is better left in the hands of law authority. Too many cooks spoil the broth."

"My nephews aren't broth. And all my brothers are out there helping. And so is Shelly."

"Shelly is ex-CIA. And she's in Zach's office in Colts Run Cross doing record checks at the moment. I'm sure you could go sit there and watch her."

"No, thanks. Watching the show is not my game."

And never had been. If Jaime was involved, she usually was the show. She had never been good at taking orders, and she had a way of claiming far too much attention from cops or any other men who happened to be around— even when she wasn't trying.

Lenora ladled hot tomato soup into a blue pottery bowl. "Zach has serious doubts that the kidnapper is still in the same place that he made the calls from. He thinks he may be regrouping to make another attempt at claiming the ransom."

"Well, if we don't hear something positive soon, I'm driving up there even if I'm just in the way. I can't stand sitting around here like a helpless female."

A spoon slipped from Jaime's hand and went clattering to the floor. She picked it up and tossed it into the sink. "I can't stand the thought of David and Derrick spending one more night with that crazed monster."

A loud thump behind her startled Lenora so badly she spilled soup from the ladle, bathing her fingers with the hot liquid.

"What the hell are David and Derrick doing with a crazed monster?"

Lenora turned just in time to see as well as hear Jeremiah's banging of his cane. "I didn't know you were coming down for dinner."

"Don't change the subject. What's this about David and Derrick?"

Jaime handed Lenora a towel to wipe the soup from her fingers and took over with the ladling. "Might as well come clean with him, Mom. It is what it is."

And put bluntly, it was a living nightmare. Lenora collapsed into one of the kitchen chairs. "There's bad news," she said. "Sit down, and I'll tell you about it."

"I can listen standing up."

"Fine." It never did any good to argue with Jeremiah. "David and Derrick were kidnapped from school on Monday."

His wrinkles folded in on themselves, and his chin quivered. "Kidnapped?"

"Yes, while they were walking from the school to the church."

His face turned the color of chalk as he sank into the chair kitty-corner from hers. "Who took them? What does he want?"

She fed Jeremiah the details as succinctly and as calmly as she could, but there was no way to paint the picture that it didn't come out in shades of gray and black.

Jeremiah stopped her after practically every sentence with questions, but he was taking this much better than she'd expected. In fact, after the initial shock wore off, his face took on the defiant hardness he was famous for.

Once he'd exhausted her supply of information, he hammered his cane against the floor again. He hadn't been using the cane much of late, but apparently the flu had weakened him to the point he felt he needed it.

Odd, but tonight the sharp pounding Lenora used to dread seemed entirely appropriate. Welcome, even. A replacement for the scream of frustration she'd wanted to give all afternoon.

Jeremiah hammered again, the echo of it reverberating off the walls of the kitchen as the back door slammed indicating at least part of the family had returned.

"That kidnapper is messing with the wrong dadburned family this time. He's swallowed himself a bitter pill there'll be no recovering from."

Lenora put a hand over his thin, heavily veined one. "I pray you're right."

"Of course I'm right. All the Collingsworth men are out there with their hackles up looking for him. Becky and Nick, too. The devil and Tom Walker couldn't stop them from getting David and Derrick back."

Jaime walked over and put her arms around Jeremiah's neck. "I like the way you think, Grandpa."

Trish joined them in the kitchen, balancing

her young son on one hip. Gina, Jaclyn and Kali were a few steps behind her. They all stopped and stared at Jeremiah as if waiting for the proverbial second shoe to drop.

"Grandpa was just telling us how big a mistake the kidnapper made in going against the Collingsworths," Jaime announced.

"And I'm not talking just the adults," Jeremiah added. "I'd be willing to bet David and Derrick have given the man fits, too. Those boys have spunk. It's in their genes. No one should ever underestimate a Collingsworth."

Gina started the applause and the others joined in with the spontaneous approval of Jeremiah's much needed reassurance of faith in the family.

Lenora was thankful for it. As usual, Jeremiah was right. They would find the abductor, and he would pay. And in a perfect world they would get the boys back safely.

In this world that just might take the miracle she'd been praying for all along.

IT TOOK AN HOUR to reach the area where the car they believed to be the kidnapper's had been wrecked. The car was registered to Jake Hawkins, purchased for twelve hundred dollars on time from a sleazy used-car lot the week after he got out of prison. It smelled of whiskey and marijuana and mold.

The CSI team was still on the scene, working in the misty rain and gusty wind, searching for evidence to link the car to David and Derrick. They'd shown Becky the shoes, and she'd verified they belonged to her sons or at least were perfect matches for the ones they'd been wearing when they'd left for school on Monday.

After that, both she and Nick were forced to watch the process from her car. They couldn't see much, but it was as close as the detective in charge would let them get. It was clear he didn't see any reason for their hanging around.

Becky was losing patience, and her stress-and-fatigue-laced headache was not making things any easier. As far as she was concerned, a lot of people were standing around doing very little instead of searching for her sons. She'd complained about that every time anyone got close enough to listen. They all assured her they were doing their jobs.

But ever since they'd arrived, she'd had a feeling, almost a premonition, that the boys were nearby. She knew how saying it aloud would sound, so she'd kept it to herself, but she felt it. Their presence seemed almost as tangible as Nick's, who was sitting next to her.

Finally Zach pulled up and parked next to them. He got out of his truck and slid into the backseat of her car. "Rotten weather."

"Damn the weather. Is anyone looking for David and Derrick?" she demanded.

Zach took off his wet hat and set it on the seat beside him. "Half of Texas now that we've alerted them."

"I don't see any sign of that."

"It's difficult to see past your nose in this weather, but a half-dozen deputies and your other three brothers are all combing the area and have been for the last few hours. They're checking every house, cabin and mobile home they can find.

"And the state highway patrol is setting up a roadblock on the highway to stop and search all vehicles leaving this area."

"The kidnapper's car is wrapped around a tree. What good does it do to check vehicles?" She wasn't even trying to fight her frustration now.

Zach leaned forward and massaged her shoulders. "Take it easy, sis. Getting riled at the cops isn't going to help. The kidnapper is either still holed up in the area or he's already cleared out. If he's here, we'll find him. If he's left the area, we have to depend on law enforcement agencies around the state to track him down."

Becky pressed her fingers into her temples, where the throbbing ache was building to an explosive crescendo. "It's not enough."

Nick reached over and put a hand on her thigh. "You need to get some rest before you bite someone's head off."

"He's right," Zach said. "You can only go so long without sleep. Why don't the two of you drive into Huntsville and get a room? That way you can be nearby and still get some rest."

"In other words, you're telling me to do nothing." She started to get out of the car but was hit with a wave of vertigo. She was sick, exhausted and now dizzy. Maybe getting some rest did make sense.

"What about you, Zach?" Nick asked. "What are you doing the rest of the night?"

"I'll be out here a few more hours, checking for any houses or cabins we've missed. We're working from a grid. The major areas have been covered, but there are a few seldom used back roads we haven't hit yet."

"I'd like to join you. I'll need to drive Becky into town first. I don't want her driving these dark roads alone when she's as tired as she is tonight, but I can meet you after that."

"Are you sure that's what you want to do?"

"Positive."

"Then why don't I get one of the CSI guys to drive Becky into Huntsville and make sure she gets checked into a room. They'll be through out here shortly."

"There's no need for that. I can go wizz you two," she said.

"Would you listen to yourself?" Zach exclaimed. "You're so tired you can't talk straight. You've been living on raw nerves and strong coffee for almost thirty hours. I'm not trying to get rid of you, but if you don't get some rest, you'll end up in the hospital."

"Okay, but I don't like leaving."

"I'll go arrange for a ride for you." Zach opened the door and scooted out of the car without waiting for a response.

Nick took her hand in his and squeezed gently. "I'll go with you if you need me."

"You need your rest more than me, Nick. You're the one who's injured. You already should be in a hospital."

"When the boys are safe."

She knew it was useless to argue about this.

"I'll be fine alone," she said. "You do what you need to do."

Zach returned a few moments later, the arrangements apparently made. "They're saving you a room at Whistler's Bed and Breakfast Inn. Steve Jordon will drop you off, and he says it's the most comfortable accommodations in this part of Texas."

Zach gave her a hug. So did Nick. And then he kissed her. A quick kiss, but it was the first time their lips had touched in months. She'd almost forgotten the taste of him. Sweet. Salty. Nick.

"I'll join you in the room in a few hours," he said. "Get some sleep."

"I'll try."

She closed her eyes and imagined the boys walking out of the woods and strolling toward the car. And then it was the four of them—Becky, Nick, David and Derrick running hand in hand through a soft summer rain.

ZACH GUNNED his engine, spitting gravel as he drove away from the mobile home where the inhabitants had told them about a recent break-in. The single wide was set in a clearing at the end of a ribbon of dirt and mud that looked more like a pig trail than a road, but this area was full of those.

Most led to deserted cabins, many built years ago before some river Zach had never heard of dried up. At least that was the word from the local sheriff, a giant of a Texan with arms like a gorilla's and thighs as big around as Zach's waist. His disposition was all snarl and growl, and Zach suspected that his bite was just as bad.

Nick reached for his seat belt as Zach's truck rocked and rolled through a couple of mud holes big enough to drown a large dog. "Do you think it's possible that the kidnapper was the one who broke into those folk's mobile home Monday evening?"

"It's possible, but it's hard to believe a man who'd put as much thought into how he wanted the ransom paid and how he'd planned his escape would risk alerting the cops of his whereabouts for ice cream and sodas."

"But then ice cream, sodas and spaghetti do sound like David and Derrick," Nick said.

"That's why I told him we'd like to check the house for fingerprints. I think we can get a team on that first thing in the morning."

"I'd like to think it was the boys and that

somehow they'd escaped the kidnapper and were on the run. But if that were the case, why would he have called this morning and set up the meeting at the Conroe airport?"

Zach turned on the defroster. "Maybe he thought he could pull it off even without the boys?"

"And then changed his mind?"

"I'm just thinking aloud," Zach admitted. "The most likely scenario is that he was hiding out in one of these old cabins until he wrecked his car. He probably intended to steal a vehicle and close the deal this morning."

"But something stopped him."

"And if we knew what that something was, we'd have a handle on things and a hell of a lot better chance of finding all three of them."

The rain was more of a deluge now, and Zach was starting to seriously feel the crunch of a long day. Fortunately they had almost covered every inch of their grid—or rather unfortunately since they hadn't located the kidnapper.

Zach came across another road, this one in even worse shape than the one they were currently on. He was pretty sure it hadn't made the grid. He turned down it anyway, though he half expected it to ramble around a few curves and then dead-end into an overgrown patch of mud, grass and brush.

He hit a spot where the water from the rains completely covered the road, and he had to creep through it. Lightning cut a jagged path through the dark clouds followed by rumbling thunder. The weather might be about to get a lot worse.

Nick put his head next to the side window. "Did you see that?"

"The lightning?"

"No, but when it lit the landscape, I saw a house—or what's left of one off to the right."

"How far off the road?"

"I couldn't tell. I just got a glimpse."

Zach slowed to a stop and yanked the gear into Reverse. He backed up until he was in about the same spot they'd been in when the lightning struck. Grabbing his rain gear and a high-beam flashlight from the backseat, he opened the door. He was half out of the truck before he decided to grab a second gun from beneath his seat.

Nick did the same, and as soon as the ponchos were over their heads, they tramped through the slosh, their boots sucked into the muddy goop with every step.

Nick found the cabin again with the beam

from his flashlight. Rundown. Leaning. But there was a vehicle parked in front of it.

Zach's adrenaline level spiked. "Looks like someone might be around."

"If they are, they're either already in bed or sitting in the dark. Unless the storm knocked out the electricity."

Zach's hand rode the butt of his pistol as they approached.

"A Jeep Cherokee," Nick said once they were close enough to get a good look at the vehicle. "Isn't that what Hermann Grazier's wife said he was driving?"

"Exactly."

"Maybe Hermann and his brother-in-law found this old cabin and took refuge from the storm."

"Except that they should have been out of here long before the worst of the storm started. And this vehicle's obviously been parked here since before the rain made a lake of the driveway."

"Makes sense."

"That's why I make the big bucks." The comment was more habit than joke. Nothing about this situation was a laughing matter. If the hunters were inside, Zach was pretty damn sure they hadn't ended up here willingly.

He doubted they were. But Jake Hawkins just

might be. Which meant the boys might be inside, as well.

"Take this," he said, passing the extra gun to Nick. "I know you know how to use it. I've seen you on the driving range at Jack's Bluff. Keep your eyes peeled, and use the car for cover in case someone inside heard us approach."

Nick took the gun. "You think this could be it, don't you?"

"Yes, if by 'it' you mean that this could be where Jake Hawkins has been hanging out."

"I'd give anything to walk though that door and find David and Derrick alive and well."

"I know, but don't count on it. The place looks empty. And about the gun, I guess I don't have to tell you not to shoot unless it's a matter of life and death—then make sure you're not the dead one."

"Got it.

The hood of the Cherokee was up and rain was pouring into the car's guts. Zach failed to come up with a rational explanation for that.

"Work your way around to where you can see the back of the cabin just in case someone tries to escape that way. And stay protected."

Nick followed the order without question, staying low and near the tree line. Zach sprayed the front of the house with light, eventually letting the beam pinpoint the entrance. Gun poised for action, he walked up and knuckle-rapped the door.

"Police. Open the door and keep your hands in view."

Of course there was no response. That would have been way too easy.

He knocked and yelled the order again, sure that this time he'd shouted over the wind and rain. Still nothing. Mentally and physically geared for an ambush, he tried the knob and the door swung open.

He flicked on the light, keeping his back to the wall and his trigger finger ready. There was no movement, but chaos painted a vivid picture that left no doubt in his mind that his nephews had been in this cabin with the kidnapper. They weren't here now—unless…

A shadow moved outside the open front door. He was not the only one around.

Chapter Thirteen

"Back up. Don't shoot."

"Damn it, Nick. I told you to watch the back of the cabin."

"Nothing going on back there." And Nick had far too much at stake to be hanging around outside. "I'll cover. Let's search the house."

With each step, Nick's alarm rose. His sons weren't in this house, but they had been. David's Dallas Cowboys hat that had been signed by the whole team was on the kitchen table. Their two school bags were slung over the arm of a kitchen chair.

And everywhere he looked, the sights made him recoil in horror. Shreds of duct tape that Hawkins must have used to bind his sons. A rope. Boarded windows. A broken lamp. Empty beer cans everywhere. And blood splattered on the front door. His stomach pitched.

"This is were he held them while he did no telling what to them." His voice broke with his resolve and he buried his head in his shaking hands. "Right here, not a good two hours from the house, and I couldn't find them."

Zach put a hand on his shoulder. "Haven't found them *yet*. We're not through, not by a long shot."

But Jake Hawkins or whoever had his twin sons had fled the area, not in the hunter's car but likely in some other vehicle he'd stolen. For some reason Nick couldn't fathom, the man must have given up on getting the ransom. If that were the case, there would be no reason for him to let the boys go free so that they could identify him.

He'd refused to think that the boys could be dead, but now the possibility hardened to cement in his gut. They might have found them in time if he'd let Zach call the shots from the beginning.

But he hadn't. He'd held out for the ransom attempt. He'd only wanted to protect them, but he might have destroyed them the same way he'd done his mother. He could have saved her if he hadn't waited until it was too late.

Becky was right to want the divorce. He didn't measure up. Cheering crowds, raving sports announcers and a huge bank account couldn't change that.

He walked over and picked up the cap David had been so proud of.

"Don't touch anything else," Zach said. "We need to preserve the evidence. There should be enough fingerprints in this room alone to put Jake Hawkins away."

"Then you're convinced Jake Hawkins is the kidnapper?"

"I'd stake my claim to my part of the ranch on it."

That was as sure as a man could get.

"He could be on his way to Mexico now," Nick conceded. But if he'd killed or even hurt David and Derrick, Nick would find him or spend the rest of his life trying.

"Let's get out of here, Zach. I need to give Becky the news."

THE RAIN WAS FALLING in sheets, and Becky's clothes were drenched, her skin numb from the wind and falling temperatures. "David! Derrick?"

Why wouldn't they come? She'd been calling them for hours and, now she was lost in this pitch-dark forest. A low-hanging limb from a tree smacked her in the face when she tried to pass. Blood trickled down her cheek and across her lips. The metallic taste of it burned her tongue.

"David! Derrick? Answer me. I know you're out there."

A bird swooped down on her in the darkness, and its talons tangled in her hair. She fought it off, then tripped and fell on her face on the soggy ground.

A giant tarantula crawled across her hand. She screamed and knocked it away.

"Are you looking for us, Mom? We're right here."

She jumped to her feet and ran to them. When she reached them they were gone.

BECKY WOKE UP SHAKING. It took several seconds to realize that she was still in her car on the edge of the woods near Jake Hawkins's wrecked car. She rubbed her eyes and tried to clear the troubling remains of the nightmare from her mind.

She glanced at her watch. Eleven-fifty. She must have fallen asleep while waiting on the deputy who was supposed to drive her into Huntsville. The few minutes she was supposed to wait for a ride into Huntsville had lasted for two hours.

If anything, there were more cars here now

than when she'd drifted off. But the action was no longer centered on Jake Hawkins's wrecked car. In fact, there was no one around it. The activity was in an area of bright lights shining through the trees off to her left.

She lowered her window. The rain had stopped. The wind had died down, as well. She opened the door, got out and started walking toward the lights and din of voices.

Someone grabbed her by the arm. She turned to find the young deputy she and Nick had talked to earlier.

"I'm sorry, Mrs. Ridgely, but you can't go back there. Crime scene. Secured area. You know how it is."

"Is there new evidence?"

"Yes, ma'am. One of the deputies had gone to take a—well, you know because there aren't any bathrooms around."

"I understand." She could use some decent facilities herself. "What did he find?"

"Two bodies."

"Two bodies." She swayed, and the ground started rising to meet her face.

The deputy steadied her. "It was those hunters that were missing. It was their bodies that were found. I'm sorry. I should have said that first. No excuse, but it's been a night."

She still wasn't sure she'd heard him right. "Did you say that someone killed Hermann Grazier?"

"Yes, ma'am. Killed him and his brother-in-law. Shot one of them in the back of the head, the other in the front. Real nasty."

"Jake Hawkins must have killed them."

"I'm not at liberty to divulge any information. If I did, it would just be supposition."

But who else would it be? Surely he hadn't killed them for a phone. Only someone who'd gone totally mad would commit such an act.

The totally mad person who had her sons. The depths of her soul started to shake. She needed to get out of here.

"Would you tell Deputy Steve Jordon that I'm feeling much better now and that I'm going to drive myself back to Whistler's Inn in Huntsville? And if either my brother Deputy Zach Collingsworth or my husband Nick Ridgely shows up, you can give them that same information."

"I'll do it."

She'd call Nick when she got back to Huntsville, but not until then. He'd only insist she wait for him to drive her. She was fully capable of doing that herself now that she'd had some sleep and a new shock to steel her mind.

The deputy stayed at her side. "Do you know how to get back to the main road?"

"Probably not. Can you point me in the right direction?"

"Do you have a compass in your car?"

"There's one with the GPS system."

"Then keep turning to the west. I think it's about four turns before you reach Highway 190. That will take you right into Huntsville."

"Thanks." She hurried back to her car. Two people were dead. Nothing about this could be good. She turned the key in the ignition. "O, Holy Night" was playing on the radio. The clock said ten past midnight.

It was Christmas Eve.

THE FIRST THING Nick noticed when he and Zach returned to the spot where he'd left Becky was the action taking place in the nearby woods. The second was that Becky's car was missing. "I thought Steve Jordon was going to drive Becky back to the hotel in his squad car and leave her car for me."

"He was, but he may still be here. Judging from the lights and the crowd and that new strip of bright orange tape going up in the trees, I'd say they've uncovered some new evidence."

Which meant that Becky had probably given up on her ride and driven back alone. He pulled out his cell phone and was punching in her number when a young deputy stuck his head in the window Zach had just lowered.

"Mrs. Ridgely left about ten minutes ago, maybe less. She said to be sure and tell you that she got some sleep first and that she was wide awake. Said she was driving into Huntsville."

"Thanks," Nick said. "Did she seem all right?"

"Seemed as coherent as any of us, not that that's saying much."

Zach turned toward the site of the lights and action. "What's going on in the woods?"

"We found those two hunters who went missing—Hermann Grazier and Bruce Cotton. Well, to be more specific, we found their bodies."

They listened to the gory details. Zach interrupted with questions several times. Nick's mind had jumped ahead to terrifying conclusions. Number one was that Jake Hawkins was capable of murder.

"Never seen a man more eager to get back to prison." Zach stepped out of the car and tossed Nick his keys. "Why don't you take my truck and go join Becky? I have a feeling she needs your company and that you need hers."

Nick nodded. "What about you? You need some sleep."

"I'll get some, but I want to take a look at exactly what they found. Steve or one of the other deputies will give me a lift into town when we're done. I'll get my keys from you over breakfast in the morning."

"That'll work."

Nick drove away from the scene, glad the rain was over, and thinking of his sons.

Memories of the night the boys were born sprang to life as if it had been yesterday. He'd been overcome with emotion the first time he'd held them in his arms—David in the right one, Derrick in the left.

He was certain his life had changed forever at that point. He was a father, a husband, a second-year player in the NFL. Finally he'd be able to bury the past and lose the insecurities and guilt that drove him.

He'd been wrong, of course. If anything the secret life of Nick Ridgely pushed him even harder to prove himself after he'd become a father.

Now he might lose his career and his marriage. And if that weren't terror enough, his sons were with a sociopath who'd already killed today. And that was the best scenario.

He beat a fist against the steering wheel as he pulled onto the rain-slick road. His day of reckoning had come.

HOURS OF POURING RAIN had left the old rock and dirt roadbed formidable and the shoulders a slimy sledge. Becky crept along, afraid to drive faster than a crawl. She'd made one turn. Now her eyes were peeled for the next crossroad.

She hadn't realized earlier how narrow the roads were or how isolated they felt. Nick had been driving then, and she'd been consumed with the prospect of seeing Jake Hawkins's car and determining for certain if the shoes inside belonged to her sons. That seemed days ago.

So did Nick's shocking confession of a past she'd never even suspected. Even now, she struggled to fuse the Nick she knew with that frightened little boy who'd been forced to deal with issues far beyond his years.

The Nick she knew was driven, cocky, sexy. She'd fallen so hard for him when they met that she'd have married him that very night. Nick had been the sane one, insisting that they take it slow. Not that they had in the lovemaking department. They'd been dynamite together—until football season started the following fall.

Even then he'd been driven to be the best player on the team. She'd accepted his ambition without question, considered it a good thing. She'd been far too in love with the star of the Longhorns to ever find fault with him.

But never once in all the years they'd been together had she seen the haunting pain in his eyes that had been there today when he'd told her about his mother's death. Had he hidden his vulnerability that well all those years or had she just been too blind to see what was in his soul?

She'd been quick to blame Nick for their lack of emotional attachment, but now it seemed that she'd been as guilty as he was of not seeing beyond the superficial. She'd never bothered to look beyond the facade of the man he appeared to be to see the person deep inside.

Now it all came down to the fact that neither of them had ever really known the other.

He wanted to change. Maybe she needed to do some soul searching and some changing, as well…when this was over. When their sons were safe.

Her car went into a skid as she rounded a sharp

curve that sent her straining against her seat belt and the beams from her headlights jutting across a patch of dark woods. She tensed but managed to keep the vehicle from leaving the road.

Going even more slowly now, she caught a glimpse of movement on the edge of the illumination from her headlights. Her heart slammed against her chest as the earlier nightmare flashed across her consciousness.

She braked slowly and stared into the pitch blackness of the moonless night. She was overreacting. The movement had most likely been a deer or several of them. She'd hit a huge buck once driving back to the ranch after a function in Houston.

A heavy fog had drastically reduced visibility, and by the time she'd spotted the animal, it had been too late to stop. Just as she reached it, it had darted across the road. Her car had been totaled. Luckily she and her mother, who was dozing in the passenger seat, only suffered a few bruises.

Becky lowered the window. The night seemed eerily silent at first, and then she became aware of the cacophony of sounds made by the wind in the trees and myriad nocturnal creatures that flew through the branches and scurried through the grass.

Her finger was on the button to raise the window when she saw movement again. Not a deer but a person. She was almost sure of it—unless her mind was playing cruel tricks on her. After the past few days, that was entirely possible.

She got out of the car, rounded the back of it and stepped from the road into slush. "David! Derrick!"

The feeling of déjà vu was incredibly strong and frighteningly ghostly. It was the earlier nightmare all over again, only she was fully awake. She shivered as she took a few steps toward the thick growth of trees just feet from the road.

"David. Derrick. It's Mom."

A gust of wind slapped her in the face and jolted her from the harrowing state of hypnotic absurdity she'd fallen into. The constant stress was driving her over the edge. Her sons were with a kidnapper, not wandering the forest like spooked fawns.

She turned to walk back to the car, then stopped. Someone was here. She could hear whistling.

Chapter Fourteen

Footfalls sounded behind Becky. She spun around as a brawny arm locked her in a stranglehold.

"Jake Hawkins?"

"Yeah, but we're about to be real friendly, and my friends call me Bull."

Becky tried to break free of his hold, but a sharp prick at the base of her neck stopped her. He had a knife. One jerky move and her jugular would be sliced.

"Where are my sons?"

"Where I left them. Bleeding. Crying for their momma."

She fought the rush of panic and fury that shook her. She'd never hated another person, but she did now.

"Why? Why us? Why David and Derrick?" Her heart cried into her words. "We did everything just the way you said. We had the money. You didn't show up to get it."

"You called in the authorities."

"We didn't."

"Don't lie, you bitch. The cops swarmed my wrecked car like a hive of killer bees." He spit the words at her.

He knew. There was no use in lying. Less use to fight as long as the knife was at her throat. "We only called them after you didn't show up as planned. We thought you no longer wanted the money."

"Like you'd know about wanting money. You living the friggin' dream life of a princess. Texas royalty. You like that, don't you? You always did."

"I don't know what you're talking about."

"High school, Becky. I'm talking Colts Run Cross High School. You parading around the football field in that cheerleading outfit that barely covered your behind. Wearing that stretchy top so that your young tits taunted every guy who passed."

"That was years ago, Jake. I wore the uniform they gave us. I didn't mean to taunt anyone. I barely knew you."

His grip tightened, and he lifted the arm

under her chin, pulling her head back until she was looking up into his snarling face. "You didn't want to know me. You acted like I was dried-up paint on the wall until you started your nasty rumors. You liked thinking of me as a murderer, but you didn't know the half of it."

"That's not true. I never thought you killed your grandmother. I didn't." Not until now.

"The woman nagged me all the time. Told me I was as worthless as my tramp mother. Said I was a curse to her."

Becky fought to swallow against the pressure on her neck. "I'm sorry, Jake. I am. I didn't know."

"You didn't know. You didn't care. And now I don't care, either, not about you or your bratty kids. Not about Nick Ridgely, either."

Her face was so close to his that even in the dark she could see the rage in his eyes. The same fury he must have felt when he'd pushed his grandmother down those stairs. When he'd pulled a pregnant woman from her car and stabbed her with a pocketknife. When he'd killed two men for no reason at all.

But she couldn't give up. They'd find her body, but would they ever find David and Derrick in time?

"Nick has the money, Jake. Let me call him,

and he'll bring it to you," she pleaded. "All five million, in small bills, just like you said. You get the money, and you give us back our sons."

"Where's your phone?"

"In my handbag. I left it in the car. I'll get it and call him."

"Sure you would, right after you drove off and left me here."

"No. You can go to the car with me." Anything to give her a chance to get out of this alive.

"One call, Becky. One chance. If anything goes wrong, I'll kill you along with your sons and then wipe Nick Ridgely's face in your blood."

She would have gladly given him the money, only Nick didn't have it on him. It was back at Jack's Bluff. He'd be here in minutes if she called, but she had to keep him from walking into a trap.

"Nick will want to know where the boys are. He'll want to talk to them."

"Haggling won't work, Becky. You lost all the pawns in the game the second my knife touched your flesh."

Jake pulled her into the clearing and started to drag her toward her car. The lights from an approaching car stopped him. He yanked her back into the trees, the knife piercing her skin as he did. She felt only a quick sensation and then the hot, wet trickle of blood dripping from her neck.

A pickup truck pulled to a stop behind her car. The beams from its headlights sent a muted whisper of illumination through the trees. Jake's right hand stayed around her neck, but he pulled the knife away and exchanged it for a pistol.

"Make one sound and you're dead."

She had no doubt he meant the threat. But if she stayed silent and the driver of the truck walked toward them, he'd be the one who was dead, shot just as Hermann Grazier and Bruce Cotton had been.

A man stepped from the driver's side of the truck and walked to her car. Her heart jumped to her throat and sent agonizing stabs of dread through every fiber of her being.

The driver of the truck was Nick

NICK STARED into Becky's empty car. Her keys were in the ignition. Her purse was in the passenger seat. Her jacket had been slung to the backseat. He struggled for some positive spin to put on the situation, but there was none.

Trepidation gave way to full-scale alarm. He peered into the darkness on either side of the road and then went back to the truck for a flashlight. He shot the bright beam into the trees, searching for a sign of Becky, though he couldn't imagine any reason that she'd have ventured into the heavily forested area.

He fervently wished that he hadn't given the weapon back to Zach when they'd left the cabin where the kidnapper had been holed up with David and Derrick, but he'd had no idea that he'd need one tonight.

Muscles clenched and adrenaline pumping, he stepped off the road and toward the trees, shining the beam toward the ground to search for Becky's trail. He found it quickly, imprints of her boots carved into the muddy clay.

"Becky!"

No response. Yet he was sure she'd come this way. Or been lured this way. He called her name again, louder, panic adding a crusty crack to his voice.

Something rustled the grass to his left. He took off running toward the sound.

"Don't, Nick. It's Jake. He has a gun."

Too late. Nick saw Becky being thrown to the ground and Jake Hawkins's heavy foot stamp down on her stomach. The gun in his hand was pointed at her head.

"I want my five million, Nick Ridgely, and I want it now."

This was crazy. Becky surely hadn't come out here alone to meet the kidnapper. But she was here, a gun at her head. Nick had to think fast.

"The money's in my truck," he lied. "Let Becky go, and I'll get it for you."

"I don't like those rules. Let's try mine. You bring me the money, and I'll let your bitch live."

He obviously didn't want to risk coming out of the clearing for fear an armed deputy might come along as Nick had. That was Nick's only advantage.

"Drop the gun."

"You're not giving the orders."

"Then shoot me."

"Nick, don't." Becky was crying and straining against Jake's killer hold on her. "Just go."

"Drop the gun, Jake, or get the money yourself."

"Get the money or she dies."

"Where are my sons?"

"Dead."

Becky wailed as if her heart were spilling onto the ground.

A blinding fury roared through Nick's veins along with the sure realization that Jake had no intention of letting either of them walk away from this alive.

"Your sons didn't cooperate, so I killed them, the same way I'll kill Becky if I don't have that money in my hand in thirty seconds. One."

Nick's past flashed before his eyes in living color. The red blood as his mother had drooped against him. The plum-colored dress Becky had worn on their first date. The baby-blue blankets they'd wrapped David and Derrick in the night they were born.

"The money, Nick, or do I just pull this trigger now?"

So who would it be in tonight's game? Nick Ridgely who let everyone down? Or Nick Ridgely, star receiver for the Dallas Cowboys. Great hands. Lightning speed. Amazing timing.

Or Nick Ridgely, his own man?

Nick took one more step toward the car, then turned, diving into the air in that unexpected split second and coming down on top of Jake. His left hand cracked against Jake's right one, sending the pistol flying though the air.

Jake recovered quickly, planting a fist into Nick's injured neck at the top of his spine. Nick went down in excruciating pain, then stumbled back to his feet. He swung at Jake and missed as Jake hammered him with another right punch to the center of his back and a left jab to his collarbone.

He was hitting the right spots to make the most of Nick's injury. Delivering blow after blow. Nick stumbled away, trying to get his balance. He spotted Becky clawing in the pine straw for the gun. "Get out of here, Becky. Now!"

Jake was at him again, fists pounding into Nick's neck and spine as he jumped on his back and dug his knees into his side as if he were riding a wild bronco. The pain was so intense, Nick was afraid he'd pass out or that the doctor's fears would materialize and he'd fall into a paralyzed mass.

It would take that for him to give up and leave Becky with this madman. He fought back, finally slamming his backside into a tree with enough force to shake Jake loose and send him sprawling to the ground. Nick backed away to catch his breath and regroup. Jake came up with a knife, the blade extended. He swiped it across Nick's chest, drawing blood.

Becky was still on her hands and knees in the mud. "Take the car, Becky. Get out. Please get out of here."

Jake sliced into him again, this time across

the right thigh. Nick grabbed a broken limb from the ground and poked it into Jake's face. Jake howled but never slowed down, coming at Nick and knocking him to the carpet of pine straw that was fast turning red with his blood.

He was losing feeling in his arms and legs. His vision was blurry. In spite of all Nick's vows, Jake Hawkins was going to win.

And then a blast of gunfire exploded, and Jake Hawkins finally quit coming at him.

"Nick. Nick."

"I'm sorry, Becky. I'm sorry I let you down."

"You didn't. Oh, Nick, say you're okay. Please tell me you can move."

His brain was too hazy to know for certain if he was alive or dead and dreaming. He rolled over and spit out a mouthful of blood and what felt like a dozen teeth.

"I thought he'd killed you, Nick. I was so afraid."

Slowly the scene came into view. Becky was crying and pushing Jake's body off him. He pulled her into his arms with the last of his energy and lay in the mud with her tears running down his chest.

"Are you all right?" she whispered between sobs.

He wasn't all right. He might never be all

right again. Neither would Becky. He'd failed them, and their sons were dead.

"I'll call an ambulance," she said.

"I think it's too late for that. He looks dead."

"I meant for you."

"Not yet." He couldn't bear to have her leave his arms.

They lay in the dark holding on to each other, her sobs open and honest, his tears a burn of moisture seeping from his eyes.

He didn't know how much time had passed before the flashing blue lights from a squad car lit the area. The cops Jake had been trying so hard to avoid. He managed to stand and help Becky to her feet. There wasn't a part of him that didn't ache.

"Nick. Becky."

The deputy was no surprise. You could count on a Collingsworth. "Out here, Zach."

Zach strode to them. "What the devil happened here?"

"I saw someone in the trees," Becky said, her voice shaking and drenched in heartbreak. "I thought it might be David and Derrick, that they could have escaped from the kidnapper and were on the run. It was Jake."

"And then Nick came along and shot him,"

Zach said, jumping to the erroneous conclusion. He offered Nick a high five. "Good work, man. I didn't even know you were carrying a gun."

"I wasn't. It was his."

Zach knelt and felt for Jake's pulse, making sure he was really dead. "I guess the boys were wrong. They thought they'd taken his only pistol. He must have stolen one from Hermann Grazier."

Nick shook his head to clear it. "What are you talking about?"

"Why don't I let your sons tell you?" Zach whistled and motioned to the car. The door opened, and David and Derrick jumped out and started running to them.

"Becky wasn't that far off," Zach said. "The boys escaped and came walking out of the woods to where the cops were stringing yellow tape a couple of minutes after Nick drove off."

Becky didn't wait to hear the rest of her brother's explanation. She was already rushing toward David and Derrick. The three of them literally collided, tangling in a boisterous three-way hug before they pulled her down on top of them.

Nick couldn't move that quickly, but he did pretty well for a guy with a few new contusions to add to his medical report. He fell gingerly into the tangle of arms, legs and unadulterated joy.

THE HOMECOMING for David and Derrick was everything anyone could have expected and more. Every light in the big house was on, and every single member of the Collingsworth family had been waiting on the front porch when they arrived.

The only lull in the celebration had occurred in the short period of time it had taken for Becky, Nick, David and Derrick to shower off the mud.

Now David and Derrick were holding court in front of the fireplace, drinking hot chocolate, munching on cookies and fudge explaining for at least the tenth time how they'd lassoed the kidnapper and used his own duct tape stunt to render him helpless and at their mercy.

It was three in the morning, and no one seemed to realize that they should all be in bed.

Nick was the only quiet one, and Becky was certain he was paying the price for tangling with Jake Hawkins. He looked as if it hurt to move, but he never complained. It wasn't his style, and just maybe that wasn't so bad.

Becky slipped unnoticed from the family

room and went back to the kitchen for a glass of water. Lenora was standing by the range, wiping tears from her eyes with a Santa Claus towel.

"So this is where you disappeared to," Becky said.

"I needed some alone time to count my blessings."

Becky put her arms around her mother, enfolding her in a hug. "You always believed they'd come home safely, didn't you? I tried, but I never seem to have your faith."

"I've had years to work on it. And I believe in miracles."

"After tonight, I think we all do. But I was afraid, so very afraid. And not only for the boys. I think the divorce may be a mistake, Mom. I don't think all the problems with our marriage belong to Nick."

"Tell your husband that, Becky."

"Tell me what?"

Neither Becky nor Lenora had seen or heard Nick come into the kitchen. Now that they knew he was there, Lenora slipped from Becky's embrace and left them alone.

Nick frowned. "If this is bad news, I don't want to hear it tonight. Let me have Christmas first. Give me the holiday with you and the boys before I have to come back down to earth."

Her moment of truth. She took a deep breath. "I love you, Nick. I don't know if I ever realized how much until I thought Jake Hawkins was going to beat you into a pulverized, paralyzed mess. But I knew it then, and I know it now. I admit our marriage needs work, but…"

Nick crossed the room, slowly, the pain evident in his every step. "Oh, Becky. I love you so much. I'll do whatever it takes not to lose you. I'll give up football and move back here to the ranch. I'll talk every night about feelings until you are sick of hearing me. I'll attend every school function the boys ever have, even spelling bees. Just say what you need from me to make this work, and I'll give it my best shot."

"That's just it, Nick. I don't want you to give up football for me. I don't want you to give up anything. Our problems are not all your fault. They never were. Both of us have to work on being honest with each other about our feelings. You can't hide behind your past. I can't hide behind my stubbornness."

He cradled her face in his bruised hands. "Are you saying you'll give us a chance?"

"As many chances as we need. I don't want

to face life without you. I want to raise our sons together, have grandchildren, grow old in each other's arms. I want to love you for the rest of my life. I just want the marriage to be all that it can be."

He pulled her into his arms and then winced in pain.

She pulled away. "I'm sorry. I guess this isn't the night for you to crawl back in my bed."

"Just try to keep me out. But promise not to move—or breathe heavy." He kissed her lightly on the lips, a sweet promise of all that would come in the lifetime ahead.

"Merry Christmas, Mrs. Ridgely."

"Merry Christmas, Nick."

She wouldn't have thought there was a chance of it a few hours earlier, but Nick had called it right. This really would be the merriest Christmas of their lives.

Epilogue

Three months later

"I've never seen you so excited or secretive, Nick. When are you going to tell me what is going on?"

"I've already told you. It's spring. We're going on a picnic on the beautiful Jack's Bluff Ranch."

"Yeah, Mom. It's a picnic. Don't you get it?"

Nick stopped the truck and opened his door so the boys and Blackie could pile out of the backseat of the double-cab Dodge.

"This is the new me," Nick said. "Can't get enough of family time."

"There's more going on here. I just haven't figured it out yet. You're smiling like you just won the Super Bowl."

"That's because I have the old Becky back." He slipped his arm along the back of the seat and tangled his fingers in one of her loose curls. "The Becky who makes love like a wild woman."

She punched him playfully. "It's just that you're so thrilled to be back in the saddle again."

"You got that right, lady. And such a nice saddle. You can take a Collingsworth off the ranch, but you can't make her give up those wild bronc-riding ways in the bedroom."

"I'm just a rancher's daughter at heart."

"And don't I know it."

She had to admit she loved the weekends on the ranch, like this one. It was good for the boys, too. But she was happy in Dallas, as well. She thought she could probably be happy anywhere now that she and Nick were getting along so well—both emotionally and physically.

It was as if they'd found each other all over again. And best of all, the problems with his injury were practically behind him. He'd gone back to the doctor yesterday, and he expected the doctors to give him full clearance to start getting ready for the upcoming season any day.

Nick had parked at the spot where the creek that crisscrossed the ranch bubbled musically over a bed of angular rocks. They'd come here on his first visit to the ranch and made wild, passionate love on a blanket in the grass. He'd called it their special corner of the ranch ever since. She liked the fact that they'd come back here today.

"Can we go swimming?" Derrick called, already racing to the water.

Becky climbed out of the truck. "No. It's not summer yet. The water's too cold."

"Then can we wade?"

"Cold feet won't kill them," Nick said.

"Okay, wade, but take off your shoes and socks and watch out for snakes."

"Ah, the joys of ranch life." Nick walked to the front of the truck and leaned against the hood.

"It's not so bad," she said.

"Not bad at all. I was just teasing you."

She started to pull the picnic basket from the back of the truck.

"Let's wait for the food," Nick said. "I need to talk to you about something."

His voice had grown serious. She felt a sudden tightening in her chest. "This isn't about the doctor's report, is it? Did you hear something today?"

"Actually, I did."

He'd gotten bad news. That's why he was smiling—to hide his anxiety. She'd said she wanted him to share all his feelings with her, but she wasn't sure she was up to this.

Becky walked to the front of the car and snuggled next to him. He circled his arms around her.

Finally she got up the courage to ask the dreaded question. "Was the verdict bad?"

"Could be worse. I have some mild ligamentous injuries that are healing. Nothing to keep me from playing again, though I might be at slightly more risk of future injuries."

She breathed a sigh of relief, though the possibility of his having a serious injury never went down easily. "So you can still play?"

"I can." He kissed the back of her neck. "I've decided that I'm not."

She turned to face him, unsure she'd heard him right. "You can't give up football. You love it. It's your life."

"It *used* to be my life. Not that I'm knocking it. I've had a great career. Football was my salvation, but I don't need it anymore, not the way I did. I want to move on to new challenges and I'd like to do that here."

"In Colts Run Cross?" She was having difficulty buying this.

"Here. On Jack's Bluff Ranch. On this spot

where we're standing. Our hideaway. Don't you think it's the perfect place to build our dream house?"

"I love it, but…I don't see you as a rancher, Nick."

"Whew. Now, that's a relief. I have no intention of being a rancher. I've talked to the school board. They need a head coach for the Colts Run Cross high school football team. I'd like to take that job. Football has given me a lot. It's time I gave something back."

He nudged her chin so that she was looking into his gorgeous brown eyes. "It's taken me a while to get here, but this is what I want. I was hoping it's what you want, too."

"Pinch me, Nick. I'm sure I'm dreaming."

"How about I just kiss you instead?"

His lips took hers hungrily, the passion as consuming as it had been when she'd first fallen in love with him.

"I love you, Nick Ridgely."

"That's good, Becky, because there is something else I need from you to make me totally happy."

"Name it, Coach."

"A daughter."

With pleasure.

"Or two."

She could handle that.

"And another son."

Now he was pushing his luck.

"Maybe even another set of twins."

She covered his mouth with her lips, cutting off his words before he'd talked her into a whole football team.

* * * * *

Here is a sneak preview of
A STONE CREEK CHRISTMAS,
the latest in Linda Lael Miller's acclaimed
McKETTRICK *series.*

A lonely horse brought vet Olivia O'Ballivan to Tanner Quinn's farm, but it's the
rancher's love that might cause her to stay.

A STONE CREEK CHRISTMAS
Available December 2008
from Silhouette Special Edition

Tanner heard the rig roll in around sunset. Smiling, he wandered to the window. Watched as Olivia O'Ballivan climbed out of her Suburban, flung one defiant glance toward the house and started for the barn, the golden retriever trotting along behind her.

Taking his coat and hat down from the peg next to the back door, he put them on and went outside. He was used to being alone, even liked it, but keeping company with Doc O'Ballivan, bristly though she sometimes was, would provide a welcome diversion.

He gave her time to reach the horse Butterpie's stall, then walked into the barn.

The golden retriever came to greet him, all wagging tail and melting brown eyes, and he bent to stroke her soft, sturdy back. "Hey, there, dog," he said.

Sure enough, Olivia was in the stall, brushing Butterpie down and talking to her in a soft, soothing voice that touched something private inside Tanner and made him want to turn on one heel and beat it back to the house.

He'd be damned if he'd do it, though.

This was *his* ranch, *his* barn. Well-intentioned as she was, *Olivia* was the trespasser here, not him.

"She's still very upset," Olivia told him, without turning to look at him or slowing down with the brush.

Shiloh, always an easy horse to get along with, stood contentedly in his own stall, munching away on the feed Tanner had given him earlier. Butterpie, he noted, hadn't touched her supper as far as he could tell.

"Do you know anything at all about horses, Mr. Quinn?" Olivia asked.

He leaned against the stall door, the way he had the day before, and grinned. He'd practically been raised on horseback; he and Tessa had grown up on their grandmother's farm in the Texas hill country, after their folks divorced and went their separate ways, both of them too busy to bother with a couple of kids. "A few things," he said. "And I mean to call you Olivia, so you might as well return the favor and address me by my first name."

He watched as she took that in, dealt with it, decided on an approach. He'd have to wait and see what that turned out to be, but he didn't mind. It was a pleasure just watching Olivia O'Ballivan grooming a horse.

"All right, *Tanner,*" she said. "This barn is a disgrace. When are you going to have the roof fixed? If it snows again, the hay will get wet and probably mold…"

He chuckled, shifted a little. He'd have a crew out there the following Monday morning to replace the roof and shore up the walls—he'd made the arrangements over a week before—but he felt no particular compunction to explain that. He was enjoying her ire too much; it made her color rise and her hair fly when she turned her head, and the faster breathing made her perfect breasts go up and down in an enticing rhythm. "What makes you so sure I'm a greenhorn?" he asked mildly, still leaning on the gate.

At last she looked straight at him, but she didn't move from Butterpie's side. "Your hat, your boots—that fancy red truck you drive. I'll bet it's customized."

Tanner grinned. Adjusted his hat. "Are you telling me real cowboys don't drive red trucks?"

"There are lots of trucks around here," she said. "Some of them are red, and some of them are new. And *all* of them are splattered with mud or manure or both."

"Maybe I ought to put in a car wash, then," he teased. "Sounds like there's a market for one. Might be a good investment."

She softened, though not significantly, and spared him a cautious half smile, full of questions she probably wouldn't ask. "There's a good car wash in Indian Rock," she informed him. "People go there. It's only forty miles."

"Oh," he said with just a hint of mockery. "*Only* forty miles. Well, then. Guess I'd better dirty up my truck if I want to be taken seriously in these here parts. Scuff up my boots a bit, too, and maybe stomp on my hat a couple of times."

Her cheeks went a fetching shade of pink. "You are twisting what I said," she told him, brushing Butterpie again, her touch gentle but sure. "I meant…"

Tanner envied that little horse. Wished he had a furry hide, so he'd need brushing, too.

"You *meant* that I'm not a real cowboy," he said. "And you could be right. I've spent a lot of time on construction sites over the last few years, or in meetings where a hat and boots wouldn't be appropriate. Instead of digging out my old gear, once I decided to take this job, I just bought new."

"I bet you don't even *have* any old gear," she challenged, but she was smiling, albeit cautiously, as though she might withdraw into a disapproving frown at any second.

He took off his hat, extended it to her. "Here," he teased. "Rub that around in the muck until it suits you."

She laughed, and the sound—well, it caused a powerful and wholly unexpected shift inside him. Scared the hell out of him and, paradoxically, made him yearn to hear it again.

* * * * *

Discover how this rugged rancher's
wanderlust is tamed in time for
a merry Christmas, in
A STONE CREEK CHRISTMAS.
In stores December 2008.

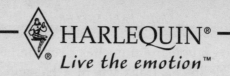

"Am I in trouble?"

He snapped his attention to her. "You're conscious."

"Disappointed, huh?" she teased.

Nate ripped his gaze from her adorable face. "This isn't funny."

"No, it most certainly is not. I was just doing my job and found a body. Is she dead? Please tell me she's not dead. At first I thought maybe she just collapsed and hit her head. I've passed out before from not remembering to eat."

Her nonstop chatter convinced Nate she was okay. "Cassie, take a breath."

"You're angry with me," she said.

"I'm not angry."

"You seem angry. Why, because I'm down here? I was only trying to get away." She hesitated. "That man, there was a man."

"It's okay, he's not here now. You're safe."

An eternal optimist, **Hope White** was born and raised in the Midwest. She and her college sweetheart have been married for thirty years and are blessed with two wonderful sons, two feisty cats and a bossy border collie. When not dreaming up inspirational tales, Hope enjoys hiking, sipping tea with friends and going to the movies. She loves to hear from readers, who can contact her at hopewhiteauthor@gmail.com.

Books by Hope White

Love Inspired Suspense

Echo Mountain

Mountain Rescue
Covert Christmas
Payback
Christmas Undercover
Witness Pursuit

Hidden in Shadows
Witness on the Run
Christmas Haven
Small Town Protector
Safe Harbor

Visit the Author Profile page at Harlequin.com.

WITNESS
PURSUIT

HOPE WHITE

HARLEQUIN®LOVE INSPIRED® SUSPENSE

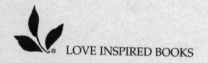

LOVE INSPIRED BOOKS

Recycling programs
for this product may
not exist in your area.

ISBN-13: 978-0-373-67776-4

Witness Pursuit

www.Harlequin.com

Printed in U.S.A.

Wherefore putting away lying, speak every man truth with his neighbor: for we are members one of another.
–*Ephesians* 4:25

For Lar, my real-life hero

ONE

Cassie McBride got out of Ruby, her little red car, and froze.

The front door to the Whispering Pines cabin was ajar. That wasn't right. Was the renter still on the premises? How awkward. The woman was supposed to have checked out by noon and it was nearly eight o'clock in the evening.

Cassie pulled out her phone to call Becca, her best friend. Becca had helped Cassie get the job as a property manager for Echo Mountain Rentals, which rented out private cabins to vacationers in the Cascade Mountains. Perhaps Becca had dealt with this type of situation and could offer advice.

No, if Cassie wanted people to think of her as independent, she needed to act more and ask less. She decided not to bring in the fresh linens and toiletries until she'd resolved this issue. Who knows, she might even have to call security.

"Be strong," she coached, but she abhorred conflict. If she were to keep this good-paying job, she'd have to do the uncomfortable tasks like kick out renters who'd overstayed their welcome. She straightened her shoulders, marched to the front door and eased it open. "Hello? It's the property manager."

Silence.

"Anyone here?"

Nothing.

She sighed with relief. Perhaps the door didn't latch properly when the renter vacated the premises.

Her gaze drifted to the picture window and the incredible view of the Cascade Mountains. She would miss these mountains when she left on her travel adventures overseas where she'd discover new mountains and beautiful places in foreign lands.

But she wasn't there yet.

To get the cabin ready for tomorrow's renters, she pulled her phone out of her purple bag and opened the checklist. She glanced toward the back of the house and noticed the patio door wasn't locked.

"Not a very responsible renter," she said to herself. She'd let Mr. Anderson know not to rent to that woman again. She crossed the room and locked the door.

Turning her attention to the kitchen, Cassie got busy with her assignment. Her report needed to be filed tonight, and if anything was damaged they'd send maintenance to fix the problem before the next renter checked in.

To help her focus, she plugged earbuds into her phone and hit Play. This was the perfect job for Cassie, and she couldn't thank Becca enough for recommending her to her boss. The money earned during the high season would pad Cassie's bank account so she could escape Echo Mountain sooner rather than later.

Starting in the kitchen, Cassie turned the appliances on and off—the toaster, blender and microwave. She checked the garbage disposal and oven. All seemed in working order.

During a break between songs, she thought she heard something. It sounded like scratching. Another song started, and Cassie hit Pause. Pulled out the earbuds.

Scratch, scratch, whine.

She followed the source of the sound into the master bedroom.

Whine, whine, scratch.

It was coming from the closet. Thinking a critter might have sneaked in through the open door, she grabbed a pillow off the bed, ready to shoo it out of the house.

She took a deep breath, counted to three and slid the door open.

A flash of fur dashed out of the closet.

Cassie gasp-shrieked, startled by the sudden movement of a little dog sprinting across the room. She caught her breath, her gaze trained on the terrier mix scurrying into the master bathroom.

"Where did you come from, Dasher?" The name seemed appropriate, although not so much his presence. Whispering Pines was a no-pet property. Cassie followed him, stepped into the bathroom doorway and froze.

A limp female body lay sprawled across the edge of the Jacuzzi tub.

"Oh no, ma'am?"

Cassie rushed to the fully clothed unconscious

woman. As she knelt beside her, Cassie noticed blood trailing down the side of the woman's face. Had she hit her head? Cassie felt for a pulse, but couldn't find one. The dog barked frantically as if trying to revive its master.

"Gotta get help." Cassie ran into the kitchen, the dog practically underfoot. She could barely think over the constant barking, so she picked up the dog to soothe him. "It's okay, buddy," she said, stroking his head.

She grabbed her smartphone off the counter, and with trembling fingers she called 911.

"911 Emergency," the operator answered.

"My name is Cassie McBride. There's a woman, she's injured, maybe dead I'm not sure, in Whispering Pines cabin on Reflection Pass Drive."

"What's the address, ma'am?"

"I…I… Hang on a second." Cassie fiddled with the phone, opening a map program. Becca had given her landmarks, not an actual address, when she'd asked Cassie to cover for her tonight.

The map program was taking too long to load. A woman could be dying in the next room.

She held the phone to her ear once again. "Just take the first right after Craig's Gas and Grub on Highway Two, then a left at the blue bear mailbox and you'll see the cabin up ahead."

"Ma'am, we need an address."

"I don't have it. I'll have to call my manager and call you back."

"Ma'am, I need you to stay on the line. Give me your manager's phone number."

Cassie rattled it off.

"We'll get in touch with him," the dispatcher said. "Please tell me what happened."

"I'm a property manager and was checking one of our rentals and I heard scratching. It was a dog and he ran out of the closet and into the bathroom and when I followed him, I…I found an unconscious woman. You need to send someone, quick!"

Cassie hoped she was making sense, but adrenaline flooded her brain and jumbled her thoughts. She took a few steps into the main living area, hoping the peaceful view would ground her somehow. She glanced out the window…

And spotted a man heading toward the cabin carrying a shovel over his shoulder.

She dropped to the floor, clutching the little dog.

"Someone's here," she whispered into the phone.

"Who's there?"

"A man, he's coming toward the house with a shovel. What is he doing with a shovel? Oh my God, he dug a grave, he dug a grave and he's going to bury her."

"Ma'am, please stay calm."

"I need to get out of here. I'll leave the line open, but I can't talk. And don't talk to me because he might hear you." She pocketed the phone and crouch-walked across the living room, carrying the dog under her arm like a pro quarterback clutching a football.

She swallowed her panic, her fear. Maybe he wasn't a killer preparing to dispose of a body. Maybe he was with maintenance doing a little grounds work. No, he wasn't in a dark green uniform. He wore jeans, a black T-shirt and a leather jacket.

Cassie needed out of here. She needed to get safe. Glancing at the kitchen counter, she eyed her keys lying beside her bag. Just as she started toward them she heard the rattling at the back door. He was there, trying to get in. She'd locked him out, which meant he knew someone was inside.

She was inside.

And if she reached for her keys now, he'd see her for sure.

Dread gripped her chest. She was next.

She counted to three. Calmed her breathing.

She hadn't survived a childhood fraught with illness to become a victim of random violence. She had things to do and places to explore, places on the other side of the world that she'd promised herself she'd visit once her health stabilized.

She stroked the dog's soft fur, which both helped keep him quiet and calmed her fear.

The door rattled. More violently this time.

Maybe the police would get here before he broke in. Maybe—

A crash was followed by a click and footsteps.

Cowering in the entryway, she heard floorboards squeak as he crossed the room. The sound of keys scraping against the kitchen counter sent a shudder of fear down her spine.

He'd found her keys. He knew she was still here.

She had seconds until...

The pounding of footsteps sprinted toward the bedroom. Of course, where he thought he'd find Cassie, the intruder, potential witness to murder.

This was her chance.

She slid open the side window and climbed through, still clinging to the dog. Only then did she realize taking care of Dasher was keeping her somewhat sane.

Once outside, she sprinted in the opposite direction of the master bedroom, assuming the guy might come looking for her.

If only she could escape in her car, but that was impossible without her keys. She focused on her breathing, taking slow, calming breaths.

The dog released a quick bark. "No, Dasher, no bark."

She spotted a trail up ahead leading to the next property, about half a mile away.

Half a mile. She could do it. She wouldn't be the victim of circumstance, a victim of "wrong place, wrong time." There were so many things she had yet to accomplish, things she ached to experience.

Like love.

As she ran steadily, the dog flopping in her arms, she scolded herself for losing focus and thinking about such trivialities. Yet with danger barreling

down on her, she was haunted by her biggest fear:
she would never experience romantic love.

Because her childhood illness had left her so damaged that no one would want her.

Knock it off, she mentally scolded herself. This
kind of thinking would not keep her alive.

She made it to the trail and clenched her jaw with
determination, thinking what a great story she'd be
able to tell her friends when this was over. When she
was safe.

Towering trees reached for the sky on either side
of her; the trail was well worn and easy to navigate.
Which meant if she could navigate it, so could Shovel
Man. She glanced over her shoulder. Didn't see anything.

She turned back to the trail. Increased her speed.

A few minutes later he called out to her. "Hey!
Stop!"

He knew she was there, running for her life. She
skidded as she took a sharp turn, but caught herself
and managed not to slide over the edge into the abyss
below.

She peeked to her right, down into the steep drop,
and it gave her an idea. If she could find a way down
at the next turn, her pursuer might think she'd continued on the trail. Yes, that's it.

Somehow she needed to disappear, and quickly.
She uncoiled her scarf from around her neck and
wrapped the dog in it, then secured him against her
chest. Thank God he was a little guy, probably seven

pounds soaking wet. This was not something she could do with a golden retriever like Fiona, her sister's dog.

"Let's go, Dasher." Cassie peered over the edge. She needed to stay out of sight only until police arrived. "Emergency, this is Cassie McBride," she said, speaking into the phone, still in her shirt pocket. "I'm climbing down the mountain to a safe spot, out of view."

"Is the perpetrator following you?"

"Yes, I think so. I'm about a quarter of a mile south of the cabin. Send help." She eyed the perfect spot to grab a tree root and lower herself.

"Deep breathing, doggie," she coached, as if the dog understood her. She grabbed the tree root jutting out from the mountainside, and lowered herself until she found a firm rock on which to plant her feet. The next step would be landing on a small ledge, about ten feet below.

"Just like REI," she said, referring to a rock-climbing class she'd taken months ago.

She took a slow, deep breath. She could do this.

With a grunt, she edged her right foot onto a thick tree branch sticking out from the mountain wall. She reached for another branch to hold on to.

The branch beneath her foot snapped.

And she dropped.

Police Chief Nate Walsh had a firm grip of one end of the stretcher, and Eddie Monroe had the other. As a search-and-rescue volunteer, a sense of satisfaction gave Nate the added strength necessary to make the final trek down the mountain carrying the injured woman.

It was a good thing they got to her when they did, since it would be dark soon. Darkness would have made the mission more challenging, even though her injuries weren't life-threatening.

Although some folks in town had expected him to give up his SAR work when he was named police chief last year, helping people, saving them from the dangers of the wild, gave Nate a sense of control over the random chaos of life.

Random, like his partner's death nearly four years ago on the Chicago PD. Perhaps if Nate had known where Dean's head was at he'd still be alive, along with the witness Dean had been protecting.

The witness Dean had fallen in love with.

If Nate had only known, he would have convinced his partner to not let something like love cloud his judgment and ruin his career. Which was probably why his partner decided not to share.

Sometimes people considered Nate's firm opinions as judgmental, yet he was about protecting family and friends. Besides, Nate wouldn't be arrogant enough to pass judgment, since he was far from perfect.

These days he'd strive to be as close to perfect as possible for the citizens of Echo Mountain. Volunteering for SAR kept him connected with his community, even if some of these folks wondered how he had the time given his chief duties.

He and Eddie carried the wounded hiker, a twentysomething female named Sylvia, to the command center where an emergency vehicle waited.

"Thanks, thanks, everyone," Sylvia said. "Thanks, Chief."

"You're welcome. Take care of yourself."

"Chief," SAR volunteer Luke Winters said. "Dispatch needs you to call in."

"Thanks." He shook hands with a few of the volunteers and went to his truck. When he'd taken over as chief, he'd directed dispatch to give him immediate updates on criminal activity calls, however minor. Kids in a small town had a tendency to grow bored and get into mischief.

He fired up his truck and pulled away from the command center, grateful for the successful mission. Another life saved.

"Dispatch, this is Chief Walsh, over."

"Sir, there's been a 911 call reporting a wounded, possibly dead body, and the female witness says the killer is still on the premises, over."

Adrenaline rushed through his bloodstream. "Address?"

"We're looking it up, over."

"The witness couldn't tell you?" What kind of fruitcake didn't know where she was?

"She had directions, but no address. She works for Echo Mountain Rentals, over."

Nate's blood ran cold. Cassie worked for Echo Mountain Rentals. Cassie, his best friend's sister with the sparkling blue eyes and a contagious smile.

"Did the caller give you her name?"

"Cassie McBride."

Nate gripped the radio so hard he thought it might crack in his hand.

"I need that address, over," he said.

"One minute, over."

He didn't have a minute. A sweet, lighthearted young woman who looked at the world through a veil of optimism was in trouble. Cassie trusted too easily and believed in the goodness of all and the glory of God.

She hadn't been tainted by life's tragedies, and wouldn't be able to cope with a crisis, much less a violent perp.

"The address?" Nate snapped, pulling onto Highway Two.

"5427 Reflection Pass Drive. We still have an open line to her phone, over."

"Patch it through, over," he said.

"Yes, sir, over."

"Alert all available officers. Did you dispatch an ambulance, over?"

"Yes, sir, over."

Nate gripped the steering wheel with his left hand and held on to the radio with his right. Coordinates indicated he was about five minutes out.

Hang on, Cassie. I'm coming.

What was she doing up there at this time of night? She should be relaxing in her apartment above the tea shop with a good book, not working. Then he remembered why she'd taken a second, part-time job with the rental company: to earn money for travel.

The thought of her traveling alone didn't sit well with Nate or her big brother, Aiden. If she could stumble into trouble in her own hometown, Nate shuddered to think what could happen to her in a foreign country.

But she wasn't gone, not yet. She was in danger right here in Echo Mountain. Nate pressed down on the accelerator and flipped the lights. It might get folks talking, but he didn't care.

All he cared about was getting to Cassie. Making sure she was okay.

His phone rang, and he recognized Aiden's number.

"Chief Walsh," he answered.

"Sorry to bother you, but my little sister was supposed to stop by Mom's and she's late and hasn't called."

"I'm heading up to Reflection Pass now."

"Reflection Pass? Why?"

"Cassie called 911," Nate said.

"What's wrong? Is she okay?"

"I'll let you know as soon as I get to her. Just hang tight."

"Where is she? I'm coming."

Just then, sounds from Cassie's phone echoed over the radio.

"I've gotta go." Nate ended the call. He held his breath as he listened.

"Deep breathing, doggie," Cassie's gentle voice whispered through the radio.

Nate's fingers wrapped tighter around the steering wheel.

"Just like REI," she said.

He realized she was climbing down the mountain to get away from danger.

"Cassie, no," he ground out. She didn't have proper gear and wasn't a seasoned climber.

A few seconds later, a soft shriek echoed through his car. His heart pounded against his chest. What happened? Did she fall?

"Where did you go?" a male voice called.

The perp was there? Stalking her? Nate slammed his palm against the steering wheel.

"Cassie McBride?" the man called.

How did he know her name? Nate grabbed the radio. "Dispatch, how close are the patrol cars to Reflection Pass Drive, over?"

"About a minute out, over."

"Tell them to hit the sirens."

"Copy that."

A woman's moan floated across the inside of his truck. He glanced at the radio, then back at the road. Two minutes; he had to be only two minutes out.

"Is that you down there?" a man said.

Nate flipped on his siren and floored it.

The next few minutes were a blur. It took all of

Nate's self-control to keep the panic from turning him into a raving lunatic. He reined in his temper. Locals had been worried about giving the chief's position to a thirtysomething like Nate, from a big city. Folks didn't think he had the patience for being chief of a small town.

He was determined to prove them wrong. Echo Mountain had become his home. He'd moved here three years ago to support his sister and her teenage son. He'd been absent from their lives far too long, playing protector for the rest of the world. He'd been pretty good at it, until he'd failed Dean.

He would not fail Cassie.

As he pulled onto Reflection Pass Drive, two patrol cars turned the corner up ahead. Nate sped toward the house, parking behind Cassie's little red car. He whipped his door open and motioned to officers James "Red" Carrington and Ryan McBride. "Red, search the house. McBride, you're with me."

Nate hoped that seeing her cousin Ryan McBride might comfort Cassie. Red drew his weapon and entered the house.

Nate grabbed rope from his trunk, then called dispatch. "I need the last known location for Cassie McBride, over."

"Quarter of a mile south of the cabin, over."

The ambulance peeled up the driveway and the paramedics hopped out; one was Cassie's cousin, and Ryan's sister, Maddie McBride.

"Wait until Officer Carrington gives the all clear."

Nate took off toward the trail, Officer McBride right behind him.

Nate withdrew his firearm. The guy still had to be here, right? Jogging up the trail, Nate steadied his breath, occasionally glancing over the edge. She could be anywhere down there.

The trail forked, and Nate pointed for Officer McBride to go left. Nate continued another few minutes.

The sound of a barking dog echoed from below. Nate knelt to look over the edge.

"Cassie! Cassie, you down there?"

The barking intensified, but there was no response from Cassie.

Had the guy climbed down there and…

Nate would not allow himself to go there. He holstered his gun and secured the rope around a tree trunk nearby. He had to get down there and make sure she was okay.

Because if she wasn't…

Something slammed against Nate's back and he lurched forward, over the edge.

TWO

Nate had experienced his share of falls, and that experience taught him how to survive even in impossible situations. As he tumbled off the trail gripping the rope he'd secured to the trunk, his back smacked against the mountain wall. He clenched his jaw against the pain. He glanced up, but didn't see his attacker peering over the edge.

"McBride!" he called out to his junior officer, as Nate clung precariously to the rope.

Silenced echoed back at him. He planted his boots against the mountain wall and lowered himself. A few seconds later, a splash of bright blue caught his eye below, in contrast to the rich green surroundings.

Cassie. It had to be. She usually wore bright colors, much like her bright personality.

Totally inappropriate time to be thinking about her fashion choices, Nate.

"Cassie?" he said, getting closer.

Nothing. He released the rope and dropped to the ledge. He was desperate to check on Cassie, but needed to alert his men.

"This is Chief Walsh," he said into the radio. "The perpetrator is still on the premises, over."

"Are you okay, over?" Red said.

"Affirmative. McBride, check in, over."

Silence.

"Red, we need backup. Call County, over."

"Ten-four."

Although Ryan McBride was an exceptional police officer, Nate worried that the perp had surprised and attacked Ryan before coming after Nate.

The dog growled, protective of the woman he guarded.

Nate knelt beside Cassie. "Good dog. Now let me have a look."

She lay on her side, unconscious. "Cassie?"

He hesitated before checking her pulse. *Don't be stupid. She's a young, healthy woman. A fall like this wouldn't kill her.*

Pressing his fingers against her neck, he caught himself wanting to ask God for a favor, not for Nate, of course, because he knew better, but for Cassie.

Her pulse tapped steadily against his fingertips. He took a deep breath. With a trembling finger, he trailed golden-blond strands of hair off her cheek. Redness discolored her head above her right eye, but he didn't see any lacerations. He wished she'd open her eyes.

"Chief, what's your twenty, over?" Red asked.

"About a quarter mile south of the cabin off the trail on the right. We'll need SAR to lift Cassie McBride off a ledge, over."

"Aiden McBride is already here, over."

"Of course he is," Nate muttered to himself. "What about Officer McBride?" he said into the radio.

"He hasn't checked in, over."

"Be on the lookout, over."

"Ten-four."

Nate glanced across the mountain range. The sun had already started its descent. He wanted to get Cassie off this ledge so they wouldn't have to do this in the dark.

"Am I in trouble?"

He snapped his attention to her. "You're conscious."

"Disappointed, huh?" she teased.

Nate ripped his gaze from her adorable face. "This isn't funny."

"No, it most certainly is not. I was just doing my job and found a body. Is she dead? Please tell me she's not dead. At first I thought maybe she just collapsed and hit her head. I've passed out before from not remembering to eat."

Her nonstop chatter convinced Nate she was okay. "Cassie, take a breath."

Cassie and Nate couldn't be more different. While many thought of Nate as a reserved enigma, Cassie was bubbly and upbeat. Her brother, Nate's friend Aiden, said she'd drive any man crazy with her constant questions and observations about life, especially a man like Nate.

Drive him crazy? Sometimes, yet other times he enjoyed the pleasant sound of her voice.

"You're angry with me," she said.

"I'm not angry."

"You seem angry. Why, because I'm down here? I was only trying to get away." She hesitated. "That man, there was a man."

"It's okay, he's not here now. You're safe."

"He was carrying a shovel and broke into the house and—"

"Cassie." He placed a hand on her shoulder. "You're okay. I'm here and your brother's on his way with rescue gear."

She sighed. "Great, Aiden and his lectures. Look, I'm fine." She sat up and winced, gripping her head. "This must be what a hangover feels like."

Of course, she wouldn't know firsthand because she never drank, unlike Nate, who at one point found himself using alcohol to ease the sting of grief and the bitter taste of shame.

That was another reason he didn't like spending too much time around Cassie—he worried he'd somehow sully her goodness.

"I'm glad you're here," she said.

He snapped his attention to her, trying to read her expression. Was she teasing? Because he knew he often came off like a jerk, abrupt and cold.

She watched him, as if waiting for him to respond to her comment.

He had no response, fearing if he opened his mouth he'd give her a lecture about being out so late alone.

"Are you okay?" she said.

Something snapped.

"Am *I* okay?"

The dog jumped into her lap, and she stroked its fur. "Yeah, you look more worried than usual, and your shirt's torn and you're clenching your fist like you want to hit a punching bag at Bracken's Gym. So it's logical to ask if you're okay, not that you consider my questions logical but—"

"No, Cassie, I'm not okay," he interrupted. "What were you thinking coming out here so late?"

"It's only eight o'clock."

"But by yourself without protection?"

"What, like a bodyguard?" She smiled.

Which only frustrated him more.

"It's Echo Mountain," she said. "Besides, I have pepper spray in my bag, not that I could get to it because it was on the counter and I was hiding in the front hallway."

"Pepper spray?" he said.

"Yeah."

"You think pepper spray is going to protect you from guys like this?"

"Guys like what? I don't even know who he was."

"Well, he knows you." He immediately regretted his words when her face went white.

"How is that possible?" she said.

"Didn't you hear him calling your name from above?"

She shook her head. "How did you hear him?"

"You left your phone on. Dispatch put it through. Speaking of which, give me your phone." He stuck out his hand.

The dog dived between Nate and Cassie, frantically barking.

"It's okay, Dasher," Cassie said. "He's not really angry. That's just Chief Walsh." She restrained the dog with one hand and gave Nate her phone with the other.

"Dispatch, this is Chief Walsh. I'm with Cassie McBride. Rescue is on the way. I'm closing the line, over." He handed it back to her.

"If you give me a boost I can climb back up and save search-and-rescue from having to come get me."

"I'd rather you relax until they arrive."

"This is silly." She struggled to stand.

Since she wasn't going to listen to him, Nate reached out to steady her. That's when he noticed the blood smearing her sleeve.

"Cassie, did you touch the body in the cabin?"

"Only to feel for a pulse, why?"

"You've got blood on your jacket." He motioned to her sleeve.

"Oh, wow, I didn't see that before. You'd think I would have noticed, especially since it's so…bright." Her legs buckled.

Nate caught her as she went down, the dog wedged between them. He lowered her to the ground and examined the wound. It wasn't bad, yet it had caused her to pass out. Concerned, he ran his hands over her clothes searching for other wounds, but found none.

Then he remembered her reaction when her brother had suffered a knife wound last year.

"Can't handle the sight of blood," he said under his breath.

It was okay; she was okay. He examined her wound closer. The four-inch gash didn't look deep.

She probably snagged her arm on a sharp branch on her descent.

He pulled gauze from the earlier rescue out of his jacket and wrapped her wound as the dog hovered close by. They hadn't even discussed how she'd ended up with the dog. He knew she didn't own a dog, because it would interfere with her travel plans. Which meant she'd rescued a dog while being stalked by a killer and rappelled down the side of a mountain with the pup in her arms. This woman was…

"Nate, the team's here," Aiden called from above.

"Great!" Nate called back.

Cassie awoke in an ambulance, confused and worried.

"Where's Dasher?" she asked her cousin Madeline, the EMT.

"Who?"

"My dog."

"You don't have a dog."

"I had him on the ledge with me. What happened to him? You didn't just let him go, did you? He could get eaten by wild animals or—"

"I didn't do anything but tend to the laceration on your arm and check your vitals. You were passed out cold. Didn't even wake up when they strapped you to a litter and lifted you up the mountain."

"I need to find Dasher."

"Cassie—"

"Please Madeline, I need to find him!"

"Calm down. I'll have Rocky call and check on the dog, okay?"

Cassie nodded, unsure why she was freaking out about a little dog that wasn't even hers. But there was something about him—his protectiveness and vulnerability—that made her feel connected to the terrier mix.

Then there was the way Chief Walsh interacted with Dasher, how Nate's tone softened when he praised the dog for protecting Cassie.

Good dog. Now let me have a look.

She'd heard him speak, although she thought she was dreaming at the time. Then she cracked open her eyes and saw Chief Walsh's intense expression studying her. With a gentle touch, he brushed hair off her face. Who would have guessed such a hardened man could be so caring?

She blinked away a tear. She was being ridiculous, yet the truth was she'd felt safe when he touched her. All the trepidation that flooded her system had dissolved in the very instant she felt the warmth of his fingertips against her cheek.

"What's wrong?" Madeline asked.

"What do you mean?"

"You're crying."

"Allergies."

"Cassie," Madeline said in that motherly tone, the tone everyone in Cassie's family used when speaking to her.

That's why she needed to get out of town, to explore other places in the world where people didn't know her as Baby McBride with the strange autoimmune disease.

"Cassie?" Madeline pressed.

"I'm fine," she said, closing her eyes.

"You're not fine. Do you want to talk about it?"

"Nothing to talk about."

"Finding a dead body—"

Cassie's eyes popped open. "So she *was* dead?"

"You didn't know?"

Cassie shook her head.

"I'm sorry." Madeline patted Cassie's shoulder.

It was just the beginning, Cassie thought, the beginning of her family and friends smothering her until she could no longer breathe.

God, please help me cope.

She suspected all the prayer in the world wouldn't change the way people looked at her: like a fragile doll, a sick little girl who could barely manage on her own. But she wasn't a little girl anymore, and she'd outgrown her illness, although the technical term was *remission*.

That fact wouldn't change the way people treated her. She decided to take the offensive.

"Have you assessed my injuries?" she asked her cousin.

"Your arm will need a few stiches, and the ER doc will probably order a CT scan of your head."

"I didn't hit my head."

"You might not remember hitting your head, but you're exhibiting symptoms of head trauma."

"Like what?"

"Obsessing over a random dog."

"An orphaned dog."

"And you're anxious."

"Rocky's driving too fast."

Madeline shook her head and bit back a smile. "Rocky, this is base, over," a voice said over the radio.

"Go ahead."

"Chief Walsh has the dog, over."

"You hear that, Cassie?" Rocky said over his shoulder.

"Yeah, thanks."

"Okay?" Madeline said.

Cassie nodded and closed her eyes, wanting to avoid arguing with her cousin. She'd save her energy because she knew there'd be more discussion, more arguments about her choices today as she defended herself to her mother, older brother, sister and whoever else jumped on the "help Cassie" bandwagon.

She thought about her bank account, now up to two thousand dollars and change. It wasn't enough to support herself for six months to a year overseas, even if she stayed in hostels. After tonight's fiasco, she might lose the awesome-paying property manager job. At the very least, her family would forbid her from going anywhere by herself for a while.

They reached the hospital, and Rocky and Madeline wheeled Cassie inside. Once transferred to an ER bed, Madeline slid the curtain closed.

"The doctor will be here shortly. I think Dr. Rush is on duty. You'll like her," Madeline said.

"I need to speak with Chief Walsh."

"Oh yeah?" Maddie said with a raised eyebrow.

"Stop fooling around. It's important."

"I think he's at the cabin managing the investigation into the woman's death."

"Oh, right." Cassie wanted to call and give him a description of Shovel Man. She reached into her pocket. "Where's my phone? Can you check the ambulance?"

"Sure, if you promise to stay here and wait for the doctor."

"As opposed to going dancing?"

"See? Sarcastic. That's not like you, which is why I suspect a head injury. So relax. I'll be right back."

Cassie laid her head against the pillow and closed her eyes. She knew she didn't have a serious head injury, and was upset that her cousin wasn't listening to her. Cassie needed to call Chief Walsh and describe the man who'd stalked her. She could still picture those heavy eyebrows and thin lips. He reminded her of Mr. Gruner, a curmudgeon who used to yell at Cassie and her friends whenever they'd pass by his boat at the Emerald Lake Pier. They were terrified of him, until the day he saved Izzy Bingham. No one knew Izzy couldn't swim. After the save, the kids had changed their opinions of Mr. Gruner. He was just lonely, not mean.

She had a feeling Shovel Man didn't fall into that same category.

A shiver snaked down her arms. She slipped into her jacket to get warm. The more agitated she appeared, the more her family would close ranks and suffocate her. She had to show them she was strong, healthy and capable, that she wasn't that sick little girl anymore.

The curtain slid open.

"Did you find it?" she said, assuming it was Madeline.

"I'm here to take you for a CT scan," a male voice said.

"Oh, okay."

She opened her eyes, but he stood behind her as he pushed her bed out of the examining area.

"I was hoping you were my cousin with my phone," she said.

"Nope, sorry."

"How long does a CT scan take?"

"Not long."

She knew they wouldn't find anything, but she couldn't fault the doctor for being cautious. They entered the elevator, and he pressed the button for the bottom floor.

"How did you get injured?" he said.

She glanced at the orderly, who wore a surgical mask. A surgical mask?

"I've got a cold," he said in explanation.

Yet even behind the mask she recognized the thick eyebrows of the man who'd been carrying the shovel.

The elevator doors closed.

THREE

Cassie was alone with the killer.

A ball of fear rose in her chest.

No, she wasn't going to give up without a fight.

She had nothing with which to defend herself, nor did she have her phone to call for help. But she was a smart woman and would use her best weapons: her wits and her words.

She took a quick breath for strength. Wait, she remembered she had her emergency house keys in her side pocket. Locking herself out last month had become a blessing after all. She launched into chatter mode to distract him.

"I can't believe they want a CT scan," she started. "I told them I didn't hit my head. I can see just fine and I know my own name."

"So what happened?"

"I'm a klutz. I fell off a trail. Can you believe that?" She deftly reached into her jacket to palm the keys. "I mean, I've lived here forever and Dad used to take us hiking, and you'd think I'd be an expert with all my experience, but I wasn't paying attention and went over the side of the mountain. Isn't that the most ridiculous thing you've ever heard?"

"Why weren't you paying attention?" he asked.

She slipped the keys between her fingers, thinking she could jab him in the eye if necessary. "I was scared," she said.

"Of what?"

"I'd found an unconscious woman at a rental house and there was all this blood." She shuddered.

"Was she dead?"

"I have no idea, but me and blood? Not a good mix. Last year my brother was attacked by a guy with a knife and there was blood everywhere, all over the kitchen, and I completely freaked out. I guess that's what happened today. I took off and lost my footing and fell off the trail. Quite embarrassing if you think about it."

She hoped she could convince him she hadn't seen his face at the cabin. She certainly didn't want to get into hand-to-key combat.

She clutched the keys tighter. "Have you ever done anything dumb? It would make me feel a whole lot better if you had."

"Nothing comes to mind."

The doors opened and he wheeled her out of the elevator. Jumping off and running didn't seem like the best plan, since he was much taller than Cassie and therefore a lot faster. She strategized her next move as she chatted away.

"I'm going to get a huge lecture from my family, but what else is new?" she said, laying it on thick. "I'm the flaky one. This won't surprise them one bit. The woman probably fell and hit her head, yet I freaked and tore off like a scared cat. Oh well, at least I wasn't totally irresponsible, because I called 911 for help."

She pretended to be relaxed, not easy considering Shovel Man's hands were pushing her from behind—hands of a killer hovering dangerously close to her throat.

Dear Lord, give me wisdom and courage to know how to convince this man he does not have to take another life.

My life.

That's when she spotted a fire alarm on the wall. Perfect.

She suddenly sat up and sniffed. "Wait, do you smell that?"

"What?"

"I smell smoke!" She hopped off the bed and yanked the alarm.

She took off running and glanced over her shoulder. Shovel Man stood there with a quizzical frown.

"Hurry!" she shouted. She had to keep up the pretense that she thought he was an orderly, not a killer.

Staff rushed out of rooms and flooded the hallway, puzzling over the alarm. Shovel Man was no doubt puzzled, as well. But at least she was away from him.

She shot another quick glance behind her.

He'd disappeared.

Relief settled in her chest, but only for a second. If he could disappear that quickly, he could reappear just as fast. Or worse, what if he was working with a partner who was waiting outside in a car to whisk Cassie away? Shovel Man could have given his partner Cassie's description: short with blond hair, wearing a bright blue jacket.

As she marched toward the exit, she shucked her jacket, wincing in pain from her injured arm.

Once outside, she tossed the jacket onto a bench and practically sprinted into the parking lot.

But where should she go? She didn't know which of these strangers she could trust, and didn't have her phone to call for help.

Across the parking lot she spotted the one place she knew she'd be safe, Nate's truck. Which meant he had to be close. Scanning the parking lot, she didn't see Nate, only frantic employees and patients being herded out of the north side of the building.

Feeling badly about causing the commotion, she waved down an orderly who was arriving for work. "It's a false alarm. I pulled it because someone's after me. Tell them they don't have to evacuate the building!"

She ran off, hoping he'd relay the message before too many patients were inconvenienced. Head down, she motored toward Nate's truck and tried the door, but it was locked. She climbed into the flatbed. It seemed like the best place to hide.

Truth was, she felt safe because it was Nate's truck. Eventually he'd have to return to it, and he'd find her.

The reality of what just happened shot a chill down her spine: Cassie had faced off with a suspected killer. Her hands started trembling, then her arms and legs. She gasped for breath, determined to stay conscious.

* * *

Nate shoved down the panic threatening to pull him off course.

Cassie was missing.

He clenched his jaw and retraced her steps through the hospital, hoping to find a clue as to where she'd gone.

Hoping to find her safe and sound in a hospital room.

Instead, it was like she'd vanished in the mist.

The hospital alarm suddenly clicked off. Through the ominous silence, his fear grew louder, more insistent: *She's been taken against her will. She's been killed and her body will be found in a laundry bin.*

He had to stop these torturous thoughts and think like a detective–turned–chief of police.

"Why'd the alarm go off?" he asked into his radio.

"I'm checking, sir."

Nate had locked down the cabin crime scene, called the lab tech and brought Officer Ryan McBride to the hospital to get checked out. He'd been assaulted and suffered a head wound. Nate assumed from the guy who shoved him off the trail.

Anyone could have driven McBride into town, but Nate wanted to check on Cassie.

"Apparently it was a false alarm, over," Red called through the radio.

"How do you know that?" Nate asked.

"A staff member encountered the woman who pulled the alarm."

"Why would she—" Instinct struck him square in the chest. "What did this woman look like?"

"Blond, short, twenties."

"Where did he see her?"

"Back entrance, heading into the parking lot."

Nate rushed to the exit, wondering if Cassie had pulled the alarm because she'd been in trouble.

"Should we continue checking the lower level?" Red asked.

"No, meet me in the back parking lot. And bring the employee who spoke with her."

"Copy that."

Nate jogged outside, navigating the sea of staff members headed back into the hospital. What made Cassie pull the alarm?

He scanned the parking lot for her wavy blond hair. Had she changed into a hospital gown, or was she still wearing her electric blue jacket? That would make her easy to spot.

Out of the corner of his eye, a pop of blue caught his attention. He went to a nearby bench and picked up Cassie's jacket.

"Chief?"

Nate glanced to his left. Red and an orderly approached.

"This is Kevin Wright, the man who spoke with the woman who pulled the alarm," Red introduced.

Nate pulled out his phone and found a picture of Cassie and Aiden taken at the Christmas Lights Festival last year. He flashed the image at the orderly. "Is this the woman you spoke with?"

"Yes sir."

"When did you see her?" Nate asked.

"About ten minutes ago."

"What did she say to you, exactly?"

"That she pulled the alarm because someone was after her."

Nate's fingers dug into the down-filled jacket. "Who was after her?"

"She didn't say."

"Where was she going?"

"She took off into the parking lot." He pointed. "That way."

"Thank you." Nate dismissed the orderly and pulled Red aside. "Put out a BOLO on Cassie McBride. See how fast a few of the guys can get here to help search the woods bordering the parking lot."

"You think he dumped her body—"

"Call Spike and Harvey," Nate cut him off.

"What about SAR?"

"Too many personal connections."

"You mean Aiden and Bree?"

"Let's leave them out of this for now."

"I think it's too late for that." Red nodded at Aiden, who sprinted toward them.

"What happened?" Aiden demanded.

"Cassie is missing," Nate said.

"Wait, what? How is that possible?"

"Officer Carrington, continue the search."

"Yes, sir."

Nate turned back to Aiden. "She hasn't been gone that long. It appears that she felt threatened, pulled the fire alarm and ran."

"She ran?" Aiden's voice pitched.

With a firm hand on his friend's shoulder, Nate said, "We'll start by searching the woods bordering the hospital. Knowing Cassie, if she was in danger she would have taken off, but perhaps didn't think it through to the end."

"She never does. She's so impulsive sometimes." Aiden's phone rang. He glanced at the screen. "It's Mom."

"We don't need more frantic people down here, Aiden. Let's focus on finding Cassie and then you'll call her back with good news, okay?"

Aiden nodded and paced a few steps away. "Hey, Mom. I have to call you back…in the middle of something. Soon, love you, bye." Aiden turned to Nate. "She knows something's up."

"Let's get to work. I've got a flashlight in my truck."

"Yeah, okay," Aiden said, dazed with worry about his sister. "I'll get mine, too."

Nate walked away, proud of himself for holding it together in front of his friend. He had no choice. As police chief, folks depended on him to be the grounding force in a crisis, and usually he excelled in that role.

Today was different. Someone was after Cassie.

He never should have let her go to the hospital alone. He should have stayed with her, protected her. Right, and how ridiculous was that considering he had a potential murder on his hands?

He struggled to bury his concern and not let anyone see the utter panic tearing at his insides. But as he approached his truck, the bottled-up frustration got the better of him. He slammed his palm against the quarter panel.

A woman's cry echoed back at him.

Nate froze, his heart pounding.

Leaning forward, he peered into the flatbed. Cassie blinked her bloodshot, terrified eyes.

"You're in my truck," he said.

"D-d-disappointed?" She broke into a round of shivers.

He grabbed a blanket from the backseat and climbed into the flatbed beside her. As he gently covered her body, a wave of calm washed over him. She was okay. For now.

"Aiden!" He motioned to his friend who'd gone to get a flashlight. "Over here!"

"I knew you'd come."

Nate snapped his attention to Cassie. "What happened? Why did you run?"

"A guy…in the hospital…the guy with the shovel… from the cabin."

"Is it…?" Aiden stopped short and looked at her. "What are you doing in there?"

"Aiden," Nate warned, wanting him to soften his tone. "She's trembling."

"Let's take her inside," Aiden said.

"Nooooo." She clamped her hand around Nate's forearm. "Not back in there."

"Cassie, you need medical attention," Aiden argued.

"That man got to me in there. I can't go back." Her pleading blue eyes tugged at Nate's heart.

"She's delirious. She doesn't know what she's saying," Aiden said.

"I am n-n-not!" she protested.

"Come on, I'll help you out." Aiden reached for her.

"Wait," Nate said. "I've got another idea."

Cassie couldn't believe it. Nate had listened to her. He'd respected her fear of going back into the hospital and found an alternative.

Nate drove her to the urgent care, where Dr. Spencer was on duty. He was a good friend to both Nate and Aiden, and he'd done his share of triage with search and rescue. Cassie knew she wasn't suffering from anything serious, but she did need medical attention for the gash in her arm.

Closing her eyes, she relaxed under the heated blanket in the examining room. She appreciated the warmth that finally drove the chill from her bones.

"Cassie?"

She blinked her eyes open. A frown creased Nate's forehead.

"What's wrong?" she said.

"I thought you passed out."

"Why, because I stopped talking?" she joked.

Instead of smiling, he glanced down at his hands, holding his Echo Mountain PD cap. He seemed regretful, and she couldn't understand why.

"Thanks," she offered.

He looked at her. "For what?"

"Bringing me here. Listening to me, I guess. Not many people do that, especially not my brother."

"I almost forgot." He pulled her cell phone out of his jacket pocket. "Your cousin found it in the ambulance."

"Awesome, thanks. Where is my bossy brother, anyway?"

"He went outside to call your mom."

"Oh boy, now the whole town is going to know."

"Maybe that's not a bad thing," Nate said.

"You've got to be kidding."

"People will be on the lookout. They'll keep an eye on you."

"Right, because I'm so fragile and incapable of taking care of myself. They should consider the fact that I escaped this guy—" she hesitated "—twice, and the first time with a dog in my arms." She sat up. "Speaking of which, what happened to Dasher?"

"Relax, your sister and my sister are fighting over custody."

She sighed and lay back down. "Thanks, I'll pick him up after I get out of here."

"You should worry more about yourself than some scruffy dog."

"I have lots of people to support me, but Dasher? He's got no one. And besides, he's not scruffy, he's got character."

She thought Nate smiled but couldn't be sure.

The door slid open and Dr. Spencer poked his head into the room. "Sorry, had an emergency. I'll be back as soon as I can."

"Thanks," Cassie said.

Dr. Spencer smiled and shut the door. Cassie glanced at Nate. "When my brother comes back, you can go. I know you should be figuring out what happened to the dead woman, instead of hanging around here."

"Detective Vaughn is leading the investigation."

"Why?"

"I delegate in order to keep a broader perspective on things. I hope you don't mind me asking, but—" he pulled his stool close to Cassie's bedside "—do you think you can identify the man carrying the shovel?"

"Absolutely, and I wanted to call you with that information, but I'd lost my phone."

"I'll try to get a forensic artist to come by tomorrow. Where will you be staying?"

"You know where my apartment is, over the tea shop."

He straightened. "It would be wiser if you didn't go back to your place for a few days. The perpetrator knows who you are."

"I still don't understand how."

"Where's your wallet?"

"Back at the cabin. Oh…so you think he went through my things?"

"It's likely, yes."

"But I did a good job of playing a daft property manager who runs from the sight of blood. I was pretty convincing that I didn't see him at the cabin."

"Cassie, he came after you in the hospital and knocked out the orderly who was supposed to take you to imaging."

"Wait, what? Is he okay?"

"He's fine. That's not the point."

"I feel so bad since it's my fault that—"

"Cassie, stop talking, just for one minute."

She bit back more questions she wanted to ask about the injured orderly. At least she'd like his name so she could add him to her prayer list.

"We can't take chances with your safety," Nate said. "You need to be in the most protected environment possible until we solve this case."

"Well, I could always leave the country. I have enough money saved to travel for a while, not as long as I'd originally intended, but a few months should work, right?"

Nate didn't answer at first. He clenched his jaw and his green eyes darkened. "I'd rather you not."

"You said I'm in danger here, so the most logical choice is to—"

He stood abruptly. "You're a witness. I need you to stay in town."

"Oh, okay." She glanced at her fingers in her lap. Arguing with Nate was pointless. He was the police chief, after all, and his primary concern was the murder case, nothing more, nothing like…

He actually cared about Cassie.

Nope, Nathaniel Walsh was all business. He wanted to get his man, and Cassie was a means to that end.

"You're upset with me," he stated, studying her.

"I want to go home."

"To your mother's farm. Good idea."

She cocked her chin. "When did I say that? I never said that."

"But you agree that it's a good idea?" He sat back down beside her.

"No, I don't want to stay at the farm. Mom will hover and forbid me from leaving the house."

"It's probably a good idea to lie low for a while, stay at your mom's and do your blogging stuff."

"Hey, my blogging stuff doesn't pay the bills. I've made a commitment to Echo Mountain Rentals and it's good money."

"Right, it's about padding your getaway fund."

"You say that like it's a bad thing. You know what? Let's not talk about this. What do you need?"

"Excuse me?"

"What can your primary witness do to help you solve this case?"

"You're injured. I can conduct an interview tomorrow."

She continued anyway. "He was about six feet tall,

with thin lips and bushy eyebrows. Oh, and a bump on his nose, here." She reached out to illustrate on Nate's nose, but he jerked away, like she was contagious.

"Wow, okay." She swallowed the hurt burning her throat and pointed to her own nose. "A bump right here. He's got dark brown eyes and he smelled of something...I can't put my finger on it, something pungent."

"What did he say to you?" Nate pulled a small notebook out of his jacket pocket.

"I did most of the talking. Especially after I figured out who he was. I did my best flaky girl impression, and told him I ran away from the cabin because of the blood, then tripped and fell down a mountain."

"You think he bought it?"

"He seemed to. I'm not dead." The inappropriate comment awkwardly slipped out.

Nate's fingers froze as he gripped the pen.

"Sorry, that was morbid," she said.

"Is there anything else you can tell me about him?"

"No, sorry."

He glanced up. "You have nothing to be sorry about."

In that moment she felt caught by something in his green eyes, something intense and sad. She struggled to form words.

"I... You... Thanks," she uttered.

She didn't like this feeling, a feeling of being derailed, yanked off course. It seemed to happen only when Chief Walsh was looking straight at her.

The door swung open. "How's the patient?" Dr. Spencer asked, approaching her.

His presence ripped Cassie out of the intense moment with the chief. She smiled at the doctor and said, "Pretty good, considering."

"Attitude is everything," the cheerful doctor said. "Let's stitch you up and send you home."

Nate stood. "I'll get her brother."

"Wait," she said. "Would you mind staying?" For some reason she didn't feel overly judged by Nate, whereas every word that came out of Aiden's mouth felt like a criticism.

"Are you sure?" Nate said.

"Yes, but you probably have to get back."

"I've got a few minutes." Nate offered to hold her hand for support.

She accepted the gesture, appreciating the warmth. As she focused on a spot across the room, the doctor raised the sleeve of her hospital gown and explained how he was numbing her arm in preparation for sutures.

A few minutes later she felt a tugging sensation, but no pain.

"Not so bad, right?" Dr. Spencer said.

She glanced at him. "That's it?"

"Only needed ten stitches. A little more paperwork and you're good to go." He smiled.

The sound of gunfire echoed through the door.

FOUR

Nate instinctively withdrew his firearm.

"Stay here," he said to Spence.

As Nate tried to pull away from Cassie, she clung tighter to his hand. Her face had drained of color.

"You're okay, Cassie, but I need to get out there and make sure everyone else is, too."

With a reluctant nod, she let him go, and he rushed to investigate.

"Be careful," she said.

He nodded, slid the door open and peered into the main area. It looked empty, as if staff had suddenly abandoned the urgent care. He left Cassie's examining room and shut the door.

Taking a few steps toward a computer station, he hesitated. Whimpering echoed from below. He knelt and peeked beneath a desk. Two staff members, young women in their twenties, were huddled together, fear coloring their eyes.

"Where did the shot come from?" he whispered.

One of the women pointed toward the reception area.

Just then the reception door flew open. Aiden and a middle-aged woman stepped into the examining area with their hands raised. Someone was obviously behind them. Nate took cover beside the desk to better assess what he was dealing with. If he exposed himself now he could lose his weapon in exchange for sparing someone's life. Without a weapon he had no control of the situation.

"She needs help now!" a male voice demanded. "Where's the doctor?"

"I—I don't know," the woman beside Aiden said.

"How can you not know?"

"Hey, can't we talk about this?" Aiden argued.

"Get down, facedown on the ground, and put your hands behind your head!"

Aiden must have hesitated, because another shot rang out and the two women beneath the desk shrieked.

"Okay, okay." Aiden dropped to the floor and made eye contact with Nate.

The assailant placed his boot on Aiden's back. "Now stay there. And you, get in a room!"

The front-end receptionist who'd entered with Aiden did as ordered.

If the guy would just move a few inches to the right Nate could get him from behind, the goal being to disarm him without the gun going off again.

"Where's the doctor? The nurses? I heard them scream."

The women under the desk eyed Nate. He shook his head, warning them off, not wanting to put more innocents in the line of fire.

The shooter turned. Nate saw the man's reflection in an examining room window: the shooter was holding on to a young, barely conscious woman.

"Nurses, get out here!"

Nate got ready to take his shot.

A door slid open. "I'm Dr. Spencer."

Nate froze. Spence was sacrificing his own safety to protect his patients and staff.

"What happened here?" Spence said calmly, as if the man wasn't threatening him with a gun.

"She's hurt, she's hurt and needs help and they said I had to wait for a doctor, but we can't wait!"

"I understand. Where is she hurt?"

As Spence engaged the shooter, Nate debated firing his weapon with so many innocents around. The last thing he wanted was to get into a heated exchange of gunfire.

He holstered his gun. The minute the perp's gun was no longer aimed at Spence, or anyone else for that matter, Nate would make his move. He'd take the guy down, hopefully before he could get a shot off.

"She's bleeding, can't you see that?" the guy said.

"I can't tell from this vantage point. How about we get her into a room?"

There were only three rooms: the receptionist was in one, an emergency patient in another, and Cassie in the third.

And hers was the closest.

"How did this happen?" Spence asked.

"Stop asking so many questions!" To drive home his point, the shooter pointed his weapon at the ceiling to fire off another shot.

Nate charged the guy from behind, the force making him release the injured woman. Distressed about letting her go, the guy lost his focus. Nate slammed the shooter's fist against the wall and the gun sprang free, dropping to the floor. Nate swung the guy to the ground, pinned him with a knee to his back and zip-tied his wrists.

"You've gotta help her," the man groaned.

Nate glanced at Aiden. "Help Dr. Spencer get the female victim into a room."

Aiden got up off the floor and assisted Spence.

"Ladies hiding beneath the desk?" Nate said.

Their heads popped out.

"Call 911. I need backup."

"I already did," Cassie said from the doorway of her examining room.

On cue, the wail of sirens echoed from the parking lot.

"You okay?" Nate asked Cassie.

"Yep."

Aiden approached Nate. "Doc says she'll need to be transported to the hospital. It's a gunshot wound."

"It was an accident," the perp said.

"You're under arrest for reckless conduct and aggravated assault," Nate said.

Red rushed into the examining area, gun drawn.

"Don't need the weapon." Nate stood, pulling the perp to his feet. "Take this guy to lockup."

"Yes, sir." Red led him away.

"Good job, Chief," Aiden said.

"Thanks." He glanced at Cassie. "Ready to go home?"

"Beyond ready."

"I'll take her to Mom's," Aiden offered.

"I don't think she wants to stay at the farm," Nate countered.

"It's okay. I'll go," Cassie said.

Nate guessed that after what just happened, she was upset and could use the support of family.

"But…" Cassie hesitated. "Can you drive me, Chief?"

"Come on, Cassie," Aiden said. "Nate has more important stuff to do."

"It's fine," Nate said. "I'll take her."

When she'd asked him to drive her to Mom's farm, she hadn't expected the chief to hang around as long as he did. He'd been here over an hour.

Mom, who lived alone since Dad's passing more than ten years ago, kept hammering him with questions about the dead woman, but he explained he couldn't discuss an ongoing investigation. She'd even bribed him with food, but he declined, opting for coffee instead.

He had a long night ahead of him. Not only had Cassie found a dead body, but then she wouldn't go back into the hospital, and ended up in the urgent care, where a man went nutty and shot up the place.

Her mom politely asked another question and Cassie jumped in for the save. "I think he needs a refill."

Mom glanced at his mug. "Oh, of course." She went into the kitchen to get the pot.

"I'm sorry," Cassie said to Nate.

Nate glanced up from his mug. "For what?"

"I feel like I'm a trouble magnet."

"I don't understand."

"The dead woman in the cabin, having to rescue me, Jesse James in the urgent care. You wouldn't have been there at all if not for my fear of the hospital."

"It was a good thing I *was* there or more people might have been seriously injured."

She shrugged. Her mind still spun about everything that had happened…and in one night!

"Here we go," her mom said, returning with the coffee. "We're so glad you could stay and chat for a bit. I'm sure it makes Cassie feel less anxious to have the chief of police here. It's important to keep her anxiety at a minimum."

"It's important to keep everyone's anxiety at a minimum," Cassie said.

"True, but we don't want yours triggering an episode."

Cassie shook her head, mortified. To have her illness mentioned in front of Nate made her feel broken and pitiful.

"Could I get some cream?" Nate asked Mom.

Not *what kind of episode*? Or *how bad is Cassie's issue with anxiety*?

Her big brother had probably told Nate the whole ugly story.

"Of course." Mom went back into the kitchen.

"I'm okay," Cassie said to Nate. "You don't have to stay."

"But your mom said—"

"I'm fine." She stood and paced to the front window. "I'm not going to freak out if you leave, and I haven't had an episode since I was a teenager."

"Oh, okay."

She turned to him. He was staring into his coffee.

"Go ahead, ask," she said.

He glanced up. "Ask what?"

"About my anxiety, my—" she made quote marks with her fingers "—episodes."

"It's none of my business."

"You mean Aiden hasn't told you?"

"No."

"I'm shocked. Well, you should probably know since everyone else seems to. I had a childhood autoimmune disease," she started, wandering back to the sofa. "Juvenile idiopathic arthritis. It's hard to diagnose in kids since there's no blood test for it. I'd be stiff in the morning, tired throughout the day, and not the most coordinated person on the planet. Aiden used to call me lazy bird. Since the symptoms would flare up and go away, it took a while to diagnose. Mom blames herself for not figuring it out sooner."

"Wasn't that the doctor's responsibility?"

"Sure, but she was the one who took care of me, saw me wince when I'd get up in the morning. I've outgrown it, but Mom can't see me as anything but that sick little girl."

"She loves you. It's her job to worry."

"But not her job to shame me in front of people."

"Shame you?"

"Telling you how my anxiety could trigger an episode? It's like I have no control over my health, but I do. I follow an anti-inflammatory diet and get my share of exercise."

"She might have some post-trauma issues related to your illness, Cassie. Try to see it from her point of view."

"Here we go," her mom said, breezing into the living room with cream for Nate's coffee. "Sorry it took so long, but I was looking for an appropriate accompaniment to the coffee. I know you said you weren't hungry, Chief, but I thought I'd tempt you anyway." She placed a tray of pastries on the coffee table and sat on the sofa beside Cassie. "So, what are we talking about?"

Nate's phone buzzed and he eyed the screen. "They need me." He glanced at Cassie as if waiting for her permission to leave.

Cassie stood and motioned toward the door. "Thanks for bringing me home."

"Wait," her mom said. "Let me put some sweets in a container to take with you."

Before he could respond, she'd dashed into the kitchen. Good old Mom, always feeding people to make them feel better.

"You'll be okay?" he asked Cassie.

"Yeah, don't worry about me. I'm tough."

* * *

The container of sweets on the seat beside him, Nate pulled away from the farmhouse. Glancing in the rearview, he couldn't ignore the pit in his stomach.

Don't worry about me.

Which was asking the impossible. Sure, the house had a new security system installed after the break-in last year, but the property was off the beaten path, and if Cassie and her mom needed emergency services it would take a good ten minutes to get to them.

A lot could happen in ten minutes.

Yet Nate couldn't be in two places at once. They might not have a large staff at the Echo Mountain PD, but SAR had its share of former military. Nate decided to see if Harvey, retired security manager for Echo Mountain Resort, could watch the farmhouse.

Harvey answered on the second ring. "Hey, Chief, heard you've had a busy night."

"Word gets around."

"How's Cassie McBride?"

"That's why I'm calling. She's staying at her mom's temporarily and I was wondering—"

"I'd love to."

"I haven't asked the question yet."

"You want me to keep an eye on Margaret and Cassie."

"If you've got time."

"Got plenty of that. Fishing trip was canceled so the timing is perfect. Besides, Margaret makes a dynamite cup of coffee."

"That she does. I'll let them know you're coming."

"Roger that."

Nate ended the call and pressed the speed dial for Cassie's cell phone. It rang a few times and went to voice mail. He fought the urge to turn the truck around and speed back to the farmhouse. He was overreacting. Cassie must be away from her phone, or maybe she'd gone to bed. She'd looked exhausted.

"Hi, this is Cassie. I can't take your call right now, but leave a message and I'll call you back. Have a blessed day." *Beep.*

"Cassie, it's Chief Walsh. I've asked Harvey to stop by and check on you and your mom. I didn't want you to be alarmed when he arrived." He hesitated, as if he wanted to say something else, something like everything was going to be fine, or how much he admired her for surviving a brutal childhood disease. "Okay, well, have a nice evening." He ended the call.

Maintaining his professionalism was key with Cassie McBride. Wasn't that why she called him Chief instead of Nate? It was a reminder to both of them that they didn't have a personal relationship. No matter how often she pestered him with questions for her blog, or seemed to show up whenever he was hurt on the job, Nate would never cross that line, a line his partner had crossed, which had cost him.

It could put her life in danger if Nate lost focus because of his attraction to Cassie.

His attraction to Cassie? Whoa, where had that come from? Well, who wouldn't be attracted to her?

She was kind and engaging, independent and optimistic. Which made him wonder why she wasn't in a serious relationship.

When Nate asked Aiden about Cassie's social life, her brother said she blamed her family for scaring away suitors because they were so overprotective. Aiden countered that she was too picky—either that or she didn't want to get involved because of her travel plans. No one in Cassie's family approved of her taking off on her own to see the world. On one hand, Nate could understand why, yet he couldn't fault her for wanting to explore life outside of Echo Mountain.

Fifteen minutes later, Nate arrived at Whispering Pines cabin to check in with Detective Sara Vaughn. Before he went inside, he glanced at a text message from Cassie: Thanks for sending Harvey. Mom is excited for more company. ☺

Nate texted back: Glad to help. He hit Send and considered sending another text, something like *Have a good night* or *I'll see you in the morning*.

"I'm losin' it," he muttered and went into the cabin. He found Detective Vaughn conferring with a forensic specialist.

"Hey, Chief," she greeted.

The forensic officer retreated into the bathroom where they'd found the body.

"Initial cause of death looks like blunt force trauma, but there were no defensive wounds, no sign of a struggle, no evidence he restrained her. Nothin'." Her eyebrows furrowed. "So, what? She let him whack her head against the side of the tub? It makes no sense. We'll know more once they get her on the table."

"How about identification?"

"License reads Marilyn Brandenburg of Moscow, Idaho. We found an emergency number in her cell phone for a sister. I've called, but it keeps going to voice mail."

"Did you find Cassie McBride's purse on the premises?"

"There's a purple bag on the kitchen counter, why?"

"The killer came after her at the hospital. I'm trying to figure out how he knew who she was since she claims he didn't see her face."

"Wait, so she saw him, called for help and took off with a dog in her arms?"

"That is correct. I'm wondering if the perp took her wallet, which was how he identified her."

"I saw a wallet on the counter."

Nate went to the kitchen where Cassie's wallet, made from colorful duct tape, lay next to a bright purple bag. Cassie probably made the wallet herself, he mused. A few inches away he spotted a key chain with small charms: silver cross, flower, Union Jack flag, Eiffel Tower and kangaroo.

Fingering the keys made him wonder about the killer.

"Vaughn?" he called.

She popped her head out of the bedroom. "Sir?"

"Are we thinking the suspect escaped on foot? There were no cars in the area other than Cassie's."

"Someone spotted a black sedan at the Snoquamish trailhead. We're looking into it," Vaughn said.

"Good." He redirected his attention to Cassie's wallet.

He started to analyze the contents. Her round face smiled back at him from her driver's license. The killer would only have to glance at the license to determine Cassie's name and address.

Nate's fingers dug into the plastic wallet.

The address on her license was the farmhouse.

FIVE

Cassie tossed and turned in bed. Couldn't sleep. She hadn't spent the night at the farmhouse in months. Being back here, staying in her old room, brought back memories of a darker time, a time when she felt weak and helpless.

As she glanced out the window at a familiar tree, memories rushed back, bringing with them the irrational and paralyzing fear of being stuck in bed for the rest of her life.

She hopped out of bed, put her fleece on over her pajamas and grabbed her phone. A sip of water would stop this line of thinking. It always had in the past.

Heading toward the stairs, the sound of voices drifted from the first floor. Her mom and Harvey were talking in the living room.

Cassie hesitated at the top of the stairs.

"You should try and go back to sleep," Harvey said.

"I can't. I keep thinking about my daughter finding a dead body. She must be traumatized," her mom said.

"She's a tough cookie, Margaret."

"But she's not talking about it, at least not to me. I don't know what I ever did to put such distance between us. We were so close when she was a child."

Cassie gripped the cherrywood railing. If only she could articulate how her mom's overprotectiveness made Cassie feel like she couldn't breathe. But she struggled to find the right words. She'd never want to come off as disrespectful, and she'd certainly never want to hurt Mom's feelings.

"Kids go through awkward stages, then they grow out of it," Harvey offered.

"Yeah, when they're sixteen, not twenty-six," her mom answered. "I wish she would open up. I could help."

"Maybe she doesn't want to worry you."

"Too late for that."

A moment of silence, then, "How about some more coffee?" her mom offered.

"That would be great."

"And cookies?"

"If you got 'em."

"I always have cookies."

Cassie could just imagine the wry smile playing across her mother's lips. She was known as the "sweet queen," the woman who baked every day, always trying out a new recipe.

Too bad Cassie didn't inherit the baking gene. Her sister Bree seemed to get all the talent in that department.

Hearing her mom walk into the kitchen, Cassie decided to join Harvey in the living room. The sixtysomething former security manager, with a crewcut and kind blue eyes, had a grounding presence she appreciated. She went downstairs, and he looked up as she paused in the doorway.

"Couldn't sleep?" he asked.

She shook her head, entering the living room and flopping down in a chair.

"You've had quite the night," he offered.

"No kidding."

"You hanging in there?"

"Always do." She offered a smile.

Suddenly the lights went out, plunging them into darkness.

"Harvey?" Mom's concerned voice called.

He clicked on a small flashlight and pointed it toward the kitchen. "Probably the wind, Margaret. We're coming to you."

Just then his phone beeped with a text. The blue light illuminated his frown of concern as he read the message.

"What is it?" Cassie asked.

"Chief's on his way. The suspect might know this address." Harvey pulled a firearm out of his boot.

Panic stung the back of her throat. It wasn't only *her* life being threatened, it was her mom's life, as well—the nurturing, compassionate matriarch of the McBride clan.

"Should we call 911?" Cassie asked Harvey.

"Chief took care of it. Let's get to your mom."

The nearly full moon lit the house through the sheer curtains covering the windows.

As Cassie and Harvey went into the kitchen, her heartbeat quickened. This was where they'd found Aiden, bloodied and semiconscious after the break-in last year. When Cassie glanced up and noticed the pale look on her mom's face, she shoved back the traumatic memory. She had to be strong.

"It's okay," Harvey said to her mom. "I'm not gonna let anything happen to you ladies."

The image of the dead woman in the Whispering Pines cabin flashed across Cassie's mind. Shovel Man had no problem killing or trying to kidnap a witness from a public place.

A red light blinked on the panel beside the back door.

Someone had triggered the alarm.

It was a good thing the system was on a separate electrical circuit.

"He's...someone's trying to get in," her mom said in a terrified voice.

Cassie put a comforting arm around her. "It's okay. Police have been alerted and Harvey's here. We need to stay calm."

"Do you have a fire extinguisher?" Harvey said.

"Under the sink," Mom said.

"We can use it to stun him."

Cassie went to retrieve it. "Mom, get in the pantry."

"What about you?"

Cassie had no intention of hiding while Harvey fought off the intruder by himself.

"We both won't fit in there," she said. "I'll find another place." Gripping the extinguisher, she led Mom to the pantry.

"There's room for both of us," her mom whispered.

"Try to keep quiet," Cassie whispered.

"But—"

"Mom, please, I know what I'm doing." Cassie gently shoved her mom into the pantry, then shut and locked the door. She had to; she wouldn't risk Mom popping out during a dangerous encounter. Her parents had put the lock on the outside of the door, out of reach of the kids so they couldn't raid the cookie jar.

Cassie dreaded the lecture she'd get when this was over, but Mom was safe. That's what mattered.

Harvey nodded at an antique oak credenza beside the door leading to the living room. "Help me push this into the doorway."

It was a good plan, Cassie thought. By blocking the door between the kitchen and living room, the intruder could get to them only through the back of the house.

And they'd be ready.

The credenza firmly in place, Harvey motioned for Cassie to get on the opposite side of the back door, out of view. She crouched beside the kitchen cabinets, clutching the extinguisher to her chest.

"What if this is just a blown fuse?" she said.

"That'd be okay with me," Harvey answered. "But I don't believe in coincidences. You sure you won't go into the pantry with your mom?"

"I'm sure."

"Trying to prove how tough you are, huh?"

"Not proving anything. But I can take care of myself."

"I don't doubt that."

"Then you're the only one," Cassie said, noticing how their voices had grown softer in pitch as they spoke.

A few seconds of silence stretched between them. She thought she heard the echo of a police siren, but it was probably wishful thinking.

She glanced down at the vinyl flooring. Even in the darkness, the moonlight illuminated a mark on the floor Aiden's football cleats had made years ago.

A mark she had fixated on when he'd been attacked and wounded last year.

"Hear that?" Harvey whispered.

Cassie took a deep, calming breath and focused.

Wooden boards creaked on the porch just outside the kitchen. Someone approached the back door.

Please, God, give me courage.

Creak, creak...

The door handle rattled.

Cassie took another deep breath and removed the pin on the extinguisher. A crash made her shoulders jerk. Mom really needed to replace the multipaned door.

Scratching echoed across the kitchen. The intruder was trying to unlock the door, but that wasn't happening since it was the kind you locked with a key from the inside.

Another crash echoed through the kitchen. The guy had broken the window above the sink, probably in search of another way inside.

"I know you're in there," he said. "Tell me what you did with it and I'll leave you alone."

What she did with what?

Cursing under his breath, the intruder smashed all the kitchen windows. Was he going to climb into the house?

Right above Cassie's hiding spot?

Harvey grabbed her, protectively shoving her behind him.

Shovel Man popped his head through the window.

Harvey aimed his weapon. "I wouldn't."

The shrill sound of sirens echoed in the distance.

The guy retreated. Footsteps pounded across the porch. She waited a good few minutes before speaking. "Think he's gone?"

"Probably. But we'll stay here until help arrives."

The sirens grew louder, easing the tension in her shoulders.

And then the terrible sound of screeching brakes and crashing metal made her straighten. Cars must have collided on the farm road outside.

Chief's on his way, Harvey had said.

She jumped up and went to the window. "I can't see anything."

"Calm down," Harvey said.

She rushed to the pantry and opened the door.

"Listen, young lady—"

"The key to the back door, where is it?" she interrupted her mom.

"Above the phone."

Cassie dashed to the wall phone, grabbed the key and stuck it in the door.

"Hang on, Cassie," Harvey cautioned.

"There was a crash. People could be hurt." *Nate could be hurt.*

But she didn't say it. She couldn't.

"Cassie, you can't go running out there," her mom said.

Cassie whipped open the door and sprinted to the edge of the porch for a better look. She spotted a black sedan's grill buried in the side of the Chief's truck.

Harvey blocked her. "You need to wait until emergency shows up and we know it's safe."

She clasped her hands together, fighting the panic. The chief had to be okay. She whispered a prayer of hope, wondering how he had become so important in her life.

She was grateful to the chief, that's all. He'd saved her life more than once. Of course she'd be worried about his well-being.

Two squad cars peeled up the long dirt drive, followed by an ambulance. It felt like they took forever to approach the mangled cars.

Cassie squeezed her fingers tighter, fighting the urge to leap off the porch.

The patrol cars screeched to a halt, and the officers got out and drew their guns, aiming at the sedan.

"Okay?" she said to Harvey.

"Not yet."

She ached to see Nate open the passenger door,

since the sedan had pinned the driver's door shut, and climb out of his truck. One of the officers pulled a guy out of the sedan and threw him to the ground.

Cassie took off. Mom called out to her, but Cassie didn't care. The threat was neutralized. As she got closer she recognized the driver—Shovel Man. Good. He was in custody. All was well.

Yet Nate hadn't opened his door.

She raced to the truck, spotted the white air bag, but couldn't see Nate's face, so she went to the passenger side and flung open the door.

She gasped at the blood smearing Nate's forehead and the side of his face. She would not fall apart like she had before.

"Nate?" she said, climbing into the front seat beside him.

Fingering the blood seeping down the side of his face, he glanced at her, confusion coloring his green eyes.

"Cassie?" he said, as if he wasn't sure he recognized her.

"You're okay," she said. She wasn't a doctor and couldn't be sure he was, in fact, okay, but figured he needed to be reassured out of his confused fog.

He studied her with a disoriented expression. Her pulse raced. Did he suffer a serious head injury?

She gripped his hand. "You're going to be just fine."

"Cassie, get out of the truck," her cousin Madeline said from behind her.

But Nate wouldn't let go of her hand. Cassie offered a gentle smile. "The paramedics need to clean your head wound. I'll be right out here."

With a nod, he released her, and she slid out of the truck. "He's conscious, but disoriented," she informed her cousin as she climbed into the front seat.

Cassie's eyes stung with unshed tears. Nate was a strong, healthy man, yet he seemed so vulnerable and lost.

She hovered beside the truck, hugging herself. Worrying, praying.

A gentle hand patted Cassie's back. She glanced sideways at her mom.

"He's a strong man," Mom said.

Cassie nodded, only then realizing she was in her pajamas, in public. And she didn't care.

"Here, I think this is yours," Madeline stuck out her hand, clutching Cassie's shoulder bag.

"Thanks." Cassie took it without looking inside the truck at the chief. It upset her too much to see him that way. Confused and broken.

Harvey joined Cassie and her mom. "Thanks for protecting us," Cassie said.

"My pleasure." He winked.

They waited.

A few minutes later, Madeline slid out of the truck, looking back at Nate. "Stay there until—"

"I'm coming out," Nate's angry voice argued.

"But we need to—"

"I'm fine."

Madeline shook her head in frustration and motioned for Rocky to bring the stretcher.

Nate shifted out of the truck, took one look at Cassie and said, "What are you doing out here?" He glanced at Harvey. "I told you to protect her."

Apparently the fog had lifted. No longer confused, the chief seemed steaming-hot mad.

"He did protect me," Cassie argued.

"You shouldn't have left the house."

"I had to make sure you were okay," she said, miffed that he was being so rude.

"Sorry to interrupt, but we need to take you to the hospital, Chief," Madeline said.

"Not necessary. What do I have to sign to release you from your responsibility?"

"Chief, you should get checked out," Cassie said. "You're bleeding."

"It's not serious."

"Okay, Dr. Walsh," she replied.

"He's right, it isn't serious," Madeline said. "But it wouldn't hurt to get checked out."

He motioned Madeline and Rocky away. "I'm fine. I need to make sure Cassie is safe."

"I'm safe. They arrested Shovel Man."

"We don't know if he's working alone." He glanced at Harvey. "Take Margaret to the resort. Since Aiden is the manager, he should be able to find her a secure room."

"Yes, sir." Harvey turned to Cassie's mom. "Let's pack some things and call your son."

"Cassie's coming with me, right?" Mom said.

The walls were closing in. Cassie loved Mom, but spending days upon days in a room with her, listening to her fret and worry over Cassie's health, would drive Cassie bonkers.

"I'd rather go back to my apartment," Cassie said.

"Honey—"

"That way if someone comes looking for me again, I'm not putting you in danger." She gave her mom a hug, glancing into Chief Walsh's eyes.

He studied her, as if trying to figure out what was going on in her mind. She looked away, her gaze landing on the inside of his truck, the deflated air bag. He could have been seriously hurt.

Because of her.

"We'd better get going," Chief Walsh said. "I'll protect Cassie.

She broke the hug with Mom and said, "Keep your phone on and I'll text you."

"Be safe."

"I will. Promise."

Harvey led her mom back to the farmhouse. This was the best plan for so many reasons. She turned to Nate and caught him rubbing his forehead.

She touched his arm. "Does your head hurt? I'll get my cousin."

"Not necessary. I'm just trying to figure out how everything fits together, that's all."

"That's a lot. Maybe you should wait until you've had a good night's sleep."

* * *

Sleep wasn't in the plan for Nate, not anytime soon. Not until he could be sure Cassie was safe.

Since his truck had been damaged, he'd driven Cassie to her apartment in a squad car, and remained outside her building all night. Nate had an officer patrol the area to make sure it was safe, that no one was lurking and waiting for an opportunity to strike.

Although that scenario seemed unlikely, he wasn't taking any chances. Since Cassie hadn't bothered to change her address on her driver's license, it would be difficult for someone to track her down. He wished he would have known about her not changing her address on her license before she let him take her to the farmhouse. Maybe it had slipped her mind, or maybe she was in denial that the perp would come after her again.

Nate doubted anyone had tracked her to the quaint, modest apartment, but couldn't be too careful. This case grew more complicated by the hour.

The next afternoon, he spotted Cassie waving to him from her window. Nate went up to her apartment to discuss the case.

"You've been down there all this time?" she asked from the kitchen.

"One of my officers gave me a break."

He peered through the delicate lace curtains in her living room, scanning the street below. It wouldn't be easy to breach her apartment considering the two entry doors downstairs, plus Cassie's apartment door.

She lived in an older building with a mailbox vestibule, and her mailbox, 2D, did not have her name on it, which worked in their favor.

"Shouldn't you be interrogating Shovel Man?" she said, coming into the living room carrying a tray with a teapot and cups.

"Shovel Man?" He raised an eyebrow.

"I didn't know what else to call him."

"He's still at the hospital being treated for injuries sustained in the collision. I'll question him in lockup after he's discharged."

"How about some tea?" she asked, pouring herself a cup.

"You don't have to entertain me. Just pretend I'm not here."

If only Nate could follow his own advice. It was impossible to ignore the intimacy of being surrounded by Cassie's personal things, wall posters of castles and mountains overseas, and family pictures proudly displayed on oak bookshelves.

"I can't believe I slept until midafternoon."

"You obviously needed it."

"Why not sit down and take a breath?" She shifted onto the sofa.

He decided this could be a good opportunity to question her about the events of last night to help with the investigation.

Stop being so insensitive. The woman is probably still traumatized from surviving violent encounters with a criminal.

Yet the sooner he got answers, the safer she'd be.

"Tell me again what the intruder at the farm said."

Cassie poured him a cup of tea. "That if I'd tell him what I did with—" she made quotes with her fingers "—'it,' he'd leave me alone."

"Did with what?"

"Wish I knew." She handed him a delicate china cup.

He took it, noting how fragile it felt in his large hands. "Did you take anything from the cabin, other than the dog?"

"No." Her eyes widened. "You don't think they're after Dasher, do you? Why would anyone be after a dog? Speaking of which, is he okay? Who's got him? Catherine or Bree? Did Bree take him to the vet to get checked out?"

Nate cracked a smile.

"What?" she challenged.

"I can tell you're back to normal because you're firing off ten questions at once." He sat on the sofa beside her.

"Oh, sorry."

"Don't be. I'm glad you're okay. Dasher is safe with your sister. Apparently he and your sister's dog are hitting it off. They didn't take him to the vet because he didn't suffer any physical injuries."

"Speaking of which, hang on." She got up and went into the kitchen.

Nate glanced at his watch. He hoped the perp would be released from the hospital and taken back to the station soon, but Nate didn't want to leave Cassie alone just yet.

He'd left her alone last night and couldn't forgive himself for the trouble that followed.

She breezed back into the living room holding an ice bag. It amazed him that she had so much energy considering everything that happened to her yesterday.

"Here." She sat down and held the ice against his head. "To reduce the swelling. Still looks pretty red from last night."

"Thanks." He reached up and his fingers brushed against her hand.

Her skin was so warm and soft, and his breath caught in his throat. What was happening to him? He wasn't a teenager, and he'd certainly outgrown the crush stage of relationships. Why did this woman rattle him so?

"I've got it, thanks," he said.

"Oh, sure, right." She snapped her hand away and reached for her teacup. "My mother's overprotective instincts must be rubbing off on me. Sorry."

"Cassie?"

She glanced up at him with those iridescent blue eyes.

"You never need to apologize to me, okay?" he said.

She bit back a smile. "Even if I do something nasty?"

"Define nasty," he said, surprised by their sudden lighthearted banter.

"Hmmm, what if I doused your tea with happy herbs like lemon balm or chamomile?"

He glanced into his cup. "I probably deserve that."

"I'm kidding," she said. "Stop being so serious."

The lightness of the moment destroyed by his dark thoughts, he slid his cup onto the table.

"My seriousness will keep you safe." He stood and went to look out the window. "I can't afford to be distracted by tea and conversation."

Man, he sounded like a jerk.

"I get it, I do." She got up and crossed the room.

He felt her hand touch his back. Warmth spread across his shoulders. She had that kind of effect on him—a peaceful, calming effect.

"But I think that instead of getting pulled down by the darkness, we should focus on strategizing our way out of this mess."

When she put it like that it made him seem like an unprofessional, emotional head case.

"Are you worried about how all this will reflect on your position as chief?" she asked.

He turned to her, wanting to read her expression. It was authentic and open. Her eyes always seemed so honest when she looked at him.

Which meant she honestly thought he was more worried about his job than her safety. She hadn't a clue how he felt, that this wasn't just about protecting a random citizen.

No, this couldn't happen. These feelings could get her killed. He went to the coffee table to get his teacup.

"Or is it something else?" she pushed.

"I don't want to mess up."

"No one does," she said.

He turned to her. "People died because I wasn't paying enough attention." How had that slipped out?

"I'm so sorry."

"Yeah, well, you can't fix the past."

"No, but you can let it go."

"Wish I could." He sighed. "And now, well, Echo Mountain has historically been a quiet town, until recently."

"Until what, you came on board as chief? Don't even go there, big guy. We had our share of trouble long before you took over, like the guys stalking Scott, and the thugs after Nia because of her deadbeat brother. And now I find a dead body. I'm sorry it was on your watch."

"Wait, you're not blaming yourself for this," Nate said.

"No, but I feel responsible for putting the people I care about in danger."

She glanced at him with a startled expression, like she'd blurted out a secret she hadn't meant to share. Awkward tension filled the living room.

"Don't worry, your mom will be fine." Nate recovered. "Aiden will make sure of it."

She nodded, but didn't speak.

I feel responsible for putting the people I care about in danger.

Her words hung in the air between them, and Nate considered their meaning. She couldn't possibly include him on that list.

He had to redirect his thinking before it totally distracted him from his goal: protecting Cassie and finding out why "Shovel Man" killed the woman in the cabin.

"To be clear, you didn't take anything from the rental cabin?" he said.

"Just the dog," she said, breaking eye contact and walking back to the sofa.

"What were you supposed to do when you got there?"

"Check appliances, general condition of the cabin, bring in fresh toiletries and linen. But I didn't get very far because I heard Dasher scratching at the closet door." She shook her head. "I wasn't even supposed to be there."

"Explain, please."

"My friend Becca had originally been assigned the Whispering Pines cabin, but I offered to cover for her. She seemed stressed lately."

"Why's that?" Instead of sitting beside her, he chose a chair across from the coffee table.

"I think she's having boyfriend trouble. Tony keeps promising to get a better job. He does part-time work for Echo Mountain Rentals and she's been supporting them by holding down two jobs."

He pulled out his notebook. "I need Becca and Tony's last names."

"Wait, why? You think they're involved in this?"

He glanced up at her trusting and offended expression. "She might have seen or heard something along the way," he said. "I have to look into everything connected to the rental company. Detective Vaughn has already been in touch with your boss."

"Oh, okay."

Cassie gave him Becca's last name and her phone number. "I don't know Tony's, sorry."

He looked at her with a raised eyebrow.

"Oh, right, I'm not supposed to say 'sorry.' Sorry." She smiled.

He refocused on his notebook to avoid the effect her disconcerting smile was having on him.

"I'll call it in." He pulled his phone off his belt.

He called Detective Vaughn and gave her the information about Becca and Tony.

"You think they're tied to the deceased?" Vaughn said.

"I have no idea," he said into the phone. "Cassie said Becca has been stressed out. It's worth looking into."

"I'm on it."

"And let me know when the suspect is in lockup."

"Of course."

He ended the call and turned to Cassie. "We'll figure this out."

An explosion echoed through the windows. Cassie shrieked and Nate instinctively pulled her against his chest.

SIX

Cassie had never heard anything so ear-piercingly loud, yet the eerie silence that followed was even creepier.

She felt guilty about clinging to Nate like a little kid, and knew she should let go. Yet he'd been the one to reach for her. It wasn't like she'd jumped into his comforting arms that held her snugly against his chest. The pressure of their embrace dissolved the ball of fear lodged in her throat.

Then she realized Nate couldn't investigate what was going on outside with Cassie stuck to him like Velcro.

Releasing him, she stepped back. "I'm okay."

"You're sure?"

"Yes, go ahead. Do your thing."

He called it in. "This is Chief Walsh. There's been an explosion on Main Street. I can't tell what it is or from where it originated. Send a patrol car and I'll meet him in front of the Sweet Rose Teashop." He pocketed his phone and looked deep into Cassie's eyes. "I need you to stay here and lock the door behind me. Don't let anyone in but me, got it?"

"Of course," she said with false confidence. He must have read fear in her eyes because he didn't move.

"Go, go." She led him to the door and securely locked it once he left.

She stood there for a good minute, pressing her forehead against the aged wood, praying that Nate wouldn't be harmed and he'd return quickly.

"Uh," she moaned, going back to the sofa and grabbing her cup. Five minutes, she wanted five peaceful minutes to ground herself from the craziness.

Then she realized she *had* felt grounded the moment Nate pulled her into his arms. Wow, that was a first. She'd dated a few guys, sure, but she'd never felt calmed by any of them. Considering the current situation—being stalked and threatened—it was quite remarkable that she could feel grounded from a simple hug.

"Of course he makes you feel safe. He's the police chief," she said.

As the minutes ticked by, she grew more anxious about what was happening outside, wondering if Nate was okay. She padded to the living room window and peered down to the street. A cruiser with flashing lights was parked in front of her building, but there was no sign of Nate or the other officer.

"Where are you?" she whispered.

A sudden movement caught her eye. On the corner, she noticed a man standing under a streetlamp, lighting a cigarette.

And he was staring up at her.

She snapped back from the window, her heart racing. Now she was overreacting about everything. She wasn't in danger. Shovel Man was in custody. The guy outside was probably out for a walk and happened to pause at the corner to light a cigarette.

As she was about to peek outside again, someone knocked on her apartment door. She gasped. How did they get into her building?

She slowly crossed the room and eyed the peephole. The hallway was empty. Taking a few steps away from the door, she whipped out her phone to text Nate.

"Cassie, open up!" her sister called.

Cassie eyed the peephole again. Bree stood there holding Dasher in her arms. Cassie flung open the door.

"How did you get in my building?"

"Key, remember?" Bree waved her key chain. "You going to let me in?"

Cassie motioned her inside.

"Mom wanted me to check on you," Bree said, carrying the dog in one hand and a take-out bag in the other. "She told me to bring food."

"Hey, Dasher." Cassie grabbed him for a quick hug.

"Mom told me what happened. You seriously locked her in the pantry?"

"It seemed like a good idea at the time." Cassie shrugged. "Thanks for bringing Dasher, and dinner."

"I figured you could use the company."

"I had company until a few minutes ago. Didn't you see the police car out front?"

"I parked in back."

"Chief Walsh was here."

Bree quirked an eyebrow.

"Knock it off," Cassie said. "He's just doing his job."

Bree's phone beeped. She held it up. "Mom."

"Go ahead, tell her I'm okay."

Bree answered. "Hi Mom… Yeah, I'm with her now. She's okay…I'll tell her. Love you, too." Bree pocketed her phone. "Mom says she loves you even if you won't stay with her at the resort."

"It's safer for Mom this way."

"I wish you would've called me instead of me having to hear about it from Mom," she said in her hurt voice.

Bree had survived her share of violent situations, and Cassie wanted to spare her big sister more trauma.

"Cassie?" Bree prompted.

Cassie put Dasher down and watched him enjoy all the new smells of her apartment. "I'm okay…well, I was okay until we heard an explosion outside just now. Chief Walsh went to investigate. He said not to open the door to anyone but him and when you knocked, I couldn't see you through the peephole."

"I was picking up the dog, sorry. What is going on around here? First the body in the cabin, then a crazy man in urgent care, and someone tried to break into the farmhouse? How are you coping with all this?"

"I'm fine." Cassie glanced at the window across the room. "I just wish Chief Walsh would let me know he's okay."

"Want me to look?" Bree started for the window.

"No, stay away from the window."

"What? Why?" Bree studied her.

"I saw a guy out there. It's probably nothing."

"Honey." Her sister took Cassie's hand. "Never, ever ignore your instincts. If you think there was something off about the man outside, then respect that feeling."

Bree knew a lot about trusting her instincts. She'd learned the hard way after surviving a relationship with an abusive boyfriend. She'd also found a wounded man in the mountains named Scott, and trusted her instincts that told her he was not a criminal. Scott turned out to be a wonderful man who was now Bree's boyfriend.

"We'll tell Nate about the strange man outside," Bree said.

"No." Cassie pulled her hand away. "I'm probably overreacting."

"Or maybe not. Why don't you want to tell him?"

Cassie sat on the sofa and Dasher jumped up beside her. "Nate's got enough going on. He doesn't need to deal with my paranoia about some phantom stranger."

"That's not it," Bree challenged, joining her on the sofa. "Come on, out with it."

"Look, he already thinks of me as his friend's bubbleheaded little sister who talks way too much. Why add overreacting, hysterical woman to that list? I don't want him looking at me that way. I want him to see me as…" Her voice trailed off as she noticed a wry smile playing across her sister's lips. "What?" Cassie challenged.

"Nothing." Bree winked.

"What's with the wink?"

"Admit it, his opinion of you means so much because you kinda like him."

"He's the police chief. Everyone likes him."

"I'm not talking *that* kind of like. I'm talking hugging and holding hands and—"

"Stop." Cassie stood, grabbed the food bag and went into the kitchen. She had to get away from her sister's teasing comments.

More like, unavoidable truth.

Drat, who was Cassie kidding? She'd been crushing on Nate Walsh for months and kept pushing it away, telling herself he'd never be interested in a naive chatterbox like her.

She also knew he was the exact *wrong* person to date because of his dedication to his job. She wanted to take off and explore the world, whereas Nate was firmly rooted in the community as police chief. He wasn't going anywhere anytime soon.

"Cassie?" her sister said from the kitchen doorway. "I understand if you don't want to admit it to me, but at least be honest with yourself."

Cassie glanced at her sister. "Nate is not an option."

"Why not?"

"I can't stay here, Bree. I need to get out of this town."

"Okay, well, make sure you're running toward your dreams, not fleeing your problems."

The apartment buzzer went off. Cassie pressed the intercom. "Hello?"

"It's Nate."

"Come on up." She pressed the unlock button. A minute later she spotted his handsome face in the peephole. She opened the door and the dog burst into furious barks.

"Stop, Dasher, it's Chief Walsh." Cassie picked up Dasher and glanced into Nate's eyes. "What was the explosion?"

"Someone started a Dumpster fire behind the hardware store. Probably kids needing a little excitement." He glanced at Bree. "Hi, Bree."

"Chief."

He studied Cassie, cocking his head slightly. "What's wrong?"

"What? I... What do you mean what's wrong?" Cassie stumbled.

"Did something happen while I was gone?"

Cassie glanced at Bree, who bit back a knowing smile. Nate could read Cassie like a three-word text.

"Everything's fine," Cassie said, going to the sofa.

"She saw a suspicious guy outside and it freaked her out."

"Bree!" Cassie snapped.

"Where?" Nate said.

"By the lamppost on the corner," Cassie said. "It was probably nothing."

"Stop denying those instincts," Bree repeated.

"Good advice." Nate went to the window. "No one's there now. What did he look like?"

"Tall, wearing a baseball cap and smoking a cigarette."

"She's pretty jumpy," Bree added.

"You can leave now," Cassie said, half-joking.

"I don't want to leave you alone."

"She won't be alone," Nate said. "I'm staying for a while."

"Good, well, there's plenty of food for both of you."

"Guys, I can take care of myself," Cassie said, putting Dasher down.

"Bree, how about I escort you to your car," Nate offered, and then looked at Cassie. "I'll be right back."

"Hey, don't I get a say in any of this?" Cassie protested.

Bree hugged her. "Don't argue. Enjoy his company," she whispered in her ear.

"Stop." Cassie playfully shoved at her sister's shoulder.

"Did you want to keep the dog?"

"You should probably take him until all this is sorted out. He'll have more fun at your place with Fiona, anyway."

Bree picked up the dog and smiled. "Have a nice evening."

Cassie's cheeks must have reddened, because Bree darted into the hallway. Seemingly unaware of Cassie's embarrassment, Nate followed Bree, and Cassie locked the door behind him.

* * *

Nate escorted Breanna safely to her car, then decided to walk the block to see if the suspicious-looking man Cassie had noticed was still hanging around. Other than the fire department making sure the Dumpster fire was out, Main Street was relatively quiet. There was no sign of the guy.

As he made his way back to Cassie's apartment, his phone vibrated. He pulled it off his belt. It was his mentor, former Police Chief Washburn.

"Chief," Nate said.

"Heard you've had a busy twenty-four hours."

"Nothing I can't handle."

"That's what I've been saying."

Nate hesitated outside Cassie's apartment building. "Have you been getting calls?"

"Just one or two."

Which probably meant half a dozen, but the chief didn't want to worry Nate.

"Do I need to hold a press conference?" Nate half joked.

"Nothing that public. But be willing to talk to people if they ask questions. It's not every day a dead body shows up in town."

"I get it, I do, but my primary focus has to be solving the case."

"I hear frustration in your voice. If there's anything I can do to help, I'm here, trying to enjoy retirement, and failing miserably, by the way."

"Thanks. I might take you up on that offer. You're around this week?"

"Around with a honey-do list in hand. Nothing that can't wait. I'm serious, son, call if you need anything."

"Will do. Have a good night."

"You, too. And Nate?"

"Sir?"

"I recommended you for the job because I have one hundred and twenty percent confidence in your abilities."

"Thank you, sir." Nate ended the call.

What did Nate have to do to convince the townsfolk that he was a solid choice for chief, that he could protect them as well as Chief Washburn had for the past twenty years?

He went to Cassie's building and she buzzed him in. Once upstairs, he spotted her peering through a crack in her apartment door.

"You took longer than I thought." She motioned him inside.

"Got a call from Chief Washburn."

"Everything okay?"

"As long as I solve this case by tomorrow, sure."

"People have been calling him?" She sat down on the sofa.

"How'd you guess?"

"I've lived in this town for twenty-six years, remember? People worry when they hear things and don't know what's going on. It's not a personal reflection on you or anything."

"Thanks."

"No, thank you for taking Bree to her car. You should have let her stay so you wouldn't have to."

"It's my job."

An odd, almost pained expression flashed across her face. She motioned to the TV.

"I was watching television, unless you'd prefer quiet."

"Television's fine."

It didn't surprise him that the station was tuned to a travel show.

He sat down on the sofa, a safe distance away from her. "So, Ireland, huh?" he said, nodding at the screen.

"England, France, Switzerland and eventually Australia, although that's a superlong flight. I'd need tons of plane activities to get me through that one."

"Plane activities?"

"Sure, movies, puzzles, books, you know, activities."

He couldn't help but smile. This woman fascinated him on so many levels, especially her enthusiasm for life and new experiences.

"You're smiling," she said. "It's a good look on you," she teased.

Again, as they drifted into natural conversation, he warned himself not to get too comfortable. "Other than the challenges of living in a small town, why are you so desperate to travel?" he asked.

"It's a long story."

"I'm not going anywhere for a while, remember?"

She shrugged. "I made myself a promise when I was a kid. As I lay in bed, praying my body would finally work the way it was supposed to, I promised myself that when I recovered I would visit all the places I read about in books. I would climb mountains and watch the Eiffel Tower light up on New Year's. Too bad I hadn't left last week, huh? That would have made my life so much simpler."

He didn't have a response for that, realizing how much he'd miss her once she left. "I'll figure this out, Cassie," he said, hoping to ease her fears. "I promise."

A few hours later, after a pleasant meal courtesy of her sister, Nate found himself on the sofa beside Cassie as she watched another travel program. His phone vibrated with an incoming call. It was Detective Vaughn. He started to get up.

"It's okay. You can take it here," she said, turning down the volume on the TV.

He sensed she wanted him to stay close, so he leaned against the sofa and answered the call. "Detective?"

"The perp's license reads Len Pragner of Chicago. Someone saw him check into the Rushing River B&B, alone. I haven't been able to question him. His injuries were worse than we thought, so he's still at the hospital. Want me to stay?"

"No, see if Carrington can cover for a few hours so you can get some sleep."

"Copy that. The deceased has been transported to the ME's office."

"Good. I'll be posted outside Cassie McBride's apartment tonight. I can't risk her being alone, not until we figure out why someone's after her."

Nate felt pressure on his arm and glanced down. Cassie had fallen asleep against his shoulder.

"Any idea why she's been targeted?"

"When the suspect stuck his head through the kitchen window he said if she told him where *it* was, he'd leave her alone. They want something from her, but the only thing she took from the cabin was the dog."

"Strange," Vaughn said.

"Have you found any connection between Pragner and our vic, Marilyn Brandenburg?"

"Not yet. I'll do a more thorough check tomorrow when I get to the station."

"Good night, Detective." He ended the call and glanced at the blond-haired beauty leaning against him. He shifted to get up, but she was gripping his sleeve, mumbling something he couldn't make out. She'd fallen asleep, and found comfort clinging to Nate's jacket. He didn't have the heart to wake her up.

As he puzzled through tonight's events, his gaze drifted to the television program. The travel show reminded him that this, the feel of Cassie leaning against him and depending on him for comfort, was temporary. Still…there was no harm in enjoying the moment.

* * *

The next morning Cassie awoke up with a start, anxious and disoriented. She opened her eyes and focused on her antique nightstand lamp. She was in her bedroom, on her bed. Sitting up, she realized she was on top of the comforter with a blanket tucked snugly around her body.

"Nate?" she said, her voice hoarse.

Footsteps echoed down the hallway. Her heartbeat quickened.

Her brother stepped into the doorway holding a white to-go cup from the tea shop below. "Good morning, sunshine."

"Where's Chief Walsh?"

"At work. What did you think, he was going to be your personal bodyguard for the rest of the week?" Aiden motioned to his cup. "Got you some coffee." He disappeared from the doorway.

"Coffee, bleh," she muttered under her breath, and flopped down against the comforter.

The last thing she remembered was leaning against Nate on the sofa while watching television. She must have fallen into a deep sleep and he'd carried her to her room. She wished he'd stayed long enough for her to tell him…tell him what? Well, at least long enough to thank him again for protecting her.

"That's unacceptable," Aiden's voice drifted down the hall. "We need the heating system repaired by the weekend. We'll be at seventy-five percent capacity."

Cassie felt like such a burden, taking Aiden away from his managerial responsibilities at the resort, and Nate away from his police chief duties.

She felt like that little kid again, trailing behind her older siblings who cast irritated smirks over their shoulders at her. She was the afterthought, holding everybody back, dragging everyone down with her problems…her ill health.

Determined not to be that needy child, she shifted out of bed, appreciative that she'd outgrown the morning stiffness of her childhood illness. Today she was a healthy and independent woman. She must be out of danger if Nate left her apartment, right?

Heading into the living room, she waved Aiden down as he paced. "I'm going to take a quick shower and go to work," she said.

He held the phone against his flannel shirt. "What are you talking about?"

"I have to stop by the rental office and turn in my report on the properties. I'm a day late as it is."

"I'll call you back," he said into the phone. He shot Cassie a stern frown. "Email or call it in."

"Mr. Anderson doesn't do email reports, Aiden."

Aiden shook his head. "How does that guy stay in business?"

"Besides, I need to go in person and explain what happened."

"Oh, I'm sure they know."

"It's my job, Aiden."

"Don't you remember what happened over the past thirty-six hours?" he said in that condescending tone of his.

"I remember," she shot back. "I also remember the suspect was taken into custody."

"Why can't you—"

"I won't stay locked away like a caged bird. I need to get out of here and live my life." Cassie realized the words came out a little stronger than she'd intended, but she was desperate to get through to her brother.

He studied her for a second. "Fine. I'll take you to the resort. I had your car towed there this morning. Maybe Mom can change your mind."

He whipped out his phone and continued his argument with the repair company.

An hour later they arrived at the resort where she checked on her mom, who was set up in a nice room facing the grounds.

"I was so worried about you," Mom said, hugging Cassie.

"Thanks, I'm okay. Looks like you're okay, too."

"My son takes good care of me." She smiled at Aiden.

"Well, I'm off to the rental office," Cassie said.

"Cassie, no, you—"

"It's fine, Mom. They've got the suspect in custody."

"Honey, you shouldn't be gallivanting around town on your own," her mom said.

"She won't listen," Aiden said, checking text messages.

Cassie clenched her jaw to quell the protest threatening to crawl up her throat and burst out of her mouth.

"I'll be fine," she said.

"Aiden, go with her," Mom said.

Aiden's beeper went off.

"Mom, he's got a work crisis. I'll be back in an hour."

She gave Mom a hug and turned to leave, but Mom was determined to walk her to her car. Cassie felt Mom's silent guilt trip, even though she didn't speak.

"Cassie, I—"

"Love you," Cassie interrupted and kissed her on the cheek.

She got behind the wheel of Ruby and spotted the manila envelope in the passenger seat containing completed reports from the other cabins she'd visited.

As she drove away from the resort, the swell of frustration loosened around her throat. This was why she needed to build her travel fund and get out of town. She loved her mom and siblings but felt smothered and didn't know how to communicate her frustration.

She avoided glancing in the rearview mirror, not wanting to see her mother's worried expression, the one that still haunted Cassie from childhood.

The expression that reminded her how broken she was.

Was, but not anymore.

Make sure you're running toward your dreams, not fleeing your problems. Bree's comment taunted Cassie.

"I'm not running away, I'm not," she said.

Fearing she wasn't being completely honest with herself, Cassie flipped on the radio as a distraction and found a country station. Lyrics about sacrifice in the name of love filled the car.

She clicked it off. She wasn't going to give up her dream of traveling in order to make her family happy, no matter how much she loved them. Nor should they expect it.

As far as romantic love was concerned, Cassie had plenty of time for that later, after she'd seen the world. Who knows, maybe she'd even find the love of her life overseas and decide to relocate to Europe. Wouldn't that fry everyone's fritters?

"Oh, grow up," she scolded herself, realizing how juvenile she sounded. Yet sometimes the way they hovered made her feel like the walls were closing in, and she couldn't breathe.

A few minutes later she pulled into the parking lot of Echo Mountain Rentals. She got out of her car, preparing to apologize for being late with her incomplete report. As she approached the entrance, she noticed the front door was ajar.

Just as it had been at the Whispering Pines cabin.

The hair prickled on the back of her neck.

Never, ever ignore your instincts.

She scanned the parking lot and noted only one other car, not her boss's. She darted out of sight, her back hugging the side of the building, and called Nate.

"This is Chief Walsh. Please leave a message and I'll call you back. If this is an emergency call 911."

Cassie texted him instead: SOS @ EM Rental office. Front door open. Danger?

She sent the text. But if he was in a meeting or interrogating Shovel Man, he wouldn't be able to respond immediately.

Never, ever ignore your instincts.

Cassie debated.

A crash echoed from inside the office.

She dialed 911.

"911. What is your emergency?"

"I'm at the Echo Mountain Rentals office," she whispered. "I think someone's breaking in."

"What's your name?"

"Cassie McBride."

"Why do you think someone is breaking in?"

"The front door is open and my boss's car isn't here and I heard a crash."

She glanced up.

A tall man wearing jeans, black boots and a black jacket crossed the parking lot and approached Cassie's car.

He slid his hand into the inside of his jacket.

And pulled out a gun.

SEVEN

Nate stood at the foot of the perpetrator's hospital bed and considered his next move. Len Pragner seemed to be enjoying this—Nate asking questions; Len not answering. A half smirk curled the guy's lips like he had a secret, like he thought the handcuffs were going to magically open and he'd walk out of the hospital, all charges dropped.

"We've got you on attempted assault, breaking and entering—"

"I didn't enter," Len said.

"Because someone was pointing a gun at your head."

"And I didn't assault anyone," he argued.

"You smashed the windows and tried getting into the farmhouse. That'll keep you in town for a while."

Len shrugged. "It's a nice town. Friendly people."

"My witness says you were looking for something."

"Your witness, you mean Cassie McBride?"

"What were you looking for?"

"She's cute, not my type, but cute."

Nate struggled to keep his temper in check. "Why are you in Echo Mountain?"

"I think I might ask her out," he taunted.

Nate narrowed his eyes, but kept his cool. Len couldn't possibly know how Nate felt about Cassie.

"You keep playing games, Len," Nate said. "We've got a nice cell waiting for you when you're released."

Nate left the guy's room and motioned to his officer on duty. "When the doctor releases him, he goes straight to lockup."

"Yes, Chief."

Detective Sara Vaughn approached Nate. "From the look on your face I'm thinking he isn't being co-operative."

"He's enjoying pushing me around. Feel free to give it a try." He glanced at his phone. A text popped onto the screen from Cassie.

An SOS.

"I've gotta go." Nate rushed to the stairs, made it to his squad car and took off. As he listened to the radio chatter, he heard an officer responding to a B&E call at the Echo Mountain Rentals office.

She shouldn't have left her apartment; then again, the suspect was in custody, so she didn't seem to be in immediate danger.

Unless Len had a partner. The man standing on her street corner, perhaps?

Nate pressed down on the accelerator, struggling to quiet the shame coursing through his mind: *You never should have left her.*

Yeah, and how unrealistic was that? He was the police chief; he had a job to do, a homicide to solve.

A town to keep safe.

He turned into the rental company parking lot and spotted Cassie's red car, a black sedan, and a patrol car, lights flashing. He didn't see anyone in cuffs.

Nate approached his officer, who stood beside his car speaking with a taller gentleman in his forties.

"Officer Hough?"

Officer Hough turned to Nate. "A misunderstanding, Chief. The caller thought this man was a burglar, but he's with the FBI."

"Agent Steve Nance." The agent reached out and shook Nate's hand. "I'm investigating a case that led me to Echo Mountain Rentals. When I arrived to question the owner, I found the door open, the office ransacked, and no one inside. I guess your witness assumed I was the perp." He nodded toward the building where Cassie sat on the front steps, her chin resting on her upturned palms.

A rush of relief washed over Nate. She was okay; not hurt, just frightened.

"I'd like to be brought up to speed on your investigation," Nate said to the agent. "Perhaps our murder is related."

"Of course. I have a lead I'm following up on in twenty minutes. Can we meet for lunch?"

"Sure. Healthy Eats Restaurant, one o'clock?"

"Sounds good."

Nate went to Cassie, rehearsing his lecture in his head before he said the words. Then he remembered how she didn't like being bossed around. If he wanted to keep her safe, he needed her cooperation, not her defiance. He couldn't afford to push her away.

"Cassie?" he greeted.

She looked up, her cheeks red. His gut clenched.

"Hey, you okay?" He sat beside her.

She shook her head. "I'm ashamed."

"Ashamed? Why?"

"I obviously overreacted. I mean the guy is an FBI agent, but the door was open and I got this feeling, and Bree said never to ignore that feeling, and then the guy comes outside and he's got a gun."

He placed a gentle hand against her back. "Cassie, you did not overreact. Someone *did* break into the office. That's a crime. You did the right thing by calling 911."

"I guess."

"It's not a guess. You acted responsibly."

She frowned slightly, fiddling with her key chain.

"What is it?" he said.

"No one's ever said that to me before." She glanced at him. "I appreciate it."

His heart raced, but not from fear or adrenaline. He slipped his hand off her back. "You know what I'd appreciate?"

"What?"

"If you didn't go anywhere alone for a while, just in case Len Pragner has friends in town."

"You think he does?"

"It's possible."

"Did you interrogate him?"

"I tried."

"What did he say?"

Nate ripped his gaze from her hopeful blue eyes.

"Nothing helpful," he said. "But he knows who you are, which is why I'm concerned for your safety."

As he scanned the parking lot for signs of trouble, a silver minivan pulled up beside his patrol car.

"It's Mr. Anderson," she said.

The owner of Echo Mountain Rentals got out of his vehicle and cast a worried glance at the chief.

Nate stood to greet the middle-aged man. "Someone broke into your office."

Mr. Anderson glanced at Cassie. "Are you okay?"

"She called it in," Nate answered for her.

"I'm fine," Cassie said. "I showed up after the fact. You're lucky you didn't come in right at nine this morning."

"My assistant and I had a few stops to make."

A small blue sedan pulled into the lot. Mr. Anderson's assistant, Carol Trotter, got out of the car. "What's going on?" she asked, rushing up to them.

"Someone broke into the office," Mr. Anderson said.

The sixtysomething woman glanced at the building with rounded eyes.

"It's okay, he's gone," Nate said to ease her fear.

"But why?" she said. "We don't keep cash or anything valuable in there."

"Do you think this is related to the dead woman at the Whispering Pines cabin?" Mr. Anderson said.

"We're not sure," Nate said. "I'd like you to go

through the office and see if anything's missing. That might help us determine motivation for the break-in."

"I can help," Cassie offered.

"Okay, but let's all wear gloves so as not to interfere with forensics."

Nate retrieved four pair of gloves from the patrol car. When they went into the office, he noticed Cassie's rattled expression. Then she lifted her chin as if to say, *this isn't going to bother me.*

That's what he admired about her: her ability to act strong when she was feeling anything but powerful.

Cassie bent to pick up papers scattered on the floor. "Where would you like me to put these?"

"Stack them on the table," Mr. Anderson said. "We'll go through them."

"How about your files, Mr. Anderson?" Nate asked. "Does anything look off?"

"Carol is my file pro."

Carol analyzed the files strewn haphazardly on the floor. "It doesn't look like anything's missing."

They continued to go through the mess for a few minutes.

"This isn't good," Cassie said.

"What?" Nate questioned.

She held up an empty file folder, then another. "My personnel file is empty. So is Becca's."

"It probably just fell out somewhere." Carol got down on the floor and sifted through paperwork.

"What did you keep in those files?" Nate asked Mr. Anderson.

"Job applications, work reviews, property assignments."

"Our addresses and Social Security numbers were on those applications." Cassie glanced at Nate.

"Which address was on your application?" he asked.

"The farmhouse."

"That could be a good thing." Nate turned to Mr. Anderson. "Didn't you keep that type of sensitive information secured?"

"I lock it every night," Carol answered for her boss. "They must have picked the lock. What on earth would they want with personnel information?"

"I've got to warn Becca," Cassie said and raced out of the office.

Cassie paced outside, pressing her cell phone to her ear. "Come on, come on," she said under her breath. Why wasn't Becca answering? Was she in trouble?

Her voice mail picked up. "Hi, this is Becca. I can't take your call right now, so please leave a message."

"Becca, it's Cassie. Be careful. Someone stole our personnel files from the office so they know where you live, and we need to talk because I don't know what's going on and we could be in danger, or at least we were in danger until they arrested that guy last night, but still we don't know if he has a partner—"

A solid hand rested on her shoulder. She glanced into Nate's green eyes. "Take a breath," he offered. "Tell her to meet us at the police station."

Cassie nodded. "Becca, come to the police station. Chief Walsh and I will explain everything." She ended the call and nibbled at her lower lip.

"Come back inside." With a hand cupping her elbow, Nate led her into the office. "Was Becca working for you this morning?" Nate asked Mr. Anderson.

"No, she's off until Wednesday."

"She has a second job with Blackburn Adventures guiding tourists into the mountains," Cassie said. "Maybe she took a group out today."

"I'll check into it," Nate said. "In the meantime, other than personnel files, does anything else seem to be missing?" Nate directed his question to Mr. Anderson, who glanced at his assistant.

"Not that I can tell," Carol said. "I'll keep looking."

"Thanks. When forensics arrives, you and Mr. Anderson should clear out. Do you have another location where you can conduct business?"

"We can work out of one of the empty cabins," Mr. Anderson said.

"I'll have a patrol car stay here until you're finished. Also, Cassie needs a few days off until we sort this out."

"Nate—"

"Cassie, don't argue with me on this," he said.

"We completely understand. We're pretty slow for the next few weeks, so no worries," Mr. Anderson said.

"Thanks." Cassie handed him the manila envelope. "Sorry my paperwork is late."

"Totally understandable," Mr. Anderson said. "I'm glad you're okay."

Nate escorted Cassie outside to her car.

"You didn't have to apologize for late paperwork, either," he said.

"I don't want to lose this job."

"He seems like an understanding boss."

She narrowed her eyes at him. "Why do I get the feeling you've only said sorry, what, twice in your entire life?" she teased.

"Maybe three times," he countered.

She was surprised he'd joked back. "Wow, a whole three times."

"Hey, you don't have to point out my faults. I know them intimately."

Pointing out his shortcomings was not what she'd meant to do. "I wasn't trying to—"

"So, you'll head back to the resort now?" he interrupted.

"I'd like to help you find Becca."

"Cassie, this is a police investigation."

"At least let me call Blackburn Adventures. I have the number in my phone."

"Okay, go ahead."

Cassie called Blackburn, a family-owned company founded more than thirty years ago with an excellent reputation.

"Thank you for calling Blackburn Adventures. Sorry we missed your call. Please leave your name—"

Cassie glanced at Nate. "No one's answering. I don't like this. I'll run by her place to see if she's okay."

"Cassie—"

"What if she's in trouble?"

"I need to know you're safe at all times. That means going back to the resort. I'll swing by Becca's apartment."

"Okay, Chief." She got behind the wheel of her car and turned the key, but it wouldn't start. She tried again. Nothing.

She opened the door. "What else could possibly go wrong today?"

"Could be your battery," he said.

After a few minutes of trying to jump her battery with no success, Nate suggested it might be her alternator, or possibly something more serious.

"Come on," he said. "I guess you're with me."

With him? She liked the sound of that. Cassie walked a little too excitedly beside him but couldn't help herself. He motioned to a police officer.

"Officer Hough, keep an eye on Mr. Anderson and his assistant until they leave the premises. Get keys so you can give forensics access to the office."

"Yes, sir."

"Chief?" Carol said, coming toward them. "The only missing personnel files are Cassie and Becca's." She nodded at Cassie's car. "Is there a problem?"

"It won't start," Cassie offered.

"We'll be here for an hour or so if you want to leave the keys with me and call for a tow."

"That would be great." Cassie started to hand Carol her keys and hesitated. The key chain was her touchstone to the future and her glorious travel plans. She removed the car keys and handed them to Carol. "I appreciate it."

"Of course." Carol went back into the office.

Cassie made the call to have Ruby towed, and Nate led her to the squad car. "I'll drop you at the resort and I'll go check on your friend."

"Nate, please take me with you. I'm worried about her. I've even got a key to her apartment for when I feed the cat if she's out of town." Cassie jangled her keys.

"I noticed you wouldn't part with the key chain. Those charms mean a lot to you, don't they?"

"Oh yeah. The cross and flower charms represent God and nature, and these three remind me I'm going to England, Australia, and France," she said, pointing to the respective charms. "Although I keep thinking I should add a charm for Switzerland, but haven't figured out what that is yet."

Realizing she was chattering away again, she stopped and glanced at Nate. A half smile curled his lips.

"Hang on, were you trying to change the subject? You were, weren't you?" she said. "Nate, come on, we need to check on Becca, and the resort is half an hour in the opposite direction of her apartment. That's a whole hour lost. Let me go with you."

Nate shook his head in surrender and opened the car door. "Okay, on one condition."

"What?" She shifted onto the front seat and buckled up.

"Follow my orders. I know you don't like to be told what to do, but I can't worry about you *and* do my job effectively, understand?"

"Of course."

He shut the door. He was worried about her? Could it be more than just an officer of the law worrying about a witness? It felt like more, but then Cassie didn't have a lot of experience reading between the lines when it came to men.

When he got behind the wheel of the car, he reached for the radio to call in. "Base, this is Chief Walsh. I'm heading to Becca Edwards's apartment at…" He glanced at Cassie.

"543 Wilshire."

"543 Wilshire," he said into the radio.

"Copy that, Chief."

He pulled out of the lot and headed toward town.

"Thanks," she said.

He shot her a quick glance, then refocused on the road. "For what?"

"Listening to me again."

"What… I don't understand."

"You respected my need to make sure my friend is okay."

"I respect a lot of things about you, Cassie."

"That's a first," she muttered.

"Meaning what?"

"It'll sound dumb."

"Try me."

"I don't feel like I get a lot of respect from my family."

"You mean Aiden?"

"And my mom, and Bree. Then again, Bree isn't too bossy, but my cousin Madeline…" She shook her head.

"What about her?"

"Never mind." Cassie glanced out the window, wondering why on earth she was exposing herself like this to Nate, of all people.

"I'd like to understand why you're thanking me, so maybe I can do it again," he said.

She snapped her gaze left and noticed a hint of a smile playing at the corner of his lips.

Frustration eased from her chest. She liked it when he smiled. She could almost feel it herself.

"Your cousin?" he prompted.

"Sometimes she makes me feel, I don't know, small. She's patronizing, and she teases me, and not always in a good way."

"Have you talked to her about it?"

"No."

"Don't you think you should?"

"I wouldn't know what to say," she admitted.

"Finding the right words is the toughest part."

"Did you ever have an uncomfortable talk with someone you cared about?"

"I did."

"What happened?"

"I lost her for a little while, but eventually it strengthened our relationship."

"Oh." So there *was* a woman in Nate's life. Cassie puzzled over that one, since he lived alone and never seemed to be with a woman during his off-hours.

"My sister," he clarified.

"Catherine? But she's so lovely and caring and patient—"

"Too patient. Do you know why she moved to Echo Mountain?"

"To open a restaurant?"

"To distance herself from Dylan's father, an abusive jerk."

"I had no idea."

"It's not something she's proud of, and the guy was sneaky about it. He'd scream in her face one night, act like nothing had happened the next morning and then bring her flowers after work. She never told me about it—Dylan did. It was about the time Dylan wanted to defend his mom that I got involved. I went to college with Chief Washburn's nephew, and we'd come to Echo Mountain to visit family on break. I thought it would be the perfect place for Catherine to get a fresh start."

"And she stopped talking to you because…?"

"She resented me telling her what to do, not that you can relate to that." He smiled.

Cassie smiled back and felt herself blush.

"Anyway, she fought me on the move until one day her ex chased Dylan around the house swinging a wooden chair. That was it. She called me and I made arrangements for her to move here. She got a job at a local restaurant, and a few years later the owner sold it to her. Shortly after that I—" he hesitated "—I had a career shift and Chief Washburn offered me a job. I was glad to move near my family. Catherine's got a wonderful life in Echo Mountain."

"But why was she upset with you for trying to help her?"

"Months after they'd moved here, she admitted she was ashamed that her little brother had saved her, and she said a part of her felt her husband's violent behavior was her fault."

"Nate, no, that's nonsensical."

"Human emotions. They don't always make sense. Like a mother who's overly protective of her grown daughter because she was sick as a child."

"But I'm not sick anymore."

"Emotions don't have to make sense to be real, Cassie. Your mom's worry is real."

"I know." She hesitated. "But it drives me nuts."

"Then tell her."

Cassie shook her head. "I could never hurt her feelings like that."

"And you won't hurt her when you take off on

one of your trips because you're trying to get away from her?"

That gave her pause. "I never thought about it like that. What would I say to her?"

"You've got a solid relationship with God. Why don't you pray on it?"

Nate could hardly believe the words that had come out of his mouth. *Pray on it?*

Sure, why not? It made sense for a woman like Cassie to pray, a woman who needed to find her voice with her family or risk losing them forever.

And family was everything. Catherine and Dylan were Nate's family, along with the former chief, Aiden McBride, and a few search-and-rescue friends. Truth was, Nate's family had grown exponentially since his move to Echo Mountain.

After losing his partner, Nate would never take family for granted again.

A few minutes later, they pulled up to Becca's place. Nate eyed the building for signs of trouble, yet all seemed quiet in the neighborhood.

Cassie placed a gentle hand on his arm. "Thanks."

The warmth from her hand drifted up and settled across his shoulders. "For what?"

"Helping me get perspective about my mom."

"That's the second time today you've thanked me. I'm getting pretty good at this." He shot her a smile and reached out. "Keys?"

She dropped them into his palm.

"You stay put, got it?" he said.

"Sure."

But halfway to the apartment building, a nagging sensation told him not to leave her behind.

He turned back and motioned for Cassie to join him. As she opened the door, her blue eyes widened with curiosity. "What's wrong?"

"Nothing. Just want to keep you close."

A contented smiled eased across her adorable face.

"In order to keep you safe," he clarified.

Her smile faded. "Of course."

He refocused on the apartment. Why did he have to say that?

Because he was being professional.

Because he wanted to keep the line firmly drawn between them.

Because you're a jerk.

They approached the building in silence, Cassie a few inches behind him to the right. The key gave them access to the front door, so they let themselves in and took the stairs to the second floor.

"Her apartment is around the corner," Cassie said.

"I'm sorry," he said, wanting to apologize for his rude nature.

"For what?" She led him down the hall and froze.

Becca's apartment door was cracked open.

"Nate," she whispered.

He grabbed her arm and pulled her behind him. He withdrew his firearm.

Here he thought keeping her close was the safe

thing to do. He had no idea what he was walking into, but couldn't send her back to the squad car alone.

Focus, Nate. Focus.

Senses on high alert, he moved slowly toward Becca's door, Cassie right behind him, her hand against his back.

A crash echoed down the hall from inside the apartment.

He had no intention of leading Cassie into a dangerous situation. Pointing to the stairs, he leaned close, his lips practically touching her hair.

"Go upstairs and stay out of sight," he whispered.

She nodded and brushed soft fingertips against his cheek as if to say "be careful." The warmth gave him an added confidence he couldn't explain.

Still focused on the partially open door, he waited a good ten seconds until he knew Cassie was safely hidden. He shot a quick glance over his shoulder. Couldn't see her.

With the toe of his boot, he eased the door open and stepped inside.

EIGHT

Cassie clasped her hands together and prayed. She prayed that Becca was okay, and she prayed for Nate's safety.

She wasn't sure why she'd touched his cheek the way she had. It was instinctive. She needed to make that connection before he stormed into whatever was waiting for him in Becca's apartment.

Squeezing her hands tight, she prayed: *Dear Lord, please keep my friends safe in Your loving embrace. Let Your light shine upon us, Your love flow through us, and Your glory protect us.*

She realized, and not for the first time, that her stomach twisted into a pretzel-like knot at the thought of Nate being hurt, or worse.

Please God, keep him safe.

Because she wasn't sure how she would manage if anything happened to him. The image of his disoriented expression last night in his truck flashed through her mind. The look in his eyes, that faraway, confused look, stuck deep in her core. Nate was a tenacious, capable man who'd been broken trying to protect her.

"Cassie?"

Her eyes popped open, and she spied around the corner to the floor below. Nate motioned to her. "It's clear."

She released the breath she didn't know she'd been

holding. It must have sounded like she gasped for air, because Nate was suddenly beside her.

"You okay?"

She nodded. "Who knew praying could be so exhausting?"

He pulled her against his chest in a brief hug as if to convince her she was safe. Which was exactly how she felt whenever he held her in his arms. The hug didn't last nearly long enough.

Not letting go of her hand, he led her to the second floor and into Becca's apartment.

"I think the cat knocked something over," he said. "Saw him run into the bedroom."

"Probably hiding under the bed. You should shut the door to keep him safe."

Nate released her. "Don't touch anything. It's a crime scene."

"Is Becca...?"

"Not here," he said as he closed the bedroom door.

She sighed with relief.

"Detective Vaughn is on the way. Could you try Blackburn Adventures again to see if they have any information about Becca?"

"Sure." Cassie made the call, her eyes scanning the disheveled living room: books strewn about, cushions ripped off the sofa and pillows shredded into pieces. The thought of a man slitting innocuous pillows with a large blade made her cringe. She clung to the hope that Becca wasn't home when the intruder destroyed her apartment.

"You've reached Blackburn Adventures—"

Cassie ended the call. "It's voice mail again."

Footsteps pounded up to the second floor. Detective Vaughn rushed into the apartment. "Any sign of Becca Edwards?"

"No," Nate said. "We've been trying to reach her employer, but they're not answering. Found the premises tossed. I'll leave you in charge here while I head over to Blackburn Adventures to see if Becca showed up for work."

"And there's a cat in the bedroom," Cassie offered.

Nate motioned Cassie toward the door, but hesitated and turned to Agent Vaughn. "I'm meeting with FBI agent Nance at one o'clock."

Vaughn snapped her attention to him. "What have the Feds got to do with this?"

"He's working a case that led him to Echo Mountain Rentals."

"Led him how?" She narrowed her eyes.

"I'll find out at lunch and I'll let you know."

"Thanks, Chief."

Cassie felt like she was missing something; there was subtext to that exchange. The way Detective Vaughn reacted to the mention of FBI involvement ignited a spark of tension.

Once they got downstairs, Cassie asked, "Is she… upset?"

Nate glanced at her as he opened the door and led her outside.

"About the FBI?" Cassie prompted.

"Nah, it's a territorial thing. Sometimes various law enforcement agencies don't play well together in the sandbox. She's probably worried the agent won't share information."

They got into the squad car and pulled away.

"Sharing information is crucial, it's—" he hesitated "—well, it can affect a man's life."

"Yeah, I'm worried about Becca's life right now."

"Hey, don't go there. These guys usually don't like breaking in when someone's home. It complicates things. The assailant probably waited until she left for work this morning."

Cassie glanced out the window, wondering how yesterday at this time life seemed so simple, so easy: work to make money so she could travel. No complications, no second thoughts.

"Cassie?"

His deep voice speaking her name set off a round of second, third and fourth thoughts about her leaving Echo Mountain.

She glanced at him, steeling herself against his concerned expression.

"I'll do everything within my power to find and help your friend," he said.

"I know, thank you. That gives me great peace."

"I wouldn't go that far," he muttered, eyeing the road.

"Why not?"

He shook his head as if the conversation was over, but she wasn't giving up. She'd openly shared her frustrations about family and the challenges of battling her childhood medical condition. It would help her understand this guarded man if she knew a little about his past.

"You said you used to come here with Chief Washburn's nephew on break?" she started.

"Yes."

"So you went to college?"

"I did."

"And studied what, criminology?"

"Actually, got a degree in psychology. Was going to do law school, but decided to join the Chicago PD instead."

"What was that like compared to being a police officer here?"

He shot her a wry smile. "Different."

"I'll bet. Why did you leave? To be near Catherine?"

"Mostly."

Cassie waited. She sensed he wanted to talk, but rarely opened up. To anyone. Who would he confess his past to, anyway? As the local police chief, he had to maintain a strong, professional demeanor. Revealing any flaws or imperfections could make people feel insecure.

How unfair, Cassie thought. People were human, not perfect. But it was also human nature to want to look up to people in leadership positions, sometimes even put them on pedestals.

"I don't mean to be nosy," she said.

"Oh yes, you do." He shot her a quick glance and

winked. "Just promise me none of this will end up in the community blog."

"Nate, do you honestly think I'd—"

"I'm kidding."

"Because I want you to trust me as much as I trust you, and with everything I've told you over the past twenty-four hours, you're one of the most trusted people in my life right now."

"I'm honored."

Redirecting her attention out the window, Cassie felt offended by his quip about her publishing his life story in the community blog. She thought he knew her better than that, knew that she wouldn't ever share a confidence. Then again, how could he know that? It wasn't like they were good friends, or something more serious like boyfriend and girlfriend. He was the police chief doing his job, and she'd been randomly targeted for some reason.

The constant threat of danger must be wearing on her, that's all. It was silly to be offended because Nate wanted to keep his secrets to himself.

"My partner was killed."

She snapped her gaze to study his profile. He would not look at her.

"Along with a witness he was guarding," he added.

"Oh, Nate, I am so sorry."

"I feel responsible."

"What? Why?"

Again, he shook his head, as if to indicate that was as much as he could share.

She waited, interlacing her fingers to remind herself that God was present and listening, and could hopefully ease the burden she knew was weighing on Nate's heart.

They reached a stoplight and he glanced at her. "He didn't trust me with the truth."

"Which was?"

"He and the female witness—" He hesitated and redirected his attention to the light. It turned green and he pulled into the intersection. "They'd grown close."

"And that isn't allowed, right?"

"It's ill advised. If you're distracted by a pretty face you can't do your job."

She wondered if they were still talking about his partner, or if the comment was meant for her as another warning. Like he hadn't given her enough warnings, drawing a firm line between them over and over again. Suddenly it hit her why it was so important for him to maintain his distance.

"I don't understand why your partner's death is your fault," she said.

"Maybe I could have prevented it if I'd known what was going on. I would have at least been there as backup, knowing he couldn't be in love with the witness and effectively protect her."

"You can't blame yourself for his choices."

"Yeah, well…" A few seconds passed. "I was devastated by his death. When I pressed one of the guys, he said Dean didn't tell me about the affair because he knew I'd judge him. It was just like my sister taking that garbage from her ex for years and not telling me. Why are people afraid to tell me things? Am I that intimidating or scary or what?"

Cassie actually welcomed Nate's uncharacteristic rant. When she'd share her frustrations with God, it often eased the pressure in her heart.

"By your silence, I guess that means yes," he said.

"Actually, I was waiting to see if you were done." She motioned with her hands. "Come on, there's gotta be more in there."

"You're teasing me."

"I most certainly am not. I'm impressed by your honesty, and now don't freak out, but also your vulnerability."

"That's not what a man likes to hear, Cassie, especially one who's supposed to be protecting you."

"It means you're human. You feel things just like the rest of us."

He frowned. "That's how the town sees me? As some kind of unfeeling robot?"

She touched his arm. "No, but sometimes the whole strong, silent type thing makes people uncomfortable. When someone's unusually reserved, like you, people wonder what you're thinking, and because they don't know what's going on up here—" she touched the side of his head "—they make things up. Stuff like 'he thinks I'm an idiot' or 'he doesn't like my choices.' It's just human nature."

"So what, I'm supposed to talk all the time like—" He stopped abruptly.

"Like me?" Cassie finished for him. "It's okay, I know I'm a chatterbox. But no, you don't have to jibber-jabber to ease the tension with other people. Just be a little more open, you know, softer, like your friend Will Rankin."

"Will's got two little girls to soften his edges."

"Well, you have friends, lots of friends, to help you practice your communication skills."

"Maybe if I'd had better skills my partner would have confided in me."

"And you would have said what?"

"I would have told him it was a bad idea, that getting romantically involved on the job was insanity."

"Which would have felt like he was being judged."

"Being brutally honest is the only way I know how to communicate. I was hoping a little of that would rub off on you."

"What is that supposed to mean?"

"You could be more honest with your family."

"I can't risk hurting their feelings. I told you that."

"Look at us, I'm brutally honest and you're brutally careful not to hurt anyone's feelings."

"It creates a kind of strange balance, doesn't it?" she said, not censoring her words before they left her mouth. She wondered if she'd scared him back into his cave.

"Yeah, it sort of creates balance," he said in a soft voice.

"Do you have anything else to get off your chest?" she said in a teasing tone.

"Actually, I'm good for now."

"Then will you do me a favor?"

"What's that?"

"Stop blaming yourself for your partner's death."

"I'll try."

"I've got an idea, how about surrendering the guilt to God? Does that sound doable?"

"I've never…I don't really have a connection to God."

"That's okay. He has a connection to you. Open your heart to the idea?"

"I guess I can do that."

Nate wasn't sure why he'd agreed to opening up to God, but for the first time in his life the idea didn't seem all that foreign. It was probably Cassie's nurturing personality and hopeful attitude that got through to that empty spot in his heart where he knew others found their faith.

He'd envied his friend Will, a man of faith who always seemed so grounded, even as he balanced being a single parent with work and volunteering for SAR. But Nate figured the window of opportunity had passed, that he'd ignored God for too long and he'd missed his chance.

Cassie thought differently.

She continually amazed him by the way she talked, listened and counseled. Which was great, except that she was a witness in danger and this was a repeat of his partner's situation. If Nate would have gotten in

Curt's face about falling in love with a witness, Nate deserved to give himself that same lecture.

Falling in love? Was that what was happening between him and Cassie?

No, Nate wasn't thinking clearly due to lack of sleep. He knew the reality of the situation, and his focus had to be about protecting her. After they arrested the perpetrator or perpetrators and closed the investigation, *that* would be the time to see if there could be something more between Nate and Cassie.

Only one problem: it was her life's dream to travel, and he'd be a jerk to do anything to get in her way, like asking her out on a date.

"You think she's in trouble, don't you?" Cassie said.

Nate snapped his attention to her. "I'm sorry?"

"You get this look when you're worried about something. You think Becca's in serious trouble?"

"No, I was thinking about something else."

I was thinking about you.

"Care to share?" she said.

"Not at present, no." Could he ever speak his truth to Cassie?

Cassie's phone rang. "It's Blackburn Adventures," she said, eyeing the screen.

"Could you put it on speaker?"

She pressed the speaker button. "Hello?"

"This is Blackburn Adventures. I saw multiple calls from this number. Can I help you with something?"

"This is Echo Mountain Police Chief Walsh. With whom am I speaking?"

"Wendy Longmire, trail guide."

"May I speak with whoever is in charge, please?" Nate asked.

"Sure, I'll get my boss."

Cassie nibbled her lower lip. Nate shot her what he hoped was a reassuring nod, but even he didn't know where this would lead.

"This is Jeff Porter, can I help you?"

"Police Chief Walsh here. I'm looking for Becca Edwards."

"She's leading a group up the west side of Echo Mountain. They left at six this morning."

"I need to contact her. Is that possible?"

"Let's see…by now they'll be a few miles west of Rattlesnake Pass. I can try, but reception tends to be hit or miss on that side of the mountain."

"I'll be there in about five minutes. In the meantime, can you tell me how she seemed this morning when she came to work?"

"Hang on. Hey, Wendy, how was Becca this morning?"

"She seemed okay," Wendy said from the background. "Excited about some trip she and her boyfriend were planning. I think they were leaving after today's hike."

"Did she seem anxious or worried?" Nate asked.

"No, sir."

"Thanks."

"Do you want me to try to contact her before you get here?" Jeff said.

"No, I'd rather you wait."

"Will do."

"See you soon." He nodded at Cassie, who ended the call. His fingers tightened around the steering wheel. None of this made sense.

"What?" she said.

He shot her a quick glance.

"You're gripping the steering wheel so tight your knuckles are turning white."

"I can't seem to make sense of this. Someone's after Becca, and she's planning to leave town, but she takes a group up into the mountains? If she's fleeing the jurisdiction she must know she's a target, right? But then why go to work and act like everything's fine?"

"You almost make it sound like she's a suspect."

"Right now she's acting like one."

A few minutes later they pulled into the Blackburn Adventures lot. Jeff, the manager, introduced himself.

"I'm Chief Walsh and this is Cassie McBride."

"Right, Aiden's little sister," Jeff said.

"That's me."

He led them into the office and clicked on a high-powered radio.

"Becca, this is base, over," Jeff said. "Becca, come in, over." A few seconds passed.

"Why isn't she answering?" Cassie said.

"Like I said, bad reception," Jeff explained. "If they're in trouble someone will hit the locator beacon."

"How many people did she take up there?" Nate

asked with concern. Not only was Becca in danger, but potentially her entire group.

Jeff eyed a clipboard. "Looks like seven."

"Could you give her another try?" Nate pressed.

"Becca, this is base. We need you to check in, over."

Scratchy silence echoed across the line.

"When do you expect them back?" Nate asked.

"About one o'clock."

Nate had agreed to meet the FBI agent at that time, but needed to be here when Becca returned.

"Hello? Hello, are you there?" a voice said through the radio.

"Becca, is that you, over?" Jeff responded.

"No…she's gone!" a female voice said.

NINE

Cassie's heart leaped into her throat.

"Gone, what do you mean, gone?" Jeff said. "Who is this?"

"Tanya Holmes. I've got a little hiking experience so they put me in charge."

Jeff clicked the radio so Tanya couldn't hear them. "This is a novice group," he said to Nate. "Little or no hiking experience to speak of."

"Let me." Nate took the radio.

"Tanya, this is Police Chief Walsh. When did Becca go missing?"

"About an hour ago. We stopped to eat lunch. She said she was going to check the trail up ahead because of bear sightings. She never came back."

"Is everyone okay?"

"For the most part, but one of the gals twisted her ankle when we tried to find Becca."

"The hiker who injured her ankle, is she mobile?"

"We were just trying to figure that out."

"Please assess the situation and let me know."

"Okay, hang on."

Cassie studied Nate's profile and marveled at his calm and confident demeanor in the midst of a crisis. Somehow his controlled reaction took the edge off the panic swirling in Cassie's stomach.

"Chief?" Tanya said through the radio.

"Yes, Tanya."

"Carly is unable to put pressure on her ankle."

"I'll dispatch search and rescue. Do you know your exact coordinates?"

"We're at the Lake Mirage Overlook."

Jeff pinpointed it on the map.

"Tanya, it should take them about ninety minutes to get to you," Nate said.

"A few of the guys want to head back down," she said.

"I'd prefer everyone stay together."

"I'll tell them."

"Which direction was Becca headed when you last saw her?"

"North on Chinook Trail."

"Hang tight. Help will be there ASAP."

"Okay, thanks."

Nate clicked off the radio and pulled out his phone.

"Ninety minutes is pushing it," Jeff said.

"You're not familiar with SAR," Nate countered. "It becomes a contest to see who can get there first."

As Nate drove Cassie to a safe location so he could join the search, she considered what could have happened to her friend, a seasoned climber.

"I'll find her, Cassie," he said.

She glanced across the car at Nate, realizing he knew her so well he could sense what she was thinking.

"I want to go with you."

"Not an option. You know that." He pulled onto

Resort Drive and only then did she realize where he was taking her.

"Nate—"

"Echo Mountain Resort has the best security in the county. I know you don't like being told what to do, but this once, could you be okay with my plan to keep you safe?"

Her automatic reaction was to argue, to come up with all sorts of reasons why she didn't want to be dumped at the resort into the midst of her overbearing family, but she stopped herself. There was something about his voice, a hint of desperation that made her reconsider.

"What's the plan?" she said.

"You'll stay at Echo Mountain Resort while I'm gone, either in your sister's cottage or in a resort room, but please don't go anywhere alone." He paused. "I'm sorry if that sounds like an order, but I don't know a nicer way to say it."

"I understand."

And she did. Somehow she was able to appreciate Nate's concern for her well-being without growing defensive.

"What's wrong?" he said.

"Why do you think something's wrong?"

"You're being too agreeable. I mean it, Cassie, no leaving the resort."

"I know."

"And stay out of sight if possible."

"Ten-four, Chief."

He pulled up to the front of the resort, got out of the car and opened the door for her, his eyes scanning the parking lot.

"I got it from here," Aiden said, approaching them.

"I thought you'd be on the team heading up to Lake Mirage Overlook," Nate said.

"Too much going on here today. Besides, I heard it was just a sprained ankle."

"And Becca's missing," Cassie said.

"Missing?" Aiden questioned, looking at Nate.

"I'll know more when I get up there."

Aiden nodded at Cassie. "Okay, I'll take care of trouble here."

Cassie would have normally shot off a retort to her brother, but she couldn't be bothered. Not when she feared for Nate's safety. Who knew what trouble he'd find once he reached the spot where Becca had disappeared?

"Be careful," she said, only this time she didn't touch his cheek. She wrapped her arms around his waist and gave him a hug. When he didn't return the gesture she thought maybe she'd crossed a line. But it was her way of wishing him well.

Just as she released him, his arms tightened around her back and he held on for a few seconds. He leaned forward and whispered, "Be safe. Promise?"

"Promise," she uttered, barely able to speak against the ball of emotion tightening in her throat.

He released her and without making eye contact, got into his car and drove off.

* * *

It was almost as if the hug had energized him, Nate thought as he practically sprinted up the incline of the trail. The first team radioed that they were nearly at the site, and Nate wanted to get there as quickly as possible. He'd called his sister at Healthy Eats, described the FBI agent, and asked her to let him know Nate wouldn't be back for their meeting.

Joining Nate on the mission was Officer "Red" Carrington and Nate's friend Will Rankin, a widower who was dating Detective Vaughn. None of the men spoke much as they motored up the mountain with purpose.

The other team would probably take the lead on assisting the injured hiker, while Nate and Red would search the surrounding area for clues as to what happened to Becca. He'd send Will back down with the first team, not wanting to put the single father in danger.

"Hey, speedy," Will said, short of breath.

Nate glanced at his friend.

"I'm in good shape and you're killin' me here. Trevor's team is perfectly capable of dealing with a sprained ankle."

It wasn't just the thought of the injured hiker that made Nate run uphill. It was the look on Cassie's face, the look of worry about her friend being in trouble.

Nate would do anything to ease her fears, to make her smile.

"Nate, say something, grunt, anything," Will pushed.

Red chuckled.

Nate slowed down a bit. "Sorry."

"What's really going on here?" Will asked.

"Guess I'm worried about Becca Edwards. She's gone missing."

"I know that, but I assumed she slipped and took a tumble or something. Is there more to this?"

Nate motioned for Red to hike ahead, while Nate hung back with his friend. "Her apartment was tossed. We can't rule out foul play, which is why I want you to head down with team one once we get to the injured hiker."

"What are you going to do?"

"Red and I will search the area for clues, some indication as to what happened to her."

"Well, if she needed help, she should have activated her locator beacon."

"True. In a way, I'm hoping she intentionally disappeared."

"That makes no sense. A trail guide wouldn't abandon her tour group."

"There's a lot that hasn't made sense since we found a dead woman at the Whispering Pines cabin."

"Yeah, I heard about that."

Nate glanced at him. "News gets around in a small town."

"Smaller when you're dating the lead detective." Will smiled.

Nate hadn't seen him smile like that for years, since his wife had died.

For a brief second Nate wondered if that's how he looked when he thought about Cassie.

"Speaking of dating…" Will started. "You been out on any lately?"

"No time."

"You seem to be spending a lot of time with Cassie."

"She's a witness in a murder investigation."

"I meant before that."

"She comes into the station to get ideas for the community blog."

"She's a sweet lady."

"Who's traveling to the far corners of the world once she gets enough money."

"Maybe she just needs a good reason to stay."

"Can we focus on the mission?" Nate said.

Will winked. "Which one?"

"Chief, I see the group up ahead," Red called out.

Nate and Will picked up their pace and reached the tour group within minutes. The first team seemed to have it under control. They had wrapped the ankle, secured the hiker to the litter, and were ready to head down.

"Sorry if this was a wasted trip for you," Nate said to Will.

"Any day out here in the mountains is a blessing, not a waste. I'd be happy to stay and help you look for Becca."

Nate recalled the incident when Will suffered from amnesia after being injured by a criminal in the mountains. He would not put his friend at risk again.

"No, we're good." Nate looked at the hikers, who assembled to head back down. "May I have your attention?"

They glanced in his direction.

"I'm Chief Walsh with Echo Mountain PD. Who spoke with your trail guide before she disappeared?"

A woman raised her hand.

"Are you Tanya?" Nate asked.

"Yes, sir."

"I'll need to talk to you for a second. Anyone else speak with Becca Edwards?"

They shook their heads that they hadn't.

"I'm asking for a refund, that's for sure," a fifty-ish man said.

"Don't be so heartless, Roger," a woman about the same age scolded. "What if something happened to the poor girl?"

Roger shrugged.

"So, no one else spoke with the guide, or noticed anything unusual?" Nate said.

"She seemed nervous," a man offered. He was in his midforties, wearing a blue ski cap with the letter *B* on the front, and dark sunglasses.

"And you are?"

"Owen Banks." He shook Nate's hand.

"How did she seem nervous, Owen?"

"The way she looked around, like she was worried about something."

"There are bears out here," Will offered.

Nate looked at Tanya. "Did you sense Becca was nervous?"

"Not particularly."

"Thanks." Nate motioned for them to rejoin the group.

"You sure you don't want me to help search for her?" Will offered.

"I'm sure."

Nate sent the hikers back down. He and Red got to work following the trail in the opposite direction, looking for clues.

About an hour later, Nate spotted a small glove on the ground. He picked it up. "Could be Becca's."

"Chief," Red pointed up ahead. A woman's hiking boot lay in the middle of the trail.

Twenty feet from the boot was a dark green jacket.

"What happened out here?" Red muttered.

"Let's pack this stuff up and keep moving."

A few hours later the sky grew dark and Nate sensed a storm brewing. Rather than backtrack, Nate decided to consider other options.

"Hang on a second." Nate pulled out his binoculars and the topographical map. He handed the map to Red. "Can you find us the quickest way down?"

Nate peered through the binoculars, scanning the immediate area for signs of Becca. Could she still be out here, held captive by someone? He didn't figure this for an animal attack because her jacket wasn't torn, nor were the other items of clothing they'd found: the other glove, a scarf and a knit hat.

"Huh," Red said.

"What?"

"If we veer left in about half a mile, the trail leads straight down to Echo Mountain Resort."

A chill raced down Nate's spine. Cassie was at the resort.

"Let's move."

It had been nearly five hours without word from Nate. Through a slit in the resort room curtains, Cassie watched the sky grow dark with angry clouds. She couldn't stop thinking about Nate, worrying about him. To distract herself, she'd turn the television on and then turn it off, irritated by the inane programs that seemed to be on every channel. She wanted him to call or text or something.

A soft knock echoed across the room. She rushed to the door, hoping...

Instead of seeing Nate through the peephole, she saw Bree with Dasher in one arm and a grocery bag in the other.

Cassie swung open the door. "Hey."

"Brought you dinner," Bree said, waltzing into the room. "Ham and cheese melt sandwiches, fruit salad and raspberry brownies." She turned and narrowed her eyes, studying Cassie. "No? I thought you liked raspberry brownies."

"I do, it's not that."

"What then?" She put Dasher down and the dog sniffed his way around the room. "Wait, did Mom say something to make you feel guilty about not staying with her? I know she was upset when you said you wanted your own room. I guess I was a little miffed you didn't want to stay with me either, but—"

"I haven't heard from Nate."

"Where is he?"

"He went to search for Becca. She disappeared while leading a tour group up Echo Mountain," Cassie said, her voice pitching.

"Oh honey, I'm sorry." Bree gave Cassie a hug and patted her back. "I'm sure he'll find her." She broke the hug and looked into Cassie's eyes. "Becca's a resourceful woman. If she's in trouble, she'll figure out a way to signal the chief."

"I hope you're right."

"C'mon, let's eat something. Chocolate always makes you feel better."

Within the hour Cassie had managed to consume a sandwich and two brownies. "I was hungrier than I thought. Thanks for bringing all this food by."

"Sure. Guess you're lonely without your bodyguard." Bree smiled.

"Don't start."

"You guys do make a cute couple."

"How is that possible? He's intense and brooding, and I'm chatterbox Sally."

"It's perfect. He never has to talk and you don't have to compete for attention like you always had to do with us growing up."

Cassie picked up Dasher and held him in her lap. "Don't get me wrong, Nate's a nice guy, but we want completely different things out of life."

"Like?" Bree leaned back and nibbled a brownie.

"He's got a good job in town as chief, versus me wanting to travel."

"Police chiefs get vacation."

"Not for months at a time." She shook her head. "What am I talking about? We've never even been on a date."

"Maybe because you haven't been quiet long enough for him to ask?" She winked.

"Or he's not interested."

"Trust me." Bree started packing up the plates. "He's interested. Are you?"

Cassie considered the burn in her stomach. She'd just eaten, so it wasn't hunger. She was deeply worried about Nate. On some level she knew she liked him a lot more than as a friend.

"You're taking a long time to answer," Bree said.

"I can't be interested. It makes no logical sense."

Bree chuckled. "And when did you become Miss Pragmatic? Love isn't logical, little sister. Look at me and Scott. There is no way I should have fallen in love with a wounded stranger in the mountains. But I did."

Bree reached out and touched Cassie's arm. "Love is surprising and wonderful and glorious. You need to trust it." She stood. "I'm going to the lobby to get a cup of tea. You want one?"

"Sure."

Bree went to the door. "Do you have a preference?"

"Anything will be fine," Cassie said, gently stroking the dog's fur.

"Hey, Cassie?"

Cassie glanced at her sister.

"I'm sure Nate will call soon."

Just then the nightstand phone rang.

"See," Bree said with a smile and shut the door.

Still holding Dasher, Cassie went to answer the phone, wondering why Nate hadn't called her cell.

"Hello?" she answered.

"Your friend is dead," a deep male voice said. "You're next, unless you—"

Cassie slammed down the phone and stepped back. It rang again. And kept ringing. What should she do? Nate ordered her not to go anywhere alone, so she shouldn't leave the room. But now a threatening man was calling. Did he know her room number? No, the front desk wouldn't give out that information.

She couldn't stand the ringing phone, so she unplugged it from the wall. She was safe. No one could get to her in this room.

Her cell rang and she hesitated before answering. Now she was being paranoid. She pulled it out of her pocket and eyed the screen. It was Nate. Relief washed over her.

"Nate, they keep calling so I unplugged—"

Pounding on the sliding glass door made her shriek.

TEN

The dog burst into a round of high-pitched barks.

"Cassie, what's wrong?" Nate said.

"The slider, someone's trying to get in."

"Cassie, it's Tony!" a muffled voice called from the other side of the glass. "Open the door! I need to talk to you!"

"Cassie!" Nate said through the line.

"It's Tony, Becca's boyfriend. Maybe he knows what happened to her."

Cassie whipped open the curtain. A wild-eyed Tony motioned to the door. Sliding it open, Cassie said, "What are you doing here?"

He eyed the phone. "Who are you talking to?"

"Chief Walsh, he's—"

Tony snatched the phone out of her hand and turned it off.

"Hey, I was talking."

"Listen to—"

"You owe me an explanation. Becca disappeared from her tour group and they sent out a search team and—"

"Enough!" he said.

Cassie bit her tongue, wanting to give him a piece of her mind for raising his voice. Instead, Dasher protested for her, barking his displeasure.

"Shut that thing up," Tony said. "I've gotta talk to you."

"Don't speak to us that way."

He reached for the dog, but Cassie turned away in a protective posture. "I'll put him in the bathroom." She marched across the room and kissed the dog on the head. "Just for a few minutes, Dasher."

She shut the door and turned to Tony. "Give me my phone."

"After we talk." He slipped her phone into his pocket.

Trusting her instincts, Cassie kept her position a good ten feet away from Tony. His wild black hair practically stood straight up, and his skin was unusually pale, almost white, accentuating dark circles under his eyes.

"What happened to Becca?" she demanded.

"It's a long story."

"Give me the quick version."

He paced the small room. "It was supposed to be easy. No one would notice."

"Tony, I have no idea what you're talking about."

He stopped right in front of her. "You need to come with me."

"I don't think so."

"You have to, Cassie. Becca needs you."

"Why, is she hurt?"

"Just come, please?"

Three soft knocks echoed from the resort room door. "Hey, I've got tea, open up," Bree said.

"Yes, let us in," her mother added.

As Cassie started for the door, Tony grabbed her

arm. "If you want to keep your family safe, you won't involve them in this."

"In what? Let me go." Cassie tried to wrench free.

Tony whipped out a gun. "I didn't want to use this, but you're not listening to me." His eyes flared with panic.

"If you're in trouble, Nate can help," she offered.

"No one can help, especially not the police."

"Cassie!" Bree pounded.

Tony flung out his arm and pointed the gun at the door. Panic flooded Cassie's chest.

"Don't you dare fire that thing."

"Then come with me."

Cassie grabbed her purple bag as Tony pulled her toward the sliding door. Bree's insistent pounding and the dog's echoed barking filled the room with chaos.

Going with him was her best choice. She didn't think Tony was a violent guy, but right now he seemed irrational beyond words. She wouldn't risk him discharging the weapon out of frustration and hurting her family.

Tony led her outside into the dark night, his fingers pinching her arm. He picked up his pace, half jogging toward a beat-up car. Cassie kept her head down and her eyes averted, not wanting to draw attention from innocent bystanders. She didn't know what Tony might do.

"Cassie!" Aiden shouted from the south entrance.

She was simultaneously relieved and terrified. Aiden would jump into a burning fire for someone he cared about, which meant he'd charge Tony and get a bullet in the gut for his trouble.

"I'm fine!" she shouted back. "Going to see a friend!"

"You're not supposed to leave!"

Tony rushed to his car and shoved her into the passenger side. "Move over. You're driving."

She did as ordered, glancing once in the rearview mirror. Both Aiden and the resort's security manager, Scott, Bree's boyfriend, were racing toward them.

"Go!" Tony shouted.

Her trembling hands put the car in Drive. Pressing down on the accelerator, she felt a tear warm her cheek.

I can't die yet. I haven't been to Australia or France. I haven't been on a date with Nate Walsh.

Oh, what ridiculous thoughts flooded her brain when her life was being threatened.

"Faster!" he shouted.

She applied more pressure and they sped off. Her fear dissolved into anger. Once again, she was at the mercy of someone else's control, just like the disease that had dominated her childhood.

"If you're going to kill me you should at least tell me what's going on," she snapped.

He sighed, and it seemed like all the air was sucked out of him. "I'm not going to kill you," he said, and lowered the weapon.

"Then what's with the gun?"

"I need your help and I can't involve the police."

"Because you broke the law?"

"No...maybe...I don't know."

He sounded so defeated that she started to feel sorry for him, but caught herself.

"Don't you ever threaten my family again, you hear me?" she said.

"Yeah."

"I want my phone back."

He tossed it onto the dashboard.

"Is Becca okay?" she said, pocketing her phone.

"I don't know."

"You mean you're not taking me to see her?"

"No, sorry. I had to do something to get you to come with me."

Cassie raised an eyebrow at the gun in his lap. "Like that wasn't enough?"

"You're more stubborn than I thought. You have to help. I'm freaking out here."

"Tell me what happened."

"Becca was supposed to meet me at three this afternoon, but she didn't show up. No call, no text, nothing."

Cassie couldn't bring herself to tell him about the mystery phone call from a man claiming Becca was dead. It could send him into a downward spiral, and besides, the call might have been a manipulation to rattle Cassie's nerves.

"I went by her apartment and cop cars were everywhere," he continued.

"That's because someone broke in. They slashed

cushions and tossed furniture. Do you know what they were looking for?"

He leaned back against the headrest. "Maybe."

"Clue me in."

"Money."

"Becca works two jobs to make rent. What money?"

He shook his head. "I can't."

"You'd better."

"I messed up, okay? There was so much of it and I didn't think they'd notice."

"Notice what?"

"Stop asking so many questions!"

"Hey, bub, you've taken me hostage so I'm allowed to ask as many questions as I like. Where are we going, by the way?"

"Somebody wants to meet you." He glanced at her, then away. "He'll help us get Becca back if you meet with him."

"Because he thinks I have something he wants? I don't have anything, Tony. You're dragging me into—"

"Just shut up!" he shouted.

Cassie pursed her lips, wanting to give him a lecture of a lifetime. Instead, she strategized ways to get help without being accidentally shot by Becca's crazy boyfriend.

"What's that?" Tony said, staring out the front windshield.

A car straddled the two-lane road up ahead, blocking traffic.

A patrol car.

"Go around it! Go around it!"

"But there's a drop off!"

Tony pressed his foot on top of hers, gunning the engine. To avoid a collision, she jerked the wheel right. They clipped the cruiser and slid off the road, barreling into the forest.

Heading straight for a tree.

"No!" she cried.

She jerked the wheel.

The car spun.

The back end slammed into a tree. The engine sputtered and died. She pinched her eyes shut, her heart pounding in her throat.

Breathe, she coached herself. *You're okay.*

"Cassie!"

Hearing Nate's voice made her feel better than okay.

She pried her eyes open and tried to focus on the man running toward her in the distance.

Then she remembered: Tony had a gun. She wanted to call out to Nate, to warn him, but struggled to get her voice back.

Backup was on the way. Nate couldn't wait. He sprinted toward the car Aiden had described as the kidnapper's.

Whoever had taken Cassie was in for a long night's interrogation. As he got closer, Nate could tell Cassie's eyes were open and she looked fairly coherent. He reached for his firearm, but was hesitant to use it. Opening fire on an assailant with Cassie in the middle was not an option.

"No!" she shouted at Nate just as…

A gunshot pierced the crisp night air.

Nate ducked, but not quick enough. A slow burn seared across his upper arm. Nothing, not even a gunshot wound, would stop him from getting to her. He'd have to be smart about it. Dropping to the ground, he crawled toward the car, clenching his teeth against the pain.

A young man in a black hoodie and jeans took off into the forest. Nate was about to pursue him when the perp turned and fired off multiple shots in Nate's direction.

With the car still between them.

Nate could only hope Cassie had the presence of mind to duck.

Staying low, Nate continued toward the car, assuming the perp's goal was to get away quickly and he couldn't do that with a hostage. Nate peered above the surrounding brush. The guy had disappeared into the forest. It made no sense for Nate to pursue him. The perp had the advantage of camouflage, and Nate would be an easy target.

He reached the car and cracked open the driver's side door. The old car didn't have an air bag. Nate searched Cassie's face for cuts and bruises.

"You okay?" he asked.

She glanced at his jacket and her eyes widened. "You've been shot." She started to unbuckle her seat belt.

"Don't move until the ambulance comes."

"I'm not hurt, but…" Her voice trailed off. She closed her eyes and took a deep breath, then another.

He suspected the full impact of what just happened—kidnapping and gunfire—must have finally hit her.

"Cassie?"

"I'm okay," she said. "Just scared."

He stroked her golden-blond hair. "There's nothing 'just' about being scared. Did the guy threaten you with a gun?"

She nodded. "It was Tony, Becca's boyfriend."

"Why did he take you hostage?"

"To meet someone who would help Tony find Becca, I think, I don't know for sure. But before that, at the resort, a man called my room. He had a deep, scratchy voice and said my friend was dead and I'd be next unless, but I hung up. Tony banged on the door. I let him in, I shouldn't have, because Bree and Mom wanted to come in and Tony pulled a gun and aimed it at the door and—"

"Shh, it's okay. Breathe." He continued to stroke her soft hair, hoping it would ease her anxiety.

She glanced at him. "I should be helping you. Let me out so I can put pressure on your wound."

"It's a flesh wound, no big deal. Relax until the EMTs check you out."

The wail of a siren echoed down the two-lane highway.

"What happened in the mountains?" she asked.

He hesitated, not wanting to upset her further.

"Nate, what is it?"

"We'll talk about it later." He took her hand. "I'm glad I got to you in time."

"Me, too." She brought his hand to her cheek and smiled.

An ache exploded in his chest. She could have been hurt or even killed. He slipped his hand from hers. "I'll flag down emergency. Stay put."

"Yes, Chief."

Nate stood, waving down the ambulance and squad car. Maddie, Cassie's cousin and a local EMT, came bounding toward them.

"Cassie?"

"She's okay."

She noticed Nate's wound. "Whoa, what about you?"

"I'm fine. Take care of your cousin."

Detective Vaughn screeched to a stop and flung open her car door. She marched toward Nate.

"Tony Miller took Cassie at gunpoint," he said.

"Where was he taking her?"

"Not sure, something about meeting a guy that would help find Becca."

"You want me to question her?"

"No, I'll take care of Cassie. I need you to figure out what they want from her. She received a threatening call at the resort."

Nate's phone vibrated, but he didn't recognize the number. "Chief Walsh."

"It's Agent Nance. I have some information to discuss with you."

"I'll send Detective Vaughn."

"I'd rather speak with you."

Nate wanted Detective Vaughn to take the lead so Nate could protect Cassie. But he was police chief and couldn't shirk his duties.

"Meet me at Healthy Eats in an hour," Nate said.

"Will do."

Nate ended the call and studied his phone.

"Who was that?" Vaughn asked.

"FBI agent wants to meet." He glanced back at Tony's car. Maddie was checking Cassie's vitals. Cassie smiled at Nate.

"Want me to meet with the Fed?" Detective Vaughn said.

"Actually, we're all going."

An hour later Nate and Detective Vaughn were seated across a booth from Agent Nance, while Cassie hid in the kitchen. That was the best way to keep her safe: make her invisible.

Nate's sister, Catherine, owner of Healthy Eats, was happy to brew them a pot of coffee after closing. Not that they'd stay long. Nate wanted the meeting with Nance to be quick so he could take Cassie someplace safe.

"That's what we suspect," Agent Nance said. "The Sartuchi family is smuggling their guys, who are out on bail, out of the country by way of Echo Mountain, Washington."

"Why here of all the places in the country?" Nate said.

"Haven't figured that out yet."

"Well, figure faster, people are getting hurt," Detective Vaughn shot back.

Agent Nance narrowed his eyes at her. "Did I do something to offend you?"

"Smuggling, how?" Nate redirected before Vaughn and the agent got into a shouting match.

"We think they hide out in the cabins for a week or two where they're given passports for their new identities, money and plane tickets," Agent Nance continued.

"But Sea-Tac airport is two hours away," Detective Vaughn said.

"They could take the airport bus," Nate offered. "For that matter, they could take a bus north into Canada."

"Whatever the case," Agent Nance continued, "we think they book lodging through Echo Mountain Rentals, and Becca Edwards and Tony Miller were hiding the passports and money in the cabins."

"Becca Edwards has no criminal record, and

her employers say she's a hard worker," Detective Vaughn said.

"Yet she's disappeared and her boyfriend took Cassie McBride hostage," Agent Nance countered. "Where is Cassie, anyway?"

"Safe," Nate said.

"She could be our best leverage to get Len Pragner to talk."

Nate didn't like the sound of that.

"How do you figure? She didn't see him commit the murder," Nate said.

"No, but she can put him at the scene." Nance leaned back in the booth. "I could take her off your hands, put her in federal custody to protect her, and give you time to work the murder case."

That wasn't happening. Before Nate could say so, Vaughn spoke up.

"How is Marilyn Brandenburg, the dead woman Cassie found in the tub, involved in this?"

"We've found no connection between her and the mob." Agent Nance glanced at Nate. "I was hoping you could share what you've got so far. Maybe we can piece together some answers."

Nate nodded at Detective Vaughn. "Go ahead."

"Marilyn was a nurse from Moscow, Idaho. Worked at Pullman Regional Hospital. Her sister said she wanted a little time away in the mountains. She'd been stressed out at work. She's divorced, kids are grown and married. She's squeaky clean, so why kill her?"

"Maybe she came across something at work?" Agent Nance said.

"She's a pediatric nurse," Vaughn countered.

"We're not going to solve this tonight," Nate said. "We appreciate you filling us in, and we'll give you information on the case as it develops."

"Becca and Tony could be the key to shutting this thing down and sending these guys away for serious jail time," Agent Nance said.

"So let's work together and make that happen," Nate said.

Agent Nance slipped out of the booth. "I'm getting a to-go coffee. Want one?" he asked Nate.

"Sure, thanks."

The FBI agent crossed the room to the coffee station and grabbed a few cups from the counter.

"He didn't offer to get me a coffee," Detective Vaughn said, crossing her arms over her chest.

"You don't drink coffee," Nate countered. "What do you make of all this?"

"Something feels seriously off."

"Agreed. For now, I'm taking Cassie someplace safe. I'll call Chief Washburn back in to help out."

"You sure you wanna do that? It might look like—"

"I don't care how it looks. Having his experience on the team is invaluable. This kind of thing shouldn't be happening in our town."

"No kidding," she said softly.

"I'll fill in Chief Washburn. His presence will keep people calm. You need to find Becca. Pull Red off patrol if you have to. I know he's been wanting to do more detective work."

"Will do. And the Marilyn Brandenburg murder?"

"Keep on forensics for results. Dig into her past. If she's involved, there's got to be a trail. I'll have the chief do background on Len. If he's a mob enforcer, we could use that to help the ADA build a case against him."

Agent Nance returned to the table with the coffees.

"Thanks." Nate got out of the booth and shook the agent's hand. "I'll be in touch."

"Sounds good." With a curt nod at Detective Vaughn, Agent Nance left the restaurant.

Vaughn frowned. "I don't trust him."

"Go home and get some sleep."

"What about you? I could relieve you at three a.m."

"No, I need one of us functioning on a full night's sleep. I'll conference call with you and Chief Washburn tomorrow morning at eight."

"You got it, Chief."

As Nate drove away from the restaurant, Cassie noticed how tired and defeated he looked, which only made her more determined to figure out a solution to this mess. It wasn't even her mess; it was obviously a mess of Tony's making, and he'd put Cassie's friend in danger.

"It was nice of Catherine to lend you her son's car so no one would recognize us," she said.

"Yep."

"Did it go well with the FBI agent?" she asked.

"Well enough."

She wanted to be a part of the investigation, to help solve the mystery of the dead woman and demanding stalkers. But it seemed like Nate wasn't up to more than one-or two-word answers. He kept checking the rearview mirror to make sure they weren't being followed.

"Did the agent have information about Tony?" she asked.

"Some." He took a sip of coffee.

"Can you share?"

"Tomorrow."

"Well, I could tell you what Tony said about getting into a mess because he didn't think they'd—"

"Cassie, save it until we get there, okay?"

"To the resort?"

"No, a safe house."

"Can you at least tell me who Tony and Becca got involved with?"

He shot her a quick glance. "We suspect this is mob-related."

"Wait, what, here? In Echo Mountain?"

He nodded. "Which is why we need to stay off everyone's radar. Be invisible for a few days."

"That's crazy. I mean there's like no crime in Echo Mountain. It's a nice town with good people and charming little shops."

She felt suddenly embarrassed by her chatty nature.

The poor guy needed quiet, needed to think, yet he was stuck with Cassie, jabber-jawing like a teenager.

She stretched her neck and closed her eyes. She'd be sore tomorrow from the car collision with the tree. Wherever Nate was taking her, she hoped it had a soft bed. A good night's sleep would certainly put her in a better frame of mind to piece things together. She'd start with Tony's comments, and then consider Becca's stressed behavior as of late, and rack her brain for anything she might have in her possession that didn't belong to her.

The car suddenly swerved and her eyes popped open. "Whoa." Gripping the dashboard, she glanced at Nate.

His eyes kept opening and closing, like he couldn't stay awake.

"Nate?"

"Sorry, I'm…I'm—"

A horn blared.

She glanced out the front window and was blinded by headlights of an oncoming car.

ELEVEN

Cassie instinctively grabbed the wheel and yanked it right to steer them out of the path of the car. Nate must have snapped out of his fog because he hit the brakes and the car swerved, coming to a stop on the shoulder.

Cassie shoved the car in Park and caught her breath. Then she leaned over and examined Nate. It looked like his wound had bled through his bandage.

"Nate, your arm." She glanced up. He seemed to be drifting in and out of consciousness. Could it be from blood loss?

"Nate? Nate, can you hear me?" she said.

"Cassie," he said, his voice weak.

A kind of determination shot through her that she didn't know existed, determination that would give her strength to get help for Nate and protect them from the mysterious threat.

She glanced out the back window. The driver of the vehicle that almost hit them was gone.

Nate said they needed to be invisible, which meant she shouldn't call 911 because an ambulance would transport them to the hospital, a very public place.

She hit the hazard lights so they'd be visible to motorists on the dark road, and then plucked his phone out of the holder on the dashboard. With unusual calm, she scrolled through his contacts. She spotted Dr. Spencer's number and made the call, holding her breath.

"Hey, buddy, I heard you were in a gunfight," he answered.

"It's Cassie," she said. "I need your help. Nate is semiconscious and needs medical attention."

"I'll send an ambulance."

"No, we have to stay under the radar because they think the mob is somehow tied to all this and...and..." She composed herself. "We need to hide out where no one will find us."

"What's his condition?"

"Groggy, drifting in and out of consciousness, and he's bleeding through his bandage."

"Where are you?"

"Highway Two, about five minutes north of Healthy Eats."

"My cabin is ten miles northwest of your location. Take Highway Two four miles and turn left on Rushing River Drive. Follow that until it becomes a one-lane road, then look for the rooster mailbox and turn left. That's my driveway. I'll meet you there as soon as I can."

"You're not home?"

"At the hospital. I'll leave right away. Is his wound seeping or oozing?"

She carefully pulled his jacket down off his shoulder and eyed the dressing. "It seems to be seeping through his bandage."

"Okay, meet me at the cabin."

"Thanks." She shifted Nate's jacket back on and placed her palm against his cheek. "Hey, you'll be okay."

"Cassie," he muttered. "Gotta keep her safe."

"We're safe. But I need you to move over. Here, I'll get out and—"

He gripped her hand and his intense green eyes popped open. A chill danced down her spine.

"I have to protect you." His voice cracked.

"You are protecting me. It's all good. Trust me?"

He nodded, his eyes drifting shut. She slipped her hand out of his and went around to the driver's side. She opened the door and knelt beside him. "Nate, I need you to move over, can you do that?"

"Yeah, what?"

"Move to the passenger seat."

He nodded and started to shift across the seat. She was grateful that the old car had a bench seat or this would be quite challenging.

"That's it," she coached.

He hesitated. "Cassie?"

"I'm here. Move over so I can drive."

A car honked and she jumped, startled. So focused on Nate, she hadn't sensed a motorist pull over on the other side of the highway. She had to pay more attention to her surroundings.

To the potential danger.

The driver lowered his window. He was an older man, in his sixties. She didn't recognize him.

A part of her wondered if he was with the mob,

while another part countered that he could be a local. Even if he was, she didn't want him telling stories about a nearly passed-out chief of police. She blocked his view of the front seat.

"Everything okay?" he asked.

"Yes, thank you. We're good."

"I saw the hazard lights so I thought I'd stop, offer to help."

"That was awfully nice of you. My friend suddenly took ill while driving, but we're A-okay." She tried not to sound too forced.

"Are you sure?" He started to get out of his truck.

"Absolutely." With a pleasant smile, she slid behind the wheel of the car, shut and locked the door, and buckled up. Putting the car in gear, she waved at the man and pulled onto the highway. Glancing in the rearview mirror, she watched the Good Samaritan get back into his truck, but he didn't pull away.

Cassie pressed down on the accelerator, wanting to put distance between them. She simply couldn't trust anyone she didn't know, and even some people she did know.

Becca. Cassie still couldn't believe how Becca had fallen under Tony's influence. It started months ago when Becca broke dates with Cassie because Tony wanted Becca to stay home with him. Cassie would never get romantically involved with a controlling man like that, a controlling and potentially criminal man in Becca's case. What kind of trouble had Tony gotten them into?

She eyed the rearview mirror, but there was no one behind her and she could no longer see the Good Samaritan's truck parked on the side of the road. He must have been exactly who he said he was: a motorist who'd stopped to help.

Cassie didn't like feeling suspicious of everyone she encountered. Maybe if Nate had shared more about what he'd learned from the FBI agent that would have given her some solace or peace. But he'd been short with his answers, and now she understood why: he was struggling to stay conscious to fight off whatever was plaguing him. She hoped it wasn't an infection from the bullet wound.

She stopped herself from slipping into panic mode. Her new role was that of protector, not protectee. She had to take care of Nate for a change, and so far she was doing a decent job. They were on their way to meet the doctor who would treat Nate and assess his condition.

"Wait…where are we going?" he said, opening his eyes.

"We're meeting Dr. Spencer."

"No, can't go to the hospital," he said in a panicked voice.

"We're going to his cabin. No one will find us there."

He nodded and leaned back against the seat. A moment later he mumbled, "I had a place, a better place…they wouldn't find you…"

"Shush. I've got this. And you know why?"

He glanced in her direction, his eyes unfocused.

"Because I'm smarter than I look, big guy. And you know how I can prove it?"

He shook his head indicating that he didn't.

"Because I climbed down a mountain with a dog in my arms and hid from creepy Shovel Man."

"Shovel Man," he repeated.

"He might have called out my name, but he didn't know where I'd gone." She tapped her finger against her temple. "I used my head. Just like I'm doing now. I've got my eye on the rearview to make sure we're not being followed. We're not. And we'll go to Dr. Spencer's cabin for private medical attention. See how smart I am?"

"Y-e-ah," he said, slowly.

She realized by talking to him, she could ease his anxiety. So she'd keep at it.

"You're in good hands, and you don't need to worry about anything. We'll take care of you. I'm just sorry I don't have EMT training like my cousin Maddie. I could have assessed your wound better and maybe even re-dressed it. Then again, I don't have first aid supplies with me. That wouldn't stop Aiden, of course. He was always finding solutions to problems, even as a little kid. Dad called him Mr. Fix-It. I think that's why Aiden's so good at being a resort manager. He knows how to fix things—well, most things. His relationship with his sister? Not so much."

She glanced across the front seat. Nate's eyes were

closed. Smiling to herself, she was proud that her non-stop chatter had actually soothed him.

"What happened?" Nate said.

"What do you mean?"

"You stopped talking."

"I thought you were asleep."

"Don't stop."

She smiled and launched into her plans to explore castles in Europe.

Nate drifted. Half awake, half asleep. He wasn't sure what was real and what was a dream. He couldn't remember what day it was, or even where he was.

But he remembered her voice, that sweet, melodic voice of Cassie's that somehow eased the tension from his muscles, and the dread from his thoughts. She talked about castles and islands in Ireland, and cliffs overlooking the Atlantic Ocean. He drifted, picturing the Irish countryside and the vast ocean.

Then she'd said, *You're okay*, and he went dark, passed out or fell asleep.

Leaving her vulnerable. The sweet girl with a big heart. He'd left her at the mercy of mob thugs. The image of Becca's boot and jacket haunted him. What if they got to Cassie, what if…

"Cassie." He opened his eyes and sat up.

"I'm here."

He glanced to his left and saw her get up from the kitchen table. She was beside him in seconds, placing her warm hand on his shoulder, his bare shoulder. He glanced down at his naked chest.

"How are you feeling, Chief?" Spence asked, coming into view over Cassie's shoulder.

Spence must have taken off Nate's shirt in order to treat his wound. "I... How did I get here?"

"Cassie called me last night with an SOS so I had her meet me at the cabin," Spence said. "Needed to re-dress the wound and check you out."

"I don't remember that," he said.

"You were pretty out of it," she offered.

"I passed out?"

"It's okay," she said. "I got us here. And you even had a good night's sleep."

"Someone could have followed us." He stood and wavered.

"Whoa, take it easy." Spence gripped his arm.

"What time is it?" Nate asked.

"Seven thirty," Cassie said.

"I've got a conference call at eight a.m." He looked around for his shirt.

"Here." Cassie grabbed a throw blanket off the sofa and draped it across his shoulders. She and Spence stayed close as Nate shuffled to the table. With each step he seemed to get his strength back.

He shifted onto a chair and Spence checked his vitals. Cassie grabbed mugs out of a cupboard.

"I'm fine," Nate said to Spence.

"You're not fine or you wouldn't have passed out

last night," Cassie said. "Then again, maybe it was my chatter that put you to sleep."

Oh yeah, her melodic voice telling him stories about her family, Aiden's fight with his dad about joining the army, and Bree's decision to move to the city against her parents' wishes.

Nate also remembered a wave of calm washing over him as she chatted away. How was that possible? The answer was too simple to ignore: he was falling for her.

"I'm okay, right, Doc?" Nate asked.

"Your vitals look good this morning. Last night your blood pressure was unusually low, so we took turns keeping an eye on you. You didn't lose that much blood from the bullet wound, and without blood work I can't make an official diagnosis. You could be suffering from exhaustion or dehydration or a combination of both. When was the last time you ate or slept?"

"I haven't seen him do much of either since he rescued me from the mountain ledge," Cassie said.

She slid a bowl of oatmeal in front of him along with a mug of tea. "Drink this." She sat at the table.

"I was hoping for coffee."

"Tea is healthier than coffee."

Nate glanced at Spence for help.

"Sorry, buddy, but I'm not getting in the middle of this," Spence said.

"Not to lecture or anything," Cassie started. "You're

great at taking care of everyone else, Chief, but not so much yourself."

"I've been a little busy," he shot back.

"I know, I'm sorry."

"Hey." He reached out and took her hand. "No more apologizing for things that aren't your fault."

"Well, if it weren't for my predicament you'd be sleeping and eating better, that's for sure."

"You're not responsible for what's happening, got it?"

"Yeah, thanks."

He tried releasing her hand, but she wouldn't let go.

"So what is happening, exactly?" she asked. "What did the FBI agent tell you?"

He spent the next twenty minutes going over the details of the case, from the smuggling of bail jumpers, to the suspicion of someone at Echo Mountain Rentals being involved.

Nate respected Cassie's need to know what kind of trouble she'd been pulled into, and it was important that Spence be kept in the loop, especially since he was offering to shelter them from criminals.

"And what about Becca?" Cassie asked.

"No sign of her. We found her jacket, a boot, hat, gloves and a scarf up in the mountains."

"Oh, Becca." Cassie interlaced her fingers and closed her eyes.

Nate assumed she was praying for her friend. He bowed his head and waited, wishing he could pray. If he did, it would be for Cassie's safety.

"Amen," she whispered, and looked at Nate. "What happens next? How do we put these guys in jail?"

"The FBI is building a case, but they need witnesses, and we're hoping Becca and Tony would step forward to testify."

"And if they can't find Becca and Tony?"

"You saw Len Pragner at the cabin. You're the best thing they've got to putting him at the scene of the murder."

"But I didn't see anything other than him carrying a shovel."

"They want to use that as leverage."

"Huh," she said.

Nate sensed something was brewing behind her bright blue eyes. "Cassie?"

"I'll get more firewood," Spence offered, probably to give them privacy.

"No, you should hear this, too," Cassie said.

"Hear what?" Nate said.

"I made a decision while you were unconscious last night."

He eyed her. "I have a feeling I'm not going to like this."

"My bad timing will not prevent you from solving this case."

"Bad timing?"

"You know, wrong place, wrong time."

"Cassie—"

"You should be investigating that woman's murder, not babysitting me."

"You're a potential witness to a homicide, and someone is after you because they think you have something that belongs to them. My job is to keep you safe until we solve both the murder and the smuggling operation."

"Well, my new goal is to stop being a victim and help you do just that." She hesitated. "If you're up to it."

"I'm fine."

"Good." She glanced at Spence. "Do you have paper and pens?"

"I think I might have some in the office, hang on." Spence disappeared into a spare room.

She pushed Nate's oatmeal closer to him. "Eat."

"What's with the paper and pens?"

"I'm going to help you do your job."

He started to protest.

"I may seem like a ditz," she said, cutting him off. "I talk too much and act happy all the time. But when I was stuck in bed as a kid, I read anything and everything to help me escape my life. I'm pretty smart, Nate, and I plan to help you solve the murder and find Becca."

Although he was tempted to tell her there was no way he'd allow her to get more involved in these cases, he had to appreciate her enthusiasm.

"I suppose nothing I say will change your mind," he half joked.

"You know me so well. Now eat, or do you need me to feed you?" She reached for the spoon.

"Don't even think about it." He grabbed the spoon and caught her smiling at him. They were sharing a playful moment while embroiled in a crisis.

But he couldn't risk the distraction.

He took a bite of his oatmeal and considered ways of distancing himself without hurting her feelings.

"Who's the call with?" she asked.

He swallowed his oatmeal. "Detective Vaughn and Chief Washburn."

"Chief Washburn? But he's retired."

"I called him in to handle things while I'm out in the field."

"Oh, you don't think, I mean, will that look like—"

"I don't care."

"But you like your job."

He glanced into her eyes, but had no words. What could he say? That he liked his job, but he liked her more? That somehow over the last year her sweet nature had gotten under his skin and he hadn't realized until just today how much he cared about her?

No, he couldn't say any of that.

"The chief's presence will make folks feel safe," he said.

Cassie didn't look convinced.

"I'd better call in." He started to get up, but she stopped him.

"Oh no, you stay right there. And put it on speaker so I can hear."

"I don't think—"

"I won't say a word, promise."

Spence came back into the main living area and placed paper and pens on the kitchen table. "How can I help?"

"When's your next shift?" Nate asked.

"I'm supposed to stop by the urgent care later this morning, but I can find someone to cover."

"No, don't. Continue your normal routine. I don't want to put you in danger because they suspect you're helping us."

"Got it. You two can stay here as long as necessary."

"How many people know about the cabin?" Nate asked.

"Well, you're my first guests, so no one."

"I'm sorry we had to impose on your sanctuary," Cassie offered.

"It's not like that. I just haven't had time for a social life."

Nate sensed there was more to it. Spence was a skilled doctor and a dedicated SAR team member, but he kept his secrets to himself. Nate suspected Spence had experienced some sort of trauma before coming to Echo Mountain that haunted him.

"We appreciate everything you've done for us," Cassie offered.

"Of course." Spence bundled up. "I'm off to get more wood. There's an extra SAR T-shirt for you on the end table." Spence left and the cabin grew oddly quiet.

Nate and Cassie usually seemed comfortable with

each other, but for some reason tension stretched between them.

"I charged your phone last night." Cassie went to the counter and grabbed Nate's phone.

"You think of everything."

"I hope so." She placed it in front of him.

"You may not want to hear this call," he said. "If they found Becca—"

"It's okay. I can handle it. I need to help, Nate."

With a nod, he called the station.

"Good morning, Chief," Chief Washburn said.

"Good morning. Is Detective Vaughn with you?"

"Yes, sir," she responded.

"And Cassie McBride is with me," Nate said. "Do we have an update?"

"Got preliminary forensics," Vaughn said.

"That was quick."

"I called in a few favors," Chief Washburn said.

"Thanks."

"Our victim in the cabin died from blunt force trauma, but they found no blood evidence on the shovel to indicate it was the murder weapon. It confirms what we suspected, that she hit her head on the tub," Detective Vaughn started. "Not helpful, I know."

"What about prints?"

"Couldn't find Len Pragner's anywhere. He's in the system so they should have popped pretty quick."

"So we can put him outside the cabin, but not inside," Nate said. "Must have been wearing gloves."

"The thing that bothers me is there's no connection

between Marilyn Brandenburg and this whole mob thing," Chief Washburn said.

"Okay, so let's look at this as two completely different crimes: Marilyn's murder, and smuggling bail jumpers out of the country. Vaughn, you've interviewed people in the victim's life. Is there any clear motivation why someone would want her dead?"

"None, sir."

"Maybe she's like me," Cassie interjected, then placed her hand over her mouth.

"Go ahead," Nate encouraged.

"Well, maybe she was in the wrong place at the wrong time. She was late checking out of the cabin and Shovel—I mean Len Pragner was looking for Tony or Becca, but found Marilyn instead. I mean, Becca was originally supposed to be there."

"Which still doesn't explain why Marilyn was murdered," Detective Vaughn said. "Why risk killing a random tourist?"

"Finding Becca and Tony will help us fill in the blanks," Nate said. "Let's focus our efforts in that direction." He glanced at Cassie. "What did Tony say to you in the car?"

"That someone wanted to talk to me and in return that person was going to help Tony get Becca back."

Nate fisted his hand at the thought of Cassie being taken to a meeting with mob thugs.

"Sounds like the mob's got guys in town," Chief Washburn said.

"We have to assume so, yes," Nate said.

"Tony also said something about messing up, that there was so much of it and he didn't think they'd notice?" Cassie offered.

"Now it's making sense," Nate said. "These two were skimming."

"From the mob," Chief Washburn added. "What were they thinking?"

"We have to find them before the mob does," Nate said. "If they haven't already."

"Maybe it's time to enlist the town for help," Chief Washburn said.

"I don't want to cause panic or put innocents in danger," Nate countered.

"It wouldn't hurt to have a few key folks keep an eye on things, let us know about strangers in town," Chief Washburn said.

Nate stood, feeling suddenly like a failure. "It's my job to protect them. I don't want to put them at risk."

"You won't, son. I'm talking about folks like Harvey, and Grace Longfellow of SAR. They always know what's going on in town. It's in their nature."

"If you think they will respect the boundaries and not risk their safety."

"Absolutely," Chief Washburn said.

"Then I trust your judgment," Nate said. "Detective, put out a BOLO on Becca and Tony."

"Yes, sir."

"You keep that young lady safe," Chief Washburn said.

"That's the plan. I'll check in later."

Nate collapsed against the wooden chair. Cassie offered a halfhearted smile. "You didn't finish your oatmeal."

"Lost my appetite."

"Hey." She touched his hand resting on the table. "You're doing the best you can. That's all anyone can ask."

"I've been chief for less than a year and it feels like it's all coming apart on me. You'd think, with my experience, I could get ahead of things."

"No one could have expected something like this to happen in our town. The mob? Come on."

Nate eyed her. "Hang on, you're right."

"I am?"

"There has to be a direct connection between the mob and Echo Mountain." Nate stood and paced to the sofa. He shucked the blanket and put on the long-sleeved shirt Spence had left him. "We need to approach this from a different angle. The mob wouldn't randomly pick Echo Mountain, so what's the connection?"

"That's why I've got pen and paper. We'll write everything down and—"

The front door burst open and Spence hovered in the doorway. "You've gotta get out of here. Now!"

TWELVE

"What happened?" Nate said.

"An SUV is coming up the drive. Take this." He grabbed a jacket off the coatrack by the door and tossed it at Nate. "It will keep you warm in the mountains. Cassie, get my spare pack out of the closet. It's well stocked with food and supplies for a couple days."

Cassie did as ordered, trying not to think about the potential danger headed toward them. She flung her shoulder bag across her body and waited for further instruction.

Spence grabbed car keys off the table. "Let's go."

Cassie handed Nate the backpack, and they rushed out of the cabin.

Once outside, the doctor pointed toward a trail that disappeared behind a cluster of spruce. "The other end of that trail will drop you at the mouth of Lake Serene. You can find your way back to town from there."

Nate gripped his friend's arm. "You're coming with us."

"No, I'll throw them off by driving your car in the opposite direction."

"Spence—"

"Go, I know what I'm doing."

"But—"

"I'll call 911 if I need help. Move it."

As they headed for the trail, Nate glanced over his shoulder.

"I've got this!" Spence called.

Nate shifted Cassie ahead of him and they practically sprinted into the woods. Neither spoke for a good few minutes. Once out of sight, Nate touched her shoulder. "Hang on a sec."

Nate peered through the thick mass of western red cedar and Douglas fir trees to the cabin below.

Cassie looked as well, trying to calm her frantic heartbeat. The SUV slowly rolled up the driveway as if the men inside were deciding the best way to approach the cabin.

"Come on, Spence, get out of there," Nate muttered.

The air seemed colder, crisper, than a minute ago as they anxiously waited to make sure their friend had escaped. The front door to the cabin was still open and Dr. Spencer was nowhere in sight. She automatically dug her fingers into Nate's arm.

The ominous dark SUV stopped at the end of Dr. Spencer's driveway. Was the doctor still inside?

"Call for help," Cassie said to Nate.

"They wouldn't get here in time."

Three men got out of the SUV. One wore a black trench coat that could easily conceal a weapon. They scanned the mountain range, as if looking for Cassie and Nate.

"Hang on," Nate said. "I recognize one of those guys from Becca's tour group. The one with the ski cap."

The obvious leader in the trench coat said something to the other men. They approached the cabin.

"I need to help Spence," Nate said.

Panic shot through Cassie's body. "He said he had a plan." She was desperate not to lose Nate to these violent men.

He took her hands in his and looked into her eyes. "Cassie, I can't abandon my friend."

She nodded, understanding that guilt about his partner's death was driving him to protect the doctor. He leaned forward and kissed her cheek.

It was a goodbye kiss.

"Follow the trail like Spence told you," he said, taking off the backpack. "And don't look back, no matter what you hear, got it?"

She didn't nod this time; she couldn't.

He turned to hike down the trail when Cassie noticed something out of the corner of her eye.

A car speeding away from the cabin.

"Wait, look," she said.

It was Dr. Spencer driving Nate's nephew's car. "He must have been hiding in the car the whole time."

"He was waiting for them to go into the cabin so he could get a head start."

The guy in the trench coat hit the horn and the men scrambled out of the cabin. One got into the car with trench coat man, while the third remained behind.

The SUV took off after Dr. Spencer, just as he'd hoped.

"Why aren't they both going?" Cassie said.

"They can't be sure we're in the car." The third man went into the cabin and shut the door.

"So they're leaving him in case we come back?" Cassie said.

"Looks like." Nate pulled out his phone and called Detective Vaughn. He gave her the make, model and license plate for the car he'd borrowed from his sister. "Spence is driving and he's being pursued by some suspicious-looking men. Get him help. Also, they left one of their guys at the cabin. Yep…we're headed into the mountains, gonna attempt to disappear for a while." Nate pocketed his phone and nodded at Cassie. "All right, let's go."

They hiked for hours, and Cassie figured it was nearly noon when they finally reached Lake Serene. She had been pretty good about monitoring her questions and general chatter. Asking Nate every ten minutes if he was feeling okay wasn't going to make him any healthier, and would probably drive him nutty. Still, she worried about his bullet wound and his energy level.

"We should probably stop for a snack," Nate said.

She touched his jacket sleeve. "Are you tired? Hungry? Dizzy?"

"Cassie." He paused and offered a smile. "I'm fine. But it's been at least four hours since you've eaten. I imagine Dr. Spencer has snacks in his backpack."

He shucked the pack and eyed her. "What's wrong?"

"What do you mean?" Cassie sat down on a nearby rock.

Nate took out a bag of trail mix. "You've been too quiet. Are you worn out from hiking?"

"No, hiking is invigorating."

"But you haven't said much."

"I figured you liked the quiet."

He offered her the trail mix and she dug out a handful.

"I like it quiet, sometimes," he said, scanning their surroundings. "Other times I appreciate the sound of your voice."

"Yeah, it's like background music," she joked.

"It's more than that." He reached over and tipped her chin with a bent forefinger.

"You know I'll do my best to protect you, right?"

"Yes."

With a confident nod, he popped some trail mix into his mouth. They ate in companionable silence. It struck her that she didn't feel the need to jabber away when she was with Nate. Totally comfortable in his presence, she was simply enjoying the fresh air and a moment of peace.

Nate's ringing phone shattered the serenity.

"Detective?" he answered, then frowned. "I see." He stood and took a few steps toward the lake.

Cassie wondered if he didn't want her hearing details about the case. Bad news, perhaps? As she watched him pace back and forth, she realized he was frustrated.

"I'm not sure yet. Our goal was to make it to Lake Serene… Yes. Thanks." He glanced at Cassie. "They lost track of the car following Spence, but he's okay."

"You don't sound happy."

"I shouldn't have let him lure those guys away like that. It put him in the eye of the storm."

"It was his idea, and he's okay, right?"

Nate nodded. "He took the risk because he wanted us to be safe, so we should keep going." She picked up the backpack, but Nate took it away from her.

"I got it."

"Your wound—"

"It's fine." He strapped on the pack and motioned her ahead.

The trail was wide enough that they could walk side by side, a good thing since she sensed he needed to talk.

"What's the plan, Chief?" she said.

"Find temporary shelter until we can get to the safe house, which has been a challenge. I still can't figure out how they found us at Spence's cabin."

"Speaking of temporary shelter, I have an idea. Echo Mountain Rentals has a few properties under construction. What if we stayed in one of those?"

"But the work crews—"

"Construction is on hold for two of the cabins due to some kind of contract issue or something, I don't know the details. The properties are sitting vacant. I think the closest one is Horizon Point."

"How far?"

"I'm guessing about three miles east of here? Let me check the map." Nate hesitated and she dug it out of the side pocket of the pack. "Yep, here it is. Actually, we might be able to avoid major roads and cut through here." She pointed to a trail. She folded the map. "We should probably notify Mr. Anderson so no one calls the police on us."

"Not a good idea. I don't know who I can trust."

"Mr. Anderson's a good guy, a little scattered, but that's why he has Carol."

"Yet she couldn't keep the personnel files safely locked."

"We all make mistakes. Even you," she teased.

Nate didn't smile and seemed to fall into deep thought. She wondered if he was still beating himself up about Dr. Spencer.

Rather than try to talk him out of his self-recrimination, Cassie silently asked God to lighten the burden from his heart. He was such a good, kind man, a man who could seem impenetrable on the outside, but she knew he was gentle on the inside. He didn't deserve to suffer.

"I know what you're doing," he said.

"Excuse me?"

"You're praying for me, aren't you?"

"What if I am?" She glanced sideways at him.

"I guess—" he hesitated "—I'd say, thank you."

"You're welcome."

They continued along the trail, Cassie pleased that he appreciated her prayers. Silence once again stretched between them like a line connecting a boat to a buoy. Even in silence they'd become close. She never imagined that could happen, especially with a man like Nate.

"I've been negligent," Nate suddenly said.

"What do you mean?"

"With God. Actually, I've been without God since, well, I'm not sure I've ever had a relationship like that."

"God is always there for you, Nate. 'An ever-present help in trouble,' according to the Bible."

She took his hand, thinking the contact might make him feel less alone, less distanced from both her and the Lord.

"You are…remarkable," he said, squeezing her hand.

In that moment she felt something much stronger than friendship blossoming between them, and it wasn't one-sided on her part. Could it be that a life-threatening crisis had brought them together and made them realize they had feelings for each other? The corners of his lips raised slightly as he glanced at her.

Sudden movement caught her eye over his shoulder. Before she could register what was happening, a man hurled himself out of nowhere at Nate.

"No!" she cried.

Nate automatically pushed her aside and whipped around as the attacker slammed into him. The men hit the ground and rolled a few times, the guttural sounds sending shivers down her arms. The awkward pack put Nate at a disadvantage.

Cassie scanned the immediate area looking for a weapon and spotted a thick branch a few feet away. But could she use it on the attacker? The guy, in his forties wearing a blue knit cap, wrapped his arm around Nate's neck and strangled him from behind.

"Let him go!" she shouted.

The man tightened his grip. Nate swung his arms, trying to break free.

The guy jerked his arm again.

Nate's legs buckled.

Both men went down.

"God forgive me," she whispered.

She grabbed the branch, about the length of a base-ball bat, and swung, hitting the man in the back.

He jerked in response, but didn't let go of Nate.

She was not going to watch a criminal murder Nate.

The love of her life.

"I said, let go!" she warned.

The guy squeezed tighter. Nate's arms went limp by his sides. Complete and utter panic drove her to swing the branch again and again. The third swing connected with the guy's head.

He suddenly let go of Nate and stumbled to his

feet. Nate rolled onto his side, coughing and gasping for air.

He was alive. She sighed with relief.

The attacker took a step toward her, his eyes flaring with rage.

She fought back paralyzing fear and considered her next move. Much bigger than her five-foot-three-inch frame, the guy could easily take away the branch and even use it on her. Yet she knew they didn't want her dead because they thought she had something of theirs.

"Stay away," she threatened, clinging to the branch. She just needed to buy enough time for Nate to regain his strength.

The man took another step toward her.

She was not a defenseless woman. She'd taken a self-defense class with her sister, Bree, when she'd returned to Echo Mountain.

He took another step.

"What do you want?" she demanded.

A sinister smile eased across his lips.

He stepped closer.

She jabbed the branch at his crotch. He instinctively pitched forward to protect himself and she swung the branch, hard, nailing him on the side of the head.

He collapsed, seemingly dazed. She stood there for a few seconds, heart pounding in her ears, a little dizzy from the adrenaline rush.

Cassie scrambled to Nate. "Are you okay?"

"Yeah."

The attacker moaned.

Adrenaline reignited her body. She grabbed Nate's gun out of his holster and aimed at the guy.

"Don't move!" she threatened, even though she didn't know much about guns and the safety was probably still in place.

The guy went still, either because she'd threatened him or because he was unconscious.

She glared down the barrel of the weapon, hoping the threat of being shot would be enough to keep him from coming after her or Nate.

"Cassie," Nate said, his voice hoarse.

She couldn't speak. Couldn't even form words. A metallic taste filled her mouth. She could see her hands trembling as they gripped the gun, but she was not letting go.

Had to protect Nate. He'd been hurt enough.

"Cassie."

She felt Nate's hand touch her shoulder from behind, then slide down her arm. "It's okay. Release the gun."

With gentle pressure, he eased her arm down so she was no longer aiming at their attacker.

"Let go," he said.

She nodded, but her fingers were locked in place, like they were glued to the cool metal.

"It's okay," he whispered against her ear.

The warmth of his breath filtered down her arm, easing the tension from her fingers.

"That's it, just relax."

A burst of air escaped her lips. She'd been holding her breath.

"Shh, you're doing great," Nate coached.

She willed herself to unclench the gun, but it was like someone else's hand was attached to her body.

Nate wrapped his fingers around her hand. His warm palm blanketed her knuckles and seemed to melt her frozen joints. She stretched her fingers, releasing the gun. Nate eased it out of her grip.

"That's it," he hushed.

"I…I was protecting you."

"Yes, you were. And you did an excellent job."

Nate steadied his hand as he retrieved the gun from Cassie, not wanting her to see that he was shaking, as well. She might be trembling from the adrenaline rush of violence, but Nate's body trembled from the lack of oxygen. He'd almost been strangled to death.

In front of Cassie.

He'd been distracted by her beauty and kindness, and had almost gotten them both killed. Well, Nate would have been killed. It was pretty clear they wouldn't kill Cassie until they got answers.

"Are you okay?" he asked, his lips touching her soft blond hair.

"Yes."

He aimed the gun at their motionless attacker, the guy from Becca's tour group. It never should have gotten this far. Cassie shouldn't have been put in the position of having to shoot a man. The trauma of wounding or killing another human being would have stayed with her forever.

Changed her forever.

It was Nate's fault. He'd drifted into a false sense of security out here in the wilderness while looking into her expressive blue eyes.

Nate approached their attacker. Blood trailed down the side of the man's head. Nate nudged him with his boot, but the guy didn't respond. He knelt and pressed the barrel of the gun against the guy's forehead.

"I will pull the trigger if you make a move," he warned.

Again, no response.

Nate pressed two fingers against the man's neck to feel for a pulse.

"Is he… Did I?" Cassie uttered in a shaky voice.

"He's alive. Can you go into the backpack and find a first aid kit and some rope?"

When she didn't move, Nate glanced at her. Eyes wide, she continued to stare at the wounded man. It was as if she had just awakened from a dream and realized what she'd done, that she'd inflicted the head injury and caused all the blood.

"Rope and first aid?" he prompted in a firm tone.

Her gaze shot up to meet his. "Oh, right."

She dug into Spence's backpack, strapped to Nate's back. A moment later she handed him rope.

"You need to bind his wrists." With the gun still pointed at the guy, Nate rolled him onto his stomach.

Cassie pulled his wrists behind his back and bound them as tightly as she could. Nate holstered his gun and pulled the knot even tighter.

Nate used remaining rope to secure the man to a nearby tree, where he assessed his injuries.

"Head wound doesn't look too serious." Nate wiped the gash clean and applied a bandage. "That's all we can do for him. We'd better go. He may not be alone." Nate packed up the supplies.

"We…leave him here?"

"Yes, but I'll get him help." Nate led Cassie away and called in. "This is Chief Walsh. I need a law enforcement team to retrieve a suspect, midforties, just north of Lake Serene on the trail. He's tied to a tree and unconscious. I administered first aid, but he's dangerous. Proceed with caution, over."

Cassie glanced at their attacker. "He was going to kill you."

Nate put his arm around her, hoping to ease her anxiety. She didn't push away, yet he felt her body stiffen.

He let his arm slide off her shoulder and they walked in silence. It was a different kind of silence than before. He felt like he was losing her somehow.

Hours later, utterly exhausted by the day's journey hiking through the mountains, Cassie was starting to feel weak for the first time in many years. She fought anxiety about her condition possibly flaring up. These could be normal aches and pains, nothing related to the autoimmune disease that plagued her as a child.

Don't give in to the fear, she told herself.

Not so easy.

Nate would start a conversation with her, probably because she was too quiet, and she'd struggle to find the strength for small talk.

That jerk almost killed Nate.

Right in front of her.

She shuddered at the memory of Nate's arms going limp.

"Cassie," Nate started. "Next time someone comes after me, promise you'll take off and find a safe place to hide."

"I can't make that promise."

"Look." He stopped and gripped her arms. "If I die trying to protect you, I'd like some peace of mind that at least I saved your life. Promise me you'll put yourself first."

There was desperation in his serious green eyes, and pain. Lots of pain.

"Okay, okay." She glanced away and he released her.

After hiking in awkward silence for another half an hour, she spotted the cabin. "There." She pointed to the one-story rental in the clearing below, with a gravel driveway and wooden porch.

As she started down the trail, Nate blocked her. "I'll go first. You stay back until I signal that it's safe."

"No," she said.

"Cassie—"

"You would have been killed if I hadn't been with you. We stick together, Nate. We're better together."

She walked around him, realizing she'd never been that direct with anyone in her life. Maybe it was exhaustion. Maybe it was hunger.

Or maybe she'd finally found her voice.

"Hey, hey," he said, catching up to her. "I'm just trying to keep you safe."

"I know, and I appreciate that."

"But?"

"I guess I'm hungry and tired."

"There's dehydrated food in the pack. We can heat that up for dinner."

Twilight illuminated the property as they approached the cabin. Cassie punched in the override code that unlocked all property doors.

"At least let me go in first," Nate said.

She stepped aside, understanding his need to take the lead. He placed the backpack on the porch, turned the door handle and went inside.

The door slowly eased shut behind him.

Cassie put her hand on the heavy oak to keep it open.

And saw something come down against Nate's head from behind.

THIRTEEN

Cassie snapped her hand back in shock.

The door clicked shut.

Heart pounding, she darted to the side of the cabin, spotted a small shed and ducked inside. It was her instinct to run, find safety and regroup. She could call for help, but they wouldn't get here in time to do any good. No, she was on her own.

Nate would want her to flee, hike to safety. He'd made her promise to leave him behind.

A light sparkled through the crack in the shed door. Someone was searching the area with a flashlight. And he was headed in her direction. Cassie dug into her bag for keys.

The ball of light grew bigger, brighter.

Her fingers touched a small canister of pepper spray Bree had given her. She calmed her frantic heartbeat and waited for the door to open.

God give me strength.

She blinked to clear her vision.

It seemed like it was taking forever for the guy to find her.

"Who's in there?" a woman demanded.

Cassie recognized that voice.

"Becca?" Cassie flung open the shed door.

Becca lowered a two-by-four she had been gripping as a weapon. "Cassie?"

She threw her arms around Cassie and gave her

a hug. Cassie hugged her back, although she still gripped the pepper spray and keys.

Becca released her. "What are you doing here? It's dangerous, a man—"

"Nate." Cassie took off for the house.

"Cassie, don't! There's a guy—"

"Nate Walsh! It's the police chief!" Cassie called over her shoulder. She raced into the cabin and froze at the sight of Nate, unconscious on the floor. Dropping to her knees beside him, Cassie said, "Nate, can you hear me? Come on, open your eyes."

Footsteps pounded on the porch and Becca rushed up behind Cassie.

"I didn't see him, Cassie, I didn't know who it was. Honest, I never would have—"

"What'd you hit him with?"

"A two-by-four."

Cassie ran her hand across the side of Nate's head. "Go get the backpack on the porch. Quick!"

Becca dashed out of the cabin.

"Nate, can you hear me?"

When he didn't respond, she stroked her thumb across his cheek. "You'll be okay. You have to be okay," she whispered. "Ya know why? Because I love you. I've never loved anyone like this before, so could you open your eyes, please?" She waited. "Not yet, huh? Okay, take your time."

As she stroked his hair, she prayed for him to open his green eyes and speak her name.

"I got it," Becca said.

"There should be a cold pack in there, and ibuprofen. Is the water working?"

"No, and no electric. But I have some water left. And there's a creek behind the property. We can get water there if there's a filter in that pack."

"I'm assuming there is."

Becca handed Cassie the cold pack and knelt beside her. Cassie twisted the package, releasing the chemicals, and placed it against the bump on Nate's head.

"I didn't mean it, Cassie. I never would have hit the chief."

"It's okay, he'll understand."

"No, he won't." Becca shot to her feet. "I'm already in trouble because of Tony. He said we weren't doing anything wrong, but now these guys are after me, and I think Tony's working for them and—" she paused "—I don't want to go to jail!"

"Take a breath," Cassie said. "One thing at a time. Help me make him comfortable."

Becca glanced from Cassie to Nate back to Cassie.

"Find me something to prop up his head," Cassie ordered, shifting Nate onto his back.

Becca pulled a pair of jeans out of her backpack, rolled them up and handed them to Cassie. Cassie slipped them beneath Nate's head and readjusted the cold pack. "If he doesn't wake up in a few minutes I'm calling 911."

"No, those men...they'll find us, they'll kill us," Becca said.

"I won't risk Nate's life. If this is more serious than a minor concussion, we'll have to get him to the hospital."

Becca stared in horror at Nate, her eyes widening.

"I need you to tell me what's going on," Cassie said. "Who's after you and why?"

"I can't." She stood and paced to the kitchen sink.

"Really? Because you've dragged me into this violent mess and I don't appreciate it."

Becca spun around. "What do you mean?"

"They think I have something of theirs. What?"

Becca shook her head and put out her hand. "The less you know the better."

"It sounds like Tony is into something dangerous, criminal even. I want you to explain how a good person like yourself could end up going down this path."

"I love him," she said in a hushed voice. Becca's gaze drifted to the floor. "He was always so nice to me, made me feel special…and loved. He brought me flowers for no reason." She glanced at Cassie. "I'm an idiot, right?"

"No." Cassie sighed. "But you need to fix this."

"It's impossible. They're everywhere."

"Is that why you disappeared from the tour group?"

She nodded affirmative. "A guy pulled me aside and said if I didn't tell him where the money was, he was going to kill me before we got down off the mountain. Cassie, we're in so much trouble." Becca burst into tears.

Cassie felt bad for her friend, but was also angry at the decisions she'd made. Becca should have gone to the police and asked for help. Instead she was hiding out in an abandoned cabin.

"What was the plan?" Cassie asked. "Hide out here until when?"

"I don't know. I hadn't thought past getting away."

"You left your jacket and a bunch of other stuff on the trail. Why, to throw everyone off?"

"I needed the men who were after me to think I was dead."

"No, what you need to do is end this before more people get hurt."

Nate moaned and blinked his eyes open. "Cassie?"

"Hey, you're awake. How do you feel?"

"Like I was hit by a truck." He glanced around the room. "What happened?"

"Misunderstanding. Becca thought you were one of the bad guys."

Becca stepped into his line of vision. "I'm so sorry, Chief. Please don't arrest me. I had no idea it was you."

"We thought you'd been kidnapped." Nate struggled to sit up and Cassie helped him. He clenched his jaw as she held the cold pack against his head.

"I was scared," Becca explained.

"The federal authorities would like to speak with you," Nate said.

"Oh my God, am I going to jail?"

Nate stood and Cassie led him to a chair beside a worktable in the kitchen.

"That depends," Nate said. "Have you broken the law?"

"I don't think so, I don't know. I'm stupid. I trusted Tony."

"Well, try trusting me instead. Tell me what's going on."

"I can't, don't you get it? It'll put you in danger."

"In case you haven't noticed, we're already in danger," Cassie shot back. "Tell the chief everything."

Becca sighed and hugged herself.

Cassie stood beside Nate, her hand resting protectively on his shoulder.

"From the beginning," Nate encouraged.

Becca joined them at the table. "Tony worked part-time for Echo Mountain Rentals, dropping things off for guests and taking the laundry in, picking it up, that sort of thing. One day a man approached him and said he was a small businessman wanting to grow his company."

"What kind of business?" Nate asked.

"Laundry services. Tony tells the guy he should talk to Mr. Anderson. The guy says he'll have a better chance if he gets Tony's support." Becca sighed and shook her head. "That should have been his first clue, because Mr. Anderson doesn't take business advice from Tony."

"Continue," Nate said.

"The guy says he's going to offer a lower rate than

the current service. But it's a longer drive to his facility, so he's afraid Mr. Anderson won't consider him. If Tony agrees to make the extra thirty-minute drive, the man will pay him a $500 finder's fee. Then, every time he has to make the drive, which is two to three times a week, Tony will get an extra $100 cash. That would certainly pay for the extra gas, plus his time. That's like $300 a week."

"And Tony didn't suspect anything strange about this?" Nate asked.

"No, the man seemed genuine, at least in Tony's opinion, and he needed the money because he was working limited hours for Echo Mountain Rentals. Mr. Anderson is kind of cheap that way."

"Okay, so Tony was driving the laundry to where?" Nate asked.

"A facility near Mount Vernon. He'd drop off the dirty bags of laundry and pick up the nicely packaged clean linens, take them to the office where Cassie and I would pick them up and deliver to the cabins."

"But something changed," Nate said.

"One day, Tony was in a hurry, and a clean linen package ripped." Becca's eyes grew wide as she retold the story. "All this stuff spilled out, like passports and cash, lots of cash."

"That's when he should have called the police, Bec," Cassie said.

"I know, but he didn't. He brought the linens to my place. We didn't know what to do at first, but Tony couldn't resist. He took a hundred dollars cash and we bundled the linen back up, nice and neat. A week later, when no one said anything, he assumed they hadn't noticed."

"Could he honestly be that naive to think it wouldn't catch up to him?" Nate said.

Becca leaned back in her chair. "It's not his fault. He never got a fair shake in life, being orphaned and sent to live with an aunt and uncle who didn't have time for him, and then being expelled from school for no good reason."

"He sounds like he suffers from victim mentality," Cassie said.

"He hasn't had it easy, Cassie."

"We all have our struggles."

"Says the girl with the perfect family," Becca shot back.

Cassie didn't respond. Comparing personal trauma was counterproductive. Nate placed his hand over Cassie's and gave it a squeeze.

"Sorry," Becca said. "I shouldn't have said that."

"Back to the laundry," he prompted Becca.

"That's how it started, with a broken package. I didn't know he continued to take money. After a month, he'd saved over three thousand dollars between his driving fees and what he was skimming from the packages."

"You had to have known what he was doing, Becca," Cassie said.

"No." She hesitated. "Maybe, I don't know. I suspected, I guess. He kept saying how he was planning this amazing new life for us, because he loved me so much. A few days ago, he shows up at my place with plane tickets to Maui. Said he had a job offer down there and wanted to marry me. We were going to leave right after I brought the group back from the hike. But while I was up there, this guy threatened me. You know the rest."

"You haven't spoken with Tony since you took the group up the mountain?" Nate asked.

"No."

"The man who threatened your life, what did he say?"

"That I wasn't going to make it down the mountain alive unless I told him where the money was." She stood and paced to the window. "Tony said everything was going to be okay."

"He was stealing from the mob," Nate said.

"What?" She turned to them. "No. Tony said it was just some guy moving cash around, you know, because he was being paid under the table for things like fake passports."

"The mob was sending bail jumpers to Echo Mountain Rentals cabins to hide out until they could flee the country with new identities."

Becca came back to the table. "You mean he was helping criminals escape?"

"It looks that way," Nate said.

"And I'm a part of this. I'm going to jail, aren't I?"

"That's yet to be determined," Nate said. "Help us solve this case and you may be able to stay out of jail. There's a federal agent in town who'd like to speak with you."

"What about Tony?"

Nate and Cassie shared a look.

"He's not a bad person," Becca protested. "He didn't know the laundry owner was involved with the mob."

"We'll sort it out once we get safely back to town," Nate said. "It would help to know why they're after Cassie. Any ideas?"

"Because we're friends and they think she knows about the money?"

"What, you mean like I took some of it?" Cassie said.

Becca shrugged. "I guess. I'm truly sorry you got dragged into this."

"Me, too. And I'm sorry you didn't challenge Tony on his activities sooner," Cassie said.

Becca glanced at the floor, ashamed. It was not Cassie's intent to make her feel bad, but she had to face her mistakes.

Cassie's stomach growled. "I'd better eat something before I start gnawing on the table."

"I've got a few cans of hash in my backpack," Becca offered.

"There's dehydrated food in our pack if we can heat up some water," Cassie said.

Cassie and Becca got to work pulling together a meal. They chose the canned items because it would take too long to start a fire outside and heat water.

After eating the last of the cold canned food, Nate said they should rest. He'd take the first watch.

Cassie slept fitfully, if at all, her eyes opening to the image of Nate, her protector, standing guard at the window.

Becca had fallen fast asleep. Well, at least one of them would feel refreshed in the morning. A few hours later Cassie gave up on trying to sleep and went to Nate. "Hey, your turn for some shut-eye."

"You sure?"

"Absolutely. Go on."

"Wake me if you see anything."

"Of course."

Nate brushed a kiss against her cheek and went to lie down on the sleeping bag.

As Cassie kept watch, she thought about everything that had happened in the past few days. Not wanting to be dragged down by fear, she said silent prayers of gratitude: she and Nate were still alive and safe, and they'd found Becca. Plus, Cassie had been able to dig deep down to find the strength to defend Nate from the attacker in the woods.

There was one more thing: Nate had kissed her on the cheek. She smiled to herself.

A few hours later, the early sunrise sparked a sense of peace across the property. She heard rustling behind her. Becca stepped up beside Cassie at the window.

"Did you get any sleep?" Becca whispered.

"Not much."

"Go lie down. I'll keep an eye out."

"Thanks."

"How long has the chief been asleep?"

"A few hours. Wake us if you see anything."

Becca nodded and gazed out the window.

Feeling utterly exhausted, Cassie lay down near Nate. She wished she could reach out and hold his hand, feel his warmth, but sensed it was inappropriate. Yet the ache to touch him made it painfully clear that she'd have to confront him about their relationship at some point.

Something amazing had grown between them, and she planned to hold on to it.

"Cassie?" Becca whispered.

Cassie sat up. "What's wrong?"

"Nothing. I have to go outside for a few minutes." She went to her backpack and took out some tissue. "Be right back."

Cassie lay back down and waited for Becca to return.

And waited.

Something wasn't right.

Cassie got up and started for the door.

The glass window shattered.

FOURTEEN

Nate sat straight up and was about to pull Cassie out of harm's way when she dropped to the floor. He scrambled to her, a ball lodging in his throat.

"Cassie, honey, are you hit?"

She didn't answer at first. He rolled her over, looking into her wide blue eyes.

"I'm okay, but I'm getting seriously tired of this," she snapped.

He pulled her against his chest and hugged her tight.

"Becca," she said against his shoulder.

Nate released her. "She's out there?"

Cassie nodded. Staying low, he made his way to the window and peeked outside, recognizing Tony's hoodie and wild black hair. He shoved Becca into the passenger side of a car.

Nate whipped open the cabin door and withdrew his firearm. "Tony, stop!"

Tony fired off a couple of shots.

Nate dodged back into the cabin. "He's out of his mind shooting at a cop again."

The car screeched as it sped away from the cabin. Nate rushed outside, but was too late. At least he got the make and model, probably another stolen vehicle. Tony was racking up the charges.

"Nate," Cassie called from the cabin.

He holstered his gun and went back inside. She

stood at the kitchen table, holding a note in her hand. "It's from Becca. She says she's sorry and begs my forgiveness." Cassie slapped the note on the table. "This is wrong. She wouldn't go willingly with someone so unstable and dangerous."

"I need to alert my team." He called in, giving Detective Vaughn the make and model of the car Tony was driving.

"Wait, he shot at you again?" Vaughn said.

"Yes, add that to the list of charges. This kid is falling fast, and he's got Becca Edwards with him. I'm not sure if she went willingly or not."

"She didn't," Cassie called out.

"We'll find them," Vaughn said.

"Any other developments I should know about?" Nate pressed.

"The guy who attacked you in the mountains yesterday lawyered up."

"Big surprise. Anything more from Len Pragner?"

"Nothing. He's hiding behind his attorney, some guy from Chicago."

"Fantastic," he said, sarcastic.

"What?" Cassie asked, touching his arm.

He glanced into her eyes, realizing how much she trusted him to do the right thing.

"Detective," he said into the phone, "I'm rethinking our current strategy. Our disappearing act is obviously not working, and now Tony knows where we are. If they find him first, it won't take much to pressure Tony into giving up Cassie's whereabouts. I'm bringing her in."

"Yes, sir. Where are you going to keep her?"

"I'll contact Aiden about commandeering Quinn Donovan's fortress apartment at Echo Mountain Resort. If that wing of the resort is empty, it's our most secure location. Also, Becca filled in some of the blanks about the case. We need to be more aggressive in shutting this thing down."

"What have you got in mind?"

"I'll explain it when I see you."

"Want me to send a cruiser to pick you up?"

"Yes. Who's on?"

"McBride and Carrington."

"Send McBride. We're at the Horizon Point property. Have you spoken with Agent Nance this morning?"

"No, sir."

"Once we're set up at the resort I'll want him in on the plan."

"Roger that. Stay safe."

"Thanks." He ended the call and hit speed dial for Aiden.

"My baby sister's driving you nuts, isn't she?" Aiden answered.

"No, actually, she's good. But I need a favor."

"Name it."

"Is Quinn Donovan using his apartment at the resort?"

"He's not expected back for a week. Why, you want to stash my sister there?"

"Yes, if that wing of the resort is mostly vacant."

"I'll relocate the few guests who are there and I'll put extra security on that end of the building."

"Do you need to check with Quinn first?"

"Nah, he gave me blanket permission to use it in case of emergency. I think this qualifies."

"Great, thanks. We'll see you within the hour."

He ended the call but didn't rip his gaze from the property surrounding the cabin. Tony may no longer be a threat, but Nate's adrenaline still hummed just below the surface. For all he knew, Tony could be in direct contact with the mob guys, maybe even told them he'd give up Cassie's location in exchange for Tony's and Becca's freedom.

Which still made no sense—why were mob guys after Cassie? Nate could only assume it was guilt by association.

"I'm so disappointed," Cassie said.

He glanced at her. "I'm sorry."

"Not in you, Nate. You've been amazing. You've been shot, and beat up, and shot at again, and all because my friend fell in love with the wrong guy. I'm so disappointed in Becca."

He refocused out the window. "I think she got that message last night when you challenged the poor decisions she'd made. I was actually quite proud of you."

"You were?"

"Yes, ma'am. You spoke your truth. Not always an easy thing to do."

"I hope that's not what drove her away. I'm upset

with her, but I'll always forgive her, even if I don't appreciate being dragged into this, all because of laundry."

Laundry containing passports and cash. That gave him an idea. "Cassie, did you put the clean linen in the Whispering Pines cabin the other night?"

"I didn't have time."

"Which means it's still in your car." He pulled out his phone and called Detective Vaughn.

"Yes, Chief?"

"Cassie McBride's car, I need you to find it and check the trunk."

"What am I looking for?"

"Passports and cash stuffed into linen packages."

"I'm on it, sir."

Nate pocketed his phone. "Now it makes sense. Cassie, how many other rentals did you cover for Becca besides Whispering Pines?"

"Let's see—Hidden Hollow, Serenity Lake and Sunset Vista."

"And each time you delivered a fresh package of laundry?"

"Yes."

"Which you picked up at the office?"

"I did. As a matter of fact, it was weird because some of Becca's packages looked different from the other ones I delivered."

"Did you report that to Mr. Anderson?"

"I mentioned it to Carol and she said she'd check

into it, but didn't seem all that concerned. Wait, you don't think Mr. Anderson is involved?"

"We won't know until we do some digging into the mob connection to Echo Mountain. My gut tells me they didn't randomly choose our town to set up their smuggling operation."

"When we get back to the resort I'd like to help so I can feel like I have some control over my life."

"How about you do internet research?"

"Wow, you didn't say no," she said with a smile.

Nate realized saying *no* to Cassie was becoming harder and harder to do.

They didn't talk for the next half hour and from Nate's expression, Cassie figured he needed quiet time to think and process. She sensed he was upset with himself for the direction of this investigation. Why else would he automatically assume she was disappointed in him?

Or was it something else? Was he withdrawn because somewhere in his unconscious brain he'd heard her confession of love and wasn't sure how do deal with it?

Well if that were the case, they should talk about it, right?

She caught herself. This wasn't the time nor the place to discuss a heady issue like love.

Finally, unable to stand the silence any longer, she approached Nate as he stood guard at the window, waiting for her cousin to show up. She offered a piece of beef jerky. "Breakfast?"

"Thanks."

As he gnawed on the jerky, she followed his gaze out the window to the surrounding property.

"I'm sorry," Nate said.

She snapped her attention to him. "For what?"

"That you had to experience this kind of trauma."

"Well, at least I've got you with me." She looped her arm through his and leaned against his shoulder.

She felt him sigh, and she looked up into his green eyes. "What was that for?"

"What?"

"That heavy sigh."

He shook his head and wouldn't look at her.

"Nate?" She hesitated. "You don't like people keeping things from you, yet you're awfully good at clamming up. It makes people who care about you feel terribly insecure."

"People who care about me," he said in a flat tone.

"Yep, that would be me."

"Well, you shouldn't."

"Too late, and I think you feel the same way. Unless I've been reading your signals all wrong, which I doubt because I've been paying pretty close attention to your body language these past few months. Wait, that makes me sound like a stalker."

Nate pulled his arm free of Cassie's and went to another window.

"I'm not really a stalker," she teased, sensing he was about to shut her out completely.

He snapped his attention to her for a quick second, and the intensity of his eyes was nothing short of alarming.

"Whoa, what was that?" she said.

When he didn't answer, she went to him.

"Nate? You looked at me like...like you hated me."

He stared deeply into her eyes. "I could never hate you."

She felt utterly lost when he looked at her like that. Was this what love felt like? Mature, adult love?

"I hate myself," he spoke so softly she almost didn't think she heard him right.

"What? Why?"

"Because I'm unable to keep you safe, unable to shield you from the brutality of what's going on."

"Hey, you've done a great job protecting me. I'm unharmed and alive."

And in love. For the first time in my adult life.

He ripped his gaze from hers and glanced out the window. "Your cousin's here."

As he started to walk away, she grabbed his arm, stood on tiptoe and brushed her lips against his.

"I'm alive because of you," she said.

When she released him, his brow furrowed like she'd spoken another language, one he didn't understand.

But Nate was a grown man who surely had been in a relationship before.

He had to understand what the kiss meant.

With a tightly clenched jaw, he opened the door and went out to greet her cousin, Officer Ryan McBride. She packed up trail mix and beef jerky, a little dazed by the impact of the kiss. That was awfully forward of her, but it felt right and necessary. She had to let him know there was more to this whole cop-protecting-the-witness thing, a lot more.

Was he so dense that he didn't get it? No, he was purposely dodging the issue, but why? Not because he didn't care about her, because she sensed he did.

At any rate, she'd help with the case because she wanted it solved quickly. Then she could explore her relationship with Nate.

It struck her that she hadn't thought about travel for a while now, not since she and Nate had gone off together, not since he'd challenged her to speak her truth—which she had to Becca.

Thankfully she was getting better at saying what she needed to say with clarity and compassion. The next subject of her honesty would be Nate. If he wouldn't accept the kiss as an indication of her feelings, she'd have to come out and say it: she wanted to date him, explore a future together.

"Wow, can I do that?" she whispered to herself, zipping up the pack.

"Do what?" her cousin Ryan asked from the doorway.

"Um…stay at the resort without Aiden driving me loony birds," she recovered.

"I wouldn't count on it. Come on, coz," Ryan said, shouldering the backpack. "Staying at the resort's gotta be better than being stuck in the wilderness with the silent chief."

Nate cleared his throat from the doorway.

Ryan snapped around. "Ah, sorry, Chief, that's not what it sounded like, sir. I meant the resort is better than being out here with no running water or—"

Nate put up his hand to silence Ryan. "It's fine. Let's go."

"Yes, sir." Ryan rushed out of the cabin.

Cassie glanced around, looking for anything she might have left behind. She grabbed her shoulder bag and marched to the door, hesitating in front of Nate. "Just so you know, we're not done talking."

An hour later they were settled at the secluded apartment on the north side of Echo Mountain Resort. Nate didn't like bringing Cassie, and the trouble that followed her, back to the resort, but the reality was they couldn't get away from whomever was after her no matter how far they went. It seemed as if the mob had eyes and ears everywhere: in the mountains, in town, possibly even in the police department.

No, he was being paranoid. He trusted the former chief with his life, and Detective Vaughn was solid. They were the only two in the inner circle, the only two who knew where Nate and Cassie were at any given moment. At some point Nate had to learn to trust, even if it wasn't second nature to him.

Neither was love.

He'd thought he'd heard Cassie say it back at the Horizon Point cabin when he was struggling to regain consciousness.

She loved him.

Not good for so many reasons.

"Are you talking background checks on everyone in town, Chief?" Detective Vaughn said, standing on the opposite side of the dining room table.

She was speaking to him, discussing strategy, yet he was so distracted by thoughts about Cassie that he barely heard her.

"Start with anyone associated with Echo Mountain Rentals," Nate said. "That's the hot zone. We also need to track down this mysterious laundry service. It all started with the owner of that company. I want to know who he is, how he got paid and where his facility is located. The Feds can assist with the search of the facility."

"Shouldn't we handle that?" Detective Vaughn said.

"We need to focus on the local angle. Let Agent Nance deal with the mob side of things."

"If he ever shows up," Vaughn shot back. "Oh, and I finally located Cassie's car."

"Finally?" Nate asked.

"There was some confusion. It was towed the other day from Echo Mountain Rentals, but at first no one seemed to know where it ended up. Found it at Rutger's Garage in Lake Stevens, but I haven't had a chance to get down there yet."

"That's half an hour away," Cassie said. "Why did they take it there?"

"Not sure," Detective Vaughn said. "Want me to head there first?"

"No, focus on the new laundry service," Nate said. "See if Mr. Anderson will give you contact information. Agent Nance and I will check on Cassie's car."

"Guys, I think I found something," Cassie said, eyeing a laptop screen.

She was determined to contribute, so Nate had given her an assignment. He'd also given it to her to keep her busy so she wouldn't demand more conversation about their relationship. The time and place for that was after everyone involved in this smuggling operation was behind bars.

"What've you got?" Nate asked Cassie.

"Over the past three months, six men reserved cabins through Echo Mountain Rentals." She glanced up. "But not together and not at the same time."

"They've smuggled six perps out of the country?" Detective Vaughn said. "Were they all originally from the same city?"

"No, actually, different cities across the US, but three from Chicago."

"We need to weed out which ones worked for the mob and which ones were innocent tourists," Nate said.

"I'm on it," Cassie said.

"How are you going to figure that out?" Detective Vaughn asked.

"I'll do searches to see if any of these guys went on hiking trips or local tours. I'm assuming the criminals wouldn't want to be seen in public so their names won't show up on those lists."

"Good point," Vaughn said, and glanced at Nate. "I'm off to talk to Mr. Anderson and track down the laundry service."

"Maybe I should go with you. I can have Agent Nance check out the car."

"No need, Chief," Vaughn said. "I've got this."

"You sure?"

"I'll call if I need backup, promise," she said, and left.

"You're worried about Detective Vaughn," Cassie said.

Nate sat across the table from her. "When I offered her the position of detective I thought she'd be dealing with teenage vandals, not mob criminals. I don't want anything to happen to her."

"Because of Will and the girls?"

Nate nodded. Will had suffered enough after the loss of his wife, and then physical abuse at the hands of white-collar criminals. He'd survived an intense, dangerous situation, and ended up falling in love with Sara Vaughn, a former FBI agent who'd joined the Echo Mountain PD.

Will deserved a little peace. He deserved his happily-ever-after.

"She's a smart cop," Cassie offered. "She'll be okay."

A tap sounded at the door. "That's probably agent Nance." Nate got up and eyed the peephole. He spotted Cassie's mom, sister and big brother Aiden in the hallway.

"You have company." Nate swung the door wide. "Come on in."

Cassie's mom and sister, holding the little dog, rushed to her side and bombarded Cassie with questions about the last twenty-four hours.

"How's it going?" Aiden asked Nate.

"We're good. Thank Quinn for letting us set up base here."

"Will do. So, have you lost your mind yet?"

"Not yet, but another few days of these guys running around my town and I might."

"I wasn't talking about the case. I was referring to my sister." Aiden nodded toward Cassie. "Nonstop chatterbox, that one."

"Doesn't bother me," Nate said.

"No kidding?" Aiden raised a brow in question.

"She's your sister. You're supposed to get on each other's nerves," Nate said, studying Cassie.

She wore a strained smile she'd never flashed at Nate, a smile that he suspected covered what she was truly feeling. Probably something along the lines of, "leave me alone, you're hovering again."

Another knock sounded at the door and Nate let Officer Ryan McBride into the apartment.

"Whoa, family reunion," McBride muttered.

"Actually, ladies, can I have your attention?" Nate said.

Cassie, her mom and her sister looked up.

"I'm sorry, but we need to keep this visit short. Cassie is doing some work for me on the case. Time is essential if we're going to catch these guys before they come after her again."

"She's helping you?" Cassie's mom said. "Are you sure that's a good idea, Chief?"

"Mom, I'm doing research on the internet," Cassie explained.

"I have to get back to work anyway," Bree said, standing. "I have a strict boss."

"Hey, I let you leave early yesterday for a special date with Scott," Aiden countered.

"A special date?" their mother asked. "What kind of date?"

"Thanks a lot," Bree shot at her brother. "Now she's going to expect us to announce a wedding date."

"Well, shouldn't she?" Aiden pushed.

This is what family looked like, Nate realized. They didn't always agree on everything, and this particular family loved to tease one another. But the love they shared was obvious.

"Can we come back and visit Cassie later, Chief?" her mom asked.

"Yes, but call first. Please be as discreet as possible. These guys could be keeping an eye on your entire family in order to find Cassie. I've got Harvey assigned to you." He nodded at Cassie's mom. "And Scott will stick with Bree when he's off shift."

"Do you know what all this is about?" Bree asked Nate. "What they want from Cassie?"

"We have our suspicions, but I can't discuss details of the investigation at this time."

"Come on, everyone out." Aiden motioned and then eyed his younger cousin Ryan. "You're protecting her, right?"

Officer McBride nodded that he was.

Aiden jabbed a forefinger at Ryan's chest. "Don't mess up."

Once family members had left, Ryan settled at the breakfast bar with a cup of coffee.

"You'll be safe here with Ryan," Nate said to Cassie.

She glanced up from the laptop. "You're leaving?"

"I need to retrieve the laundry from your car. Finding the fake passports will help us track down the suspects."

"But those are new identities."

"Agent Nance can run facial recognition. Speaking of which…" Nate called the agent.

"Nance," he answered.

"It's Chief Walsh. I thought you'd be here by now."

"Rental car broke down."

"Need me to pick you up?"

"Nah, I got another one. Are you at the resort?"

"Yes, but I'm headed to Rutger's Garage in Lake Stevens. Cassie McBride's car is there and I suspect we'll find evidence inside."

"I'll meet you there."

Nate ended the call and glanced at Officer McBride. "I'll be back in a few hours. Keys?"

He handed Nate keys to the patrol car.

"Do not open the door to anyone," Nate reiterated.

"Yes, sir."

Cassie walked Nate to the door. "What else can I do to help?"

Nate hesitated. "Stay safe."

"But is there other research I could do, like—"

Nate pressed his fingertips against her lips, so soft, so perfect. She stopped talking, and her blue eyes widened.

"I can do my job better if I know you're okay." He smiled. "Okay?"

She nodded and gave him a quick hug.

"I'll see you later." Nate glanced through the peephole to make sure the hallway was empty, opened the door and left the apartment.

The burn of worry simmered in his gut as he walked to the squad car. But he couldn't be in two places at once, and he had to trust that between Officer McBride and Aiden watching over her in the fortress apartment, Cassie would be safe, at least until he returned.

Besides, Nate hadn't been all that successful at keeping her safe. It had been one disaster after another up in the mountains, starting with him practically passing out in the car. What was that about? His gunshot wound wasn't that serious and Spence didn't think the bleeding had caused Nate to drift in and out of consciousness.

Well, he was feeling okay now, and ready to take on the men who were terrorizing Cassie. Hopefully he'd find the cash and passports in her car, and get the word out that she was no longer in possession of the items. Then, maybe, they'd leave her alone.

If only it were that easy.

When he arrived at Rutger's Garage, the place looked abandoned. He slowly approached the building, eyeing the closed sign. Closed in the middle of the day?

Nate withdrew his firearm, went to the front door and peered inside. No one was at the counter. He twisted the door handle and found it unlocked. Taking a step into the reception area, he quietly shut the door behind him. A muffled voice echoed from the other side of a closed door a few feet away.

Carefully crossing the small office, he flipped the bolt and flung open the door.

A man rushed out of the closet wielding a broom. Nate pinned him against the front counter.

"I'm a police officer," Nate said, flashing his badge in the guy's face. "Okay?"

The guy nodded. Nate released him. "I'm Chief Walsh from Echo Mountain."

"Cory Rutger," the thirtysomething man said, running a nervous hand through thick red hair. "He had a gun and told us to get in the closet."

"Us?"

"Megan, you can come out," Cory said.

A young woman stepped out of the closet, arms wrapped around her midsection.

"How long ago did this happen?" Nate asked.

"It's hard to say. We were pretty freaked out," Cory said. "Five minutes, maybe ten?"

"It felt like forever in there," Megan whispered.

"Stay here and call 911," Nate ordered.

Nate continued past the counter and looked into the shop where the mechanics worked on cars. It was a small operation, with only three bays. Two of them were occupied, while the third was empty.

And neither of the two cars was Cassie's bright red compact.

"Cory, was there a red VW back there?"

"Yeah, he took the keys to that one."

"So you fixed it?"

"Yep, someone tampered with the ignition pins."

"What did the man look like who took her car?"

"Twenties, black spiked hair."

"Was he alone?" Nate questioned.

"Yes, sir."

"No," Megan said. "I remember seeing him drive up. There was a woman in the passenger seat."

Nate studied the garage. He didn't holster his gun

just in case, but suspected Tony got what he wanted: Cassie's car, along with the money and passports.

"You're the only ones here today?" Nate said.

"Yes, sir, my other mechanic is at lunch," Cory said.

"Stay here, please." Nate shouldered open the door into the bay area.

He glanced left, then right. Nothing seemed strange or out of place. Scanning the garage all the way to the back exit, he spotted the car Tony had been driving, and a sedan haphazardly parked, with the driver's door open.

Keeping his back close to the wall, Nate sidestepped tools and cords until he reached the other side of the shop.

Nate studied the sedan parked out back.

Smudges of blood smeared the trunk.

FIFTEEN

Agent Nance was supposed to meet Nate, and the sedan with the open door looked like a rental.

Nate holstered his gun, grabbed a crowbar and rushed to the car.

"Steve," Nate called, leveraging the crowbar against the trunk.

There was no response. Tony wasn't stupid enough to kill or mortally wound a federal agent, was he?

With a quick jerk, Nate opened the trunk.

Agent Steve Nance, bound and gagged, was looking up at him. Nate removed the gag.

"I can't believe that kid," Nance said. "He's going away for a very long time."

"Where are you hurt?"

"Besides my pride?"

"There's blood on the trunk."

"Not mine. His. He was pretty beat up, and that girl looked terrified."

Nate cut the agent free of the duct tape and helped him out of the trunk. "What happened?"

"The girl distracted me, said she needed my help and the next thing I know, I'm on the ground and he's tying me up."

"They took Cassie's car?"

"Yeah, with the evidence."

"At least you're okay." Nate's cell rang. He ripped it off his belt. "Chief Walsh."

"Detective Vaughn ran into trouble at the Echo Mountain Rentals office. I'm en route," Officer Carrington said.

"Ten-four." Nate looked at Agent Nance. "My detective's in trouble."

"Go ahead. I'll give my statement to police and catch up to you."

By the time Nate reached the rental office, an Echo Mountain cruiser, state patrol car and ambulance were parked in the lot.

Nate got out of his car. The trooper and Red approached him. "She's okay," Red said. "Just a little banged up. She didn't see who hit her."

Nate nodded at the trooper. "Thanks for the backup."

"Sure." The trooper went back to his vehicle.

"Should I hang around, Chief?" Red asked.

"No, go back to your patrol. I'd like to maintain a sense of normalcy in town."

"Yes, sir."

Nate went into the office where Detective Vaughn was being examined by Rocky, along with Cassie's cousin Madeline. Carol the office manager stood in the corner, eyes wide.

"Ma'am, I need to—"

"I'm fine," Detective Vaughn interrupted Rocky, jerking away from him.

Blood dotted her shirt, matted her hair and stained

her hands. She glanced at Nate and must have noticed his worried expression.

"Head wounds always bleed a lot. I'm okay, Chief. Thanks to this one." She nodded at Carol who was wringing her hands. "She found me and called it in."

"Carol?" Nate said.

She snapped her attention to him, obviously traumatized by all the blood.

"Thank you for taking care of my officer," he said.

"Oh, uh, sure."

"Why don't you check her for shock," Vaughn ordered Rocky.

"Then you'll come with us?" Rocky said.

"If I have to."

"Oh, she'll go," Madeline said, stepping up to continue the examination of Vaughn's head wound.

Rocky led Carol outside.

"What do you remember?" Nate asked Detective Vaughn.

"Everything, well, until someone whacked me."

Nate noticed a trophy with red smudges on the floor in the corner. He used a tissue to pick it up. "Maybe with this?"

"Probably that Tony punk."

"Couldn't be Tony. He was in Lake Stevens stealing Cassie's car from the garage and tying up Agent Nance."

"Unbelievable," she said, then winced as Madeline tended to her head wound.

Madeline glanced at Nate. "We should take her to the ER."

"Enough." Vaughn batted Madeline's hand away. "I need to talk to the chief alone."

"Give us a minute, Maddie?" he said.

"I'll be right outside." Madeline packed up her supplies and left them alone.

"What did you find?" Nate asked.

"The name and address of the laundry service, Viceroy Laundry, Mount Vernon, plus—" she glanced out the window and back at Nate "—a connection between Mr. Anderson and a Chicago company called Wallingford Imports that I suspect is a front for the mob. I took pictures of email printouts. They're on my phone, but I can't find it."

"We didn't have a warrant anyway. Couldn't use it in court."

"Yeah, but at least we know where to look."

"Speaking of which, how did you end up inside the office?" Nate asked.

"I thought I heard something and climbed in through an unlocked window."

"Heard something?" he challenged.

"A man yelling."

"And when you got inside?"

"No one was here, and the back office was locked. I guess that's where the guy was hiding. Anyway, I did a little, ya know, looking around."

"Which is against procedure. You should have left once you realized no one was in trouble."

"Chief—"

"Pushing the limits is what got you in trouble with the FBI. I told you when I offered you this job that that kind of behavior is not acceptable if you're going to work for me."

She glanced down and sighed. "Sorry, Chief."

Nate would have probably done the same thing if he thought it would give him insight into this case, insight to help him plan a strategy to put these guys away and keep Cassie safe. Still, he didn't want criminals to elude charges because his department hadn't followed proper procedure.

"Come on, you need to get your head looked at by a doctor," he said.

She stood and went white. Nate grabbed her as her legs buckled.

"Madeline!" he called.

She glanced into the office, then called over her shoulder, "Rocky, we need the stretcher!"

Madeline rushed inside and checked Vaughn's vitals. Rocky brought in the stretcher and they secured her in place.

"I'm okay," she said in a strained voice.

Nate fisted his hand in frustration. This had to end.

"Chief, find my phone," Detective Vaughn said as they wheeled her out.

"I will."

Shelving his concern, he refocused on finding the phone. He knelt on the floor and searched under tables and chairs and behind file cabinets. The phone seemed to have disappeared from the tidy office.

The attacker must have taken it with him.

"Chief?"

He stood and glanced at Carol, who hovered in the doorway.

"I was going to lock the office," she said.

"Are you okay to drive?"

"I'm not sure, so I called a car service."

"I could drive you home."

"Thanks, but you've got more important things to do."

"Give me a minute?" Nate searched for Vaughn's phone but with no success. He left the office and Carol locked the door.

"Do you know where Mr. Anderson is?" Nate asked.

"He went to lunch about half an hour ago."

"Have any idea where?"

"No, I'm sorry."

He handed her a business card. "Can you ask him to contact me when you speak with him next?"

"Sure." Eyes downcast, she took the card and walked to a minivan in the parking lot.

Carol would be traumatized by today's events, and it struck him that no one was exempt from the brutality of these criminals, not innocents, not even law enforcement.

Marching to his cruiser, he wondered how he'd tell

his friend Will Rankin about Sara's injuries. This was exactly what Nate had been trying to avoid.

He pulled out of the parking lot and called Will on speakerphone.

"Hey, Chief, got a SAR call?" he asked in cheerful voice.

"Actually, I'm calling about Sara."

"What happened?" Will said, his voice suddenly flat.

"She was taken to the hospital with a head injury."

"How serious?"

"She was coherent, but nearly passed out when she tried to stand up. She went into a situation alone—"

"Why didn't you order her to wait for backup? You know she thinks she's some kind of superwoman, but she's not. She's breakable like the rest of us."

"Will, I—"

"I've gotta go."

The line went dead. Okay, that went about as badly as expected.

Nate's next call was to Agent Nance. His voice mail picked up.

"It's Chief Walsh. I'm following a lead at Viceroy Laundry in Mount Vernon. This might be where it all started. Call me back and let me know if you can meet me there."

Nate was about to call Cassie when his phone rang. He thought it might be the FBI agent calling him back. He hit the speakerphone button.

"Chief Walsh."

"Hey, it's Cassie. I wanted to check in. How are you?"

"Frustrated."

"What happened?"

"Tony assaulted the FBI agent and stole your car. Becca was with him."

"What are they thinking?"

"And Detective Vaughn was assaulted."

"Nate, I'm so sorry."

"It's not your fault."

"Are you sure about that?"

"Cassie, let's not go there."

Silence. Then, "I'd better go. Mom and Bree are on the way."

"Be nice," he teased.

"I'm always nice. That's my problem. Talk to you later."

He wanted to call her back, but thought better of it. He knew she was feeling responsible for everything that was happening. Nothing he said could persuade her otherwise.

The best thing Nate could do was chase the Viceroy Laundry lead and gather evidence to end this thing.

"Why did you lie to the chief about your mom and Bree?" her cousin Ryan asked.

"I didn't lie," she said, petting Dasher, who lay content in her lap. "They'll be back shortly, trust me."

"Semantics, coz. What's the deal?"

"I hate putting Nate through this."

Ryan leaned against the kitchen counter, his brows scrunched together. "What are you talking about?"

"Never mind. You wouldn't get it."

"Ya know, not all of the McBride men are thick-skulled, macho types like your brother."

"Uh-huh."

"Maybe I can help?"

"Thanks, but I need to be alone with my thoughts for a while."

"That sounds ominous."

Tapping sounded at the door.

Cassie sighed. "See? Mom and Bree."

Ryan looked through the peephole. "Not quite. It's the FBI agent."

He opened the door and let Agent Nance into the apartment.

"Officer, Cassie," Agent Nance greeted. "Is the chief here?"

"No, he's following up on something. I heard you were assaulted by Tony. I'm so sorry." She sighed and glanced down at the dog.

"Hey." Agent Nance joined her at the dining table. "I'm okay, and we're close to solving this case."

"Not close enough. I can't stand that people are getting hurt because of me."

"Shut up, Cassie," Ryan said.

Agent Nance shot Ryan a disapproving look.

"It's okay," Cassie said to the agent. "He's my cousin."

"Well, he's on duty and should act professionally." Nance nodded at Ryan. "Why don't you take a break?"

"My orders are to stay here, sir."

The agent redirected his attention to Cassie. "None of this is your fault."

"That's what the chief says, too."

Ryan's phone buzzed and he answered, walking into the other room.

"Then believe us," Nance said. "We know what we're talking about."

"I want this violence to end so things can go back to normal."

"Did you feel like Becca was a willing participant, that she knew Tony was stealing money?"

"I'm not sure. I think she got in over her head."

"That's a shame because these guys won't believe that. She's a target, like you. And trust me, Tony and Becca are not smart or resourceful enough to elude them for long."

"You mean...?"

"Whether your friends have the money and passports or not, the mob will put a hit on them."

Cassie closed her eyes.

"But if we bring them in first—"

"It's Bree," Ryan said, rushing up to Cassie. "She's missing."

SIXTEEN

Cassie stood. "Missing, what do you mean missing?"

"They can't find her."

"Scott was supposed to—"

"He got pulled away on a guest emergency, not long, like ten minutes. He's been texting and calling, but she's not responding."

Cassie put the dog down and paced to the door. "I need to find her."

Ryan blocked her. "You're staying here."

"I'll protect Cassie," Agent Nance said. "You go help find your cousin."

Ryan looked from Cassie to the agent, then back to Cassie.

"If you don't go I'll break out of here and search for her myself," Cassie threatened, feeling utterly helpless.

Ryan pointed his index finger at her. "Don't leave this apartment." He whipped open the door.

"Text me when you find her," she called after him.

The door slammed shut. Cassie paced to the sliding patio door, covered by a curtain meant to hide her presence.

"There's got to be something I can do. I can't stand that the people I love keep getting hurt."

"You want to protect them," Agent Nance said.

"More than anything."

"I might be able to help with that. Actually, we'd be helping each other."

Before she could respond, the door opened and Aiden stormed inside. "We're on lockdown. Mom's safe, Scott's out looking for Bree, Officer Carrington is checking out Bree's cottage." Aiden finally noticed Agent Nance standing there. "Where's Ryan?"

"I told him to help find Bree," Cassie said.

"I'll watch your sister," Agent Nance offered.

"What can I do, Aiden?" Cassie asked.

He ran a nervous hand through his thick blond hair. "Nothing, just—" He hesitated. "Don't do anything. Don't call anyone. Just stay out of trouble."

Aiden blew past the agent and left.

Don't do anything. Like always. The world continued around her and she couldn't do a thing to participate, and in this case help get her family and friends out of trouble.

A slow burn rose up her chest. *Just stay out of trouble.* Is that what everyone thought? That Cassie had somehow caused this? She'd blamed herself from the beginning, yet Nate had almost convinced her she was not responsible for anything that had happened.

Bree was missing. Cassie's fault.

She narrowed her eyes at Agent Nance. "You were saying something before about helping me stop this madness?'

"You can start by calling Becca. We'll set up a meeting place."

"Are you going to arrest her?"

"Not if she cooperates."

"I should tell Chief Walsh."

"Let's get Becca into custody first. I'll convince her to give up Tony and testify against him. When the chief returns with evidence from the laundry facility, we'll have everything we need to shut this down. It will be over."

Finally. Cassie would be out of danger, her family, her friends…

Nate would be out of danger.

Cassie pulled out her phone and made the call.

Becca answered in a frantic state. "Cassie, I'm scared and now Tony's gone and I don't know where he is, and he said if he didn't come back to leave town but the bad guys will follow me!"

"Becca, listen, the FBI can protect you."

"They'll arrest me!"

"Agent Nance won't arrest you if you cooperate. I'm with him right now. Meet us somewhere so he can keep you safe."

"Tony said—"

"Stop listening to him. Hasn't he gotten you into enough trouble?"

The agent scribbled something on a piece of paper and slid it across the dining table.

"Bec, I'm sorry, I didn't mean to sound cross, but I'm worried about you, and my family."

"Your family?"

"Bree is missing. Becca, please help me. Meet me at—" she glanced at the slip of paper "—Sammish

Park on Route Two, north end parking lot. Okay? Do you have a car?"

"I have your car."

"Can you meet us at the park in about—" She glanced at the agent.

"An hour," he said.

"In about an hour?" Cassie said to Becca.

"I don't know, maybe—"

"Becca, please, so no one else gets hurt. We can fix this, Bec. You and me."

"Okay."

Cassie pressed End and nodded at the agent. "She'll be there."

Nate contacted the local authorities to keep them in the loop about his investigation of Viceroy Laundry.

He pulled up to a large white building tucked away in the corner of an industrial park and double-checked the address.

A patrol car eased up next to him and an officer got out. "I'm Officer Panko with Mount Vernon PD."

"Chief Walsh, Echo Mountain."

They shook hands.

"My chief asked me to meet you here in case you needed assistance."

"Thanks." Nate eyed the building. "I'm a little surprised there's no signage identifying the company."

"Maybe because it's not a direct-to-consumer business?" the officer suggested.

"Perhaps." Nate and the young officer headed for the building.

"Can you tell me what this is about, Chief?"

"Smuggling bail jumpers out of the country. It's a federal case, but somehow landed in my town—" he glanced at Officer Panko "—and now yours."

"How did it lead you here?"

"They hide passports and cash in clean linen and deliver it to cabins. The criminals check in and it's waiting for them. What do you know about this place?"

They reached the front door.

"I've cruised by a few times," the officer said. "It never seemed occupied."

Hands cupped against the glass, Nate peered through the window into a reception area. The lights were off and no one was stationed behind the desk.

"Could you take that side of the building and I'll go around the other side?" Nate said.

"Sure, what am I looking for?"

"Signs of life, access inside. Finding an employee would be helpful."

"You got it."

Nate went around the left side of the building, peering through windows, trying to figure out if this was a legitimate company. It had to be since the linen was being washed and pressed somewhere before being stuffed with contraband, and delivered to Echo Mountain Rentals.

A crash echoed from the back of the building. Nate

withdrew his gun. Could be nothing, but he wasn't taking any chances. He took a few more steps, ready to peer around the corner.

"Come on, faster!" a man shouted.

"Don't rush me," another answered. "Gotta set the timer."

"Just let 'er rip."

"Not until we're clear."

Wait a second, that sounded a lot like…they were setting a bomb?

"Police, freeze!" Officer Panko shouted.

Three shots rang out. Nate rushed around the corner and aimed his weapon.

Two men took cover behind a black SUV and opened fire. Nate darted back behind the building.

"Get in, get in!" one of the men shouted.

Nate peered into the parking lot and a bullet shattered the window above his head. He dodged back for cover, but not before he spotted Officer Panko on the ground.

Nate called for help. "Code Three. 8713 Industrial Boulevard. Send an ambulance, over."

Tires squealing, the SUV peeled out of the lot.

Nate aimed his weapon and hesitated in shock when he saw who was behind the wheel: Len Pragner.

How was that possible?

Nate refocused and fired, hitting the back quarter panel. The vehicle sped out of the parking lot. He got the make and model number and would call it in to Chief Washburn.

Just let 'er rip.

Not until we're clear.

Suspecting they'd set an incendiary device, Nate raced to Officer Panko. They had to get clear.

Nate didn't know how much time he had.

How big of an explosion to expect.

He grabbed Panko under the arms and dragged him across the parking lot behind a metal Dumpster. He did a quick check of the man's torso. No blood.

"Wore your vest. Smart kid," Nate said. Then he spotted blood staining his sleeve. He put pressure on the wound.

The wail of sirens filled the air. No, no, no, Nate had to keep emergency vehicles away from the building, away from the—

An explosion rocked the ground. Nate automatically ducked as flying debris sailed over the Dumpster into the adjoining parking lot.

Officer Panko moaned and started to cough.

"It's okay," Nate said. "You're okay."

"What was that?"

"They destroyed the building." And with it, any leads to connect the mob to the smuggling operation.

Nate hung around for a few hours, hoping to get inside the demolished building, but local fire officials weren't giving anyone access because they deemed it unsafe.

"I doubt there's anything left between the incendiary devices and water damage," the fire chief said.

Nate offered him his business card. "Let me know if you find anything."

Nate headed back to Echo Mountain. His phone rang and he hoped it was Cassie calling to check in. He pressed the speakerphone button.

"Chief Walsh."

"Len Pragner has escaped," Detective Vaughn said. "They were transferring him from the hospital and two guys—"

"I know. He just blew up the laundry facility."

"You're kidding."

"Wish I were. How are you feeling?"

"I'm fine."

"She's not fine," Will said from the background. "She's taking the rest of the day off to bake cookies with me and the girls."

"Will, stop," she said.

Nate's phone beeped with another call. He glanced at the caller ID. "Chief Washburn's calling. Gotta take this."

"I'll check in later," she said.

"Sounds good." He switched over. "Chief?"

"You're not going to believe who owns a black SUV like the one that fled the scene of the explosion: Bill Anderson of Echo Mountain Rentals."

"We need to pick him up. Also, it was Len Pragner—"

"So you heard he's escaped."

"Yes. Send a patrol car to Anderson's home and I'll swing by his office."

"No, I'll go to his office—you need to get to the resort. Both McBride girls are missing."

SEVENTEEN

Cassie and the FBI agent anxiously waited for Becca.
Three hours later, she was still a no-show. As twilight illuminated the mountain range in the distance,
Cassie considered the fact that her friend had changed
her mind, or worse—the mob guys had found her before Becca could get to Cassie.

Agent Nance spent much of his time making calls,
pacing and looking worried. He asked Cassie to remain in the car, hidden from view.

She sensed he didn't appreciate her nonstop chatter, which was worse than usual because she was nervous, worried about Becca and Bree. She kept texting
Aiden, asking if they'd found Bree, and he responded
to stop bugging him.

She almost texted Nate, but didn't want to distract
him. Even now, by helping the FBI track down Becca,
a solid lead, Cassie didn't feel like she was doing
nearly enough.

Agent Nance opened her car door. "Can I see your
phone?"

"Sure, why?"

"We're going to try to trace Becca's phone."

"Oh, okay." She handed it to him and he walked
a few feet away, holding his phone to his ear while
analyzing the screen of hers.

Cassie, in the meantime, kept watch out the window, praying Becca was okay and that she would

show up with a perfectly logical explanation as to why she took so long to get here. Optimism and prayer were Cassie's best defense against the panic threatening to drive her bonkers.

"Did they track her down?" she asked the agent.

"Not yet." He turned and glanced over the top of the car. "Someone's coming."

Cassie looked through the window. "It's Becca, driving my car." She started to get out.

"Wait," Nance said, putting out his hand.

Becca pulled up next to them. Cassie offered a wave, and got out of the agent's car. Becca opened the car door.

"I was so worried about you," Cassie said.

"I didn't know if I should come."

"I'm glad you did."

Agent Nance pulled Becca out of the car.

"Hey!" Cassie protested.

"Becca Edwards, you're under arrest." He cuffed her wrists in front.

"You said you weren't going to arrest her!" Cassie protested.

"We have to follow procedure, then offer her a deal." He read her her rights and led Becca to the back of Cassie's car.

"I didn't mean it, I didn't mean it." Becca sobbed.

Cassie was not liking this one bit.

"Let's see what you've got." Nance opened the trunk of Cassie's car. It was empty. He squeezed Becca's arm. "What did you do with it?"

"I didn't do anything. Let go, you're hurting me!"

"You and your boyfriend are done."

"Knock it off!" Cassie shouted, grabbing his arm.

Agent Nance was losing it, big-time, and he still had her phone so she couldn't call for help.

"Stop it!" Cassie said.

He shoved her away, just as…

A black SUV screeched into the parking lot. Three men got out, including Len Pragner. Cassie's heart dropped. The other two men aimed guns at Cassie, Becca and the FBI agent. A smile curled Len's lips.

"I'll take it from here, Agent Nance."

Nate tried not to break every speed law in the county as he raced back to the resort.

Cassie was missing.

When he tracked down Officer McBride, the cop was pacing the hallway outside Quinn's fortress apartment like a caged animal.

"What happened?" Nate said.

"I was helping search for Bree. Cassie told me to go, she told me she'd be fine with Agent Nance." Ryan hesitated. "He's FBI. He's good at protecting people, right?"

"Continue."

"I was gone maybe an hour. We found Bree in the shed outside. Someone locked her in and she was pounding and yelling, but it's way out there and—"

"And when you returned Cassie was gone?" Nate said, calmly.

"Both she and the agent were gone."

Nate whipped out his phone and called Agent Nance. It went directly to voice mail. He tried Cassie's phone. Again, voice mail. Needing to locate the agent, he called Chief Washburn. "Is Agent Nance at the police station?" Nate said.

"No, why?"

"He's missing, along with Cassie. We need to find them." Nate's forced calm was slowly slipping away.

"Maybe Bill Anderson will have answers. I just pulled up."

"On my way. Wait for me."

Nate glared at Officer McBride. "We need to find your cousin before they do. There's a guy at the resort, I think his name is Kyle. He's a tech genius. Check with Aiden. See if he can track her phone." Nate raced to his car.

At least they didn't toss Cassie and Becca out of a moving vehicle. What a morbid idea. But strange thoughts popped into your head when you faced death.

Regret whipped through Cassie as she considered what she'd be missing.

With Nate.

The man she should be spending the rest of her life with, a long life filled with laughter and children.

Children? She had never considered being a mother until she fell in love with Nate. A tear formed in her eye, but she swiped it away with her sleeve. She would be brave. She would not concede defeat just yet.

Len had put Cassie and Becca in the middle seat of the SUV as one of his men drove, and the other sat behind her and Bec. Cassie still couldn't quite believe they'd been taken hostage considering the way Len's men beat up the FBI agent, bound his wrists, and locked him in the trunk of Cassie's car.

Her empty car. Who could have stolen the linen from the trunk that hid contraband these violent men were after? A better question, what did Len and his mob friend want from Cassie and Becca?

"For the record," Len started, "I didn't kill that woman in the cabin."

Cassie thought his confession odd.

Len glanced at Cassie. "Not that I haven't killed before, but that was an accident."

"How was it an accident?" Cassie decided to placate him, try and make a connection.

"My boss sent me to the cabin to find her." He pointed at Becca. "She and her boyfriend have been stealing from us, and apparently kept stealing even when they knew we were after them."

"No, I didn't take the stuff in the trunk," Becca whimpered.

"Be that as it may, you'd better hope true love Tony returns it to us."

Becca shot a worried look at Cassie.

"What happened to Marilyn, the lady in the cabin?" Cassie redirected.

"I thought she was the property manager," Len said. "Didn't know what Becca looked like. Let myself in. The woman screamed and ran into the bathroom. Slipped and hit her head. Her mutt wouldn't shut up so I threw him in the closet."

"And the shovel?" Cassie said.

"Figured I'd dispose of the body. A murder would draw too much attention, and we weren't done with our business in town."

"Are you going to kill us?" she asked. Not knowing was the worst part.

Len frowned. "I have no reason to kill you, Cassie McBride."

"You chased me down—"

"I thought you were working with Becca and her brainless boyfriend."

"You were going to hurt me in the hospital, and at the farm and—"

"I wanted to find out where you stashed the money and passports. But you're not a part of this idiot scheme. You are not my enemy."

His bizarre integrity puzzled her considering who he worked for. Then again, maybe he was toying with her.

"I'm not naive," she said. "I've seen your faces."

Len burst out laughing, as if she'd told a joke.

"You watch too much television. It doesn't matter. Everyone knows who we are now, which is why guys like us need the passports, to start new lives somewhere." He patted his jacket pocket. "I always keep mine handy in case of emergency. But my friends here were supposed to get their new passports." He glared at Becca. "So we'll need those back."

He redirected his attention out the front window. Cassie studied her friend. Becca shook her head that she had no idea what happened to the laundry containing the contraband.

Cassie decided to be strong instead of scared. "Len?"

He turned to her.

"How can I help?"

Nate got confirmation from the organized crime unit in Chicago that Wallingford Imports was tied to organized crime, and there had been communication with Echo Mountain Rentals.

Nate had his connection, a direct link from the mob to Bill Anderson. As they questioned Anderson, he pretended to be baffled by their accusations.

"I don't understand," he kept repeating.

"Drop the act," Nate said, fisting his hand. "You've been letting the mob use your cabins to smuggle bail jumpers out of the country."

Bill shook his head. "No, honestly. I don't know what you're talking about. Do I need a lawyer?"

"What you need is to help us find Cassie McBride before we add murder to your list of felonies," Nate said.

The front door opened and Carol entered the living room, holding a stack of files. "Oh, I'm sorry. I didn't know you had company, Bill."

"Come in," Nate said. "Maybe you can convince your boss to be straight with us."

"About what?" She laid her purse and files down on a table by the front door.

"They think I'm involved with the mob," Bill said in a panicked voice.

Carol's jaw dropped and her eyes widened.

"Carol, you know me better than anyone. Tell them they're wrong," Bill said.

Nate took a step toward Bill, towering over him as he shrank into the sofa. "People might die, today, because of you."

"Come on, Bill. We all make mistakes," Chief Washburn said, taking the soft approach.

Bill shook his head, looking genuinely dumbfounded.

This was going nowhere, and time was running out. There had to be a way to break this guy. If only Nate could directly connect him to the evidence...

Of course, Detective Vaughn's stolen phone.

Bill must have taken it to prevent the police from acquiring evidence against him and the mob. Eyes focused on Bill, Nate took out his phone and hit Detective Vaughn's number.

A moment later, Vaughn's unique ring filled the room.

But it wasn't coming from Bill's pocket.

Nate slowly crossed the room, following the source of the sound. It originated from Carol's purse.

"Ma'am? The phone, please," Nate said.

She dug it out of her purse and handed it to him.

"I don't understand," Bill said.

"How did you get involved in this?" Nate asked.

The woman collapsed in an easy chair and burst into tears. Nate didn't have time for tears. He had to find Cassie.

"I'm sorry, I'm sorry," she said.

"Explain what's going on, please," Nate pressed. "And quickly."

"It's my grandson. He's in jail back in Chicago, and they said they'd protect him if I made sure the laundry was delivered and the reservations coincided with the deliveries." She looked at Nate. "Todd's the only family I have. I tried to get him to move out here with me, but he got caught up with a bad group of boys. He was so lost when his parents died."

"What was he incarcerated for?"

"Drug possession with intent to sell. He's not a tough kid, Chief. He was beaten up in jail and I thought they'd kill him. I had no choice."

Nate glanced at Chief Washburn and then knelt beside Carol. Threatening her with jail time wouldn't inspire her cooperation.

"Carol, I could call my contacts in Chicago to see what I can do to help your grandson, but you have to know that your days working with the mob in exchange for their protection are over."

She nodded.

"I'll make some calls, too, Carol," Chief Washburn offered. "But you need to help us."

"Please," Nate said, "I can't lose Cassie. Do you have any idea where Len would take her?"

She shook her head that she didn't. "I have Len's phone number and the laundry everyone's been looking for."

"Isn't it in Cassie's car?" Nate asked.

"No, I took it before it was towed from the rental office."

"And they think she still has it," Nate muttered.

A call came in and he answered, "I'm in the middle of—"

"They found Cassie McBride's car," Red said. "Agent Nance was stuffed into the trunk. Cassie and Becca were taken."

Two hours later Carol was scheduled to drop off the laundry with Len Pragner near an abandoned barn north of town. There was no reason Len would suspect she was working with the police.

Nate was careful whom he involved at this point. He no longer trusted Agent Nance, who admitted to persuading Cassie to help him bring in Becca even though it could be dangerous. Apparently Nance was tired of chasing his tail like the rest of them, and had planned to set a trap for Tony.

Using Becca and Cassie as bait.

Nate spoke with Agent Nance's boss, who wanted

Nate to wait for federal agents before making the laundry drop. With Cassie's life in danger, Nate wasn't waiting on anyone. He said if the Feds wanted to close the mob smuggling case, they were welcome to pick up the perpetrators tomorrow morning at the Echo Mountain jail.

Nate, Chief Washburn, and Officers McBride and Carrington assembled at the meeting spot to go over the plan.

"I'll be in the backseat of Carol's car for protection," Nate said. "After she drops off the laundry, I'll get out of the car here—" Nate pointed to the map "—and hide in the trees. I'll let you know when I see them approach. Radio County, they'll be waiting, and the three of you close ranks. These guys aren't going to be happy if they check the bag on site and find only laundry. If they do, we'll have minutes before they hurt Cassie and Becca."

Hurt them. He couldn't even think *kill them*.

"How many do you think will be in the SUV?" McBride said.

"I'm guessing two or three," Nate answered. "Everyone's wearing a vest?"

They all nodded.

"Let's focus on getting the hostages back unharmed."

Carol stood beside the car with a blank expression on her face.

"Carol?" Nate said.

She glanced at him. "Your help tonight will go a long way during your sentencing."

She nodded. "Love makes you do such stupid things."

Nate only hoped love *would not* make him stupid tonight.

Love. He loved Cassie.

"Nate?" Chief Washburn said.

Nate snapped his attention to the three men who looked to him for leadership and strength, men he knew attended Echo Mountain Church.

"I'd like to say a prayer," Nate uttered, surprising himself.

As they stood there, in the cool, quiet night, Nate led a short prayer asking for courage, strength and protection.

"Amen," they said, and took their positions.

The car rolled slowly across the uneven dirt road.

"You're doing great, Carol," Nate said, hiding in the backseat.

"I'm scared."

"It's okay, I'm here."

A few minutes later she stopped the car, got out and grabbed the laundry bag from the front seat.

"Quickly," Nate said.

She disappeared from view.

I'm coming, Cassie.

Carol returned, got behind the wheel and peeled out.

"Slow down. I need to jump out by the trees, re-member?" Nate said.

"Right, sorry."

"Did you see anyone?"

"No."

"Chief Walsh, I see a black SUV parked on the south end of the barn, over," Red said through the radio.

"Ten-four."

Carol made a turn, out of view of the barn. Nate opened the door and jumped out, rolled, and took cover. He had a clear sight line of the white laundry bag.

As he hid in the trees, he felt like time passed so slowly, as if he'd been crouched there for hours, not minutes.

Out of the darkness, an SUV crawled toward the laundry. Closer, closer.

It stopped a good twenty feet from the bag.

A door opened.

Cassie, hands bound in front, got out of the SUV.

"I have a visual, over," Nate said in the calmest voice he could manage. "It's Cassie."

She walked slowly across the wide open space, as if she fully expected an assault.

Just as she reached the bag...

A car screeched across the property, heading directly toward her. Nate automatically stood.

He recognized the driver: Tony.

"Move in, everyone move in!" he ordered, and charged into the open field.

It was like everything clicked into slow motion. Cars were honking, people were shouting, and Cassie was frozen in place, inches from the white laundry bag she was sent to retrieve.

"Cassie, grab the bag and get in!" Becca called from the open truck door.

All Cassie could do was stare at the bright lights blinding her.

Gunshots pierced the night air, ripping her out of her trance. Had Len changed his mind and decided to kill her?

She took off running, even though she doubted she could outrun a car, or a bullet.

Someone tackled her and threw her to the ground. She fought him at first, and then recognized the woodsy scent.

Nate.

The man she loved.

"You're okay," he said.

The sound of screeching tires was followed by a crash.

"Freeze, police!" someone shouted.

Multiple gunshots pierced the night air, then silence. The sound of sirens, the wonderful sound of sirens echoed across the field.

Relief edged its way into her heart, not only because of the sirens, but because Nate held her close, physically shielding her with his body, protecting her life with his own.

"Okay, I give up!" a man called. It wasn't Len Pragner, it was one of his thugs.

New worry flooded her stomach. Had Len escaped the SUV? Was he coming after her?

"We're clear, Chief!" her cousin Ryan called.

She peeked around Nate's arm and saw Len sprawled on the ground, blood staining his shirt. One of his men lay a few feet away, and the third man was in handcuffs, pinned to the SUV by her cousin.

"Where's Becca? I'll kill him! I'll kill him!" Tony shouted, racing toward Len's motionless body.

"Calm down," Officer Carrington ordered, shoving him against the car and cuffing him.

"I'm here," Becca said, edging out of the SUV.

Cassie released a sigh. Her friend was okay and the mob guys were no longer a threat.

Chief Washburn rushed up to Cassie and Nate.

"Is she okay?" he asked.

"Cassie?" Nate said, with a concerned voice.

She turned and looked into his emerald-green eyes.

"Are you okay?" he said softly.

"Yes. As long as you don't let go."

EIGHTEEN

The next day at the police station, Cassie gave her official statement about what happened when Len had taken her hostage. She noticed Nate repeatedly clench and unclench his jaw as she told the story.

Mom, Bree and Aiden demanded to go along. Cassie had a feeling that after everything that had happened, her family was going to be even more protective than usual.

"What is with people? Are they stupid?" Aiden said, shaking his head. "What were Tony and Becca thinking?"

"We all make mistakes, not that you'd understand, Mr. Perfect," Cassie teased.

"Money is a powerful motivator," Nate said. "Tony thought money would solve all his problems and he'd get the girl."

Nate glanced up briefly at Cassie, and then he looked away.

Nate had his girl. He had to know that.

"I'm so glad it's over," her mom said. "It is over, right, Chief?" When she addressed her question to Chief Washburn, he pointed at Nate.

"He's the chief."

"Of course." She glanced down.

"Mom?" Cassie prodded. "Do you have something to say?"

She snapped her attention to Nate. "I'm sorry, you

know how people talk. Once Chief Washburn came back, they thought, well…"

"That I couldn't handle my job?" Nate offered.

Her mom shrugged.

"Mo-ther," Cassie admonished.

"I didn't say it. I'm just repeating what I've heard."

"Well, I'd appreciate you repeating this," Chief Washburn started. "If it weren't for Nate, the town would still be in danger. He's the one who pieced it together. He figured out Carol was the mob's contact in Echo Mountain. And he's the one who threw himself into the line of fire to save Cassie's life."

"That's my job, to protect the citizens of Echo Mountain," Nate said.

Cassie didn't like the sound of that. She was more than an ordinary citizen, wasn't she?

Aiden extended his hand to Nate. "Thanks, buddy."

"Wait, so Carol was a part of this scheme because…?" her mom asked.

"The mob was providing protection for her grandson who was incarcerated." Nate turned to Cassie. "I'm surprised Len was so forthcoming with you about the supposed accidental death of Marilyn Brandenburg, and giving you details of how their operation worked."

"It was strange, but on some level I think he had his own measure of integrity."

Aiden snorted. "Come on, Cassie, you can't be *that* naive after all this."

"Everything isn't just black or white, Aiden. There are shades of gray, ya know," she countered.

"The FBI agent was definitely gray," Bree said. "I can't believe he bamboozled me into thinking Cassie was in the shed, then locked me in."

"I also suspect he spiked my coffee at Healthy Eats," Nate said. "Which is why I nearly passed out while driving. He'd hoped I would question my ability to keep Cassie safe and turn her over to him. He wanted to be in charge from day one."

"He manipulated me into helping him draw out Becca," Cassie said. She looked at Nate. "I am sorry about that."

"What are you sorry about?"

"That I went with him when you told me to stay at the resort. I was so desperate to put an end to all this violence."

"Well, it's over now. The Feds will take Tony, Becca, Carol and the mob guys into custody."

"Poor Becca," Cassie said.

"And Carol," her mom added.

"Why did she have the linens?" Cassie said.

"Carol was considering her options, turning the evidence over to the Feds in exchange for her grandson's safety, or continuing to work with the mob. She was playing a dangerous game," Nate explained.

"Because of her poor grandson," Mom offered. "How long do you think she'll be in jail?"

"If she and Becca cooperate, their sentences could

be reduced, but Tony, he'll be going away for a while," Nate said.

"I know Becca is desperate to make amends," Cassie said.

Aiden's phone beeped and he glanced at it. "Gotta go."

"We should let the chief get back to work," Mom said, touching Cassie's arm. "Ready?"

"I've got some things to do in town."

"If you think we're letting you out of our sight, you're wrong," her mom said.

"Mom—"

"She's right, Cassie. You must be traumatized," Bree said. "Move back in with Mom for a while. I'll come by for dinner and—"

Cassie stood. "No."

Her mom's eyes widened, Bree's jaw dropped, and Aiden froze at the door, turned and looked at Cassie.

Nate shot Cassie an encouraging nod.

"I love you guys," Cassie started. "I love you so much, but you tend to smother me, probably because of my illness, and now because of the last few days. I get it, I do. I appreciate how much you love me, so much so that you always want to help."

"Cassie—"

"Please, let me say this," she interrupted her mom. "I successfully escaped a killer, talked rationally to him and stayed alive until help arrived." She smiled at Nate. "I'm a mature woman, and would like to be treated like one. I don't know any other way to put it but—" she hesitated and made eye contact with Mom, Aiden and Bree "—the way you love me can be stifling."

"That's unfair," Aiden said.

"Aiden," Mom said. "Let her finish."

Cassie took her mom's hand. "You're the greatest mom a girl could have. Have faith in your parenting skills, and give me some space. Sure, I'll stumble and fall, but that's the best way to learn, right?"

Tears formed in her mom's eyes, and Cassie momentarily regretted speaking her truth.

Mom reached out and hugged her. "I couldn't be more proud."

Cassie hugged her back, a little surprised. Bree squeezed her shoulder and offered a smile.

"Okay, whatever," Aiden said. "I have no idea what's going on. Does anyone need a ride?"

All three women said, "No." Then burst into giggles.

"Women," Aiden muttered, shaking his head.

"Just give us a minute, Aiden." Mom broke the hug and studied Cassie. "I had no idea you felt this way."

Cassie smiled. "Yeah, well, a friend taught me to speak my truth."

"I'm so glad she did."

"He," Cassie corrected.

"Oh, do tell," Mom said.

"Come on, Mom, let's go," Bree encouraged.

"I'll walk you ladies out," Chief Washburn said.

"I'll text you later," Cassie said.

"Call me later," Mom countered.

"I'll teach you how to text, Mom," Bree said.

"What if I don't want to text? I like to hear the sound of my children's voices."

"Then Cassie can send you a voice message," Bree said as Chief Washburn held the door open for them.

"You mean her real voice or a robot voice? I don't like those robot voices, like that phone lady. She sounds so stern," Mom said before the door closed on them.

Cassie glanced at Nate, and he smiled.

"Well done," he said.

"Thanks. Is there anything else you need from me?"

His smile faded. Tension filled the room.

"No, I think we're good." He stood as if he intended to walk her to the door.

But Cassie was not done talking, nor was she done showing him how she felt. Confessing to her family gave her strength and a new sense of confidence.

She stepped up to Nate, hugged him and pressed her cheek against his chest. "Thank you."

"It's my job."

"Teaching me to find my voice? That's not in the police chief's job description."

"It's in my 'friend' job description."

"Come on, we both know there's more to this than friendship."

She felt pressure against her shoulders. He was pushing her away. She leaned back and looked into his troubled green eyes, but she didn't let go. "What's wrong?"

"It's over, Cassie. You're safe, free to take your trips and follow your dream."

She was not letting him push her away.

Speak your truth.

"Nate, I care about you, a lot."

"I know. I heard you in the cabin when you thought I was unconscious."

Heat rose to her cheeks. "You did?"

"Yes."

"Huh. I don't know if I should be embarrassed or relieved." She studied his face. "Or worried?"

He shook his head. "There's no need to be worried. You're safe, remember?"

"I wasn't talking about the mob."

Nate wouldn't look into her eyes. Then reality hit her dead-on: he didn't share the same feelings. He truly had only been doing his job both as police chief, and as Aiden's good friend.

Nate didn't love her.

Suddenly embarrassed, she released him and grabbed her shoulder bag. "Right, okay, sorry."

"I thought we agreed you never had to say sorry, especially to me."

She glanced across the room at him. "I was simply saying I'm sorry that I misinterpreted your behavior. I'm sorry I'm so naive, so immature that I misread your signals." She hesitated. "Signals I guess I imagined."

When he didn't correct her, she glanced through the window at the bakery across the street. A young couple walked out holding hands. Her throat started to close with emotion.

What would make her think a man like Nate Walsh would want to commit his life to a naive Pollyanna like Cassie? This thing between them was simply a young girl's romantic dream, a dream she'd never experienced in her teens because she didn't get out much due to her illness. She sighed and tried to focus on the good things that had come out of the past few days.

Nothing came to mind.

She'd originally thought the best thing had been the beauty of romantic love blossoming between her and Nate.

She'd fallen deeply in love for the first time and it felt amazing. Until now.

Why can't he love me?

The ball in her throat grew, threatening to cut off her voice. Cassie needed to escape his office.

She glanced at her phone. "Whoa, it's almost noon. I forgot I'm interviewing a pet sitter about watching Dasher while I'm gone." She zipped her coat. "I'm thinking two weeks in Europe will be a good test run to see where I'd like to spend more of my time. But you know Bree and Mom, they'll worry no matter where I go," she chatted away, not paying attention to what she was saying.

"Of course they'll worry. They love you," Nate said.

But you don't.

Her heart splintered into tiny pieces as she meandered to the door. Without looking at him again for fear she'd lose it, she started to say something trite in farewell, but stopped herself.

Her last words to the man she loved would not be pithy or disrespectful of her own feelings. She opened the door and said, "God bless."

She rushed outside and motored down Main Street. It didn't take long for the tears to break free.

Maybe this was a necessary lesson before she left on her trip. Perhaps she needed to experience heartbreak before she encountered men in a foreign land. Having her heart broken by Nate—the man she would have given up traveling for—would make her more discerning and guarded. A good thing, right?

She bumped into someone on the street. "Sorry," she said and continued walking.

"Cassie?"

She swiped at her eyes and turned around. Nate's sister, Catherine, studied her with a puzzled frown.

"Are you okay?" she asked.

"Sure, fine. Just late, sorry." Cassie practically sprinted away from her. Oh great, now the entire town of Echo Mountain would know she was blubbering her way down Main Street like a little girl, a child who'd lost her best friend, which in a sense she had.

Suddenly, she couldn't get out of town fast enough.

Nate leaned back in his office chair, staring at the door. It was the only way, the best way. If he'd been honest with Cassie and admitted he loved her, she might shelve her dream of seeing the world and experiencing new things.

He would not be responsible for holding her back.

Besides, she was young at heart, not cynical like Nate. She deserved more than an emotionally damaged cop as a partner in life.

He considered everything she'd done for him, showing him light where he could see only darkness, and opening his heart to a loving, forgiving God, something he'd never even considered before he'd spent time with Cassie.

God, please take care of her.

He worried about her, the way she'd rushed out of his office wearing that strained smile, the one she'd used on her family when they hovered and she wanted them gone.

The office door burst open and his sister stomped her feet on the mat.

"Hey, shouldn't you be at work?" he said.

Catherine stormed across the room and dropped a brown paper bag onto his desk. "This *was* for you, but now I'm reconsidering."

"What is it?" He reached for the bag.

She slapped his hand. "Double chocolate mini muffins, your favorite." She glared at him with steely green-gray eyes. "What did you do to her?"

"Her, who her?"

"Cassie McBride."

"I didn't do anything, other than protect her from the mob."

"Don't be a smarty Sam. You're as bad as Dylan," she said. "Now, come on, it's obvious that girl is crazy about you, overlooking your rough edges and bossy nature. She even made you smile in public. I've seen it." She crossed her arms over her chest.

"Is there a question here?"

"What did you just say to her?"

"I didn't say anything."

She snatched the bag of mini muffins. "Then why was she so upset? She was bawling her eyes out."

He fisted his hand. He knew he'd hurt her, but hearing it from his sister made it all the more painful.

"I can't give her what she needs," he said softly.

"Is that what you said to her?"

"Not exactly, no."

"Of course not, because you know she'd talk you out of such nonsense. What do you think she needs, Nate, huh?"

"To get out of town and travel, live her dream. She's earned that right."

"She's also earned the right to fall in love and be loved in return. Are you seriously telling me you don't love that adorable woman?"

"I never said that."

"Then you *do* love her?"

"Can I have my muffins?"

"Answer the question."

"Yes, I love her. That's why I'm letting her go."

"You mean, you didn't tell her the truth, that you love her?"

"I didn't want to confuse her."

"She's a grown woman. Don't you think it's up to her to decide? No, of course not, because you're Nate the great, the police chief, the guy who's going to make everything right for everyone." She turned to leave.

"Catherine—"

"Stop." She whirled on him. "You've always challenged me to speak my truth, yet you can't tell Cassie how you feel because you're afraid she'll make the wrong decision. Wrong in whose eyes? Yours?"

"You don't understand."

"Sure I do. You don't think you're a good enough reason for her to stay in town. Well, guess what, that's her decision to make. Stop trying to control everything, and stop hurting the love of your life out of some warped sense of sacrifice." With a shake of her head, his sister marched toward the door. "If you love and respect her you'll be honest instead of treating her like a child."

"I'm not treating her like—"

"Swallow your pride and apologize for being a blockhead. 'I'm sorry.' It's two words. And she's earned them."

Catherine left and slammed the door.

He tipped back his office chair, considering Catherine's lecture. Had he been treating Cassie like a child, making decisions for her like her own family had over the past twenty-five years?

Or was this something more?

You don't think you're a good enough reason for her to stay in town.

Deep down he felt Cassie deserved better than what Nate could offer. Was that a good enough reason to keep the truth from her, the truth that he loved her with all his heart?

Here he'd been challenging her to speak her truth to her family, yet he'd refused to be truthful with Cassie. What a hypocrite. That certainly wasn't what an honorable man would do, or a man searching for grace.

He sighed. *Lord, I love her. Please show me the way.*

Her family and friends wanted to throw Cassie a party at Healthy Eats Restaurant, a combination "celebrate life" and "bon voyage" party.

She wasn't in a celebratory mood. It had been only a few days since they'd closed the smuggling case, a few tense days of keeping herself busy and trying to ignite enthusiasm about her future travels.

For the first time in her life, her heart wasn't in it.

"I guess that's what heartbreak does to ya," she said to Dasher, who snoozed in a doggy bed in the corner of her apartment.

Sure, she'd shopped flights to London, but she hadn't done much else, nor had she officially booked anything.

The party was meant to be a celebration of life, of

making it through dangerous waters and coming out safely on shore.

Which she couldn't have done without Nate's help.

A part of her wanted to get a cab, catch a flight out of Sea-Tac and disappear. No, that was childish. But she wasn't sure what to expect at the party tonight and didn't want to show up in a sour mood when the guests were cheering her on and wishing her safe travels.

"I'd better not be late for my own party," she said to Dasher. The dog didn't stir, his little paws twitching as if he was having a very good dream, probably about racing through an open field.

Cassie slipped into nice black pants and a colorful top. She grabbed her purple shoulder bag and headed to the restaurant.

There were only three cars in the parking lot, and the blinds were closed. Did she get the date wrong? Was she late? Catherine had said eight o'clock.

She got out of her car and approached the restaurant. A sign was taped to the door: "Come in and celebrate!"

Cassie stepped inside. The lights were low, and soft music drifted across the restaurant.

An empty restaurant.

"Catherine?" Cassie said.

Instead, Nate stepped out of the kitchen. Dressed in a suit jacket, white shirt and jeans, he gripped a bouquet of flowers.

Cassie's breath caught in her throat.

"It's just you and me tonight," he said. "I hope that's okay."

"Sure, okay."

He closed the distance between them and offered her the flowers.

"They're beautiful," she said, loving the bright purples and pinks.

He motioned to a table covered in a white linen cloth, with delicate china plates and tulip-shaped water glasses.

Nate pulled out a chair and she sat down, still clinging to the flowers.

He joined her at the table and smiled. "Like the music?"

She nodded that she did, still trying to make sense of what was happening.

"Oh, and I got you something else." He opened a small white box and slid it across the table. "A charm to add to your key chain."

"It's the Swiss flag," she said, breathless. He remembered she wanted a charm to represent Switzerland.

"How about a drink?" he offered.

She nodded, unable to speak coherently.

"Hey, sis?" he called.

Catherine came into the dining room carrying a pitcher. "Fresh apple-carrot-kale juice with a hint of ginger." She filled their glasses.

"Cassie, can I put the flowers in water for you?" she offered.

Cassie handed her the bouquet, still speechless. Catherine disappeared into the kitchen.

"I'll bet you're wondering what all this is about," Nate said, studying her.

Cassie nodded that she was, in fact, wondering.

He smiled. "Wow, you're actually speechless."

"I don't want to ruin it," she blurted out.

"No." He sighed. "But I almost did." He pinned her with loving green eyes. "I'm sorry."

"For…?"

"For not being truthful, for trying to protect you and ending up making decisions for you."

"I'm confused."

"I love you."

Her jaw dropped.

"You had to see that coming," Nate said.

"Yes, but no…but yes?"

He reached across the table for her hand. She offered it, never wanting to let go.

"I love you so much I didn't want to ruin your dream of traveling, of going on your adventures."

"Being with you is an adventure."

"I'm not sure if that's a compliment or—"

"It is. You've made me forget my need to escape. You've taught me to speak my truth. I thought that's what love looked like."

"You were right. And I was a jerk, a bossy jerk, according to my sister."

"You've never been bossy with me," Cassie said. "You've been kind and encouraging and supportive. We are good together."

"What about your travels?"

"Traveling would be more fun if I had an adventurous travel buddy."

"I might know just the guy."

"Oh, really?" She smiled.

"If you can wait a year. I'll have earned more vacation time by then."

Cassie got up and went to Nate. "My love," she said, "take all the time you need. I'm not going anywhere."

She leaned in for a gentle kiss.

And in that moment, all her dreams had come true.

* * * * *

Dear Reader,

I'm so very excited to present to you the fifth book in my Echo Mountain series, featuring Cassie McBride and Police Chief Nate Walsh. What a great couple!

Cassie is an optimist with a lighthearted nature who's paired with Nate, the strong silent type who intimidates people just by looking at them. Yet somehow, as Nate plays bodyguard for Cassie in the rugged Cascade Mountains, they help each other work through their personal struggles, and Cassie opens Nate's heart to the concept of "grace."

The emotionally guarded chief of police even challenges Cassie to speak her truth with love to her family, something she's been unable to do. She'd rather escape her hometown and travel indefinitely than tell her mom, brother and sister that their smothering style is driving her away. But before she can speak her truth, Cassie must elude mob guys who think she has taken something of theirs. As Cassie and Nate spend time together, he feels saddened by the thought of losing her once the case is solved and she leaves town. But if he loves her, he won't hold her back from her dream of traveling.

The theme of speaking your truth with love is woven throughout the pages of this book because I feel it's essential for healthy relationships. I hope you enjoyed Cassie and Nate's journey as they learned to come together and embrace truth and faith.

Peace,
Hope White